OLD IRONSIDES

Dean Crawford

ISBN: 1544180608
ISBN-13: 978 1544180601

Want to receive a free novel and notification of new releases? Just sign
up to Dean Crawford's newsletter via: www.deancrawfordbooks.com

I

Ayleean System

Sol Date: 2418

'Our estimated time of arrival is in seven minutes, senator.'

Senator Isabel Gray nodded as her aide, Samuel, joined her on an observation post high above the vast hull of the senate cruiser *Fortitude* as the sleek spacecraft travelled at super luminal velocity through the utter blackness of the universe. At such a high velocity, all light information was stripped from the cosmos surrounding them, rendering the cruiser unable to send or receive any form of signal as it travelled toward its destination. Senator Gray often stood here upon the observation platform and stared into the absolute blackness, the hard light viewing panels providing no reflection of her ageing features and yet the darkness beyond so deep it provoked vertigo in many observers.

'We should prepare, senator,' Samuel went on. 'A meeting such as this is something we never would have dreamed possible even a year ago.'

Senator Gray glanced at the young man, his features filled with an idealistic hope that the two tribes of humanity, if humans they could all still be called, might finally settle their differences and become one race again.

'Indeed,' she replied, 'and yet as so often it required an act of conflict to create the conditions for peace. I will await the end of the conference before I hold any hope for a lasting end to the wars we have fought among ourselves these centuries past.'

Samuel peered at her curiously. 'That's not what you said in the briefing to Director General Coburn, before we left Earth.'

Gray smiled. 'That's politics, Samuel.'

The Director General of the Central Security Services, Arianna Coburn, was a long service fleet commander who had moved into politics after the end of her final combat tour a decade prior. Her tenure had lasted for the past three years and she had personally sent Senator Gray on this mission. A tall, graceful but determined person, Coburn was the rock that now held steady an increasingly nervous senate. The entire political class and the heads of the military knew what had happened just a few months before, although the public had been shielded from the worst of it: *First Contact*. Gray shuddered as she stared out into the endless and uncaring universe and reflected again on what had happened, of how close earth had come to destruction.

There was something out there, and it was heading their way.

'This isn't the time for politics,' Samuel pointed out respectfully. 'This is the time for alliance, and action.'

Senator Gray shook herself from her gloomy reverie and nodded, fresh resolve in her spirit as she turned to look at Samuel.

'The Ayleean alliance will strengthen us,' she agreed. 'They are humans just like us, though they don't care to remember it often enough. But after what happened outside Polaris Station, they know as well as we do that divided we will fall.'

Samuel nodded but she could see the uncertainty in his eyes, a fear born of history, of what mankind's estranged brethren were capable of.

Four hundred years prior to this momentous day the earth had succumbed to a plague known as *The Falling* that had taken the lives of some five billion souls and rendered society utterly broken. Entire continents had been reclaimed by nature or taken forcefully by gangs of brigands and thugs who had roamed the wilderness and the crumbling wastelands of fallen cities. Only small pockets of true humanity had remained, those cities well protected by the remnants of the military, where studies had continued until a cure for the plague had been found.

In those dark and terrible days, many possible means of eradicating the plague had been explored, and with them the darkest recesses of the human psyche. Enforced elimination programs designed to destroy, however humanely, those carrying the plague had cost the lives of millions more innocent citizens, those in power acting only in the knowledge that to do nothing would see the end of the human race entirely. Others such as the British had developed digital storage sufficient that those with the will and the means could surrender their physical bodies in preference for holographic bodies and digital brains, thus giving rise to a new species of man: *Holo sapiens*. Most, however, could not hope to achieve such immortality and instead were cut down in the last desperate days of mankind's existence.

Some of those slated for "elimination" had inevitably escaped, and in turn some of those had in fact survived the plague by virtue of losing limbs either by decay, by choice or from the radiation from countless untended nuclear reactors that spilled their toxic veil across the globe, curing the survivors of plague but in turn disfiguring them even further. Among those wandering, miserable hordes of grotesque survivors rose another new species of man, the Ayleeans, named after their leader Werner Ayleea, well versed in the art of bionic prosthetics, skeletal reconstruction and tissue regeneration, skills they used to replace their damaged limbs. By the time the war against the plague had turned in mankind's favor, millions around the world were only half human, the rest of their bodies constructed from ever more complex biogenetic enhancement and even machinery.

Two centuries later and mankind was once again a technologically advanced species, with cities and space fleets and a renewed appetite to reach for the stars. For the Ayleeans, centuries of marginalization gave them the appetite to do more than just reach, and they had been among the first to leave earth in colony ships bound for a new home several dozen light years from earth, orbiting the fearsome glare of a red dwarf star. Ayleea, a steaming tropical world and one of the first habitable planets discovered around an alien star, had evolved them even further into a race of hunters with an abiding hatred of humans, their only true brethren in an uncaring cosmos.

Decades of false histories, the distorting of tales and political games had forged a race for whom only the destruction of humanity could expunge the flames of hatred fanned by a willing political leadership. The Ayleean War was fought for the next thirty years out on the edge of the solar system between the Oort Cloud and Pluto. The last encounter between mankind and the Ayleeans had been a protracted battle that had nearly cost the lives of everybody aboard the fleet's flagship Titan and the orbital city of New Washington, when the Ayleeans had attempted to breach the solar system and attack earth in a last ditch attempt to seek revenge for their own distorted view of history. Although humanity won the war and managed to repel the Aleeyans, there was no longer any appetite for the conflict on either side and peace negotiations had begun almost immediately. Now, they were on the verge of a lasting peace treaty to be signed in the coming days on Ayleea.

A soft beeping intruded on the Senator's thoughts and Samuel straightened his uniform.

'We're coming up on Ayeela,' he reported. 'It is time.'

Senator Gray nodded, and for a brief moment they looked at each other. Isabel smiled and out of habit she reached out and adjusted Samuel's uniform.

'I'm proud of you, son,' she said as she looked down at him. 'It's more than I could have hoped that you would be with me to sign the accord with the Ayleeans that will finally reunite us as a species. Humanity has waited over two centuries for this moment.'

Samuel nodded, still a little tense.

'Let's hope they haven't changed their mind in the two hours it's taken to get here. This ship isn't heavily armed.'

Senator Gray slipped her arm through her son's and led him off the observation platform and into an elevator shaft.

'The Ayleeans are just as tired of conflict as we are and they were soundly defeated in our last engagement,' she assured him. 'There would be no tactical advantage in attacking us or taking us hostage. Their fleet was decimated and they have everything to gain now that we face a new threat.'

A slender, silver walled elevator took them down to the bridge of the cruiser. Gray led her son out onto the bridge deck, where CSS Captain Miguel Cortez held court with his crew. As a ceremonial vessel, the ship only had eight officers on the bridge deck with a support crew of thirty in engineering, technical and communications roles. The ship had no military contingent, and most of the hull was given over to dining halls and recreational facilities. Senator Gray's role aboard Fortitude was to wine and dine the political leaders of humanity's various colonies and assure the strength of the alliance.

Captain Cortez, a stocky and dark skinned man of South American descent, glanced over his shoulder and waved them forward as he sat in his command chair.

'We'll exit super luminal cruise in two minutes at the assigned entry coordinates,' he reported as they approached. 'The Ayleeans will be waiting for us.'

Samuel spoke, his voice clear but tinged with concern.

'We should come out of cruise with our shields up.'

Senator Gray squeezed her son's arm. 'That wouldn't present the kind of message we're trying to send. The Ayleeans must recognize our willingness to trust in them.'

Cortez eyed Samuel with interest, clearly missing the heavy weapons of the frigate *Valiant*, his normal command. 'I'm inclined to agree with him, Isabel. We know how often the Ayleeans have breached our trust in the past.'

'And yet their emissaries allowed us the right to come out of cruise at the closest gate to their home world,' Senator Gray pointed out. 'Close exit from super luminal was once a favorite CSS fleet tactic for ambushing Ayleean convoys, was it not?'

Cortez frowned and rubbed his chin with one hand.

'I'd be happy to oblige them in an armed frigate,' he replied. 'I'm not so sure about jumping out of super luminal one planetary diameter from Ayleea in this glorified river boat. One well placed salvo and we're history.'

'Maybe we could set an emergency leap coordinate,' Samuel suggested. 'It will allow us to jump out of the system at short notice if this all goes sour.'

'Already done,' Cortez reported.

'That wasn't part of the agreement,' Senator Gray said as she stepped up onto the command platform. 'We are an unarmed delegation. If the Ayleeans detect any attempt by us to…'

'There's risk and reward here,' Cortez cut her off, his voice gravelly but bestowed with the authority of decades of fleet experience. 'I know what's at stake, but even if the Ayleeans are in earnest for this alliance there are elements of their race who would like nothing more than to see it fail. The coordinates will be ready but we won't punch them into the computers: the Ayleeans can scan us all they want, they won't know a thing about it.'

Senator Gray clenched her fists but she said nothing as a crewman called to the captain.

'Thirty seconds.'

'Okay,' Cortez said as he turned away from Gray and straightened his uniform. 'Prepare for sub luminal cruise, and keep your eyes open.'

Senator Gray reached out for a rail surrounding the command platform and held onto it along with Samuel. Holographic display panels charted the ship's plotted course to Ayleea, a speck demarking the vessel closing on its destination at a rate of six planetary diameters per second.

'On my mark,' Cortez said as he watched the countdown displayed before him on a transparent screen. 'Three, two, one, *now*.'

Senator Gray felt the familiar tug of gravity in the direction of flight as the cruiser's mass drive disengaged. In an instant, a large screen that had previously been filled with nothing but the absolute blackness of super luminal cruise flared brilliant, bright white.

For a brief instant of time Senator Gray saw the bridge flicker with a kaleidoscopic rainbow shimmer of the light spectrum and felt a vague nausea twist inside her belly as the mass of the cruiser was restored. On the screen the brilliant flare of light faded and she saw the dark orb of Aleeya loom up out of the blackness, the steaming jungle world a paradise and yet filled with dangerous creatures and…

'We've got energy fluctuations across the board!' the tactical officer yelped as he jumped up out of his seat. 'Shields up!'

Senator Gray saw the planet grow rapidly to fill the viewing screen as Fortitude slowed to sub luminal velocity, and almost at once she saw a speck of light that soared toward them, glittering and sparkling like jewels.

'Evasive manoeuvres!' Cortez snapped. 'Get us out of here!'

Senator Gray was about to question why they would leave so suddenly when the glittering array of sparkling material around the planet resolved itself in her mind. Suddenly she realized that it was debris: vast, incalculably immense clouds of wreckage enshrouding the planet's atmosphere like a glittering veil. She could see the shape of hundreds of shattered vessels, both military and civilian alike, venting clouds of gas and glowing like embers in the night sky as fires raged within their fractured metal carcasses.

'Oh no,' she gasped.

The jungles below were smeared with endless banks of dark smoke, like black wreaths enveloping the continents, and although they were presented with the daylight side of the planet she could see what looked like city lights glowing on the surface.

'Ayleea's burning!' Samuel said in alarm as he pointed at fires raging across entire cities. 'They must have suffered a civil war over joining our alliance!'

'That's not possible,' Gray said. 'The Ayleean Council spoke to us only two days ago. Surely they couldn't have caused such destruction in so short a time?'

The helmsman hauled Fortitude into a tight turn as the navigation officer installed the escape data into the computers. Cortez bellowed orders at his crew.

'Jump as soon as the mass drive has spun up! Send a priority signal to CSS!'

A reply came back from the communications officer almost immediately. 'We're being jammed!'

'By *whom*?!' Cortez shouted.

The communications officer stared at her instruments for a moment and then looked at her captain with a stricken expression.

'Signals unknown. They're too powerful, we can't broadcast or receive and...'

Senator Gray never heard the last few words. As the cruiser turned away from Ayleea and prepared to leap into the safety of super luminal cruise, she saw something huge looming before them to blot out the stars. Bizarre tendrils of icy material enveloped the viewing screen and the hull reverberated as it collided with the mass swarming around them.

'Look out!'

A moment later and Senator Gray's world plunged into blackness as a terrible, frigid chill enveloped her in its icy grip.

***

II

Phoenix Heights

New Washington

Erin Sanders stood beneath her hard light umbrella and waited alongside a couple dozen other commuters for the Mag Rail to hum into the platform overhead 15th and Constitution, the rain clattering down around them in big, fat drops from the overhanging buildings above and falling in thin veils beyond. In contrast the sky above was a vivid blue flecked with little white clouds that drifted across the heavens, at odds with the wet ground and soaring buildings rising up around her.

Alongside the city's northern beltway was a series of high rise projects visible from her vantage point that had long been the blight of New Washington, a haven for the criminal low life packed inside. Fuelled by the drug trade, which prospered despite the complexities of living in such a city, North Four festered like an open metallic wound in the heart of New Washington. Phoenix Heights had become the epicentre of the *Shiver* trade: a new form of *bio implant* drug that caused the user to experience two lives of unimaginable ecstasy at once via an exotic and highly dangerous shifting of perceived reality, the user "shivering" between each. The drug took advantage of the fact that the human brain could "lucid dream", a near awake state that allowed dreams to be experienced as absolute reality. The phenomenon itself was natural, but short lived and hard to control. *Shiver* gave the user that control, creating an addiction that led to substance abuse, brain overload, an inability to distinguish between reality and dreams and eventually death by misadventure. The proximal cause was usually suicide, either from the use of the drug or by an individual's inability to procure more of it, forcing them to face reality on its own terms.

9

Erin hated the projects and longed to return home to her apartment amid the safer, gleaming spires of the southern quadrant. Having just finished work, she had to make the commute on the Beltway because she couldn't hope to afford a personal transport. She looked up into the bright blue sky and saw the blade like tips of the southern quadrant apartment buildings pointing toward her on the far side of New Washington's vast circumference, as personal vehicles hummed through the air above them. Behind the spires, she saw the vast blue earth turning slowly, brilliant sunshine flaring through the pillars of the space station's arms as it slowly rotated to generate the centrifugal force required for its residents to keep their feet on the ground.

The rain fell in incessant squalls, the result of countless tens of thousands of people breathing the station's endlessly recycled atmosphere. That atmosphere was tended by banks of aged dehumidifiers, carbon scrubbers and other technical wizardry totally unable to cope with a population ten times what the station had been designed to house. Water vapor built up fast and rose with the heat emitted by the urban sectors and the direct sunlight beaming in through the station's hard light ceilings, resulting in swift downpours as the humid vapor then condensed back out in the cooler, shadowed sections of the city. The constantly moving vortexes of vapor created spectacular spectral vistas as sunlight beamed in rainbow hues through the falling veils.

Erin blinked herself from her reverie as the Mag Rail train hummed into the platform and its doors opened. Erin squeezed inside with the rest of the drenched commuters and the train's doors closed as it moved off again.

The beltway, or simply the Belt, was a conveyor system that ringed New Washington and carried commuters and pedestrians along at a spritely pace without the need for the flying vehicles humming through the skies above. As the belt carried Erin away from the towering blocks of Phoenix Heights, so she got her first true sight of that sky.

The perfect blue vault of the heavens was laced with speckles of distant cloud, and Erin could see their shadows beneath them on the surface of the ocean far below. The panoramic view above spanned only a fraction of earth's surface, in this case the Atlantic Ocean three hundred kilometers below. Erin could see tiny island chains scattered amid the ocean, and across the view stretched immense girders that supported New Washington's vast ray shielding that kept warmth in and the radiation and vacuum of space out. The surface of the earth also rotated in a dizzying effect due to New Washington's movement in space.

Built before the scientists who designed such cities had been able to grasp the fundamentals of the Higgs Boson's control of mass and gravity that now allowed for super luminal velocities in spacecraft, New Washington relied instead on good old fashioned centrifugal motion: the orbiting platform spun at a rate sufficient to generate one of acceleration on the inside of its outer ring, the Belt, thus providing natural gravity for those living there. In the center of the station the docking and loading bays allowed visiting spacecraft to land without worrying about gravity – docking clamps ensured that they could unload passengers and goods safely before departing again. Not dissimilar in appearance to the ancient drawings of science fiction writers from centuries before, New Washington's ring like form was now some ten kilometers across, having been repeatedly expanded to accommodate a population that could no longer afford to live on the surface. The spread of the housing projects at the four points of the station's wheel, named the Four Corners, had become a stain of poverty on what had once been mankind's flagship orbital living space, back then ironically only available to those super wealthy enough to afford it. Erin had never once set foot on the surface of the planet, though she had once met the wife of a man whose sister had visited earth some thirty years before and talked about it still.

Erin watched the city pass by as the Mag Rail travelled around the Belt, passing through stations along the way and more occasional squalls of rain, streams of liquid that had been in the lungs of the city's residents hours before now running in rivulets across the hard light windows. The busiest stations were those at the Four Corners where the station's vast arms met the Rim and she watched through the rain soaked windows the crowds milling there, but as they got closer to the southern quadrant so the train became quieter and she began to relax.

The train eased into her station and she stepped out onto a platform still damp from recent rainfall. The air smelled a little fresher in the southern quadrant as Erin filed off the platform and down to street level. Street lights flared in the damp air and reflected off the sidewalk as though the mirror image of a vast starlit universe now sweeping through the heavens above Erin as she walked along 25th Street. The orb of the earth was now darkening, the twinkling glow from the few remaining cities along America's east coast sparkling like tiny strings of jewels encrusted in coal. Erin walked without the hovering ring of her hard light umbrella as she headed home.

The geosynchronous orbit of New Washington above the east coast of the United States meant that to some extent it shared the same time zone. Behind her as she walked the limb of the earth still blazed as the sun set somewhere across the Atlantic far below. The strange lighting of simultaneous night and day was something that stationers just got used to.

She checked her optical implant with a brief glance: *21.47pm*.

Later than usual but then her work was always busy on North Four, clients ranging from penniless street urchins to the sons of governors caught up in the drug trade and…

Erin looked up as something caught her eye, a flicker of movement high among the rooftops of the apartment buildings. She stopped, caught by a primeval instinct that told her she was being watched. Her ears moved a fraction of their own accord and the fine hairs on her neck bristled.

The brilliant sunset streaming in through the transparent arrays above the Rim cast unusual shadows around her, conflicting with streetlight and the damp air. Halos glowed in the moist atmosphere and she could see veils of rainbow light in distant rain showers far off through the city.

Erin sighed and began walking again. It was late, it had been a long day at work and now she was seeing things. Orbital life was tough for all, and more than one story had been told her as a child of the strange things people witnessed up here. Back in the day, people had apparently gone insane when separated from earth for so long, and Erin certainly felt as though…

She froze as she saw the droplets of water spilling from a nearby roof and heard the swift movement of something across the buildings above her. Dislodged rainwater splattered onto the sidewalk just ten meters from where she stood.

'Who's there?' she demanded.

A deep silence filled the narrow street around her and she suddenly realized that she was standing between two tall apartment blocks and that she was alone. Erin looked behind her, saw the last glow of the setting sun sweeping across the heavens in a golden arc that traced the curve of the earth. The street was empty but she could both hear the traffic and people back on the Belt and she could see vehicles gliding past above the buildings, their flashing navigation lights like nightclub strobes in a gloomy, damp sky.

Erin was no fool. This was no place to be if there was some drug crazed lunatic stalking her across the rooftops. She needed help and she needed it now.

She turned toward the nearest apartment block entrance and walked briskly toward it as with her optical implant she prepared to open a datalink to the nearest police precinct. The access terminal flickered into life in her right eye as she hurried to the doorway and she mentally cued the link to open.

The access terminal turned green and a voice sounded in her ear.

'South Precinct desk, how may I help you?'

Something crashed down in front of the apartment block entrance and Erin opened her mouth to scream as she saw a huge figure silhouetted in front of the entrance lights. She turned to flee as a sharp pain struck in the center of her back and knocked the air from her lungs. Erin careered off balance and landed hard on the street as the police operator's voice sounded again in her ear.

'Hello? South Precinct desk how may I help you?'

Erin opened her mouth to try to cry for help. Nothing came out but a faint squeal of pain as she tried to drag herself across the wet street toward the entrance to another apartment block. Every movement sent pain searing through her body and she knew instinctively that she could never make it to the entrance ahead before whatever it was that had attacked her reached her.

Erin stopped moving, sucked in a breath and tried again.

'Help..., me...!'

'Locating you now, ma'am. Please try to stay calm.'

Erin opened her mouth to reply when something grabbed her and rolled her over onto her back. Erin stared up at the vast girders of the space station and the hard light panels revealing the opposite side of New Washington's glittering nightscape and the darkened planet far beyond.

The figure above her leaned down and Erin screamed as something shot from its mouth toward her. Erin's scream was silenced as a savage lance of pain seared her throat and plunged down inside her body like a river of fire, her limbs and torso twitching as she was lifted bodily off the ground and her consciousness was torn away from her.

***

III

North Four

New Washington

Detective Nathan Ironside shifted his weight from one foot to another on the damp sidewalk and glancing at anything that moved around them.

'Stop fidgeting, it makes you look like a suspect. You're here to meet a family member, not get arrested.'

Detective Kaylin Foxx leaned against their squad cruiser with her arms folded and an amused expression on her features, her bobbed chromium hair reflecting a spectacular sunrise glowing between the nearby buildings. Shafts of golden light beamed over the limb of the earth and soared toward them through rainbow veils of falling rain, the light catching in metallic glints on flotillas of airborne traffic.

'I'm nervous, is all,' Nathan replied, feeling like a scolded child.

Foxx smiled. 'That's understandable, Nathan, but if you're nervous then Sula's going to be nervous too, right?'

Nathan shrugged, unsure of whether he should be presenting a confident front to veil his uncertainties in front of Sula. It was tough enough that he was meeting for the first time a descendent of his, a family member. Tougher still that they were separated by four hundred years.

'How much does she know?' Nathan asked Foxx.

Kaylin Foxx was petite, no more than five two and a hundred twenty pounds, but her small stature, elfin features and mischievous smile concealed a formidable detective and natural scrapper who had been hauled up on North Four's toughest streets. The bobbed metallic hairstyle she favoured, which made her head look like a glittering chrome teardrop, clashed with her black leather jacket and boots, and

Foxx otherwise wore no make up or adornments but for her detective's shield.

'She knows only the vague details, enough to know that this is all straight up and not some elaborate hoax,' Foxx replied for what felt like the fiftieth time. 'Director General Coburn felt that it was best if you filled her in on the rest, and now's your chance.'

Foxx nodded toward the town library where a young lady named Sula Reyon had arranged to meet them, and Nathan turned to see Sula striding toward them across a patch of worn grass amid the towering street blocks.

Sula was perhaps five eight or nine, slender, with long blonde hair that Nathan was relieved to see was not highlighted with metal striations as was the current fashion. Even though he had watched her from afar on many occasions, he was still struck by how healthy and wholesome she looked in contrast to the city's rough and weary skyline. Beside Sula was a woman with neatly bobbed brown hair, not much taller than her daughter but surrounded by an aura of cautious competence.

'Okay, I'll be nearby,' Foxx said, 'don't go making a fool of yourself, y'hear?'

Nathan smiled at her and tapped his chest. 'Hey, it's me, right?'

'Yeah,' Foxx murmured with a roll of her eyes as she walked away, 'what could possibly go wrong?'

Nathan drew a deep breath and walked toward Sula. At six two and a hundred eighty pounds he towered over the teenager. Nathan had always been a little heavy set, and his thick mop of shaggy brown hair did nothing to make him look less of the "Colorado grizzly" his mother had once referred to him as, all those centuries ago.

Nathan blinked away the thought of his family and forced himself to focus on Sula as she slowed before him, just meters away now. Despite the centuries that separated them, he could still see something in her that reminded him of his daughter Amira, lost so long ago. The slightly mischievous and lopsided smile, the twinkling green eyes and the set of her shoulders, upright and alert, ready to tackle any challenger.

'You must be Nathan,' she said.

Nathan's heart pinched and his stomach went into freefall at the sound of her voice, the tones uncannily like those of Amira. He hadn't heard his daughter's voice in four centuries and yet now it provoked a fierce pain in the corners of his eyes and his vision blurred.

'I'm afraid so,' he said meekly.

Sula smiled, more curious it seemed now than ever, and then the smile faded as she saw the raw emotion in his eyes. Nathan turned away from her slightly and sought anything to distract her. A battered, weary sign for a coffee shop beckoned him with the lights of salvation.

'You wanna grab a coffee or something?' he asked.

Sula glanced at the shop. 'In Old Joe's? Jeez, I'd be churning my guts out for a week. How about The Grain Mill on 9th?'

Nathan nearly reached up and slapped his head. 'Sure, the Mill, why didn't I think of that?'

The older woman extended her hand toward him. 'I'm Rosaline, Sula's mother.'

Nathan shook her hand gently. 'Great to finally meet you, both of you.'

'What's this about?' Rosaline asked. 'My daughter's been taken out of college this morning on Director General Coburn's say so? We've never even met the Director General. Why are we here?'

'That's my fault,' Nathan began. 'Well, it's not *my fault*, but I'm the cause of it all. Indirectly, if you know what I mean?'

Rosaline narrowed her eyes. 'Not really.'

Sula stared at him for a moment and then her smile returned. 'You're kind of funny for an old guy.'

Nathan's wrenched guts relaxed a little and he felt an odd wave of relief wash over him, as though somehow the ice had been broken in a way he had never thought it would be.

'I'm kind of a dork, most of the time.'

'I'll second that,' Foxx chirped from the cruiser nearby.

Nathan saw Sula chuckle and he realized that Foxx's presence, the detective's shields they wore and the involvement of the Director General of the CSS had provided a backdrop of trust to their meeting, which would help with what Nathan knew he had to say next.

'Sula, I need to ask you something. Do you recognize me? I'm going to tell you who I am.'

Sula inclined her head as she watched him. 'That would be ace, as I don't know who the hell you are. But…'

Nathan waited instinctively, said nothing as Sula peered at him.

'…but you look oddly familiar.'

'Funny you should mention that.'

'Are we related?'

Rosaline stepped forward. 'What's going on here, detective?'

'We need to sit down,' Nathan said, and gestured to the corner of 9th and Constitution. 'Shall we?'

They walked together across the worn grass to the corner of the intersection where The Grain Mill coffee shop stood, the sidewalks crowded as ever with citizens of the oldest of the orbital stations hurrying to and fro. The earth gazed down upon them from above with its bright blue and white eye as they stepped inside, and Nathan realized that it hadn't rained for at least a half hour as they found a seat and sat down.

Coffee arrived quickly after they had punched their orders into touch screens mounted in the table. Shops like the Mill had reverted from voice recognition and optical implant orders due to the volume of traffic confusing their ageing computer systems.

Sula watched Nathan over the Rim of her coffee cup as he took a sip of his drink and gathered his thoughts.

'We *are* related,' he said finally, figuring it was better to get it out in the open.

'How so?' Sula asked inquisitively, blissfully unaware of what was coming next and looking at her mother. 'You never mentioned a Nathan before.'

'Your mother doesn't know me,' Nathan replied, still struggling to find the right words to convey what he had to tell her. *Words.* Maybe words weren't the only way? 'Sula, I've got something to show you, to show you both actually.'

Nathan reached into his pocket and pulled out an old leather wallet, one of his few possessions that had survived to the present day.

'Man, you still carry *those* things?' Sula asked with a surprised chuckle. 'What century are you from?'

Nathan managed not to stare at her as he carefully fished out two photographs, both of them now sealed in a gel that preserved them from damage caused by handling. Although Nathan possessed a *Holo Lens* that allowed him to revisit the past in perfect virtual reality, there was still something important to him about handling something tangible from his past.

'This was my wife and daughter,' he said softly. 'Angela and Amira.'

Sula took the photographs from him and stared at them, Rosaline leaning in with her. Their features were now touched with caution, perhaps even anxiety.

'Was?' Rosaline echoed.

Nathan nodded. 'They passed away.'

'I'm sorry,' Sula replied, staring now at the images to avoid his gaze. 'They were beautiful.'

Nathan kept a grip on himself as he went on despite the trembling wave of grief he kept buried somewhere deep inside.

'Sula,' he said, quietly enough that none of the other people in the coffee shop would overhear him, 'they passed away four hundred years ago, before the plague that you call The Falling.'

Sula's green eyes snapped up to meet Nathan's.

'This some kind of joke?' Rosaline demanded.

'No joke,' Nathan said, serious now, 'you think the Director General of the CSS would invite you for a chat before this meeting if I weren't serious?'

Sula held his gaze for a long moment. 'How?'

Nathan closed his eyes and decided that there was no other way to say it other than to simply speak the truth. 'I was Ground Zero for The Falling.'

Sula reared back in her seat and dropped the photographs as though they were radioactive. Nathan could see the fear in her gaze as Rosaline almost got to her feet.

'I'm clean,' he said quickly to Rosaline, 'we all are. That's not why I'm here.'

Sula remained rigid in her seat, her jaw working as though to find words.

'How?' she repeated.

Nathan gathered his thoughts before he replied.

'I was part of a mountaineering expedition that got caught out in a supercell storm. We were forced to overnight on a high peak in Colorado. My partner didn't survive the night, and the low pressure system passed right overhead the mountain range we were on. I don't understand or remember the full details of what happened that night, but doctors said that I ingested a form of microbe that exists only in earth's high atmosphere and did not originate on this planet. The odd weather of the super cell storm brought the virus or whatever it was down low enough in the atmosphere while I was high enough on the mountain to come into contact with it, and I became infected.' Nathan hesitated and looked Sula in the eye. 'I died a few months later.'

Rosaline leaned forward in her seat. 'You *died* a few months later?'

Nathan nodded. 'I was cryogenically preserved but I had to wait a while before science caught up enough to cure the disease, the plague.'

Sula peered at him. 'When did you die?'

Nathan took another breath. 'I was pronounced dead in the year

2016.'

Sula stared at Nathan for a long moment. 'So you're a *Holosap* now? How come you can hold your coffee?'

Nathan smiled, relieved that in the 25th Century such a bizarre tale was not so hard to swallow given all of the technological advances that had been made. He glanced out of the shop window and saw among the crowds a glowing, humanoid figure walking down the street. *Holosap* was short for Holo sapiens, a new species of human conceived when the great plague, *The Falling*, had decimated mankind and it had seemed that only by evolving into digital form could humanity survive. A mixture of holographic technology and "freespace" data storage, there were around ten thousand or so *holosaps* still in existence, many of them nearly as old as Nathan. Mostly they comprised individuals who had died or chosen to abandon their bodies during The Falling, in favour of a holographic existence to await a cure, who for one reason or another were unable to return to their bodies due to malfunctions in cryostasis capsules or damage to body tissues and organs. A few however decided by choice to stay as they were, preferring life as an immortal computer program, because, as one famous *holosap* had once said: "You can't catch a plague if you're not actually alive."

'No, I'm not a holosap,' he replied finally. 'I was cryogenically frozen to preserve the original specimen of the plague in the hopes of finding a cure. Ultimately the cure was found but by then I had been long forgotten. It was only recently that I was thawed out and revived, then cured at the same time.'

Rosaline seemed to relax a little in her seat, but she was still keeping her distance from him. She glanced at his detective's shield hanging around her neck.

'And now you're a cop? How'd that work out?'

'I was a detective in Denver, Colorado in 2016,' Nathan explained. 'Once I'd settled in here in the present, it seemed a natural choice and the New Washington Department offered me a place. Detective Foxx is my partner.'

Sula and Rosaline glanced out of the shop windows to the cruiser parked on the far side of the square, Kaylin Foxx visible inside watching the traffic with a bored expression. The teenager looked back at Nathan and then she suddenly gasped and leaned forward, all mention of the plague forgotten.

'We *are* related,' she realized. 'That's why we're here.'

Nathan nodded.

'I'm your great, great, great, great grandfather,' he replied, and managed a brief smile. 'Which makes me kind of great.'

Sula stared at him and then sank back into her chair as though absorbing everything that she had heard.

'I don't know if this is the coolest thing ever to happen or the creepiest,' she said finally.

'Can we go with the coolest?'

'You're like, four *hundred* years old?' Rosaline said.

'And not a gray hair in sight.'

'How come we still talk the same language?' Sula asked.

'It's a bit different, but not so much has changed really,' Nathan said, 'and the medicine has sure changed for the better.'

'And worse,' Sula pointed out. 'The Ayleeans, the enhanced criminals, drugs, black market ID chips and optical implants.'

'There's still a lot of crime out there,' Nathan conceded. 'Like I said, not everything's changed so much.'

Sula watched him again for a long time. Nathan felt as though he was being assessed, which in many ways he guessed he was. He sat patiently and waited for Sula to speak but it was her mother who broke the silence.

'Why have you come to us with this?' she asked.

'You're my only living relatives,' Nathan replied, 'yourself and Sula here. Well, actually there was another called Arwin Minter, but he turned out to be a criminal and then he became a dead end, literally.'

Sula's lips curled up at one end in a smile. 'You've got a strange sense of humor.'

'I need one,' Nathan replied. 'Anyway, I just wanted to reach out and say hi, y'know? I don't have any family here and I lost mine...' He broke off for a moment. 'I'm not looking to be a big part of anybody's lives or anything, you didn't sign up for this. I don't know, I just felt that it was the right thing to do now that things have settled down for me a bit.'

Sula's eyes narrowed.

'My mom's not looking for a boyfriend, y'know?'

Rosaline's eyes flicked to her daughter's in surprise as Nathan panicked.

'What? Oh, no, it's not... I'm not... I didn't mean it like...'

Sula's smile cut through Nathan's defense and he recognized the mischievous twinkle in her eyes once again, although this time the nostalgic pain in the corners of his eyes was a little less potent than before.

'Take it easy,' she said. 'I'm just bustin' your chops, okay Mister Cop?'

Nathan relaxed and forced an awkward smile onto his face. 'Sure.'

'So,' Rosaline said, 'now what? You think that we all go out to dinner and play happy families?'

'I don't know, I guess all of that's up to you.'

Sula looked down at the photographs, of Angela and Amira. Her mother looked at them again also.

'This is a bit of a shock, detective.'

'It's Nathan.'

'We're going to need some time,' Rosaline added, 'to think about all of this. We don't want somebody else getting involved already, okay?'

'I'll be in touch,' Sula said, ignoring her mother.

'You'll do no such thing!'

Sula rolled her eyes. 'Mom, I'm not a kid anymore okay?'

'That's exactly what you are young lady and we don't know this…,' Rosaline glanced at Nathan: 'Gentleman.'

'It's Nathan, really, and I don't want to cause any trouble here, okay?'

'You're not,' Sula said as she smiled sweetly at her mother. 'Right, mom?'

Rosaline peered at Nathan but said nothing. Nathan watched Sula, and he figured that he must have been wearing a puppy dog look because Sula chuckled and patted his forearm with one hand.

'I *promise* I'll be in touch, okay?'

Nathan chuckled, shook his head. 'Sure, sorry, I just…'

'I know,' Sula said softly.

'Are all teenagers this grown up in the 25th Century?'

'No, they're not,' Rosaline murmured. 'That's what worries me.'

'Oh, come on mom,' Sula groaned. 'What harm can it do?'

Before Rosaline could reply Nathan's optical implant flashed and he saw a ghostly image of Foxx appear genie like before him.

'We've got a homicide,' she said, her disembodied voice clear in his ear. 'Sorry, we gotta move.'

'Duty calls?' Sula asked.

'I got to go,' Nathan said as they stood. 'Can I give you my contact details?'

'Sure,' Sula replied as she looked up at him, ignoring her mother's silent glare. 'Long as you don't mind me being out of touch for a while?'

'Why, where are you going?' Nathan asked as they walked outside onto the sidewalk and into a faint drizzle falling in rainbow hues around them.

'Induction course for the fleet,' she replied. 'I'm hoping to follow my father's footsteps and join up.'

'Wow,' Nathan said, suddenly concerned. 'You sure that's a good idea, the fleet can be a dangerous place?'

'Remember that not getting too involved thing?' Rosaline piped up.

Nathan mentally pulled back. 'Yeah, right. Sorry.'

Sula smiled again. 'It's okay. I think it's kind of cute you're already trying to look out for us. Gotta go, 'morrow!'

And with that she was gone, rushing away into the crowds in a flash of blonde hair and lengthy stride. Nathan stared after her and then belatedly raised his hand to wave.

'Morrow!'

Rosaline moved to stand before Nathan, and although her face was pinched with anger he knew instinctively that her concern was for her daughter.

'You know about what happened to her father, right?'

Nathan nodded and said nothing.

'She's all I've got,' Rosaline said, 'and we only just got our lives together again. Don't start coming around here screwing things up, understood detective?'

'Understood, and it's Nathan.'

Rosaline turned without another word and stalked away into the crowds. He watched her until she was out of sight, and then yelped as a squad cruiser hovered into view inches from his right leg.

'Hey, grandpa!' Nathan turned as he saw the cruiser's gull wing doors open and Foxx beckoning him inside. 'You wanna get the hell back to work here?'

***

IV

South Two

'What the hell are we doing up here, it's not our jurisdiction?'

Foxx guided the squad cruiser through the towering blocks a hundred feet off the deck, weaving smoothly between the traffic streaming in uniform flying lanes around the Belt. Sunlight flared through the vast ray shielding above them, the shadows of massive support beams drifting by rhythmically overhead.

'Chief of police called us in,' she replied to Nathan. 'Vasquez and Allen are already there.'

'Wow, I didn't know North Four cops were in such demand.'

From his seat Nathan could look down on the spires of buildings passing by below, the streets teeming with citizens demarked by the glowing blue rings of hard light umbrellas shimmering through the veils of rain spilling from the atmosphere. Above, the metal sky of the upper rim was interspersed with periodic shafts of brilliant sunlight from huge observation panels that revealed a dizzying view of earth and the sun outside the station, along with the far side of the Belt dominated by North Four's dark streets.

'The victim worked on North Four as part of a street team counselling drug addicts near Phoenix Heights,' Foxx explained as she flew the cruiser. 'Local PD think that she might have been targeted as part of her anti narcotics work.'

'Gang slaying?' Nathan guessed.

'That's what they're thinking, due to the unusual nature of the crime.'

'Unusual how?'

Foxx shrugged but said nothing as she descended toward the southern quarter. Already Nathan had noticed the dark, dank buildings of the northern quarter give way to the more aesthetically pleasing financial district and urban south side. Like any city there were wealthy areas and there were slums, and nowhere was the line more clearly demarked than in the orbital stations. New Washington, New Chicago, New Los Angeles and others all carried the burden of social decline in their vast populations, most of whom had never visited their home world in their lives. Earth's surface was now a haven for the super wealthy, the elite.

'There they are.'

Foxx pointed to where a flashing red icon on the hard light windscreen hovered over a pair of police cruisers that had landed in a narrow street off 25th and West San Antonio. Foxx descended carefully through the traffic and hit her landing lights, a small group of uniformed officers and detectives stepping back as the cruiser descended onto its landing pads near the crime scene, the thrusters blowing rippling veils of vapor off the damp street as it touched down.

Nathan climbed out as the cruiser's engines whined down and with Foxx he walked to the crime scene, marked as ever with glowing hard light barriers to keep out curious members of the public. He could see the overlooking apartment buildings surrounding them, faces within watching the activity in the street below.

Waiting for them were two detectives attached to Kaylin's Anti Drug Unit; Lieutenant Jay Allen and Lieutenant Emilio Vasquez. Jay was a career officer who had joined the force from high school in New Chicago, while Vasquez was a former CSS Marine who had switched to law enforcement for the better pay and the increased chance of picking up hot dates due to his uniform. The pair could not have been more different, and duly were inseparable partners with five long years' service behind them in the unit.

'Hey Ironsides,' Vasquez chortled as they approached. 'What's with the momma in the coffee shop?'

'Have you been following me?' Nathan asked.

'We've been lookin' out for you,' right Jay?'

'Watching your back,' Detective Allen agreed with a somber nod.

'Putting your concerns before ours. Riding shotgun. Watching your as…'

'As far as I remember I'm a grown man who can look after himself,' Nathan pointed out.

'Your memory's not that hot,' Vasquez replied.

'Guys, I don't need you behind me all the time okay? Foxx had my back.'

The two detectives glanced at each other and shrugged. Despite their covert observation of his morning meeting Nathan was grateful that the two of them were around. Both men knew what Nathan had been through and how much he had lost.

'Yo, Foxx? You wipe your feet before you got out of that cruiser?'

Detective Foxx strode through the barrier with a grin on her face as a tall, black detective shook her hand. Nathan followed with Vasquez and Allen, all of their implanted ID chips automatically recognized by the barriers.

'Emmanuel,' she greeted him. 'What brings you to let us dirty northerners set foot on your pampered little manor?'

'Needs must,' Emmanuel replied as he shook Nathan's hand. 'Lieutenant Emmanuel Stone.'

'Nathan Ironside, what happened here?'

'Homicide,' Stone replied as he gestured behind him to a dark stain on the street, partially washed away by recent rainfall.

'There's no body,' Vasquez observed.

'He's a keen eye, isn't he?' Emmanuel winked at Nathan with a brilliant white smile.

'Doesn't miss a trick,' Nathan confirmed. 'What's the story? We don't usually get pulled up here.'

'That's the rub,' Emmanuel replied as his smile melted away and his eyes turned dark. 'The vic' worked your patch by day, lived here by night. Normally we'd just inform your precinct and get uniforms on the canvassing from your side, but the scene just doesn't sit right.'

'Where's the body?' Foxx pressed.

Emmanuel jabbed a thumb up into the air.

Nathan looked up, to where the high rises reached up toward a steel gray sky of upper rim panelling and brilliant white lighting, uniform rows of illumination demarking the interior wall of the Rim above them. To the right, atop one of the apartment blocks, Nathan saw two figures looking down at them that he identified as uniformed officers guarding a second scene.

'The victim was a jumper?' Foxx asked in confusion.

'No,' Detective Allen said as he looked down at the blood stained street. 'Not enough blood for that.'

'That's right,' Emmanuel replied. 'The body was moved up there *after* death, and here's the thing. The apartment is securely locked at night. All of the residents have alibied out and none of the internal surveillance caught anything out of the ordinary. Yet this victim supposedly died here in the street and then wound up sixty feet in the air on the roof of that building.'

Foxx craned her neck up and looked at the rooftop. 'Could've been dumped there from a cruiser.'

'Or we could be looking at two different crimes,' Nathan pointed out.

'Bloodwork's already been done,' Emmanuel said. 'The victim definitely bled here, and that's what doesn't make any sense. There's not enough blood.'

'We already established that,' Foxx said, 'the victim didn't jump.'

'That's not what I mean,' Emmanuel replied. 'You haven't seen the vic' yet.'

Foxx and Nathan exchanged glances as Emmanuel waved for them to follow him into the apartment building. They travelled in silence in an elevator to the top floor and then up a staircase and out onto the roof of the building.

Although they were only fifty or so feet above street level, Nathan could already feel a lightness in his belly as the force of gravity was reduced. The closer one moved to the station's hub, the lower the centrifugal force acting on a body of mass became, which was why aerial traffic and elevated landing pads made sense as less thrust was needed to take off. High above them the central hub and spaceport experienced permanent zero gravity, facilitating the landing and departure of spacecraft entering New Washington or leaving for earth or the solar system's various colonies and bases.

Nathan saw at once another hard light barrier around a corpse strewn in the center of the roof. He could see the clothes of a young woman but they seemed odd, not hugging the victim's frame but almost hanging off it like limp sails from a ghost ship's rigging. As he followed Foxx to the scene, Emmanuel spoke to them.

'This is how we found her, or at least what's left of her.'

Nathan slowed as he saw the woman's face and for a brief moment his brain could not process what he was actually looking at. A moment later and the grim visage resolved itself into a skull that seemed to have been crushed inward from all sides, the black orbs of the eye sockets empty and the skin pulled taut across warped and shattered bone.

'Jeez,' Foxx uttered as she crouched down alongside the corpse.

Nathan could see that the woman's long, damp brown hair snaking across the rooftop and the nearby high heeled boots that had slid off her desiccated feet. Her limbs and torso were a shell, the bones of her ribs and chest poking up from beneath her shirt, her ankles narrow as twigs.

'What the hell happened to her?' Vasquez asked Emmanuel.

'That's the first thing we asked,' the detective replied. 'We've got nothing, and the paramedics and doctors we've called and sent data to have no idea what could have caused this. All we know is that her name's Erin Sanders and that she lived in a block just over the street. This was her route home from the Mag Rail station down the block.'

'Did they establish a time of death?' Foxx asked, still staring at the mummified remains.

'Best guess from what tissue remains would be between nine and eleven yesterday evening, which ties in with an emergency distress call made at the same time.'

'She called in?' Foxx asked, standing up.

'Just before half ten last night,' Emmanuel confirmed. 'The local precinct sent a cruiser out but there was nothing to be found and the uniforms didn't notice the blood stains here initially because it was raining so hard. They put out an alert for the missing woman, who they couldn't find at her apartment, but beyond that there wasn't much they could do. It was only when the administrator of the building conducted a routine safety check and came up here that the body was found.'

'Which means that the vic' must have been taken elsewhere and then returned here afterward,' Nathan said, 'otherwise the uniforms would have seen the body on the rooftop when they landed.'

'That's what we figured,' Emmanuel confirmed, 'but it beats the hell out of me why somebody would do that. This woman looks like she's literally had the life sucked out of her and that's what the coroner's first impression was.'

Allen winced. '*Sucked* out of her?'

'Yeah,' Emmanuel said, noting their expressions. 'There's not a drop of body tissue remaining inside her body. It's like she's been mummified, bone dry, 'scuse the pun which ain't intended. I've never seen anything like this and neither has anybody else in the precinct. We got no witnesses, no evidence, nothin' to work on. We figured maybe black market organ traders, but we don't get so much of that on south two and thought you might give us a heads' up here.'

Nathan crouched down alongside the woman's body and thought for a moment.

'What about her ID chip?'

Every person alive within human space was fitted shortly after birth with a personalized Implanted Designator, or ID for short. A liquid cell quantum storage chip the size of a fingernail, everything about a person was recorded and stored for future use. The law stated that no ID chip was ever to be tampered with, but a vibrant market existed for those able to afford tinkering with their ID and thus evading law enforcement.

'Gone, and non functional, or so we assume as we haven't been able to locate it,' Emmanuel replied. 'Whoever did this to her took the ID chip with them.'

'Which means they either knew that the chip existed,' Nathan said to Foxx, 'and wanted to get rid of it.'

'Or they didn't know about the chip and it's now been destroyed,' Foxx went on and then gestured to the woman's neck, the skin of which was heavily bruised and discolored. 'That bruising, right there. Is that consistent with strangulation?'

'Quite the opposite,' Emmanuel said, 'according to the coroner it looks like the result of swelling and haemorrhage. Like something was shoved down her throat.'

Nathan and Foxx exchanged a glance. 'We're gonna need help with this,' he said.

Foxx pulled out a communicator and contacted CSS. 'Can you send Doctor Schmidt here, if he's available?'

'Oh no,' Nathan sighed, 'not him, surely?'

'He's the best qualified physician we have,' Foxx said as she shut off the communicator. 'Trouble is he's still posted aboard Titan and we don't know when he'll get here.'

'Good,' Nathan said. 'That'll give us the chance to finish up and leave before he arr...'

'Too late!'

The voice burst into life from within Nathan's head and he leaped in fright, jumping to one side as though he had been ambushed as he saw Doctor Schmidt's ephemeral holographic form shimmering into life where he had been standing.

'Will you cut that out!' Nathan snapped.

Doctor Schmidt stood with his hands clasped calmly before him, a serene smile on his features that never seemed to slip. Middle aged in appearance, Schmidt was in fact well over two hundred years old and one of the most experienced *holosap* physicians in the fleet.

'I apologise, Detective Ironsides,' Schmidt intoned, 'but Detective Foxx's call came in on a high priority channel and I didn't have time to choose a clear spot to project myself. I was forced to target the nearest ID chip instead.'

'So you projected yourself straight into *my* head, *again.*'

Schmidt offered him an ingratiating smile. 'It was the one that had the greatest available empty space.'

Nathan refused to be baited and said nothing as Foxx gestured to the corpse. 'What do you make of this?'

Emmanuel activated his optical implant. 'Sending you all the data we have on the victim now.'

Doctor Schmidt blinked as he accessed the data, and then he looked down at the corpse.

'My, interesting.'

'Yeah,' Nathan said, 'I'm sure she said that as she was being turned inside out. Any jewels of wisdom you wanna share with us?'

Schmidt's smile faded gradually as he looked down at the victim's body. 'So young,' he murmured. 'My assessment based on the haemorrhaging around the thorax, the upper chest cavity and the absence of any detectable bodily fluids is that this poor woman was subjected to some kind of biological procedure.'

Foxx frowned. 'Biological?'

'Yes,' Schmidt replied. 'The only thing that could possibly do something like this would be mechanical, a machine of some kind. The rupturing and internal injuries, as well as the warped skull cavity and fractured chest plate, suggest that force was applied but without sharp edges.'

Nathan looked again at the corpse.

'What the hell would do something like that?'

'An utter psychopath,' Vasquez replied.

'I agree,' Schmidt said. 'A killing such as this absolutely has to be planned and prepared, so it's not likely to be a one off event. Whoever you're looking for is capable of absolutely anything and will likely strike again, soon.'

***

Dean Crawford

V

CSS Headquarters

New York City

Hurry.

The word echoed through Director General Arianne Coburn's mind as she walked upon a travellator through the enormous complex of CSS Headquarters. Behind her strode a phalanx of CSS Security guards and with them several senators. Nobody knew why the call had gone out for the director general to attend an emergency security meeting, but the fact that the call coincided almost perfectly with the expected arrival of CSS Fortitude at Ayleea plagued Arianna's mind as she willed the travellator to move faster.

The Central Security Services complex was located in north Manhattan, surrounded by landing pads and hundreds of giant holographic icons denoting the flags of all earth's historic nations united under the banner of the CSS. They were not there just to advertise the unity of CSS: rather, they reminded all of the fragmented and untrusting nature of history's warring nations and the reason for the existence of the CSS and its archaic forbearer, the United Nations. *Defensionem ut impetum* : *Defense as attack*, or so the old motto of the CSS went. Despite its name the organization was more like a senate with no offensive role, only the ability to govern earth and its colonies and to request action by the CSS Fleet and Armed Forces if such action was required. Until Titan had been required to enter earth orbit to save New Washington from destruction at the hands of the Ayleeans a year previously, no human warship had entered earth orbit in earnest for over a hundred years.

The travellator carried Arianna to the entrance of the main senate hall, and she alighted with the grace and poise that those around her had become accustomed to seeing. Arianna had learned long ago that leaders needed to appear confident at all times, regardless of what turmoil they might be keeping inside. The fact that she felt dread with every step was something she could afford to share with nobody.

The senate's huge amphitheater was filled to capacity with senators, congressmen and other lawmakers all in heated debate, a thousand voices colliding as Arianna strode toward a central podium that looked up at the politicians surrounding her. Located atop the CSS Headquarter's highest levels, a domed ceiling revealed earth's wintery skies and a city flecked with recent snowfall. Arianna's flowing senate robes of white rimmed with gold captured the attention of the senators as the amphitheater's huge double doors thundered shut behind her. The crowd reacted to the sound, taking their seats as the rush and whisper of conversation died down and Coburn took the podium.

'Senators, Congressmen, representatives of the people, this session has been called due to unexpected events beyond the fringes of our solar system,' she said, her words echoing around the huge building as though hers was the voice of a deity. 'I request that Rear Admiral Vincent O'Hara provide the explanation for this gathering.'

Arianna saw a larger than life hologram shimmer into view to take apparently solid form. The projection of the Rear Admiral, a senior officer in his early hundred twenties with wavy white hair and cold blue eyes, dominated the chamber as he spoke.

'Senators, as many of you will know, CSS Fortitude arrived in the Ayleen system some twelve hours ago. She was carrying Senator Isabel Gray and other delegates tasked with signing the agreement that would formally bring the Ayleeans into our alliance. I regret to inform you all that after arriving in the Ayleean system, all contact has been lost with Fortitude and her crew.'

A ripple of uncomfortable whispers fluttered like a live current around the amphitheater as the admiral went on.

'We have since confirmed that the ship arrived safely in Ayleean orbit, at which point her Identification Friend or Foe signal was detected as functioning normally. After approximately two minutes the signal was lost. There was no communication from the crew, and we believe from analysis of what signals we did receive that she was being jammed.'

Arianna noted that this final statement was met with silence. Politicians were not men of war, although in history they had frequently been enthusiastic war makers. She imagined that their minds would be empty of reaction because they simply had no real idea of *how* to react. The admiral's next words anticipated their lack of response.

'We believe that the Ayleeans have reneged on the deal and have either taken Fortitude as a prize of war, or destroyed her and are holding her crew and compliment hostage.'

A further silence followed, deeper than the last.

'Do we have any evidence to support this assumption?' Arianna Coburn asked the admiral.

'None,' he replied. 'But in light of Ayleean history, it would seem prudent to assume the worst. It has always been their stated goal to destroy humanity, to lay waste to the home world that we once shared. It is no secret that neither I nor any of the Joint Chiefs of Staff have believed this accord with them to be anything other than a dangerous precedent and one that leaves us vulnerable to attack.'

Now ripples of acknowledgement drifted through the senate, understanding beginning to form.

'The fate of Fortitude may not be the work of the Ayleeans per se,' Arianna pointed out. 'There are elements among them who also oppose the alliance, who may have sought through subterfuge to attack or take as a prize the vessel and her crew.'

'Risks that the Ayleean Council knew they needed to take measures against,' O'Hara countered. 'If they truly wished this accord to become formal, they would have provided adequate protection for Fortitude the moment she arrived in orbit.'

A ripple of approval fluttered through the crowd, the first hint of dissent against Coburn's long awaited alliance with the Ayleean Council.

'We moved too quickly!' called a senator representing human colonies on Proxima Centauri, a system once brutally attacked by an Ayleean force and the site of a massacre at their hands. 'Now we are vulnerable again!'

'The Ayleeans cannot be trusted, ever!' cried another. 'We warned the senate that this would happen, that any agreement with them would only be honored for as long as it served a purpose to them, not us!'

Admiral O'Hara stopped speaking as he appeared to turn to a display screen not visible in his projection from Polaris Station, the military's orbital platform around Saturn. Another senator stood. 'The Ayleeans could be attempting another infiltration of our space at this very moment!'

More ripples and murmurs of agreement from the crowd.

'Have we attempted to contact their Council?!'

'What defenses do we have in place on the Outer Rim colonies?'

'They breached our space last time and almost destroyed New Washington! How could we have let this happen?!'

Arianna Coburn closed her eyes as the wave of protests and fear rose before her like a dark wave. Slowly, she raised her hands, no longer listening to the words of the crowd and instead waiting for the raucous to die down. Slowly, one by one, the senators fell respectfully silent until Arianna lowered her hands once more and spoke.

'The admiral cannot answer your questions more than one at a time,' she said.

Admiral O'Hara inclined his head toward her and went on as he glanced at the mysterious screen in his command center.

'The Ayleean Council is not responding to our signals,' he said. 'Furthermore, we have just learned that our long range sensors are detecting no signals at all from the Ayleean system.'

Now, the senate hall fell silent and Arianna's heart felt as though it had missed a beat.

'No signals *at all* from the system?' she echoed.

O'Hara nodded. 'The Ayleeans have fallen entirely silent. All spectrographic traces of technology and industry have disappeared from sensor readings at Polaris Station.'

Now there was a deep silence throughout the senate hall. For all of their faults and their warlike nature, the Ayleeans were a technologically advanced species in their own right and they had a tendency to make a lot of noise both literally and figuratively. All industrialized colonies had a vivid spectral and radio signature that could easily be detected, the signals spilling from the colonies radiating outward in all directions at the speed of light. Earth's own fledgling society had been emitting radio waves out into the Milky Way galaxy for the past five hundred years or more. Although those signals would be weak at their greatest extent they created a beacon for any advanced civilization located or travelling within a sphere five hundred light years in diameter that loudly proclaimed: *we're here!*

For an entire world to suddenly fall silent was unheard of...

'What would you have us do?' Arianna asked the admiral.

O'Hara responded without hesitation.

'We should send an armed, fast frigate force out to the location and find out what the hell is going on. If the Ayleeans have reneged on the accord then we need to know about it as soon as possible, because whatever they're planning it won't be good.'

'And if they're not planning something?' Arianna added, letting the question hang in the air for a long moment.

'Then we have much bigger problems on our hands,' the admiral replied. 'I will dispatch the frigates *Endeavour* and *Defiance* to the Ayleean system under the strictest orders that they be prepared for the worst. O'Hara out.'

The admiral's holographic projection shimmered out of existence and left the senate hall silent for a few moments more before a lone senator stood up and spoke, her voice clear for all to hear.

'Is it possible that they have returned?'

Arianna Coburn knew precisely what the senator was referring to, and the memory of what had happened so close to earth, of how close humanity had come to extinction, shuddered through her.

'Yes,' she replied, seeing no sense in dodging the issue or uttering empty promises. 'It is possible.'

Although the public had not been made aware of it, after a closed doors senate session had voted to maintain secrecy, some months before CSS Titan had intercepted a vessel of unknown origin after detecting a distress signal from an Ayleean warship far beyond the outer colonies. The result of that intercept had been "First Contact", an encounter with an alien species that had shaken to the core all those who had encountered it. Witnesses, which included military personnel and police detectives from New Washington, had been sworn to silence.

Nobody spoke for several long moments, until Arianna shook herself from her torpor and addressed the senate.

'We should prepare as best we can,' she said.

'Prepare?' an elderly senator echoed. 'You mean for an invasion?'

Arianna nodded. 'Yes, an invasion. Whether it be by dissident Ayleeans or something else, we cannot stand by and wait. We must act now.'

Governor Sergei Vitily of New Moscow stood up.

'The people,' he said. 'The last time this happened we were able to disguise it as Ayleean aggression. That might no longer be an excuse they'll easily accept, given how CSS has trumpeted about our new accord with the Ayleean Council.'

Arianna didn't miss the veiled jibe at her policies.

'There will be panic,' said another. 'We can't hide this from the population.'

'Then we must be careful,' Arianna insisted, her stern tones silencing the senators. 'We can remain hopeful that this is a mistake, an error, a temporary failure of communication software, but it would be folly to do nothing. We must be strong and united for the people who rely upon us, and we must be prepared for whatever is waiting for us out there. Keep this news to yourselves, and especially avoid any unnecessary contact with the media.'

Arianna turned and stepped down off the podium as the senators began to disperse, pursued by the uncomfortable feeling that there was something out there that had been heading their way for millennia and that she was powerless to do anything about it.

***

Dean Crawford

VI

San Diego

California

'Give it some, man!'

The *Vampire's* EM Drive howled as the induction system drew in vast volumes of air and blasted it from the exhaust, the craft surging forward as though fired from a cannon. Above the howling engine the three teenagers in Chance Macy's ride screamed in delight as they rocketed across the open desert at two hundred twenty knots.

Chance leaned back in his seat, cruising on autopilot above the narrow metallic twin strips of the I94 north west of the city. The sun was setting out across the nearby Pacific beyond the hills, the sky a spectacular panorama of high cirrus clouds glowing against the deep blue of the heavens. He could see cruisers lifting off from the space port in the city and rising up into the evening sky, ion engines flaring white, and high above them the brilliant star–like orb of New Los Angeles dominated the sky to the north. As he watched, he saw two shooting stars arc across the sky and vanish as they burned up in the atmosphere.

'We can break three hundred!' his passenger, Freck Seavers, yelled in delight.

The *Vampire* was heavily modified, a gift from Chance's father on his graduation from college. Not that Chance gave a hell or hoot for working, despite his degree. His father owned the Macy Shipping Company out of New York City and was worth more than some small cities. Chance knew that he was first in line of his three siblings to inherit the company, so until that day came his main plan in life was to get drunk, get high and get laid, although not necessarily in that order.

The two girls in the back seats of the *Vampire's* sleek fuselage,

Candice and Evelyn, giggled and sipped alcohol from the bottle as Chance kicked the accelerator and the vehicle surged faster across the plain, turning to follow a right hand bend that would bring them down through the valleys to Lower Otay Lake on the city's south side. He glanced at the airspeed indicator and saw two hundred seventy four knots.

'Give it some more, man!' Freck yelled as he swigged beer from a chilled flask in one hand.

Chance eyed the bend and knew that he couldn't take it at more than two fifty, which itself was a hundred over the limit. The I94's boundary lines demarcated the "safe zone" where the Vampire could travel without moving out over the rocky, uneven terrain either side of the interstate. The black market location shield he'd fitted to the *Vampire* to prevent the authorities from tracking his speed was one law he could break, but Newton's Laws of Motion were pretty much out of his hands. Chance eased back off the throttle and Freck sneered at him.

'Man, you go not guts!'

'I do have a brain though,' Chance replied casually as the Vampire slowed through two hundred and some of the wind screaming past the open T Top faded away. 'I'd like to keep it in my head and not splashed across the desert.'

Freck shook his head as the *Vampire* plunged into shadowy valleys, his curly red hair and gaunt features twisted with disgust as he looked at the girls in the back seat.

'Looks like Chance's weener just shrunk a little!'

The girls giggled, but Chance didn't bite on Freck's insult. The kid was ugly to say the least, even though his deceased folks had owned a property estate and could have afforded the cosmetic re–alignment that would have fixed his twisted smile, spotty complexion and heavy eyebrows. They hadn't, something to do with "being comfortable with one's self" or some such, and though they had died in an accident and Freck had inherited their fortune, his parents' wills had created a major drag by insisting that Freck refrain from cosmetic enhancement on threat of forfeiting his inheritance.

Chance himself had no need of any enhancements, his footballer's physique and square jawed smile the very reason he didn't bridle whenever Freck tried to provoke him. Freck would be getting out of the vehicle soon, and neither Candice or Evelyn would be wanting to go with him. As ever, Chance would choose which of the girls would go with him tonight.

Or, maybe they both would.

The thought caused a smile to cross Chance's face and then he heard the screaming.

'Look out!'

Chance saw two pin prick lights appear as if from nowhere before them and he stamped down on the airbrakes as he hauled back on the throttle. The *Vampire* howled as it slowed, reverse thrusters slamming all of them against their restraints. The two lights vanished as quickly as they had appeared and the vehicle shuddered to a halt in the half darkness, its headlights glowing like beacons and the desert sky silent above them and filled with countless stars.

'Jeez, what the hell was that?!' Freck snapped.

Chance sighed and shook his head, his heart still racing. The *Vampire's* hard light shields would easily have deflected whatever animal had run out in front of the vehicle, but it was still a natural human instinct to slow dramatically when an obstacle appeared in front of such a fast moving craft. Chance recalled the last time he'd hit a wild horse while driving out here, the grim remains of the animal plastered across the shields as he'd driven his then girlfriend home, weeping all the way.

'Must've been a deer or something,' he said finally as he reached down to engage the EM Drive again, the Vampire moving off once more. 'The eyes were pretty high up.'

Freck looked about them and then glanced at the girls in the back seats

'Hey, why don't we get out here and have some fun?'

Chance looked at Freck and then at the girls. There was a furtive expression on his friend's features, and Freck's eyes flicked to Candice's long, tanned legs.

'Y'know,' Freck added as he looked Evelyn up and down, 'fun?'

Chance saw the girls' smiles vanish and Candice recoiled in her seat.

'*Eww*, no *way*!'

Evelyn burst out laughing and shook her head, her long brown hair spilling like shimmering smoke around her bare shoulders. 'Like, not in a million years, *Freak*!'

Freck withered in his seat as his skin flushed hot, and then he scowled as outrage burned him inside.

'Stop the car.'

Chance blinked. 'Do what now?'

'Stop the damned car!'

Chance slammed on the airbrakes once more and the Vampire slid to a halt amid the soaring desert valleys. Freck hit the door release and climbed out.

'Where are you going?' Chance asked, suddenly concerned.

'Home,' Freck snapped.

Evelyn pouted. 'Oh come on, I was only kidding.'

'You can't walk home,' Chance pointed out. 'It's gotta be twenty miles from here to the city limit.'

Freck shoved his hands in his pockets and stormed off. 'Better to walk twenty miles alone than spend another second with those two.'

Chance watched as Freck staggered off, the girls leaning on the back of his seat. Any concerns he might have had vanished as he felt Evelyn's hand on his chest.

'Isn't it time we got going?' she purred.

Chance sighed. 'We can't leave him out here.'

'It's not our choice, it's his,' Evelyn whispered, 'and my folks will be back by eleven so if we don't head home soon...'

Evelyn let the statement hang in the air for a moment. Chance took one last look at Freck, his shoulders set in defiance as he kept walking, his head down and his gaze resolutely averted.

'Right,' he said finally, 'the hell with him.'

Chance slammed the throttle down, the engine growling and Evelyn squealing with delight as the Vampire lurched forward and thundered past Freck. Chance saw his friend consumed by a cloud of desert dust and then his tiny figure shrank to a speck against the sunlit hills.

*

'Losers.'

Freck spat the word along with a mouthful of dust as the Vampire accelerated away into the brilliant sunset pouring like molten metal across the horizon. Freck squinted into the blazing distance and knew that he would never be able to walk the full twenty miles. Not that he had intended to.

Freck hated Chance, Evelyn and their *oh so perfect* little crowd of sycophants and fashion victims. They had more money than Freck, better looks, better homes, better educations, better everything. Hell, Freck didn't even have any parents, his education and life funded by the insurance payouts after they had died when their shuttle flight from New Chicago crashed in the deserts of Utah after a freak collision with another shuttle whose pilot had died of a heart attack at the controls. If that hadn't occurred, Freck would never have made it into the college, where money spoke louder than qualifications.

Freck pulled out his black zone communicator, an illegal device that operated on frequencies outside those of lawful communicators. He accessed a single contact and then waited as the connection was made.

'They're on their way,' he said without hesitation. 'They'll hit city limits off I Ninety Four in five minutes. Come get me when you're done, and make sure you film it.'

'Where you at?'

'Twenty miles east on the ninety four, make it fast.'

'We'll be there.'

Freck shut off the communicator, then tossed it onto the nearby desert dust and with a flourish of hate stamped one heel down upon it. The delicate, glowing screen shattered and the lights blinked out, much as he knew Chance and the girls' soon would.

Freck started walking again, feeling suddenly excited. He couldn't wait to see those girls again. Evelyn would not disrespect him or reject him again, largely because she wouldn't have a choice. Freck was done with this life; the rejections, the social awkwardness, the cold shoulder he received from most everybody around him. *Freak*, they called him. Who the hell in this day and age wouldn't give their children the surgery to rectify a thin jaw, hooked nose and wiry, tight hair? Nobody wanted to look like he did. Freck didn't want to look like he did.

Beauty is skin deep, son, his mother had always said. *It's what you're like on the inside that counts.* Freck's pleas to the effect that on the inside he looked bitter and sad at being denied a simple human right had fallen on deaf ears, but now his parents were gone and since becoming wealthy he had made some new friends who had promised they could get him the surgery he wanted "off the books". The money he had inherited would fund his bio enhancements whether the lawyers liked it or not, and as it happened the same people who could organize the black market surgery also knew a nefarious community of blowhards who could arrange pretty much anything Freck's deep pockets could afford.

Somewhere out on the city limits, four bonehead thugs were waiting. Paid half their fee up front in cash, their instructions were simple: grab the girls, bring them to Freck. He would then have his way with them, before leaving what was left to the thugs. Chance...,

Freck had decided to allow him to live and felt great pride in his magnanimous gesture. The girls on the other hand would have to die so that they could not identify him as the...

Freck whirled and froze as he heard something in the shadows behind him. He listened to the silence of the desert, suddenly aware of how alone he was out here and how far away the comforts of civilization were. He cursed himself silently for not waiting until the Vampire had been a bit closer to home before getting out, as had been his plan all along. Evelyn would surely have insulted him again anyway. This was *her* fault, and now he was stuck out here alone.

A lizard slithered down off a rock nearby and Freck sighed in relief. He refrained from walking across to it and stamping on its neck, rising above his anger as he turned and almost walked straight into a man.

Freck jumped out of his skin as he stared at Chance standing right in front of him. He glanced past his friend into the distance where the Vampire had raced away toward San Diego.

'Chance? How the hell did you...?'

Chance lunged forward and Freck saw in his eyes a blackness, that of a man with no soul. Chance grasped Freck's shoulders in his hands, his grip like an iron vice that crushed Freck's muscles. Freck opened his mouth to scream for help and saw Chance's face dissolve into a horrific maelstrom as something shot out from it toward him.

Freck felt white pain sear his body as the horrific protrusion forced its way down his throat and tore through his body in a surge of white pain. His feet lifted up off the ground and then his neck snapped like a dry twig and the brilliant sunlight vanished into darkness.

***

VII

CSS Victory

Polaris Station

Sula stepped off the boarding ramp of a shuttle and onto the deck of the frigate Victory and tried to quell the nervousness tingling in the pit of her stomach. She surveyed the scene around her and realized that this was the world into which her father had walked many years before.

The frigate was two hundred fifty thousand tons of metal, armor, plasma cannons and flight deck that dwarfed any of the ships that she had seen visit New Washington during her years growing up near North Four. As she stood with the half dozen or so other honorary Ensigns who had been flown out here to experience life aboard a serving frigate, she could see a row of Phantom fighters parked nearby, their canopies open and technicians working on and around them. Her choice of service here was no coincidence, for her father had flown Phantoms with "Fighting Eighty Fourth" to the day that he died.

'This way, please.'

A duty sergeant who looked like he'd spent centuries aboard the ship gestured for them to follow him and they walked in a narrow rank two wide, staying outside the yellow warning barriers that demarked the active engine run up areas where intakes or exhausts could cause fatal injuries. Although no fighters were flying that day, Victory was still on active duty and could theoretically be called into action at any moment.

'The ship's due to launch within the hour,' the duty sergeant explained as he led them off the flight deck. 'We'll be underway to Sol System border patrol and two visits to the Rim Colonies under CSS protection. It's a milk run so there's little danger of any live engagements, but you never know…'

The twinkle in the eye of the duty sergeant provoked a ripple of laughter among the Ensigns around Sula as they walked, but she could sense the unease it veiled. Victory had been involved in some of the heaviest fighting of the Ayleean War and still carried some of the scars to this day, her upper hull pockmarked with ageing plasma scoring and dents that had not yet been repaired. Her commander, Captain O'Donnell, reputedly liked them to remain to remind everybody who served aboard Victory what it was they were getting into.

'You've each been assigned a serving officer based on your preferences and availability,' the duty sergeant went on. 'Your active duty begins now, and your job is to assist your officer while learning the routine of life aboard an active fleet warship. What you learn here will assist you should you decide to commit to a career within the fleet, so pay attention and use the time as best you can. You all did well to beat the competition to be here, so make the most of it.'

Sula sensed the pride in those around her, but she didn't buy it. Her father had often spoken of how undermanned the fleet had been during the war, of how few people wanted to fight the Ayleeans after hearing so many horrific stories about them. The feeling back home in New Washington was that they should be left alone, Sol's borders the only thing that needed protection. Interventionist wars to "prevent" an invasion force that might never come had been unpopular as far back as she could remember, and recruitment into CSS fleet ranks barely sufficient to sustain a war footing. Sula reckoned the fleet was glad to have anybody sign up, and had sensed no great competition for places when she'd applied just two months before for the scholarship.

'Sula?

She saw the group stop and the duty sergeant pointed at a doorway, above which was emblazoned the logo of the Fighting Eighty Fourth.

'You're up,' the sergeant said. 'You're assigned to Lieutenant Tyrone Hackett. Report for duty inside, and good luck – they're a tough bunch to get along with.'

'How so?' Sula asked.

'They're pilots,' he replied with a thin smile, as though it were obvious.

Before she could reply the sergeant led the little group away to other areas of the ship. Sula sighed, turned to the door and wondered how often her father had walked through the same doorway. There were no hard light doors aboard a frigate, the ship using the old fashioned solid doors both to save on power and to help protect against the spread of fire aboard ship during battle.

Sula took a breath and knocked once on the door.

'Yeah?'

Sula opened the door and pushed through to reveal a ready room that was adorned only with a single table and two rows of lockers. The walls were freshly painted, but she could see evidence of scrawlings beneath them of which at least one read: RIP. She figured they were probably relics from the Ayleean War days.

Before her were three officers, two men and one woman, all of them pilots and all of them lounging idly around the table and looking bored, playing cards held loosely in their hands.

'I'm looking for Tyrone Hackett,' she said.

A young man with a shock of black hair, maybe thirty years old, raised an eyebrow and looked her up and down.

'And what would you want with a wonderful man like Hackett?' he asked. 'Don't be shy now.'

Sula saw the CSS wings on his flight suit and the name beneath them.

'I'm Ensign Sula Reyon and I've been attached to you as a honorary Ensign for the duration of the voyage.'

A gust of laughter burst from the three pilots and they leaned back in their chairs as Tyrone tossed his cards down onto the table.

'Man, Captain O'Donnell has really got it in for you, Tornado,' said the woman.

'Tornado?' Sula asked, confused.

'His call sign,' the woman replied, her flight suit name patch reading Lieutenant Ellen Goldberg. 'He tends to leave a trail of destruction in his wake, women and all.'

Sula narrowed her eyes as she looked at Tyrone. With jet black hair, a wide jaw and green eyes he certainly looked the part of the renegade fighter pilot, but he was clearly not pleased to see her.

'I don't want a chaperone,' he muttered. 'Take a hike, kid.'

Sula bristled and took a pace closer to the table. 'The hell I will.'

That got their attention, and for a moment Sula thought that she'd crossed a line already. The three pilots stared at her in amazement, and then the woman pointed a finger at her.

'Talking to a superior officer in that way'll get you locked in the brig before we're even underway.'

'I'm sorry, I didn't mean, I just…'

'Fortunately for you, there's nothing superior about Tornado Tyrone,' the woman added, 'so go for your life.'

Tyrone smiled and shook his head. 'And that's the support I get from my own wingman.'

'Wing lady,' the woman snapped, 'and don't you forget it.'

The woman stood up and moved across to Sula. 'Lieutenant Ellen Goldberg of the fighting eighty fourth.'

Sula shook her hand, but she was standing like a loose end in the room and wondered what the hell she was supposed to do next. Tyrone, apparently, was having the same thoughts.

'So, what exactly are you supposed to do for me? Can you fly my Phantom? Plan combat air patrols? Fuel calculation?'

'Well, no.'

'Go easy on her Tyrone, she only just walked through the damned door,' Ellen said and then turned back to Sula. 'Your job is to follow him around and clear up the chaos he leaves behind him, which he will because Captain O'Donnell's sending us over to Endeavour after they had an argument.'

'It was a disagreement,' Tyrone murmured. 'You know how we feel about the Ayleens.'

'How *you* feel about them,' Ellen corrected.

'It's that damned accord they're signing,' Tyrone complained. 'It'd be quicker if we all committed suicide.'

'It might bring lasting peace,' Sula pointed out.

'It might bring lasting extinction,' Tyrone snapped. 'The Ayleeans can't be trusted as far as they can be thrown. They're murderous, cruel, self centered sons of bit…'

'Bit of an attitude on him, this one,' Ellen advised Sula. 'Captain O'Donnell reckons he plays better when there's a woman in command 'cause he didn't play up when he served on Defiance. It's why they partnered him with me.'

Sula got the impression that Tyrone Hackett didn't play well with anybody. 'Lucky you.'

'Tell me about it.'

'How the hell did you become an officer with *that* attitude?' she asked Tyrone.

Again, raised eyebrows were directed at her and Ellen laughed out loud. 'Well girl, you two are gonna get along just fine. Grab our stuff and let's go, we'll find you a slot on a shuttle across to Defiance, they're short handed right now and you'll fit in just fine there. We've got to get over to Endeavour. The ship's leaving pronto for some reason and we need to be aboard.'

'I wanted to serve with a pilot, not a lay about, and I wanted Victory,' Sula said, and then decided not to mention her late father. 'It's what I requested.'

Tyrone chuckled bitterly.

'It's called taking orders. You joined the fleet expecting to get what you want? Man, how did you get a scholarship with *that* attitude?'

Sula frowned. 'We're not supposed to be attached to combat

frigates.'

'Because there's a danger you'll have to actually fight?' Tyrone smirked at her. 'Oh me, oh my, whatever will we do? Take a hike Ensign, only big boys get to play with big toys.'

Sula bristled as the other pilot chuckled to himself but said nothing. Ellen picked up a heavy looking kit bag and gestured to the door.

'Take no notice of them. Victory's on milk run duty but Defiance is heading out beyond the Rim, so you can add that to your C.V. You wanna stay here on Victory with the other lightweights in your Ensign group, or do you wanna see a real frigate at work?'

Sula glared at Hackett but then smiled at Ellen. 'I'm in.'

'Atta girl,' Ellen grinned back. 'You mind helping out here?'

Sula turned and opened the door for her as Tyrone hefted his own bag onto his shoulder and then thought twice about it. As he walked up to her, he held the bag out for her.

'Welcome to the fleet, Sula. Hope this isn't too heavy.'

Sula took the bag, which weighed almost as much as she did, and heaved it onto her shoulder as she saw Ellen give her wingman a dirty look.

'Hey, the kid wants to help, so let her help!' Tyrone chortled as he walked out of the ready room.

Sula sighed, and with an effort she followed the two pilots back toward the launch bays and wondered whether her father's career in the fleet had begun by dragging around the belongings of an opinionated, sexist jet jockey like Tyrone Hackett.

***

VIII

New Washington

'I hate these places.'

A fine drizzle of rain fell in thin veils as Nathan followed Kaylin Foxx across a street toward a secure complex near the precinct building that housed the coroner's office. The gigantic eye of the earth glowed far above them, filling the sky with its slowly rotating blue and white ocean and distant cloud formations as New Washington rotated about its axis. He could see the east coast of America bathed in sunlight and the advancing darkness crossing the immense Atlantic Ocean as the sun began to set far below them.

Despite having been here for a year now Nathan still could not take his eyes off the vast spectacle that dominated the station's "sky". A bizarre fusion of nature's watercolor grace, mankind's metallic fecundity and humanity's ever condensing breath falling from the city's heights, he couldn't quite decide if it was strikingly beautiful or architecturally grotesque. He had once seen a painting hanging in a gallery on the south side called *"Rainbows over metal spires"*, a digitally crafted work by an artist dead now for over a hundred years. It had perfectly captured the mood of the city and others like it, the falling veils of rain producing rainbows and sometimes mysterious sun sprites and halos as sunlight beamed through the station's towering arms to strike them.

Nathan almost walked into Foxx as she slowed, the coroner's office doors automatically interrogating her detective's shield before opening up before them.

'You need to look where you're going,' Foxx said as she glanced briefly up at the complex vista Nathan had been watching. 'Yearning for home again?'

Nathan shook his head as he followed her inside. 'Not so much, just enjoying the view.'

'I'll never get used to the idea of you admiring people's breath falling from a metal sky,' she said as they walked past the reception area where a humanoid machine waved them past with a digitized smile of greeting. 'It's gross.'

Nathan didn't bridle.

'Everybody alive today has at least one molecule of Julius Caesar's last breath inside of them,' he pointed out as they walked. 'We're all a mixture of people who have lived before us.'

'Lovely thought,' Foxx said. 'I don't want to think about having somebody's bad breath from yesterday running down my neck.'

'You spoil every moment.'

'This is New Washington, wherein dwell the dregs of orbital life,' Foxx murmured. 'You can't polish a turd, Nathan.'

'No, but you can sprinkle glitter on it.'

Foxx stifled a grin as she walked through a pair of hard light doors that shimmered out of existence before them. As they passed through into the coroner's office a wall of sparkling green light washed over their bodies, ridding them of contaminants before they entered the laboratory proper.

'Ah, Detective Foxx!'

Doctor Schmidt's glowing holographic form was standing over a mortuary slab, his hands behind his back and the familiar ingratiating smile on his face as he saw them approach. Beside him was a machine, humanoid in nature but equipped with six robotic arms wielding various surgical instruments.

'Schmidt,' Foxx greeted him with a genuine smile. 'What do you have for us?'

'Apart from smug self satisfaction,' Nathan added.

'I have that in abundance Detective Ironhead and it's all for you,' Schmidt replied jovially, but then his humorous façade slipped as he turned to the body on the slab. 'Unfortunately, our victim is a little short on mirth right now considering her manner of death.'

'You got a proximal cause?' Foxx pressed.

Schmidt tilted his head this way and that as he winced and folded his arms. 'I've got several, but the chief cause of death for the time being appears to be extreme dehydration.'

Foxx blinked. Neither of them had seen that coming. Nathan could see that the skeletal remains of Erin Sander's body were lying on the slab, but that none of the limbs had been moved from when they had first seen the body atop the apartment block on the south side. The skin was still taut across the rigid bones, sparkling like frost in the bright laboratory lights.

'She died of thirst?' Nathan asked as he looked down at the corpse.

'No,' Schmidt replied, 'and that's what is most disturbing about this case. Judging by the evidence of trauma to the throat and stomach, all of the fluid inside her body was extracted forcefully.'

Foxx winced. 'Seriously?'

'It's quite common in the animal kingdom, actually,' Schmidt said in a conversational tone. 'Most spiders use a toxin in their venom that is designed specifically to decompose the living flesh of their victim, after which the spider sucks the fluid out of the body.'

'Lush,' Nathan said, 'but unless we have a gigantic spider roaming New Washington then we're gonna have to hold off evacuating every arachnophobe on the station.'

'Some parasitic wasps perform a similar process,' Schmidt went on as though he hadn't even heard Nathan. 'They lay their eggs inside the bodies of victims that they have paralyzed with their sting. The eggs hatch inside the still living victim and proceed to eat it from the inside out. It's quite fascinating to watch if you're interested in that sort...'

'We're not,' Foxx assured him, 'and I'm pretty sure we don't have wasps the size of police cruisers wandering around New Washington either, so what's the lowdown here doc'? You figured out what kind of machine could do this?'

Schmidt sighed as he looked down at the victim, even though he had no lungs with which to do so.

'I've researched the literature and I've been able to identify several mechanical devices that could plausibly achieve what this poor young lady endured. The problem is that I have encountered absolutely no trace of cutting implements, forcible entry of foreign objects or any other evidence that would suggest she suffered these injuries as a result of a surgical procedure of any kind.'

Nathan leaned over the victim's body as though doing so might reveal some hitherto unseen evidence.

'So, you called us here, what do you think was responsible for this?'

'If I were to hazard a guess I would have to say that this is indeed some kind of parasitic animal that feeds on biological tissue, on flesh,' Schmidt replied.

Foxx stared at the doctor blankly for a moment. 'You're kidding?'

'I'm not. I can only imagine how such a creature might have got on board New Washington, or where it may have come from in the first place.'

'All inbound cruisers and shuttles are subjected to intense scans before they're allowed to land,' Foxx pointed out. 'The protocols preventing biological contamination of the orbital stations are strict and complex, but they work. Nothing could have sneaked aboard without being detected in one way or another.'

'Was there any residue?' Nathan asked. 'If something preyed upon her, then maybe it left something behind?'

Schmidt nodded. 'That was my first thought but I was able to extract nothing from the remains except this lady's own remaining body tissue, all of which was desiccated. There has been no evidence left behind or genetic material that belonged to the creature that did this.'

Foxx frowned as she looked down at the body. 'Is there *any* chance at all that this was a mechanical event disguised as a natural death?'

'It's possible,' Schmidt confirmed as he rounded the mortuary slab. 'I cannot rule out the possibility that somebody, for reasons unknown, murdered this woman in order to harvest her organs or some other ghoulish purpose.'

Aboard the orbital stations there was a small but busy market in spare organs, usually for those damaged by equally illegal body enhancement surgeries. Getting people to throw good money after bad was something at which most criminal enterprises excelled, but Nathan wasn't buying it that someone like Erin Sanders would have been targeted for her organs. There were many other, easier targets for such a gruesome slaying who lived in areas of the city where it would have been much easier to conceal the crime.

'Criminal gangs don't go to these lengths without a damned good reason. What about the crystals in her skin? Anything there that could be of use?'

'Sodium chloride,' Schmidt replied, 'or common salt. Whatever did this to her had more of a taste for sweet than savory.'

'That's an analogy I could've done without,' Foxx said. 'What about the woman herself? Anything new on her background?'

'Erin Sanders,' Schmidt replied, accessing the woman's data from CSS Central Storage in the blink of an eye. 'Twenty six years old, graduate student from the University of New Chicago. Moved to New Washington six months ago to start a job as a drug counselor at New Hope Hospital on the north side. No criminal record, few known associates outside of work here in New Washington, a model citizen. She commuted every day via the Belt's Mag Rail and was killed on her way home. Her ID went silent at about the time of death.'

Nathan shook his head in disbelief. 'Twenty six,' he echoed. 'She looks like she's been dead for centuries.'

'There's not much more that I can tell you from her remains,' Schmidt said, 'other than that she was in perfect health and that there were no other mitigating factors involved in her death. In the absence of her internal organs, blood and other internal fluids I cannot establish a proximal cause of death and cannot confirm or deny whether she was intoxicated or under the influence of drugs of any kind at the time of her death.'

'Given what we do know about her, I doubt we'd have found anything of the sort,' Foxx said. 'If you're right, it means we're not looking for organ smugglers at all.'

Nathan stared at Erin's body for a moment longer and then Foxx's communicator bleeped a warning. Foxx stood back and used her optical implant to activate the communications frequency, and immediately a life size hologram of a California State Trooper appeared before them in the laboratory.

'Sergeant Dale Wilson, Cali' State,' he announced himself in a brisk tone. 'Database says you guys are investigating some kind of homicide involving desiccated remains?'

'Yeah, we're with one now,' Foxx replied. 'What do you have for us?'

The trooper looked to one side at something Nathan couldn't see before he replied.

'You need to get planet side as soon as you can,' Wilson said. 'You've got another one right here and two more in Nevada.'

***

IX

CSS Endeavour

Ayleean System

'Cap'n on the deck!'

The bridge crew of the frigate Endeavour snapped to attention as Captain Travis Harper walked onto the command platform.

'At ease,' Harper said as he glanced at the Executive Officer. 'Status report?'

'We're five minutes from sub luminal deceleration,' the XO, Reeves, replied. 'Tactical stations are on stand by and we have four fighters ready to launch on cats one through four.'

Harper nodded as he stepped up onto the command platform and surveyed the bridge. Circular in design, with the command platform at the rear containing Harper's command seat and stations for tactical, communications and engineering, the bridge was simpler than those of the big hitters like Titan and controlled directly by its officers. Harper, a senior commander with fifty two years of experience within the fleet, disliked and distrusted the way in which modern warship commanders were often "wired in" directly to their vessel's central computer.

Harper sat down in his command seat and surveyed four holographic screens that hovered before him, presenting tactical, strategic and status information without blocking his view of the main viewing screen before them all on the bridge. Endeavour was an older frigate but she was well tested in battle and unlike the modern bells and whistles fitted to the CSS capital ships, everything aboard her was known to work correctly.

'I want all comm's channels open when we drop into sub luminal,' Harper said as he thoughtfully stroked one side of his moustache between his fingers. 'But I want all shields up and plasma cannons charged. Compute an immediate egress course before we reach orbit. I want to be able to jump out of there in an instant if something goes wrong.'

'Aye, sir,' Reeves replied briskly as he turned to relay the orders, one shoulder lower than the other where an Ayleean's plasma rifle had found its mark years earlier during the Battle of Proxima Centauri. The shot had missed his lungs but evaporated half of his ribcage, however Reeves had always refused cosmetic surgery beyond what was required to keep him alive and comfortable. Harper reckoned the XO used his deformation to remind newer recruits that life in the fleet was a serious business.

'Four minutes now,' the navigation officer reported from his post to one side of the command platform.

Harper looked at the navigation screen, the holographic image relayed from the navigation officer's console. He could see Endeavour's predicted path icon moving swiftly toward the Ayleean system, while nearby another icon denoted the predicted path and position of CSS Defiance. Both frigates had been diverted from their original missions after a priority signal from Polaris Station and CSS Command just before they had been due to jump into super luminal cruise for the Rim Colonies. The simple message, despite being of so few words, had instantly put Harper on edge.

IMMEDIATE ACTION: AYLEEAN SECTOR, IFF LOST, CSS FORTITUDE. CONDITIONAL REPORT ON ARRIVAL.

The second frigate, Defiance, had also been posted to the mission as a safeguard and would come out of super luminal sixty seconds after Endeavour and in a slightly different orbit, as he and Captain Lucas had planned before departing the Sol System.

'Alert Status,' Harper said calmly.

Instantly the bright deck lighting turned red and an alarm horn sounded mournfully through the ship as the crew prepared for battle.

Harper had not embarked on this emergency assignment expecting a fight, but he sure wasn't going to drop out of sub luminal one planetary diameter from Ayleea without taking every precaution possible. None of the crew except for the officers knew that CSS had lost contact with the senate vessel Fortitude after it had arrived in the Ayleean sector. Instead, Harper had decided to inform them only that assistance had been requested by her crew in the sector.

'You ready for this, Travis?'

Reeves stood beside the captain's seat and spoke quietly from the corner of his mouth, keeping his familiar tone from the rest of the crew. Harper looked up at the XO, who was standing with his hands behind his back but was leaning forward like a dog straining at an invisible leash.

'You look like you are.'

'I'm appalled that you'd think so,' Reeves growled, but his eyes glittered with delight as he glanced at the captain. 'At least we don't have to do what Fortitude probably did and wander in here with our eyes closed hoping for the best, our hands shoved up our backsides. I'll put fifty down in cash that the Ayleeans have reneged and are preparing for war as we speak.'

Harper stared at the big screen before them, currently jet black, the frigate's super luminal velocity rendering them devoid of information from the cosmos beyond.

'I'll take that bet,' he replied, 'and hope that you're wrong.'

'One minute to sub luminal,' the navigation officer called.

The somber wail of the battle status alarm changed to a simpler beep that alerted the crew to imminent deceleration. Reeves placed one hand on his control console nearby, favoring his lower shoulder as Harper gripped the armrests of his seat and prepared himself. Whoever was waiting for them on Ayleea would know by now that they were coming, the frigate's gravitational bow shock by now detectable at its destination. Swift maneuvering and quick thinking were their only defenses, and Harper figured they would have little time to work out what had happened to Fortitude before they would have to leave the system at full power.

'Thirty seconds...'

Harper listened to the countdown as he made his last checks and saw four Phantom fighters ready to launch on the catapults down in the launch bays. The frigate's shields were fully charged and the plasma batteries were ready to fire.

'Five, four, three, two...'

Harper grabbed the seat rests a little tighter and then the bridge seemed to lurch backward, the light momentarily split into its spectral order as the main viewing screen flared with white light and then settled as Ayleea's brown and blue, cloud flecked orb appeared before them.

'Sub luminal, shields are up!' the navigation officer called.

'No sensor contacts!' the tactical officer reported. 'No weapon launches detected, no sensor spikes or large vessels nearby, captain!'

Harper hesitated, watching as data spilled in from the system beyond. His eyes scanned the streams of information even as he saw the four Phantom fighters on the cats wind their engines up to full power, ready to launch at a moment's notice.

'Check our tail, visual scanners!' Harper ordered.

Instantly, tactical responded to the check for any vessels sneaking up behind them while sensor shielded.

'Nothing detected in all sectors, captain!' Reeves replied.

Harper nodded. 'Launch cats one and two, hold three and four in support.'

Reeves relayed the order and instantly a pair of single seat Phantom fighters blazed down the catapult tracks and were launched out into space, their engines flaring with white flame as they accelerated away from the frigate.

Harper rapped his knuckles on the arm of his seat as he watched the two fighters shrink to the size of metallic specks against the vast jungle world of Ayleea, and almost immediately the communications officer called out to him.

'I'm detecting no emissions from Ayleea at all, but the readings are off the scale for interference on all frequencies. Temperature scans indicate continent wide forest fires and major damage to cities and urban areas.'

A deep and sudden silence enveloped the bridge as all of the officers present absorbed what they had just been told.

Slowly, Harper stood up out of his seat as he saw the image of the planet resolve itself before him. Features that he had taken for cloud formations revealed themselves to be immense swathes of burning forests releasing clouds of toxic smoke into the atmosphere. Cities glowed not with street lights but with flames, carnage wrought on a global scale.

'Any ships in the area, any survivors?'

The communications and tactical officers both scrutinized their displays for a moment, and then they shook their heads in unison.

'The whole damned planet's been ravaged,' Reeves gasped, staring fixedly at the vast screen and the incomparable devastation before them. 'We don't have anything that could achieve that.'

Harper clenched his fists and made his decision. 'Ping Fortitude's IFF transponder. Show me where she is.'

Reeves froze where he stood. 'That's against protocol, captain. We're in a combat situation. If we ping their transponder any vessel within the system's going to know about it real quick.'

Harper nodded. 'I didn't come here to fail our mission, XO. Dead or alive, we need to know what happened to Fortitude before we leave or the same thing might happen to earth. Ping the transponder.'

Reeves sucked in a lungful of air and then he turned and nodded to the tactical officer. The lieutenant manning the station accessed Fortitude's Identification Friend or Foe transponder frequency, and sent the signal. In an instant a spherical energy band raced out from the frigate at several times the speed of light, sweeping the planet and beyond in all directions as Endeavour's sensors sought the automated return ping that would reveal Fortitude's location. The signal was based on the same propagation of light's wavelength technology that allowed communications between vessels across light hours in moments. Quantum fluctuations in the vacuum that also caused the uniform attraction of the Casimir Effect allowed signals emitted at luminal velocity to accelerate exponentially, as they possessed no mass. The downside was that once emitted, there was no stopping them until they were simply broken up by the competing radiation of stellar bodies, black holes and other cosmological phenomena. A tactical *"hello, here we are"*, the signals also betrayed the presence and location of the emitting vessel.

A loud beep sounded in the bridge the moment the signal had been emitted.

'Contact, oh seven four, elevation niner two.'

Harper's eyes flicked across the main screen as the frigate's sensors immediately began zooming in on a faint band of sparkling metallic debris orbiting the planet. Harper at once recognized the vast remnants of a great battle, or a great massacre, depending on how one looked at it.

'That's the Ayleean fleet,' Reeves said.

Harper could see Ayleean warships strewn in orbit around the planet, their hulks glowing with escaping gases burning from internal fires. Debris littered the field, vast chunks of metal hull plating blasted from vessels after direct strikes now rotating in the deep chill of space and reflecting the dull glow of the red dwarf star at the center of the system.

The cameras zoomed in further and finally Harper saw what he had been looking for.

'There she is,' he said.

The shape of Fortitude's hull emerged from the background debris, her slender lines and polished metal form at odds with the bulky, angular rust red hulls of the Ayleean fleet. At once Harper could

70

see that she was intact and did not appear to have been fired upon.

'Send the fighters in, one fast pass, not too close,' he ordered.

Reeves responded immediately. 'Rebel Flight, fast pass on target coordinates being sent now, weapons hot.'

'Roger, co ords received, Rebel Flight.'

A second screen flickered into life, this one from a camera mounted atop one of the Phantom fighters' fuselages as the craft swept in and accelerated alongside the debris field, the leading fighter's exhaust plume visible ahead. Harper tried to prevent himself from clasping his hands together as he awaited the pass, and he saw the names Hackett and Goldberg on the roster beside the spacecraft.

'Hackett's part of Victory's flight roster,' he growled at the senior flight deck officer. 'What's he doing out there?'

'Transferred by Captain O'Donnell,' the deck officer replied. 'I'm guessing his wingman put him up to it to avoid milk run duty on Victory.'

'Something's not right here,' Reeves said. 'Why would someone, or something, attack an entire world and then just leave it behind? You don't conquer something and then abandon it like trash.'

Harper frowned, agreeing with his XO but uncertain of whether they would ever be able to fathom the intentions of a species that they could not possibly yet understand when...

'Rebel One, I've got visual.'

Tyrone Hackett's voice on the communications channel was laden with tension as the fighters rocketed through the gloomy debris field, beams of blood red sunlight piercing the orbiting forest of twisted metal, foggy veils of billowing gas and glittering clouds of ice fragments from oxygen vented by the ruptured spaceships.

'She looks like she's in one piece,' Rebel One continued. *'No plasma cannon hits, no hull ruptures that I can see. Slowing down.'*

Harper watched in silence as the fighters gradually slowed down. Through the clouds of fog and gas the captain could see the graceful hull of the senate vessel glinting, but it looked as though her metal was dulled, perhaps by the debris around her.

'Ten kilometers,' Hackett reported.

Harper saw a veil of gas sweep across the fighters like a cloud, and for a moment they could see nothing beyond the gases swirling through the frigid vacuum and glowing a vivid red from the star light beyond.

The clouds swept past and Fortitude's hull re–emerged, and in an instant Harper's guts felt as though they had broken free of their moorings and plunged into a cold abyss as he saw the thick layer of icy material entombing the senate vessel.

Like a cocoon of ice, the material was not something that he had seen before with his own eyes but he had read the reports of CSS *Titan's* encounter and like every other member of the crew he knew what he was looking at.

'Rebel Flight, get out of there!'

Even as the words fell from his lips Harper saw the icy tomb unravel itself like the petals of a grotesque and lethal flower to strike out at the passing fighters.

***

X

'Enemy!'

The tactical officer's cry filled the bridge of Endeavour as Captain Harper saw from amid the cluttered stream of debris orbiting Ayleea vast tendrils of what looked like ice emerge, as though a silent nest of gigantic, unthinkable creatures had stirred.

The Phantom fighters turned hard to starboard and lit their engine boost, an emergency thrust reheat that diverted all available power for a limited time to the engines. Harper saw them turning toward Endeavour and a vast, seething wall of icy material surging after them.

'What the hell *is* that?!' the communications officer gasped, a woman on her first operational tour who had clearly not encountered anything like this before.

'Rebel Flight, request fire support!'

Hackett's voice was high pitched with tension.

'Plasma batteries one through four, fire now!' Harper roared.

Endeavour trembled as four of her huge plasma batteries thundered a salvo of glowing blue–white charges that rocketed away toward the growing icy mass reaching out from the debris field. Harper could hear the recoil from the four meter guns echoing like distant thunder through the frigate's hull.

The shots raced past the fleeing Phantoms and plowed into the icy mass behind them. Harper saw the enormous tendrils of material blasted apart in blossoming explosions that illuminated the darkened debris field around them, saw the specks of the two fighters silhouetted against the detonations as they raced for safety.

And then he heard words that struck fear into any starship captain coming from Lieutenant Hackett's fighter.

'Endeavour, enemy astern!'

Captain Harper barely had time to turn to shout an order for evasive action when Endeavour suddenly lurched forward as she was struck by a blast of unimaginable force. The entire ship shuddered and the lights inside the bridge flickered out as panels were blasted from the ceiling and showers of brilliant sparks exploded from the walls and control stations.

Harper tumbled down off the command platform and smashed into a console, felt bright pain lance his shoulder and neck as his collar bone snapped and he collapsed onto one knee. His lungs convulsed with the pain and he stared for a moment into empty space as his brain struggled to maintain coherent thought. The blood red lights flickered on again and revealed a scene of absolute carnage around him.

'Full power!' he yelled, his voice twisted with pain. 'Get us out of here!'

Harper looked up at the engineering station and saw that the lieutenant there was sprawled across the deck, his eyes staring lifelessly back at Harper and his tongue hanging in shreds where his teeth had bitten through it. Half of his face was a scorched mess and a tangle of shredded metal shards were poking from the dome of his skull where they had penetrated his brain and killed him instantly.

'Pulse engines are out, captain!' somebody warned him.

'Shields are down!' the tactical officer yelled. 'We're disabled!'

Harper looked desperately for his XO and saw Reeves slumped against the side of the command platform where he had been hurled after the initial blast. His eyes were closed, his features slack and his right hand was crumpled where the impact of his landing had snapped the fingers back on themselves.

'Tactical, report?!' Harper cried out.

'Enemy, rear!' the tactical officer shouted. 'No signals except massive energy readings. We've lost power to all stern guns.'

Harper staggered to his feet, cradling his right arm in his left and wincing at the pain as he turned and looked at the screen. 'Show me,' he gasped.

The screen flickered and then showed the view astern of the frigate.

Harper's guts convulsed as he saw behind them an immense craft, larger than anything he had ever seen. Her hull was adorned with two huge strakes upon which were mounted what looked like engines at one end and tremendous cannons of some kind at the front. Atop her hull was a forward facing bridge construction that was larger on its own than any two CSS capital ships. The hull was sleek, streamlined and yet oddly out of perspective, as though viewed in a mirror that had warped the image. The hull plating was an odd color, somewhat camouflaged but not appearing to be made of anything that Harper could recognize. The vessel loomed over the stricken frigate like a bird of prey over a tiny, injured sparrow.

'Can we jump?' Harper gasped.

The tactical officer glanced at his instruments and a brief glow of hope appeared on his features. 'Yes, only once or twice but we've got enough power to do it. The enemy vessel is charging weapons again!'

Harper looked at one of the few remaining tactical displays and saw the Phantoms rushing in to land. In an instant, he knew that they wouldn't make it.

'Jump,' he uttered, hating every word. 'Jump now!'

The tactical officer didn't hesitate.

Endeavour trembled as the ship's power was diverted to her Higgs Drive and a moment later the light from the viewing screen flared brilliant white and then plunged into blackness. Captain Harper felt fresh pain behind his eyes as the view of the bridge shimmered and the frigate jumped directly from orbit into super luminal cruise.

*

'No!'

Lieutenant Tyrone Hackett saw Endeavour suddenly flicker in a kaleidoscopic rainbow as the light spectrum was bent around her hull, warping the blackness of space around her, and then she vanished in a brilliant flare of white light and was gone. In her place was the huge warship now cruising directly toward them, her immense plasma cannons glowing as she plowed through the glittering shower of debris left in Endeavour's wake.

'They left us!' Ellen cried. 'They left us!'

'Break left, maximum power!' Tyrone yelled.

The Phantom fighter rolled over and Tyrone pulled back on the control column, soaring away from the massive capital ship that was looming over them. He looked over his shoulder and saw Ellen hanging close on his wing as they accelerated away.

'What the hell do we do now?!' she asked in desperation.

'Head for the cavalry,' Tyrone replied as he locked a fresh set of coordinates into his flight computer. 'Give it everything we've got, now!'

Tyrone diverted all power to his engines and rear shields and pushed the throttles wide open. The Phantom's powerful ion engines thrust the fighter away from the debris field and the alien capital ship now turning to follow them.

'Transmit the emergency distress signal now,' Tyrone ordered.

'They'll be able to follow us!' Ellen argued. 'We can't outrun them forever, we need to hide.'

'No,' Tyrone snapped. 'We need to be *seen*.'

Tyrone hit the switch and broadcast an immediate distress signal on all frequencies. Then he looked ahead and silently prayed that he would be on target, on time, because if he wasn't they were both dead.

He checked over his shoulder again and saw through his canopy Ellen's fighter alongside his in a loose formation. Behind her he saw the huge capital ship swinging around, its immense cannons moving to point at them. Both he and Ellen had seen the devastation caused by those weapons in a single salvo against Endeavour. The two Phantom fighters would be entirely vaporized if a shot came within a couple of wingspans of their…

'Gravity well, dead ahead!' Ellen warned. 'There's more of them coming through!'

'No,' Tyrone said in reply. 'Break right!'

The Phantoms rolled again as Tyrone saw a bright light flash somewhere behind him. Moments later he saw two immense plasma shots rocket past their fighters in a blaze of brilliant red light, as though two entire suns were hurtling through space.

The Phantoms rocked from side to side as the shockwave from the shots hit them, and then they passed through the gravity well ahead of the fighters and changed direction randomly as their path was bent by the warping of space and time ahead.

Something caught his eye to his left and cold dread rushed upon him.

'Look out, break right!'

A tendril of icy, pulsating material rushed upon Ellen's fighter and he saw it crash into her stern as she turned hard away and flew directly overhead Tyrone's Phantom.

'I'm hit!' Ellen yelled.

A second white flash burst into life ahead of them and Tyrone saw the aggressive lines of a warship rush into view.

'Yeah!'

Tyrone recognized the sleek, sharply raked lines of a CSS frigate the moment he saw them, Defiance surging into view with her shields up and her cannons charged. He wasted no time in hitting the transmit button on his control column and broadcasting on the emergency frequency.

'Rebel Flight, Defiance, danger close, evasive action *now*!'

Tyrone pulled up and over the frigate as it rolled hard to port and began turning to bring its guns to bear on the massive warship bearing down upon them. The voice of the frigate's commander reached Tyrone as he pulled his Phantom around in a tight turn.

'Defiance, Rebel Flight, tactical?'

'Do not engage, prepare to leap immediately, two to land!' Tyrone yelled in response as he slowed his fighter and began turning toward Defiance's stern landing bays.

'Two cleared to land, take bays two and four.'

'Cleared to land, two and four, Rebel Flight.'

Ellen's voice crackled over the comms channel. 'I'm losing power!'

Tyrone looked up and saw her fighter, its stern covered in the strange icy material that was now creeping along the hull and fuselage. Tyrone felt nausea poison his stomach as he realized that Ellen could not possibly escape the material that was rapidly creeping toward her cockpit.

'That stuff, it's on your hull,' he said to her.

Ellen's voice replied, tight with horror. 'What the hell is it?'

'Rebel Flight, landing clearance denied. Contamination is too dangerous.'

Tyrone looked over his shoulder at the huge warship bearing down upon them, and he knew that they would not have time to clear Ellen's fighter of the alien material now surging along the fuselage.

'Defiance is jumping in ten seconds!'

Ellen's voice broke through once more. 'You can't leave us here!'

Tyrone racked his brains for a solution, and inspiration illuminated his mind with a grim choice.

'Defiance, head straight past us before you leap. Rebel Two, prepare to eject!'

'What?!' Ellen screamed at him. 'I'll have nowhere to go!'

'Trust me, do it, now!'

Tyrone saw Defiance turn and head directly for them, rapidly closing the gap as the fighters fled the huge alien vessel. He spoke calmly as he guided his fighter around in a tight turn to spoil the enemy's aim.

'Rebel Two, circle around behind Defiance and line up for landing, then apply maximum power on my mark.'

'You want me to apply max power on *landing?*'

'Do it,' Tyrone said.

Ellen's fighter swung around behind Defiance, a tiny metallic speck in the distance as Tyrone lined up on Defiance's bow and accelerated. The big frigate loomed up before him and he rocketed by just a few meters over the ship's bridge.

'Maximum power, now!'

Ellen's fighter lined up and he saw her engines flare as she accelerated toward him.

'I can see them!' Ellen almost screamed. 'They're nearly at the cockpit!'

Tyrone heard a strange, crackling sound as Ellen's communications began to break up, and he knew that they were out of time. He looked over his shoulder and saw the massive alien warship's huge plasma cannons glowing brighter as an internal charge built up.

Tyrone aimed for Ellen's fighter and opened the throttles fully, knowing that if he didn't get to Ellen in the next few seconds both she and Defiance's entire crew would be trapped here forever if not destroyed entirely.

'Defiance leaping in five seconds,' came the voice of the ship's XO. *'What the hell are you doing Hackett?'*

Tyrone aimed for the frigate's stern and Ellen's fighter rocketing toward him.

'Rebel Two, nose down and eject now!'

Tyrone was coming in too fast and he knew it but there was no other option. He maintained his course as he saw Ellen's fighter pitch abruptly nose down. The Phantom presented its entire plan form before him and then Ellen's cockpit section flared with bright flame as it ejected from the main fuselage.

The ejection sequence propelled the cockpit away from the Phantom and directly toward Defiance's open landing bay door as Tyrone aimed and then squeezed the trigger on his control column. A salvo of bright blue plasma blasts seared away from his wingtips and rocketed over Ellen's cockpit to smash into the Phantom fighter and blast it into a million flaming fragments.

'Four seconds, three, two...'

Tyrone pulled up steeply and looked over his shoulder to see Ellen's cockpit sail into Defiance's landing bay and the huge doors closed behind her as the remains of her fighter and its alien attacker burned out.

'Damn me, Hackett,' Defiance's XO murmured, aware of what he had done to get Ellen safely back on board.

Tyrone looked at the enemy warship and saw its plasma cannons glowing bright red. 'Defiance, jump, *now!*'

There was no reply, nothing but silence as Tyrone hauled the Phantom around in a tight turn and saw Defiance flare white at her bow and suddenly vanish in a brief rainbow of warped light. The frigate plunged into super luminal cruise as Tyrone rocketed clear and two more tremendous blasts of red energy soared through the trembling gravity well where *Defiance* had been moments before.

Tyrone sighed as he slumped in his seat and glanced at his tactical display. Only the enemy capital ship appeared on his sensors, along with strange and shadowy features that he assumed were the icy striations he'd seen emerging from the debris field.

Ellen was safe and both Defiance and Endeavour were away. That left only him.

Tyrone craned his neck around and saw the huge vessel bearing down upon him now. Tyrone's fighter was faster in short bursts, but those huge engines would soon bring the warship into range and he would be history in a bright burst of unimaginable heat.

Tyrone didn't fancy giving them the satisfaction. He turned his fighter and aimed for the forested world far below, the huge orb of Ayleea filling his vision as he pushed the throttles open. At maximum velocity and with the planet's gravity helping, the Phantom would hit the Ayleea's atmosphere like a shooting star and burn up in a fraction of a second. He wouldn't know what had hit him.

Better to go out by choice in a blaze of glory than let some warmongering bunch of...

Tyrone glanced at his tactical display and he saw the huge warship suddenly break off the pursuit. Moments later, the ship's engines flared and it vanished into super luminal cruise. For a moment Tyrone was lost as to why they would allow him to escape, and then he realized that Defiance and Endeavour were bigger prizes than he. Plus, the enemy probably knew as he did that in a single seat fighter with limited range and endurance, there was nowhere for him to go but down. He was doomed.

'CSS Defiance, allied ground force requesting immediate assistance! Civilians in distress!'

The cry burst across the frequency and Tyrone pulled up from his suicidal dive. His voice was high pitched with disbelief and relief as he replied.

'Ground force this is CSS fighter Rebel One, what's your location?'

Tyrone had no idea what he was going to do and no idea how he was going to do it. If Defiance had held on a moment longer they would have heard the distress call too, but now Tyrone was the only human being left in orbit around the planet. About the only thing that he knew for sure was that he was on his own in a single seat fighter with nowhere to run and now he didn't even have the luxury of dying in peace because there was no way he could leave survivors of Fortitude's crew alone to die here.

'Rebel One, we're on the surface. Repeat, we're on the surface! Transmitting coordinates now!'

Tyrone looked at the savagely burning planet far below and he knew that he had no choice. The survivors might have important information on the enemy, knowledge that could help swing a battle in their favor. He banked the Phantom fighter over and began preparing for atmospheric entry, wondering all the while what he was going to find down there.

***

XI

New Chicago

Director General Arianna Coburn sat in a seat inside the executive shuttle as it pulled away from New Chicago's vast, slowly rotating bulk and began turning toward the bright blue and white eye of the earth. The visit to the governor of an orbital city was a routine event and had been covered by Global Wire Media but it had taken all of her inner strength to conceal her anxiety over the fate of the Ayleean mission. Normally the serene and silent nature of space flight enthralled her as much as it had done when she had first taken a trip into space sixty three years before, but now her eyes stared unseeing into the deep blackness.

'Penny for 'em?'

Rear Admiral Vincent O'Hara eased into a seat alongside Arianna's, a soothing smile on his features. Twenty years her elder and an experienced former fighter pilot in the CSS fleet contingent, O'Hara now served the CSS as a tactical commander and had recently joined her from Polaris Station. Solid and dependable, he had been her rock more than once since she had been voted to lead CSS. His right eye glowed with the unnatural light of an optical implant that continuously fed data streams to him in real time.

'Can't take your money,' she replied. 'My head feels empty.'

'Thinking hard about nothing,' O'Hara replied with a friendly grin. 'Any news on Fortitude?'

Arianna shook her head slightly, her gaze still directed out of the shuttle's windows as it began decelerating from New Chicago's geo stationary orbital velocity to re enter earth's atmosphere. The slender craft's wings gradually altered shape from razor thin to gracefully tapered as it prepared for atmospheric flight.

'Endeavour and Defiance will be there by now and I can't help wonder what they're going to find,' she said. 'Worse, I'm concerned that we won't hear from them either.'

'You're worrying,' O'Hara soothed, 'and worrying doesn't solve anything.'

'You think I should sit here and think about which movie I want to watch tonight instead?' Arianna snapped.

'No,' he replied, not bridling. 'There's a difference between worrying and thinking. Thinking results in a solution. Worrying just sends you round in circles and corrodes your arteries.'

Arianna raised one hand to her forehead as a faint pulse of pain throbbed behind her eyes. Re entry often did that to her, and she could see the shimmering orange glow of the heat flare as the shuttle descended, the earth's vast sphere now a curved surface and the coast of California passing by three hundred thousand feet below.

'We all have our own way of dealing with things.'

'Doesn't mean yours is the best way,' O'Hara pointed out, and he rested one hand upon hers, his skin dry and rough to the touch. 'Look, I'm not saying you shouldn't care, just that you shouldn't waste energy focusing on something that you can't act upon until you know more. Breathe, okay? Give yourself some space, and if this does become a crisis you'll be better able to deal with it.'

The pain in her head faded and a faint smile curled irritatingly across her face no matter how hard she tried to prevent it.

'I never liked you ex fighter jocks.'

A soft beeping intruded into the moment and Arianna saw a small projection of the pilot appear before them.

'Sorry to interrupt ma'am, but we've received a priority signal from CSS Headquarters. This flight is now being redirected to New York City.'

Arianna leaned forward in her seat. 'Did they say why?'

'Negative,' the pilot replied. 'Priority clearance was classed Archangel, so there was no sensitive data in the transmission. We will land at CSS HQ in eight minutes.'

Arianna felt a cold chill envelop her despite the comfortable temperature inside the cabin.

'Thank you,' she whispered as the projection disappeared.

O'Hara waited patiently beside her, the other dignitaries on the flight saying nothing as outside the deep black of space gave way to the perfect blue of a crisp winter morning. Serene layers of brilliant white cumulus were spread in crumpled blankets below them as the shuttle turned gently, her wings trembling as they encountered the first ripples of turbulence.

'Could be word from the Ayleens saying everything's fine,' O'Hara said, but this time there was no conviction in his voice.

Arianna closed her eyes and steeled herself. The black fear engulfing her heart refused to abate but she rose above it, breathing in controlled rhythm and letting her mind clear of doubts and fears. From somewhere she found the resolve to accept what was happening on its own terms. Sometimes, as she had learned in the past when commanding a warship of her own, it was better to expect the worst than hope for the best. That way, it was tough to feel let down when everything went to hell.

'What is the state of the British fleet?' she asked finally.

'Ship shape and New Bristol fashion, as the Brits like to say,' O'Hara chirped, eager to buoy her up. 'If anything comes calling, Commodore Hawker and his *chaps* are ready to answer with a plasma smile.'

'What about the Russians and Chinese?'

'They're holding their own fort as ever, but they're ready. Nobody's going to falter if this all turns nasty. We're all in the same system, remember?'

O'Hara gestured out of the window at the earth below them, and Arianna nodded as she drew strength from him.

'When you get back to tactical, I want a complete fleet assessment conducted and a strategic plan ready by the morning. If this does go to hell I want to be ready to come out fighting.'

'That's the spirit,' O'Hara grinned as he got up out of the seat and moved across to his own, accessing his communications panel.

Arianna listened as O'Hara began issuing orders to the CSS fleet as the shuttle descended down through a thick bank of cumulus. It emerged above a gray Atlantic flecked with endless ranks of marching rollers. The shuttle's wings rocked and rumbled on the gusty air as the craft turned and slowed further, and the CSS Headquarters building in New York City appeared through the gray mist ahead. Nested against the coastline she could see the glittering metal buildings of the city like a sparkling jewel encrusted into the dense forests that surrounded it.

The shuttle slowed as it approached the city and Arianna could see the occasional flare of light reflected from flying craft travelling this way and that through the skies above New York. A small number of towering skyscrapers soared up into the sky, silver and chrome reflecting the firmament above. Five thousand feet tall and with their upper floors lost deep in the clouds, the buildings all overlooked the wilderness continent and the wild Atlantic Ocean in all their untamed glory.

The Statue of Liberty stood guard over the city's harbor as it had done for hundreds of years, before the plague even, now coated with a nanotech film that ensured she was always pristine in appearance. Beyond Arianna could see a coastline and a few scattered dwellings of the super elite set against the vast forests that now covered what had once been New Jersey.

The island of Manhattan loomed into view and Arianna marvelled at the sprawling expanse of museums, mansions and the CSS Headquarters complex in the center, dwarfing the Freedom Tower that had also stood for so many centuries. Central Park's angular block of greenery housed the wildlife sanctuary, where exotic beasts were allowed to roam in large enclosures for limited times before being returned to their native habitats, allowing the children of the elite access to them for short periods to understand the nature of the planet that had given birth to the human race. Among the natural animals such as lions and elephants there roamed holographic representations of dinosaurs so vivid that it had apparently become a rite of passage for teenage boys to stand firm as a Tyrannosaur stalked toward them. Few passed the challenge.

The shuttle touched down, and as Arianna's restraints automatically retracted she saw a line of dignitaries hurrying toward the shuttle, hard light umbrellas up against the squalls of fine rain gusting across the pad. The air that filled her lungs as she stepped out of the interior of the shuttle was tinged with the sweet scent of recent rain, of distant forests and of the ocean nearby that swirled in a heady aroma as she stepped onto the landing pad.

'Director General,' an aide said breathlessly, 'you must come, quickly.'

Before she could respond a hard light arch formed over them to block out the rain as they hurried at a brisk pace toward the main buildings. Arianna could see that there were no media present, no sign of military escorts or other unusual activity. CSS was keeping events well under wraps and preventing anybody outside the organization from sensing that something, anything, was amiss.

Arianna walked into the main hall of the building and was immediately greeted by Commodore Adam Hawker. A tall, thin British officer who stood so erect it seemed as though he was permanently on the verge of toppling over backward, his cold gray eyes focused on hers like a bird of prey.

'Arianna,' he said warmly as he shook her hand. There was no light of joy in his eyes and she could feel the tension in his grip. 'The Joint Chiefs of Staff are waiting.'

Commodore Hawker commanded the British fleet contingent, which fielded a small but formidable arsenal of frigates, fast corvettes and one capital ship, *Illustrious*, a carrier with a formidable combat reputation.

Arianna gestured for Hawker to lead the way as she walked with O'Hara to a briefing room located close to the Senate Hall, CSS guards now flanking them protectively as they strode inside the briefing room and a set of hard light doors shimmered closed behind them, turning opaque to protect the security of those inside.

The Joint Chiefs of Staff all stood as she walked in, but she waved them down.

'Tell me,' she said simply.

Admiral Franklyn Marshall, the commander of the CSS flagship *Titan*, stood at the far end of the table.

'Ma'am,' he greeted her, his stony features taut, his back straight and his arms rigid by his sides. 'Approximately three hours and forty seven minutes ago, all contact was lost with the CSS station at Proxima Centauri. All attempts to re establish communications have failed. All transmissions have ceased and we have no information at all coming out of the sector.'

Arianna stared at Marshall for a long moment, her body motionless as though frozen in time. She blinked as she realized that she had stopped breathing and that the Joint Chiefs were all staring at her expectantly.

Arianna sought something to say, anything. She opened her mouth to speak but her voice rasped and she coughed briefly, her eyes watering. She cleared her throat again, acutely aware of the men watching her.

'What forces do we have in the sector?'

'Two corvettes of the British Fleet,' Marshall replied promptly, 'plus assorted Russian cruisers but they're on training manoeuvres near the Rim Colonies.' The Admiral hesitated. 'I contacted New Moscow and also the Russian contingent on Polaris Station, and they confirmed that contact had been lost with their own vessels at approximately the same time as we lost contact with Proxima Centauri.'

Finally, Arianna's strength gave way and she slowly sank into the seat before her.

'Tactical assessment?' she asked, her voice a ghostly whisper.

Marshall's voice echoed around the room as Arianna once again tried to accept the words that she had never wanted to hear in her lifetime.

'At first glance it would appear that the Sol System is being encircled,' he said, 'an enemy having first cut off our ability to communicate with our only potential allies, the Ayleeans. Isolating an enemy position effectively creates a siege mentality and helps to eliminate possible escape routes and sources of reinforcement.'

Arianna nodded, understanding perfectly but somehow unable to process the enormity of what the admiral was saying.

'First steps?' she whispered.

'First steps,' Marshall agreed. 'The enemy will complete its encircling of the system before preparing to attack.'

Again, she could only nod in response until she recovered her voice.

'Do we have any idea of the form of any first strike against us?'

Marshall sucked in a lungful of air as he considered his reply.

'In this instance we can't know for sure as we cannot be certain of the nature of our enemy, only that they do indeed represent an enemy that is intent on hostile action. Any chance of a benign approach can now be considered extremely slim due to the absence of direct communication. My best guess as to their next move is that they'll either strike from long range to avoid casualties on their side or they'll send in their infantry or whatever equivalent they may have, massed fleets perhaps or fighters, something expendable to engage and assess our initial defenses before bringing in heavier and more valuable weapons.'

Arianna nodded. Her own schooling at the academy had detailed the likely shape any kind of invasion by an alien species might take, based on how mankind had fought wars throughout history, but such schooling was purely speculative and academic. In truth, nobody had any idea what they might face when…

'Endeavour, and Defiance?' she asked suddenly. 'Have we heard from them?'

'No ma'am,' Marshall replied. 'They bypassed Proxima Centauri on the way out to Ayleea due to the urgent nature of their mission, and will have arrived in the Ayleean system within the last hour.'

Arianna closed her eyes as she realized what that meant. 'If Proxima Centauri has been forcefully occupied, they're cut off.'

Commodore Hawker stepped in to the conversation, his clipped tones reaching out to her like talons.

'We can't let ourselves worry about them right now, madam. I'm requesting that the Senate and Council hand full control of our response to the military. Unless we're very much mistaken, and I certainly hope that we are, we're facing a likely invasion from an unknown species and they're already surrounding us.'

'That's a big step to make in one day,' Admiral O'Hara cautioned the British commander. 'The Senate has not relinquished responsibility for civilian protection within the system for hundreds of years.'

'We haven't been invaded before, either,' Hawker pointed out with a stern gleam in his eye. 'Desperate times call for desperate measures and we cannot be seen to falter.'

'Nobody else knows about this but for us and the crews of our frigates at Ayleea,' Marshall pointed out. 'We're not under a microscope yet.'

'But we will be,' Hawker pressed. 'What do you think will happen when Global Wire and others start noticing fleet movements and closed door meetings like this one? It won't take long for word to spread and when it does, if we're seen to have waited too long to mobilize our forces in earnest…'

Hawker let the suggestion hang in the air and it felt like an iron weight around Arianna Coburn's neck. She sighed softly, and then she opened her eyes and looked up at Marshall.

'He's right,' she said. 'Assemble the fleet and I will inform the senate of everything that has happened, and ask for their support. Via standard protocols I hereby consent and surrender command of all initial military defenses to the Joint Chiefs of Staff, and will ensure that all support from the civilian population shall be directed into any war effort that is placed upon us by outside forces beyond our control. Provided the senate endorses my decision, the fleet will take full control of defenses from that moment on.'

A silent vacuum filled the briefing room as Arianna hesitated before speaking her final line.

'Gentlemen, until further notice or until providence delivers us otherwise, we are now at war.'

***

XII

San Diego

California

The ride out of San Diego spaceport was swift but uncomfortable as Nathan sat wedged alongside Foxx in the rear seats of the police department cruiser. Never the type of craft that had a great deal of space, the cruiser's rear seats were also caged in and designed to hold convicts rather than badged detectives.

'What can you tell us about the victim?' Nathan asked.

'Victims,' came the reply from the uniform up front, a sergeant who looked weary enough to have been working for the force for at least half a century, 'if you count the pair from Nevada found a few hours ago. The San Diego victim's name is Samuel Freck, college freshman. Barely old enough to own a license to fly let alone get his life started.'

'Any priors?' Foxx asked, her thigh squashed against Nathan's with some force although he tried to pretend that he hadn't noticed.

'Nothing,' the sergeant said. 'The friends he hung with are real clean, probably consider drinkin' alcohol to be a major crime. Most of them come from *grounded* families.'

Nathan frowned as he heard the term, uttered with something approaching contempt by the sergeant. Being called *grounded* was both a derogatory and uplifting term; derogatory because it referred to the wealthy elite who mostly lived planet side, and uplifting because most folks on the orbital stations would very much like to enjoy lives that allowed them be insulted in such a way. The grounded of the 25th Century were much like the elite of the 21st; admired, mocked and envied all at once.

The cruiser had cleared the city limits and was travelling at high speed just a few inches off the I94 navigation strips, its EM Drive growling somewhere behind them.

'We're a ways out of town,' Nathan observed, 'what was the victim doing out here?'

'Foolin' around most likely,' the sergeant explained. 'Most of these kids have fast rides, the trappings of the good life. They come out here to drink, drive fast, generally act like idiots. Every now and again we pick what's left of one of them up after a collision or similar. Serves 'em right, I say.'

Nathan said nothing, although he and Foxx exchanged a glance. The sergeant may have been serving the San Diego PD but his attitude and accent reeked of orbital. Every now and again postings planet side came up for those serving the force in the orbital stations. Competition was fierce for the postings because it allowed the officer and their family to move planet side for the duration of the tour, which might be up to five years.

The cruiser slowed, and in the dawn light Nathan could see a flickering array of hard light cordons surrounding a lonely spot on the nav' lane, nestled in a long, low valley. The sergeant parked the cruiser and the gull wing doors opened. Nathan and Foxx virtually popped out of their seats and stretched their legs, Nathan revelling in the desert air that hit his senses, fresh and clean after months on New Washington.

'Detectives?'

Nathan and Foxx turned to see a woman with blonde locks and an impossibly bright smile hurrying toward them, a hovering camera drone following her every move with a flashing Global Wire logo emblazoned above it.

'Tamarin Solly, GW Today News,' she gasped breathlessly. 'What's the story?'

'People, dead,' the police sergeant snapped impatiently at her. 'I told you to get out of here. Somebody's child is lying dead on the lane out here.'

'That's no vehicle accident with all this attention going on,' Solly retorted. 'What's really happening here, detectives?'

'We'll tell you when we know something,' Foxx said. 'We only just got here, case you hadn't noticed.'

'And *why are* New Washington detectives flying all the way down here in the first place?' Solly went on.

Foxx turned away and Nathan followed, not rising to Solly's bait.

'This way,' the sergeant said as he gestured to the cordon.

Nathan decided not to mention that it wasn't like they needed directions, the crime scene the only activity of any kind within about twenty miles.

'Were there any witnesses?' Foxx asked as they walked.

'Not to the crime itself,' the sergeant replied, 'but the kid wasn't alone just before he died. Turned out he had some kind of argument with his friends and they say he insisted on walking home. They left him, but the driver had a mysterious attack of loyalty and turned back. He found him just here.'

Nathan saw the body lying on the nav' lane, dressed in casual clothes that were draped across fragile bones visible through pale skin. The low sunlight and chill in the air made it seem as though the victim might have been frozen where he lay, his arms rigid and at awkward angles. The kid's shock of red hair was stark against the pale skin of his skull like features, his eyes empty black sockets and his jaw hanging open and slack. The skin sparkled as though it were embedded with tiny jewels that glistened in the sunlight.

'Jeez,' Foxx said as she looked at the remains, 'that's the same MO all right.'

Nathan glanced to one side where two officers were comforting a muscular teenager who was leaning against a flame red Vampire hot rod with two young girls, both of whom looked as though they'd been crying.

'I see what you mean about the wheels,' Nathan said.

'Wheels?' the sergeant asked.

'Never mind.'

Nathan was about to walk across to the teenager when he hesitated and then looked at the nav' lane. On impulse, he stepped back and began retracing his steps out of the cordon.

'Where are you going?' Foxx asked.

Nathan looked around at the desert and gestured out into the empty wastes. 'Hundreds of miles of nothing. If something killed this kid, how did it get here?'

Foxx understood immediately and moved to join him.

'Could have been someone in a vehicle,' she offered.

'Which would mean a landing would be required,' Nathan agreed. 'Or it could have been somebody on foot.'

'Out here?'

'It's only twenty miles to the city limits,' Nathan said. 'A fair way but not impossible if somebody was determined enough to kill Freck.'

'Who didn't have any real enemies that we know of,' Foxx reminded him.

'Jealousy?' Nathan suggested. 'According to the local authority's databank Freck got into college off the back of an inheritance from insurance policies. Maybe he jumped the queue and somebody got upset about that? Maybe he took somebody else's slot, one of the grounded who felt they were more deserving?'

Foxx considered this for a moment as she looked at Freck's data sheets in her ocular implant.

'Freck lost his parents in an accident. You'd have to be pretty cold hearted to come down on him for that.'

'You'd have to be pretty cold hearted to suck the kid's innards out and leave what's left out here in the desert, too.'

Nathan looked about him and then he spotted something that he hadn't noticed before. He walked across to the western edge of the cordon, no more than fifteen meters from Freck's body, and there on the desert dust he saw what he was looking for.

'Bingo.'

Nathan knelt down as Foxx moved alongside him. 'What you got?'

The desert sand was clearly marked with the impression of a pair of boots, quite large and both of them pointing toward the spot where Freck had died. Foxx wasted no time as she turned and called to one of the uniforms guarding the scene.

'Get the driver over here, and the forensics team.'

Foxx turned back as Nathan studied the prints. 'Someone was waiting here,' he said as he turned and saw a couple of fainter markings denoting where the killer had walked onto the scene of the crime. 'Then they advanced and attacked Freck on the road.'

Foxx assumed the role of devil's advocate. 'Could have been an innocent bystander or even someone hitch hiking their way across the state. Maybe it's Chance's boots from when he returned to find Freck.'

'Maybe,' Nathan said thoughtfully. 'But he'd have driven back from the west and got out on the other side of the nav' lane, the driver's side, right?'

'I guess,' Foxx said, 'and I like the way you're thinking this through, but there's no way to date an impression like that. These kids were using black market shields to hide their activities out here so we can't use their ID chips to put them on the scene at the time of the murder.'

Nathan looked up at the valley around them. 'I bet the wind whistles through here as the sun comes up and heats the land, drawing in the sea breeze as the hot air rises. Prints like this in soft dust wouldn't last all that long.'

Foxx raised an admiring eyebrow. 'Okay, but that's not enough to get this to stick to anyone, if we even had a suspect.'

'Who says we don't?' Nathan asked as he saw new information coming through on his optical implant.

Two uniforms joined them with the driver between them. 'This is

Chance Macy. He was the driver and the last person to see Freck alive, along with his two friends over there.'

'Hi Chance,' Nathan said, shaking the kid's hand and offering a smile. 'You want to run through for me one more time what happened?'

Chance sighed, obviously having had to recount events at least twice already to two different uniformed officers who would have been searching for cracks in his story.

'We drove out here, had some beers, me, Freck and the girls. We're coming home and Freck tries his luck with Evelyn, gets booted real easy but he took it hard. He insisted he get out and walk, wouldn't have it any other way. We left him about here, took off for San Diego.'

'And then you came back,' Foxx said.

'Yeah,' Chance said, 'which upset Candice real bad but I couldn't leave Freck out here, it would have taken him hours to get home. He's never really fit in with the crowd, got his money after his folks took a dive out of life. I guess I felt kinda sorry for him.'

'And you pulled up here, found the body just like it was?' Nathan asked.

'Yeah,' Chance said, his skin somewhat pale and his eyes haunted. 'I've never seen anything like that before. We were only gone like, twenty minutes. How could that have happened to him?'

'You pulled up here, got out, right?' Nathan said as he gestured to the nav' lane around them.

Chance frowned. 'No, I pulled up where my ride is now.'

'Over there,' Nathan pointed at the Vampire.

'Sure.'

Nathan let his pointing arm drop toward the imprints in the dust beside them. 'So you weren't standing right here then, waiting for Freck as he walked home?'

Chance glanced at the desert dust and then his eyes flew wide as he saw the prints, both of them the exact same size and shape as the boots he was wearing.

'No way man,' he startled. 'I pulled up over there, behind Freck!'

'That's not what these prints tell me, Chance,' Nathan said. 'They tell me you were here and that Freck was walking toward you when he was killed. Is that what happened Chance? Did you three come back here and wait for Freck so that you could kill him?'

Chance's eyes wobbled in their sockets as he looked at Nathan, pure horror etched into his young features.

'No, I didn't do that. I was in for a shot at... a night in with Evelyn. I sold her out to come and pick Freck's sorry ass up instead. Why the hell would I want him dead?'

Nathan rubbed his chin with one hand.

'Well, I guess if you found out that Freck wanted you dead, you'd have a real motive.'

'What?'

'San Diego police got a call last night,' Foxx said, having received the same information in her ocular implant. 'Turns out Freck's folks had included in their wills costs for a PI to keep an eye on Freck should they die before he turned thirty. Freck hired four goons to pick you and the girls up outside the city limits on the ninety four. The PI intercepted the calls and informed the local PD.'

Nathan watched Chance closely as the kid absorbed this new and clearly unexpected information. His reply was a faint whisper.

'He did what?'

No anger. No hate. Just disbelief and what might have been disappointment or even dismay that sucked the air from the kid's lungs.

'Freck intended to have his way with the two girls, whether they wanted to or not,' Nathan said. 'Never mentioned what would have happened to you, but I guess it wouldn't have been a night that ended well, Chance.'

Chance shook his head. 'The son of a bi.... Why would he do that? I let him hang out with us, even when nobody else would.'

Foxx stepped forward, looking up at the teenager.

'You see how this looks, Chance?' she asked him. 'You leave Freck out here, head off and then find out that he's hired four guys to kidnap you and the girls. You all get real mad, turn back, drive out here and wait for Freck, then kill him.'

Chance stared at her, his eyes widening with her every word.

'That's not what happened!'

'And these aren't your boot prints?' Nathan pressed.

'I didn't get out here!' he almost shouted. 'I swear it's true! I pulled around Freck's body because I didn't know what it was until I got closer. I thought some animal had got hit in the road and I didn't want to damage my ride so I swung out and slowed down! I only realized it was Freck when I got real close and then I hit the brakes and got out. I called you guys right after!' Chance ran his hand through his thick brown hair. 'And now you're telling me he put some kind of hit out on us? I should have left him out here! I should've run him over myself!'

Nathan had spent many years in his career talking to criminals of all kinds. Some were fabulous liars, able to convince even the most cynical and hardened of detectives that they were innocent, right up to the point that the evidence was found that led to their arrest. Others were terrible liars, incoherent with fear but still trying to cover up their heinous crimes. And then there were those who were innocent, caught up in something that terrified them.

Chance Macy looked terrified and then some.

'Then how come your prints are right here, Chance?' Nathan demanded.

Chance stared at the prints as though they were about to leap up and rip his face off. 'I don't know, I just don't know! How is this happening?!'

'It's called evidence, Chance.'

Chance's frantic anger collapsed into fear and confusion. Foxx glanced at Nathan and shook her head fractionally, as though to say *this doesn't feel right*. Nathan nodded back, and turned to Chance.

'Did you see anybody else out here?'

'Nobody,' Chance shook his head vigorously, his brow screwed up in confusion. 'it was just the three of us the whole time.' His words hung in the air and he realized what he had said. 'Man, we can't prove any of this, can we?'

Nathan took one more look at the prints.

'You blocked the signals from your own ID chips, Chance, so you're gonna have a tough time proving you were in two places at once. Either you come clean here, or you're gonna be in a jail cell by lunchtime.'

'I'm telling you the truth!' Chance wailed. 'I came back for the damned idiot and now he's dead!'

Chance's handsome young features crumbled in horror and suddenly he jack knifed on the spot and turned aside as a thin stream of bile spilled onto the desert dust at his feet. Nathan stepped back and glanced at the two uniforms nearby.

'Get him out of here, and match his statement with the two girls. Look for anything that doesn't add up before you charge them.'

Nathan sighed and watched as the uniforms led Chance's sobbing, defeated body away.

'A little hard on the kid, don't you think?' Foxx suggested.

'We've got to be sure,' Nathan replied. 'He could be our guy but I'm not feeling it.'

'Me either,' Foxx said. 'Did you see the extra data on Freck's questionable friendships?'

'Yeah,' Nathan nodded. 'Hooked up with underground cosmetic surgeons out of New Chicago, looking to rebuild his face and avoid legal repercussions to his inheritance.'

'It fits the organ smuggling theory,' she pointed out. 'Maybe there's something new on the market? But apart from that, Freck Seavers and Erin Sanders couldn't be more different. The MO matches, but the victims are random. That means we could have two perpetrators out there, and it means their MO allows them to eviscerate people in a matter of minutes. What the hell is this, Nathan?'

Nathan shook his head, as confused as Foxx was, and then he saw something catch his eye. Chance's bile had leaked into a depression in the sand, close by the footprints. Nathan looked down at it and then suddenly he saw another depression, identical to the first, behind the footprints.

'What?' Foxx asked.

Nathan said nothing as he walked behind the boot prints and saw another depression, slightly different in shape, as though something had been moving across the desert. As he stepped back so he saw others, a distinct trail leading to the spot where the boot prints were. As his eyes traced them, so he felt a chill in his bones.

'Something interesting out there, detectives?'

Tamarin Solly's voice reached out to them from where she was being held back by officers guarding the scene. Nathan glanced over his shoulder at her, saw the hovering camera drone zooming in on their position.

Foxx moved alongside Nathan to help block the camera's view. 'What are you seeing?'

'Look,' he said as he pointed at the trail.

Foxx caught the pattern and her eyes flared wide.

'They're changing shape,' she gasped in horror.

Nathan nodded slowly.

Something had walked across the desert and had changed its shape until it matched Chance Macy's. Nathan and Foxx had both seen something like that before, and they both knew what it meant.

'They're here,' Foxx said in a whisper, her voice sounding small against the vast desert. 'They're already here.'

***

XIII

Polaris Station

Admiral Jefferson Marshall sat in a hard light seat in an executive lounge of the Officer's Club and looked out over the vast expanses of Polaris Station, the fleet's headquarters. Beyond the expansive floor to ceiling viewing ports that ringed the club were the immense, curved metal plating of the orbital platform's upper level, an imposing tower ten kilometers high that was capped with a dome like structure. The officer's club, or simply "The O" as it was known, was perched atop that dome.

Beyond the station was a flotilla of CSS vessels, most arriving from elsewhere in the Sol System, others still CSS warships merely at anchor awaiting ports at Polaris for refits and re–supply as the fleet gathered. One of them caught his eye, the largest vessel visible, sleek lines and ventral strakes, a quarter of a million tons of military might that was his command, the CSS flagship *Titan*. Beyond all of that was the vast, baleful eye of Saturn, it's rings sweeping across the vast blackness.

Marshall looked in the direction of the sun, and from Saturn's relative position he could deduce the positon of the other planets and earth. He turned slightly in his seat and there, suspended in the blackness was a star just a little brighter than most of the others burning in the heavens as it reflected the sun's life–giving light and warmth. Earth looked painfully small from out here, irrelevant almost, a speck of rock in a vast Solar System that was itself a mere speck against the hundred light year expanse of the Milky Way galaxy and its hundred billion or so stars. Marshall could see that too from his vantage point, an immense band of light sweeping across the cosmos, yet even its immense scale was a mere atomic nucleus against the tremendous size of the universe, a single grain of sand on an endless, dark and uncaring beach.

He had always known that this time would come. After the

encounter they had experienced barely a year previously it was obvious that first contact had been made. Although that first contact had not been of the kind that most of CSS had been hoping for, at least the question of whether mankind was alone in the universe as an intelligent species had been answered. Sure, colony vessels had encountered strange things out there beyond the Rim but nothing that conversed, articulated, created, loved and hated: just microbes, bacteria or strange creatures that seemed to consist of little more than light drifting in ephemeral veils amid the scorching coronas of distant stars.

Now, everything had changed. First contact had been made and that contact had been brief, brutal and violent. The fear had been that it was some kind of first wave, a bizarre and frightening material that entombed entire vessels and used them as cocoons, feeding off the very materials from which they were built, and then propagating itself across the galaxy one inhabited system at a time.

Marshall stood up, never happy sitting, and paced up and down. The hard light viewing ports did not reflect his craggy features or salt and pepper hair, but his aching joints and weary gait betrayed the eighty nine years he had been alive, much of which had been spent in space. Over half way through his life, Marshall felt as though he had already lived a dozen lives and when he was honest with himself he could admit that he damned well looked that way too.

A door to the lounge opened and several fleet officers walked in to join him, flanking CSS Director General Arianna Coburn. Marshall knew Coburn well enough that he could tell at a glance that the pressure was already taking its toll on her. The Senate had endorsed the military take over of the defensive response to events at Ayleea and Proxima Centauri, and now she would be the liaison between CSS and the people of earth when the news inevitably broke.

Behind them were almost a hundred other figures, commanders of colonies or civilian politicians.

'Gentlemen,' Marshall greeted the JCOS officers as they took their seats, automatically heading for his position while the civilians moved toward the far side of the table. Even before a real war, Marshall noted ruefully, humanity was instinctively putting down its own battle lines.

Arianna passed him by with a ghostly smile. Marshall reached out and placed one hand on her shoulder, squeezed it gently. She got the message, but her eyes remained haunted. Behind her, Commodore Adam Hawker threw Marshall a crisp salute.

'And so, the game begins again.'

Marshall managed to smile at the British commander's gallows humor and shook his hand. 'Sadly, and just when we thought we'd found peace.'

'Peace is only ever a prelude and a preparation for war, admiral.'

'Good to see your optimism hasn't changed.'

'Keeping it real,' Hawker replied, 'as I think you like to say.'

'Gentlemen,' Coburn called for the attention of all of the officers in the lounge.

The JCOS and fleet commanders all fell silent. Marshall could see that military leaders from all of earth's continents and colonies were present: Russians, Chinese, Europeans like Hawker, colonists like former fleet commanders Alan Venter and Rear Admiral Wight, plus a smattering of civilians, mostly the governors of the orbital cities and grounded councils.

'Last night I received a communication from the media giant Global Wire. They recently intercepted a series of low priority signals from the Proxima Centauri system that travelled through relays here to Sol. According to their message, they have evidence that something is happening on the Rim.'

'I knew it,' Hawker muttered. 'Leave a morsel on a doorstep and the rats will come.'

Marshall frowned as he shifted uncomfortably in his seat. 'The media should be kept out of this, regardless of what they think they know. Given the chance they'll spread disinformation and panic just as fast as they can and give no thought to the consequences. You all saw what happened in the Ayleean War whenever the Wire got hold of classified intelligence.'

A rumble of discontent rippled around the room. In the middle of the Ayleean War, Global Wire had been tipped off by a CSS deserter about a possible strike being launched by CSS assets against the Ayleean fleet's supply chain. CSS commanders had identified a weakness in the enemy's frigates that had reduced their range, requiring constant fuel and munitions support from their home world. The Wire had broadcast the news, unaware that they did so just hours before the CSS strike fleet emerged from super luminal cruise in an ambush against the supply chain. The Ayleeans had intercepted the piece and managed to get two capital ships into position before the CSS strike package arrived, and the result was a massacre that had cost the lives of several thousand CSS personnel.

'Global Wire can't know much at this early stage,' Commodore Hawker said. 'Even we don't know for sure what's happening out on the Rim yet, we're just being cautious.'

'The Wire doesn't need to know anything to run with a story,' Marshall pointed out. 'Facts don't matter to them.'

Rear Admiral O'Hara looked pointedly at Marshall. 'What is the position of our fleet?'

'I've sent the fast corvettes out to the edge of the Sol System on all cardinal points,' he replied. 'The frigates are taking up strategic positions around the heliosphere, and I've pulled both *Titan* and *Pegasus* back to Polaris Station. We'll hold the capital ships here until we know what we're dealing with.'

O'Hara nodded, along with Hawker. 'What about our international allies?'

Marshall gestured with a brief wave of one hand to a holo screen nearby, which shimmered into life with an image of various star fleet assets.

'Our Russian and Chinese counterparts are fielding assorted frigates and sloops,' he said, 'while the Brits are holding the line at Sol with their carrier, frigates and ground forces. Naturally, those ground forces are at this time dispersed to avoid media interest but at some point, all leave will have to be cancelled to build up strength for any successful penetration by enemy forces. We won't be able to hide that.'

Coburn nodded and thought for a moment before she spoke.

'It is my contention that we should announce what we do know to the public now, before Global Wire puts two and two together and comes up with eighty three.'

The sound of air being sucked between teeth hissed through the room and Marshall saw Coburn's skin color up.

'That would be setting a dangerous precedent,' Marshall warned. 'We don't know how the public will react if we tell them that there may be some kind of lethal predatory species heading our way, intent on destroying us.'

'Perhaps,' Hawker shrugged, 'but they've just lived through thirty years of fearing an Ayleean invasion. They might well be ready for this.'

Marshall peered at Hawker. 'The Ayleeans might have been wiped out. What message does that send to a population who believe the Ayleeans to be virtually undefeatable? Our superior technology, warships and training won the war, but only by the narrowest of margins.'

The Governor of New Chicago spoke, his voice calm and quiet.

'The people are finally starting to settle again and are looking forward to the peace accord with the Ayleeans. Throwing this at them now, I just don't know how they'll react but if it does turn out to be true you can bet your life they'll want off the orbital platforms and the colonies will flee too.'

'Mass exodus,' Vice Admiral O'Hara agreed. 'People won't want to face an alien invader anywhere but their own back garden. We would have to lock every city down to prevent a panicked rush for the surface.'

'Most people have spent their lives on the orbital platforms,' Coburn said.

'Yes, but humanity has spent millions of years on earth,' Hawker pressed. 'You can't breed that out of people in the space of a few generations. Believe me, if this comes to blows and they catch sight of our enemy, they'll want to go home and not be blown to *smithereens* or frozen solid in deep space. And that brings us to another specter; if we *don't* inform the people and the invasion occurs, we may have cost them their last chance to escape.'

Marshall sighed and looked at the polished black surface of the table before them. The table was partially transparent to allow people to see beneath it, a popular means of sensing the mood of those within the group. Twitching legs, fidgeting, tightly folded hands in laps were all indicators of stress and he was seeing a lot of it now. The JCOS and governors didn't live and serve in a vacuum – all of them had families either planet side or in the colonies.

'Have we heard from Endeavour or Defiance yet?' Coburn asked.

'Nothing,' Marshall replied. 'If they made it out they should be back soon with a report on what they found. Given that they didn't contact us when in orbit around Ayleea, we can assume that they had to leave rapidly and must be beyond reach in super luminal cruise, or…'

Marshall didn't complete his sentence but everybody knew what he had been about to say. A long moment of silence descended on the room before Hawker spoke.

'We need a decision and a consensus on this. Either we ring the bell now, or we hold our silence and hope that Global Wire doesn't spout something dangerously close to the truth in the next forty eight hours or so. Given what they've already achieved, I think that we should pre–empt the inevitable and go public as soon as possible.'

All eyes fixed upon Arianna Coburn, who was still responsible for how to handle civilian matters even though jurisdiction of the military had passed to the JCOS. Marshall did not envy her the decision: get it right, and she could save countless lives. Get it wrong, and she would probably be the subject of Global Wire's withering coverage and a vote of no confidence in the senate, something which he knew that she ill deserved.

Coburn took a breath, composed herself and spoke.

'Gentlemen, I will…'

A loud alarm blared across the room and echoed through the entire station, cutting her off as an announcement rang out.

'Unidentified gravity well, zero point oh two planetary diameters, all stations battle status!'

Marshall was moving even before he realized it himself as he dashed to the observation ports and spotted immediately a rippling of stars against the Milky Way's vast band barely five thousand meters away from Polaris Station.

'Damn me, that's close!' Hawker uttered.

The entire JCOS and dignitaries rushed to the viewing ports as Marshall clenched his fists and hoped against hope that the incoming vessel was allied. If this was the start of the invasion, they were already doomed. He saw *Titan* already moving, turning to face the arrival as four Quick Reaction Alert Phantoms scrambled from her launch bays.

The rippling gravity well suddenly burst with light and Marshall squinted as from the fearsome glare burst the familiar shape of a CSS frigate. He heard the audible sigh of relief from the JCOS around him as they recognized the vessel, and then he felt his guts contract as he saw the trail of debris and damage streaming from the frigate's stern.

Even before Marshall could speak, he heard a broadcast coming from Endeavour as her captain accessed the emergency channels.

'All stations, execute Lazarus Protocol, effective immediately! Ayleea is gone and we barely escaped with our lives. They're coming this way!'

***

XIV

New Washington

'We've got a long way to go here and no way of knowing how to start.'

Kaylin Foxx stepped off the shuttle with Nathan right behind her, both of them switching on their gravity boots as they followed a line of passengers through the spaceport toward the terminal.

'You know what we saw,' Nathan said. 'We can't just keep it to ourselves.'

New Washington's spaceport was located at her heart, as were those of all earth's orbital stations. Without the benefit of good old fashioned centrifugal motion and with the fitting of gravitational plating far too expensive for such an old station, Nathan watched with customary amusement as people walked with their hair standing at odd angles, reaching out for items that had slipped from pockets and were spiraling up into the air to clatter against the hard light corridor around them that prevented such lost property from being ingested into the engines of shuttles.

'I can't just go into the CSS Headquarters and tell them we've got some kind of shape shifting *thing* wandering around either,' Foxx whispered back, conscious of alerting people around them to the apparent danger. 'The only person I could talk to about this is Admiral Marshall, and he's not available right now.'

'Where is he?'

'Polaris Station,' Foxx replied, 'some kind of big meeting or other that can't be interrupted. I already tried.'

Nathan showed his shield to the customs officers manning desks at the spaceport. Computers scanned both the shield and Nathan's ID chip before the guards waved him through after Foxx.

'You know what these things are,' Nathan said as they hurried toward one of the elevator shafts that would take them down to the Beltway. 'It's the same thing that the fleet encountered last year, the same stuff you saw with Allen aboard Titan.'

'I know,' Foxx uttered. 'But we can't prove anything yet unless Doctor Schmidt can come up with something about the bodies themselves. We need *proof*, just as if this was a normal homicide investigation.'

Nathan watched as they waited in line for a free elevator, and as he scanned the crowd around him he began to realize just how much danger they were in.

'It could be anybody,' he said finally. 'They could be right behind us and we'd never know it.'

Foxx winced but said nothing, obviously every bit as uncomfortable with the knowledge as Nathan was.

Nathan looked up and saw through the oval hard light portals above his head the dizzying sight of one of New Washington's tremendous arms reaching away from them toward the immense circular expanse of the city's circumference, five kilometers away. Nathan could see the tips of city spires reaching up from the streets on the far side of the Rim, all of it cast against the earth's vast surface hundreds of kilometers below. As he watched, he saw a shooting star streak across the atmosphere far below.

'How could it have travelled to the surface?' he asked Foxx as they boarded the elevator.

'I don't know,' she replied softly. 'All we can be sure of is that it can move with impunity through our security sensors.'

Nathan saw the elevator doors close and braced himself. With no gravity at the rotating station's heart, the spaceport at its center had adopted an arbitrary "deck" and "ceiling" orientated with an equally arbitrary up and down based on the cardinal points of a compass. Thus, North Four was located "above" the spaceport. Before the elevator started moving, it was required to rotate a hundred eighty degrees to prevent the increasing gravity landing the occupants on their heads as they travelled toward the Belt.

Outside, Nathan saw the rotating station's exterior begin to rotate on a further axis as the elevator flipped slowly over and began to move, now appearing to descend away from the spaceport as earth's location rolled over their heads and settled on the opposite side of the view. As the position of the earth changed, Nathan saw another shooting star zip across the blackness of space and burn up in a brief but bright trail of light.

He stared at where the light had vanished for a moment.

'Damn, what if they didn't slip through customs after all?'

Foxx looked at Nathan sharply and he realized that he had spoken out loud, several of the elevator's occupants looking at him in confusion. Nathan ducked his head and spoke softly to Foxx.

'I've seen three shooting stars in one day.'

'Congratulations.'

'What if they're landing here all the time?' he went on. 'What if they got to earth first and *then* came up here?'

Nathan saw a tremor in Foxx's eyes, a realization of something so horrific that she could barely admit it to herself.

'ID chips,' she said softly.

Nathan nodded. 'The victim on the south side didn't have their chip, and neither did Freck. If whatever did this to them was using the chip to slip through customs and other security checks, they could be anywhere.'

Foxx's skin seemed to turn pale as she looked around them at the other people in the elevator and she knew that there would be no easy way to identify a shape shifter from an ordinary citizen. Most were ordinary residents or visitors to New Washington, dressed in the popular styles of their age group: those over eighty favored the restrained two piece suit with molded boots, fold over jacket and short, center parted glossed hair. Teenagers wore shabby, loose attire emblazoned with various anarchic logos that matched their hair, which tended to be metallic or to change color every few minutes. Mothers with children, businessmen staring into the middle distance, their focus on their ocular implants as they read the latest financial reports, elderly folk engrossed in their memories, youths carefully shielding illegal bio enhancements from the two detectives.

'We've got to get this to Captain Forrester, right now,' she said finally. 'I don't care what happens after that, we just gotta let them know.'

The elevator doors hissed open and the crowd poured out in a busy little flood as Foxx stepped out and keyed her priority signal communicator. Even in North Four's so called "Black Box", where illegal disruptors attempted to hinder police communications, Foxx was able to get a faint link to the precinct.

To their surprise, it was Forrester who opened the link even before Foxx had made the connection.

'Both of you, get back here right away,' Forrester ordered. *'Doctor Schmidt is here and we need to talk.'*

'You got something on the autopsy?' Nathan asked.

'Yeah,' came the reply, *'and man am I glad it stayed on lock down. Get here, fast!'*

*

Nathan and Foxx walked into the precinct as fast as they could, a squad cruiser having picked them up from the elevator terminal and rushed them to the building. Nathan pushed his way through a rowdy crowd of prisoners clogging the "cattle pen", restrained somewhat by the hard light bars keeping them in place.

Foxx followed and they hurried upstairs to Forrester's office. The Captain came out and walked with them, his big frame taking up half the corridor as he spoke.

'Schmidt's figured something out about the remains and you're not going to like it.'

Nathan wanted desperately to say something about what he and Foxx had figured out, but Captain Forrester had not been privy to the bizarre battle fought by CSS Titan some months before or the prison outbreak on Tethys Gaol that had occurred at the same time. CSS had forbidden anybody who had been involved from discussing the events with anybody else, although Schmidt had been present at the encounter with the shape shifting mass that had infiltrated Titan.

Foxx led the way into the coroner's office, which was attached to the precinct building, within which stood Doctor Schmidt inside a hard light cubicle with the remains of Erin, Vasquez and Allen alongside him. The doctor looked up and smiled.

'Ah, Detective Ironhead. Just in time.'

Nathan ignored Schmidt's jovial mockery. 'What have you got for us?'

Schmidt saw the tension in their faces and he dropped the act.

'Poor Erin here was not disemboweled of her internal organs out of malice,' he informed them. 'She was effectively cloned.'

Nathan decided that Forrester's presence was no longer an issue: this whole thing was too important now.

'We know,' he replied. 'And we think we know how they got here.'

Forrester blinked as he looked at them both. '*They?* Something I'm missin' here?'

Kaylin Foxx replied.

'Some months ago, when you asked us to look into the case of a former prison officer convicted of homicide and sent to Tethys Gaol, something else happened up there that resulted in the CSS flagship Titan almost being overrun by an alien entity, some kind of shape shifting biological form.'

Forrester stared at them all for a long moment. 'You're tuggin' my tool.'

'I can assure you that she is not,' Schmidt replied, Erin's remains visible through the doctor's ephemeral holographic form. 'Titan was indeed subject to an attempt by a species of alien to infiltrate and infect, if that's the correct term, the human race. Fortunately, we were able to devise a means of combatting the attack and it was repelled. Sadly it would appear that our efforts to prevent the species from infiltrating our population were ultimately in vain.'

Forrester stared at Erin's remains and seemed to Nathan to be trying not to run from the room.

'You're telling me that we made first contact with something and that nobody got told about it?'

'The CSS deemed it too sensitive to report to the people,' Nathan replied. 'We were all sworn to secrecy and I'm inclined to agree with their decision. However, now we're seeing these homicides and I think that they're connected with what Kaylin and her team encountered aboard Titan.'

'It wasn't pretty,' Vasquez said. 'Damned near took out an entire platoon of Marines.'

Forrester rubbed his temples with both hands, pinched the corners of his eyes with his finger and thumb before he replied.

'This is way above my pay grade,' he said finally. 'You say that CSS has a veto on you talking about this? Great, stop talkin' to me and take this to CSS planet side.'

'I'm afraid that we cannot just pass this off to CSS,' Doctor Schmidt said. 'It's too late for that.'

'What do you mean it's too late?' Nathan asked.

'I have conducted an in depth study of the remains of Erin here, and I can report that the crystals left behind in her body are not just sodium chloride or common salt. Encased within the crystals I have found organisms that I would identify as similar, if not identical, to those discovered aboard Titan last year.'

Nathan stopped and stared at Schmidt and for a moment it seemed as though all of the air had been sucked from the room. Nobody said anything, leaving the doctor to say the words that they had all dreaded hearing for months now.

'Earth has already been invaded, we just didn't know it.'

Nathan didn't wait for anybody to speak. Instead, he turned and dashed from the room.

***

XV

Polaris Station

'Get Endeavour's crew disembarked and into quarantine for debrief!'

Admiral Marshall strode down the ramp of the shuttle and out into one of Polaris Station's massive landing bays, endless polished black deck panels and gray walls lined with white lights and flashing warning beacons. Long ranks of *Phantom* fighters and *Intruder* long range recon' spacecraft were parked inside the bay, which was well illuminated and filled with technicians working to prepare them for battle.

'We've already isolated the crew,' the lieutenant who had met him replied.

'I want to talk to Captain Travis immediately.'

'He's in the sick bay, also in isolation.'

A phalanx of armed CSS soldiers walked behind Marshall as he headed for the shuttle docking bays and the sick bay. Endeavour's entire crew would be debriefed at length but right now Marshall was in a damned hurry. Captain Travis Harper represented the only officer who had witnessed from a command perspective whatever had happened on Ayleea, and Marshall needed answers if he was to define a strategic defense of the Sol System against whatever the hell was heading their way.

Through large hard light portholes running the length of a long corridor near the landing bay he could see Endeavour hove to in a position well clear of the station as a stream of shuttle craft ferried the crew back to Polaris Station. As was standard procedure, all military crews underwent a decontamination process and medical check before being released, those checks performed exclusively by *Holo sapien* doctors to prevent undetected infections crossing into the civilian population.

Marshall reached the sick bay and entered to see small groups of *Endeavour's* personnel sitting inside hard light contamination chambers as the doctors worked. Again, standard procedure dictated that the officers were separated from other ranks and the captain was contained in a private room to allow for immediate debrief by senior personnel. Marshall strode into the holding room and ordered the Marine guards to hold station outside.

The holding room was in fact little more than a storage closet with a temporary hard light cubicle erected inside to hold the captain. Travis Harper stood as he saw Marshall walk in, clearly relieved to see someone he knew.

'Frank,' he greeted Marshall with a brief smile, all pretense of rank and protocol ignored, 'you've got to move fast.'

'Tell me, everything,' Marshall said as the hard light door shimmered closed and turned opaque behind him, blocking all light and sound from outside.

'Fortitude is lost,' Harper replied, 'and so is Ayleea. Their entire fleet, or what looked like most of it, has been destroyed along with all orbital platforms. The entire planet's burning.'

Marshall felt as though the air had been sucked out of his lungs. 'The *entire* planet?'

'Everything,' Harper confirmed. 'The cities were burning, the forests, everything. Whatever went through there utterly destroyed all life, probably by some kind of orbital bombardment. Fortitude looked intact and there was nothing on the scopes so we sent two fighters in to investigate. Turned out the ship was enveloped in some kind of ice that came to life and made a grab for the Phantoms.'

Marshall placed his hands behind his back, visions of Titan's encounter of months before flashing through his mind. 'Ice?'

'Yeah,' Harper replied, 'I know it sounds crazy but this stuff moved and it moved fast, we lost both fighters…'

Marshall saw the regret in Harper's eyes but there was no time to let him dwell on it. 'What happened?'

'We got hit from behind,' Harper said. 'No warning, as quick as I just said it. One direct hit on the stern quarter and man, that was all she wrote. We lost pulse drive, plasma batteries, most of our shields and communications. It was all we could do to turn around and leap before the next shot hit us.'

'Did you identify your attacker?' Marshall asked.

'Identify? No. See? Yeah, we saw it. Had to be a million tons plus, not CSS design, not anything I recognized. The bridge section alone had to be about twice *Titan's* mass.'

Now Marshall felt the first true stirrings of fear deep inside him, uncoiling like a cold snake probing the night for prey. Even if Harper was subconsciously exaggerating the size of their assailant there was no doubting the heavy damage that Endeavour had sustained, and Marshall reminded himself that Harper was not a captain known for embellishments. If he said it was a million tons plus...

'What about Defiance?'

Harper's head sank and he rubbed his temples with his hands.

'We were gone before she arrived,' he replied. 'We fired a single alert beacon so that she'd detect it when she dropped out of super luminal, gave her a chance to turn tail and run before she got hit by that thing. It was all we could do. Have you heard from her yet?'

Marshall shook his head.

'If it went down as fast as that, she won't be far behind you.'

'I'm just hoping she picked up Tyrone and Ellen.'

'The Phantom pilots you lost?'

'Yeah,' Harper said and then frowned. 'You don't look surprised about anything I'm saying.'

Marshall took a deep breath.

'We've seen this before,' he replied. 'CSS deemed it something that should be kept under wraps for fear of spreading panic among the populations planet side.'

If Harper felt any sense of betrayal that he and other CSS officers had not been informed about the potential dangers lurking beyond the Rim colonies, he showed no sign of it. Instead, he moved closer to Marshall.

'Forget that. Panic's nothing compared to what's going to happen when that ship gets here. It'll take half the fleet just to keep her in check. We have no idea what that vessel is capable of, but tracking Endeavour here has gotta be within their capabilities. We left a tricky trail for them but I don't hold out any hope they'll be fooled for long.'

Marshall nodded.

'I don't think they'll be fooled at all,' he replied. 'We've lost contact with about six Rim colonies in a roughly spherical area around the Sol System in the past twenty four hours.'

Harper blanched.

'They're cutting us off,' he said, his tactical training and knowledge born of the same schools Marshall had attended. 'They hit Ayleea to remove any chance of outside support or a defensive flanking manoeuver.'

'And then they strike us directly,' Marshall said. 'Report to me as soon as the docs are done with you. I need to take this to JCOS and then deploy the rest of the fleet.'

'You can't take the fleet up against that thing, it's too big to defeat in a face to face engagement.'

Marshall looked over his shoulder and grinned. 'From what you've told me, I think that we have an idea of how they're going to attack and that might just give us an edge.'

'If you go in, I'm ready for command,' Harper insisted.

'I know,' Marshall replied, 'but Endeavour's out of the game. Sit tight Travis, I'll find a spot for you.'

Marshall walked out of the room and was flanked once more by the two Marine guards as they strode out of the sick bay. He was immediately confronted by his aide de camp, a young man by the name of Morris who had been assigned to him by Commodore Hawker.

'Sir, you have a priority signal from earth, classified Archangel.'

Marshall nodded and immediately made for the nearest private conference room. He strode in even as Arianna Coburn and the JCOS were coming the other way, all looking for him. Without a word he pointed to the room and the JCOS followed him in. As soon as the guards were on station and the hard light doors were closed he spoke.

'It's confirmed,' he said to them simply. 'Fortitude is lost, Ayleea has fallen and the species encountered by Endeavour is predatory and is heading this way. We have no word yet from Defiance, but the semi biological material we encountered a few months ago aboard Titan is back and this time it's brought friends.'

Marshall let the JCOS digest this information. Hawker spoke first. 'Friends?'

Marshall nodded. 'Endeavour's data is being transferred so we'll get a look at our new enemy shortly, but Captain Harper estimated her at around one million tons.'

A simultaneous sound of escaping breath whistled from the mouths of the JCOS. Most everybody knew that *Titan* and *Pegasus*, the fleet's largest warships, each had a mass of around half a million tons. A single vessel of the type described by Captain Harper would dwarf them both.

'Its firepower was sufficient to disable the frigate Endeavour with a single shot,' Marshall went on, 'which struck her stern and disabled most of her internal systems and propulsion. She made an emergency jump with what she had left, but it's fair to say one more shot would probably have split her hull.' Marshall hesitated for a moment as he saw an image of the vessel appear on a holo screen in the room, the data from Endeavour's encounter being streamed to them automatically. 'She's a predator.'

The immense vessel loomed before them, modelled in three dimensions from the data gathered by Endeavour before she fled the Ayleean system. The immense hull was larger than any two CSS warships, and tremendously large plasma cannons were mounted on strakes below and to either side of the hull. The computer had selected an arbitrary code name for the vessel: *Marauder*.

'Any data on her weapons? Rear Admiral O'Hara asked.

'Plasma based, so not dissimilar to ours,' Marshall replied, 'but her output was far greater. Endeavour didn't get a good reading on her shields but it's fair to say they'll be powerful, more so than our own. In short, this isn't a fight we can hope to win unless we outnumber her significantly. And, of course, we don't know if there are other ships like this one out there.'

'There could be an armada of those things waiting for us,' Arianna Coburn whispered, her voice horrified. 'The entire fleet could be wiped out in a single engagement.'

'Not if we use our heads,' Marshall said, refusing to be cowed by the size of the enemy vessel alone. 'As expected, the first space faring species we've encountered in the cosmos is more advanced than we are, but they still have warships that can be recognized for what they are. That means that whatever species is behind this likely shares some attributes with humanity.'

'Tell that to the Ayleeans,' Hawker said as he saw an image of Ayleea in flames appear before them. 'That species just wiped a few billion of them out in a single strike.'

Marshall thought for a moment as he looked at Ayleea, the vast fires burning across the planet and the cities glowing with flames.

'One ship couldn't have done all that,' he said, 'not even as one as big as that Marauder.'

Both Hawker and O'Hara nodded.

'They must have had ground forces on the surface,' Hawker said. 'A bombardment from orbit would have required hundreds of ships and would have taken days to complete on that scale.'

Marshall stared for a moment into the blackness of space outside, the uncaring darkness and unspeakable age of the universe staring silently back at him. There were no other known species out there in the cosmos that could come to the rescue of Sol and its outlying systems. There were no gods to rely upon for such were the fantasies of men long gone. There were no miracles. All that he had, all that mankind had, was knowledge built up over centuries and the wits and cunning of any creature that had evolved to survive millions of years.

'They softened up their targets first,' he said finally.

'How?' Arianna Coburn asked. 'We have had no unrecorded intrusions into Sol space in the past few years, except for a single Ayleean cruiser which you yourself intercepted and destroyed before it could reach the orbital cities.'

Marshall paced up and down as he spoke, Saturn's graceful ringed arc glowing in the light from the distant sun through a nearby porthole.

'Captain Harper reported the presence of the biological material that attacked *Titan*,' he said, 'and that we once found entombing an alien vessel. It was construed from previous investigations that the material was both alive and yet a machine, an organic entity capable of transforming itself into any shape or form.'

'Where are you going with this?' Hawker asked, his normally calm and collected features pinched with concern.

Marshall nodded.

'This species, whatever it is, might send forces in advance of its fleet in order to test the defenses of target worlds. We do something similar, sending Special Forces soldiers in behind enemy lines to cause havoc and weaken an enemy.'

Admiral O'Hara glanced at the image of Ayleea's burning forests and cities.

'You think that they infiltrated Ayleea *before* they attacked?'

'I do,' Marshall agreed, 'and were able to cause the collapse of their society before the main force arrived. I think that they will do the same here and we need to be prepared for it. The question is, how do they intend to infiltrate our system?'

***

XVI

New Washington

'Will you tell me what the hell is going on with you?'

Nathan hurried into the police communications office with Kaylin Foxx close behind him, Vasquez and Allen with her. He saw a clerk at the desk inside and spoke quickly.

'I need you to put out a sensor sweep for the location of an Erin Sanders, age twenty six.'

Foxx blinked beside him. 'She's dead, Nathan.'

Nathan turned to her as the clerk initiated the search. 'That's my point. She's dead all right but we don't have her ID chip. It's got to be somewhere and I don't think that whatever killed her intended to just leave it behind.'

'But we already checked for her ID chip and it wasn't transmitting,' Foxx pointed out. 'It must have been destroyed when she was killed.'

Nathan turned back to the clerk, and as he did so a display flashed and a small icon appeared. Nathan peered at the display and saw Erin Sanders walking along a street near North Four.

'I'll be damned,' he murmured. 'Dead woman walking.'

Foxx stared at the display in amazement. 'It must take time for the chips to re–activate inside the new body.'

Nathan saw her expression collapse as she realized what was happening. Memories of the shape shifting forms on Titan from months before flashed through her mind and she understood immediately what was required.

'They need to move around,' Nathan said. 'If these things are invading, they can't remain static. They must be able to learn, and so they'll figure out they need the ID chips of their victims to travel and to *not* look unusual or suspicious.'

The clerk's head turned slowly and he looked up at them. 'Invading?'

'Keep this to yourself,' Vasquez ordered with a stern gaze. 'Word of this gets out, I'll know where to send CSS troops.'

The clerk's face blanched white and he turned back to stare at the screen.

'I'll get Schmidt on this right away,' Foxx said.

'Don't call for back up though,' Nathan warned. 'We can't afford to spook it or we'll never find it again.'

Foxx nodded as she dashed from the communications office and Nathan turned back to the display.

'I need you to track her, real careful,' he ordered the clerk. 'Relay the information to our ocular implants but don't call any support vehicles out no matter what happens, okay? Leave that to Schmidt. We need to pick this one up real quiet.'

'Understood, detective.'

Nathan hurried out of the communications room with Vasquez and Allen and followed Foxx as they made for the precinct lot on the roof of the building. Nathan jogged up the steps to the roof's access door, the building having been constructed in simpler times when ordinary doors still prevailed. The door's locking mechanism sensed their approach and cleared them to pass, and they pushed through and outside.

Nathan still felt a roiling vertigo whenever he walked out onto the precinct roof, or any other in the city. Above, the vast and curved hard light "sky" protecting the city from the frigid vacuum of space revealed the hundred meter thick North Four arm rising up toward the spaceport at the city's center. Nathan could see elevators travelling up and down it as spacecraft and shuttles moved slowly to dock with the station far above him. Beyond, the other side of the city loomed, its backdrop earth, reflecting the brilliant sunlight.

'Quit daydreaming, c'mon!'

Foxx jumped in as their cruiser detected her approach and

automatically opened its broad gull wing doors.

'Take the opposite route to us!' Nathan yelled to Allen and Vasquez. 'That way we can close it down!'

Vasquez gave him a thumbs up as he and Allen jumped into their own squad vehicle. Nathan slipped into the passenger seat beside Foxx as he heard the deep growl of the EM Drive spinning up. Within moments the cruiser lifted off the roof of the precinct building, Foxx guiding it skillfully up into the busy skies above the city.

New Washington spread out below them as Nathan activated the police computer and connected the relay from the precinct communications office to the cruiser. Instantly a marker appeared in South One with directions, estimated time of arrival and other pertinent data scrolling alongside the marker.

'Got her,' Nathan said, 'or *it*.'

Foxx hit the transmit switch on her control column. 'Allen, Vasquez, you gettin' this?'

'Dead girl walkin' on South One, we're inbound counter clockwise,' Vasquez replied.

'Roger, we're clockwise, four minutes.'

Nathan looked ahead as Foxx accelerated, the cruiser rising up amid a convoy of vehicles variously cruising, climbing or descending to their various destinations. The private vehicles and taxis were all confined to the mid lane, with the upper lane restricted to police and emergency vehicles. Foxx accelerated further and climbed above the highest of the buildings as she skimmed close to the upper surface of the station's rim.

The squad cruiser shuddered as it encountered invisible vortexes of warm air rising from the busy city below and coiling against the inner surface of the station, the updrafts more violent in areas of the city where sunlight could stream down through the hard light "skies". Brilliant shafts of sunlight illuminated the city streets in rectangular pools as the cruiser streaked overhead, the moist air rising and then cooling as it passed out of the sunlight and began to fall in diaphanous veils of rain shot through with rainbow hues.

'Two minutes now,' Foxx said. 'I've got support vehicles coming in, sirens off.'

'Good,' Nathan said as he checked his side arm. 'Where's Schmidt?'

Foxx glanced at the display and smiled. 'Already on site.'

The doctor's holographic projection allowed him to appear instantly anywhere that supported Holo sapiens projection units, which these days was pretty much anywhere due to the *Living and Non Living Sentient Being Rights Act* of 2319. Not only had it been deemed that *holosaps* were both fully deserving of all the rights cherished by ordinary people, but that they could not be denied the right to generate their projections wherever they wished as to deny that right was effectively an imprisonment. Furthermore, the permanent erasing of a *holosap's* core data bank had been legally described as an act of murder, which the media had quickly latched on to with the term "*digicide*". At least thirty living humans were serving time for the murder of *holosaps* across the colonies, one or two of the convicted themselves *holosaps* now confined inside digital prison cells after ordering the termination of their brethren at the hands of criminal gangs.

'One minute,' Foxx said.

She switched the cruiser to autopilot and slowed, allowing the vehicle to descend into the normal traffic flow above South One as she checked her side arm. Nathan could see on the display four squad vehicles arranging themselves in a quiet cordon in streets around the target, coordinated by Schmidt as Allen and Vasquez closed in from the far side of the city.

The cruiser moved into a part of the city shadowed by a solid metal ceiling. Not all of New Washington benefited from the transparent hard light surfaces as it was deemed too expensive to retrofit the entire city. Its ageing infrastructure was already badly in need of development but the Governor's office had restricted funds to more pressing needs such as upgrades to the dehumidifiers and atmospheric recirculation that life aboard New Washington depended upon.

'Setting down,' Foxx said as she programmed the autopilot, selecting a rooftop landing space within a hundred meters of the marker signal.

'I can see her,' Schmidt's voice reported on the channel. *'I'm a few paces behind, on the junction of 44th and Clifton.'*

Nathan watched as the cruiser guided itself in to a landing on the rooftop. As soon as its landing pads settled down the gull doors opened and he leaped out with Foxx as they made for the roof exit and dashed down a flight of steps. Nathan's ocular implant presented him with a glowing map that hovered over his right eye, allowing him to maintain orientation with the target while travelling.

Foxx jumped down the steps three at a time, lithe as a cat as she dashed for the main exit of the apartment building and then slowed. Nathan eased up behind her and was surprised when she reached out and slipped her arm through his. He may have been getting used to life in the 25th Century, but Nathan was still enough of an idiot to raise an eyebrow and smile down at her.

'You getting' fresh with me, Foxx?'

Foxx glanced up at him with her elfin looks and her perfectly sculptured lips curled upwards.

'Play the part Ironsides, 'cause that's all this is.'

Before he could reply she hit the door switch and it slid open before them to reveal the street outside. Foxx pulled him out of the building and onto the sidewalk, her grip on his arm like a vice as she smiled sweetly up at him.

'Coffee, or something stronger?' she asked.

Nathan grinned back down at her. 'I think I need something stronger after that performance. You really are a tiger between the sheets, Foxx. How do you keep going for so long?'

He heard Vasquez snigger down the communications channel in his ear. Foxx hugged Nathan closer, the smile still wide on her features and her gaze lovingly directed upwards at him as they walked.

'I was going to ask you the same question, out of boredom.'

More muted chuckling. Nathan's own mirth wilted but he kept his smile static as he weaved between the dense crowds clogging the sidewalk. It was almost lunchtime, businessmen and office workers flooding the streets. Clouds of steam billowed from vents in the deck where all manner of coolant pipes, sewage and ventilation systems generated heat and additional moisture that boiled up to the surface. Overhead, half of the sky above was brilliant shafts of sunlight streaming down through the hard light panels, the other enshrouded in metal illuminated by endless rows of incandescent strip lights. He could see a curling vortex of vapor rising like wispy feathers to curl over and fall back down as rain high above their heads, drifting away as it did so.

'She's heading your way, lovebirds.'

Vasquez's warning alerted them, and Nathan's height gave him an advantage as he saw Doctor Schmidt's glowing blue projection walking toward them through the crowds. His image quivered occasionally as the veils of rain falling nearby interfered with the transmission.

'I see you, Ironside. She's right in your path.'

Nathan studied the oncoming crowds, a maze of multi–colored hair, the tall and the short, the bio enhanced and the non mechanical. In their midst he spotted a pony tail of brown hair that matched their victim's, Erin Sanders barely five four in height.

'I've got her,' he replied. 'All units, move in.'

Nathan saw Vasquez and Allen suddenly emerge from the crowds to his right, where they had been studying the scene in the reflection from shop windows old enough to still be glazed. A pair of police cruisers crawled slowly into view at a junction behind Doctor Schmidt, ready to cut Erin off if she made them and tried to flee.

Nathan saw Erin Sanders scanning the crowd ahead and then she looked right at him.

There was no way that whatever entity it was looking back at him could have known who Nathan Ironside was, but in a moment of time Nathan realized that the instinct of the hunted was clearly prevalent in all species and not just humans. Sanders' expression changed to one of concern and she changed direction even as she came within arms' reach.

'We're made,' Nathan said to Foxx.

'Cut her off!' Foxx ordered as she released his arm and dashed forward.

Nathan yanked out his pistol and raised his detective's shield as Foxx made for Sanders. 'Erin Sanders, put your hands in the air and get down on your knees!'

Sander's eyes widened as Foxx reached out for her and in an instant she reacted.

Nathan saw Foxx pull her gun and then Erin Sander's chest suddenly bulged outward and a solid mass of material ripped through her shirt like a battering ram and slammed into Foxx. Nathan took aim and saw Sander's face dissolve into a hateful glare as one arm pointed at him and a whiplash of gray material flickered out and snatched the pistol from his hand before he could pull the trigger.

'She's armed!' Nathan yelled as Foxx crashed down into the crowd.

Sanders pulled the trigger on the weapon even as it was recoiling back toward her in the grasp of her grotesque, tentacle like arm and the crowd erupted into screams as panic took hold.

***

XVII

Erin Sanders glanced at the pistol in confusion as it failed to fire, the weapon uniquely linked to Nathan's DNA and his ID chip. Sanders hurled the weapon at Nathan before she suddenly took off at a tremendous pace that was far beyond what any human could achieve.

'All units, suspect heading clockwise on Clifton!'

Nathan sprinted in pursuit as the crowds split for the fleeing woman. It was good fortune that she had been intercepted in the southern quadrant and not North Four, where the crowds would likely have actively impeded Nathan's pursuit.

'We're with you!' Vasquez yelled in response from over Nathan's shoulder.

Sanders cut left onto 45th Street, her legs moving with inhuman speed as though she were bio enhanced like many of the street 'hoods on North Four. There was no way Nathan could keep pace with her but for the crowds who struggled to get out of her way quickly enough.

Sirens wailed in the sky above as Nathan saw cruisers sweeping in at the far end of 44th Street, their metallic hulls flashing in the rays of sunlight beaming down a hundred meters away.

Sanders saw them and cut left again, heading for an apartment door that Nathan knew would be locked, accessible only to those who lived there.

'She's cut off at the Lacy's Building on 45th!' Nathan yelled as he ran. 'Clear the street!'

Sanders ran straight at the door, an older style construction of reinforced plastics designed to be shatterproof. Nathan followed her close behind, waiting for the moment when she stopped and was forced to confront the police.

'There's nowhere to run to!' Nathan yelled. 'Give yourself up!'

Erin Sanders's legs pounded the street with inhuman speed and she suddenly leaped at the door. Her body transformed shape into a bizarre boulder like form that ripped her clothes into shreds and she crashed into the door. The door quivered under the blow and the hinges were torn from their mounts as the entire door crashed into the building.

Erin Sander's form resolved itself again into that of her victim and she vanished up a flight of stairs inside, trailing bits of clothing behind her.

'Damn it,' Nathan cursed as he reached the door. 'All units, she's inside Lacy's. Surround the building and cut off all escape routes.'

Nathan stepped inside as he heard Vasquez and Allen thunder up behind him. Vasquez crept in and shoved something into his hand.

'Hope you look after your weapon better than you treat the ladies, Ironside.'

Nathan felt his pistol in his hand as Allen peered at him.

'Yeah, and since when do you get to talk to Foxx like that? A tiger in bed?'

'Where is Foxx?' Nathan asked.

'Paramedics are with her,' Vasquez said, 'she took a bad hit there.'

Nathan grit his teeth and gestured up the stairwell. 'It went up there.'

Vasquez checked his pistol with a severe expression. 'Good. What goes up…'

Nathan led the way and crept up the stairwell, his eyes fixed on the route above. The stairwell doubled back on itself five or six times, each time revealing a new floor in the apartment building. Unlike those in North Four this building was well maintained, clean and devoid of noxious odors.

'It could have gone anywhere,' Allen whispered. 'Damned thing can change shape, right?'

'It's able to mimic other things,' Nathan confirmed, 'but we don't know how it does it yet.'

'Who cares?' Vasquez snapped. 'Let's corner it and get the hell out of here.'

Nathan eased up to the first floor, the corridors either side of him devoid of life. Outside, in the peculiar fusion of sunlight and shadow, he could see the reflection of flashing hazard lights as more squad cruisers and emergency vehicles arrived. Nathan spoke softly into his microphone.

'Comms, do you have a location for the suspect?'

A moment of silence, then a reply from the clerk back at the precinct.

'Two floors above you, moving north.'

Nathan hit the stairs at a run as he climbed upward, Vasquez and Allen right behind him as they headed upward for the third floor.

'Suspect now on upper floor, moving fast.'

Nathan's chest heaved and his thighs burned as he powered ever upward, pumping his arms and breathing hard. The quiet of the apartment block was broken by the sound of something crashing to the ground and a piercing scream soared through the building.

'Armed police!' Nathan yelled as he reached the fourth floor, hoping to prevent whatever horror was coming next. 'Stay still!'

He burst out onto the top floor main corridor and saw an apartment door smashed inward and swinging from its hinges. He hurried forward with his pistol pointing ahead of him, then rushed into the open doorway.

The apartment was larger than those on North Four. The walls were a pale white, one of them a vast moving image of a forest at dawn, birds singing in the glittering sunshine and the scent of fresh grass and cool, clean air filling the room. A holo screen was broadcasting the news, the presenter standing in the room and appearing as solid as a real person but for the glowing halo around him designed to prevent people from mistaking the presenter for an intruder.

In the center of the room was a young blonde woman of maybe forty years, her head trickling blood from a gash where she had fallen. Her stricken, concussed features looked up at Nathan in horror.

'My baby,' she gasped.

Nathan saw the nearby empty playpen a moment later.

'She took my baby,' the woman cried with more force.

'Stay with her,' Nathan said to Allen.

Detective Allen holstered his weapon without argument as Nathan dashed out of the apartment and sprinted down the corridor toward the roof exit. Vasquez ran out behind him, calling into his microphone as they went.

'Suspect has a hostage! Repeat, suspect has an infant hostage!'

Nathan hit the last flight of steps at a sprint and saw the roof exit was already open. He dashed up onto the roof and turned in time to see two squad cruisers hovering nearby, their hazard lights flashing. Behind them was a staggering backdrop of city streets, blazing sunbeams and falling veils of rain before a canvas of deep space and the limb of the earth, and in front of it was Erin Sanders.

'Don't move,' Nathan snapped as he aimed his pistol at her.

Sanders was standing near the edge of the building, her bare skin draped in the remains of her clothing as she cradled the child she had abducted from the apartment. The child was maybe three years old, a little boy with blond locks and a confused expression on his face.

Sanders looked at Nathan as she stroked the boy's hair. 'It's you who will stay where you are.'

The voice was female but it sounded odd, in that it didn't fit Erin Sander's appearance and was somewhat husky and low. Nathan briefly wondered if it was a recording of some kind, a default voice adopted by these creatures, whatever the hell they were. Nathan kept his pistol aimed at Sanders but double checked that the safety catch was on before he spoke. There was no way he wanted to hit the kid with superheated plasma, and at this range and with the child pressed close to Sanders, collateral would be inevitable.

'There's nowhere to run,' he said quietly as he extended one hand palm out to Sanders. 'Nobody wants to get hurt here, okay? We just want the child back.'

Sander's face was touched with a smile, as though the whole

charade was faintly amusing to her. Nathan had to remind himself again that Erin Sanders was dead and that this was merely a caricature of her, a machine masquerading as a human being.

'The child is not afraid,' Sanders replied. 'Are you afraid, Detective Ironside?'

'How did you know my name?'

Sanders shrugged and looked pityingly at the child in her arms. 'They're not so clever, are they?'

'Just let the kid go,' Vasquez said, 'that's all we care about right now.'

'And then you'll let me go?' Sanders sneered at him, her smile vanishing in an instant. 'You think that's a reason to do anything you say?'

'We don't want to hurt you,' Nathan pressed. 'We can work this out, okay?'

Sanders peered at him again. 'Hurt me? You cannot hurt me.'

'Then why'd you run?'

'I have my own reasons.'

'Then share them,' Nathan said. 'We can talk about this.'

'There is no time, because our time is done.'

Nathan saw her step back toward the four story drop behind them, still cradling the child.

'No, don't do it!'

The squad cruisers shifted position, their paintwork gleaming in the bright moving sunlight as the station revolved, heat haze shimmering beneath them in billowing clouds of distorted light. Nathan dashed for the edge of the building as Sanders laughed out loud and hurled herself backward off the edge.

'No!'

Nathan scrambled to a stop and almost toppled as he saw Sanders spiral downward, the child screaming in her arms as they fell, Sanders smiling up at him without a care as they plummeted toward the unforgiving street below. Nathan cried out helplessly as Vasquez joined him on the edge of the building, and then the street below was hit by a vivid, amber colored stream of fluid that burst from hoses being hauled into the street by police officers from the apartment's rear exit below. The fluid formed a gelatinous mound as Sanders slammed into it, the gel cushioning the blow and swallowing Sanders whole.

Nathan leaned further out and saw Foxx spraying the amber fluid all over Sanders as Doctor Schmidt flickered into existence alongside her and watched. The child in her arms clambered free of her as Sanders struggled to move, consumed by the thick, syrupy gel until it froze in place and Foxx shut off the hose. Doctor Schmidt looked up at Nathan and smiled smugly as he tapped his own skull, his finger accidentally moving in and out of his projection.

'Brains over brawn,' he called up to Ironside. 'It's tough to move and change shape when you're wrapped up in super glue.'

Foxx stepped out into the street and picked up the child, cradling him in her arms as she looked up at Nathan, clearly uncomfortable.

'You wanna get down here and take this thing back to its rightful owner?'

***

XVIII

4th Precinct Building, North Four

'How much do we know?'

Nathan walked with Vasquez and Allen into the precinct interrogations rooms to see Foxx already there and talking to Doctor Schmidt, the physician's concise tones as irritating to Nathan as ever.

'It's constructed of the same crystallized biogenic material that we found on Titan several months ago,' he said. 'Right now we have it contained inside the hard light pen in room four. I've taken the liberty of dousing the form with a solution which will break down the hemostatic agent we used to contain it.'

'The what?' Vasquez echoed as he joined them.

'A hemostatic agent,' Schmidt replied. 'It's a flashy name for glue.'

Nathan blinked. 'You glued it to the sidewalk?'

Schmidt nodded.

'We learned on Titan how they combine and maintain structural cohesion, how they stick together. In medicine we have plant based polymers that we use to clog wounds. I mixed up a larger quantity and combined it with an adhesive gel that we used to stem the flow of the entity when it infiltrated *Titan*.'

'So it doesn't have muscles and bones and stuff?' Detective Allen asked.

'No,' Schmidt said. 'It's built entirely of crystalline cells and replicates movement via a coordinated internal rippling motion, somewhat similar to the way a snake travels along the ground by alternately contracting and relaxing muscle groups. The gel we used prevents these things from moving by stimulating a clotting process by holding pressure in the cells and activates the accumulation of platelets, which bind to the cells to create a platelet mesh. The hemostasis accelerates the binding of the clotting protein, fibrin, to the platelet mesh, resulting in blood coagulation and a stable clot.'

'Just what I thought,' Nathan murmured. 'Has it communicated with us yet?'

'It can't while it's stuck in the gel,' Schmidt replied, 'but it should be able to release itself by now. Shall we?'

The doctor gestured to the nearby interrogation room and promptly vanished, transporting his hologram there in the blink of an eye.

'After you,' Nathan uttered to the thin air left behind.

Foxx led the way down a corridor to the interrogation room and opened it to reveal Schmidt standing before a hard light containment unit, the borders of which were illuminated in bright blue–white light to denote the edges.

Nathan walked in with Vasquez and Allen, the hard light door closing behind them. Schmidt gestured cheerfully to a slowly rippling mass on the floor inside the cubicle.

'It would appear our guest is reconstituting itself,' he said.

As Nathan watched, he saw the bizarre form slowly rise up from a shapeless mass into the recognizable form of a human being. However, this time it was not Erin Sanders but a taller, muscular young man whom Nathan recognized instantly.

'Chance Macy,' he said.

The colorless gel seemed to move slightly, as though shuffling its various pieces into place and then with a start Nathan saw color begin to appear within it.

'Fascinating,' Schmidt said, 'the creature appears to use crystals as prisms to bend the light spectrum to any frequency it desires. It uses the light passing through it to create its own color.'

As Nathan watched the creature took on the perfect form and appearance of Chance Macy. It looked back at him and blinked, but said nothing. Foxx moved closer to the hard light cubicle and peered at Macy.

'It's not perfect,' she said as she observed the strange being. 'It looks just like Macy but it doesn't have the arrogant stance that he had. It can't imitate character, only appearance.'

Nathan glanced at Schmidt.

'It must be able to imitate only what it sees.'

'Presumably,' Schmidt concurred. 'The entity manifests itself from countless millions of smaller entities, rather in the same way that living things are built from individual cells. Uncontained, these creatures could literally move anywhere on the planet and we would never know they were there.'

'You're telling us that these things are here all over the planet already?' Vasquez asked.

'Yes,' he replied. 'It is quite likely that they were here when Titan was attacked and remained in small numbers afterward. I studied this species after we recovered a specimen and was able to confirm that it is biological, but only partly.'

'Partly?' Allen echoed.

'Yes, it appears to consist mostly of quasi biological components. Spectroscopy reveals them to consist mostly of titanium and certain alloys. In effect this is neither a creature nor a machine, but something of both.'

'A cyborg?' Nathan suggested.

'In a manner of speaking,' Schmidt nodded. 'But it is constructed on a nanometer scale. Titan's encounter was the first known discovery of a genuine extra terrestrial artificial superintelligence. What we were also later able to deduce was that it wasn't the main force.'

'The main force?' Vasquez asked.

Foxx replied, her voice soft.

'The CSS determined from Doctor Schmidt's studies that in all likelihood the stuff this infiltrator is made of was a sort of infantry, a first in attack force that created havoc before a controlling species then came in to reap the rewards.'

'A hunter force,' Vasquez said, recalling his own service in the CSS Marines.

'If that's the advance force,' Foxx said, 'I don't want to meet their leaders.'

'They're probably close behind I'm afraid,' Schmidt said, 'and are likely some form of biomechanical species themselves.'

'You really think that's likely?' Allen asked.

'It's already happening to us,' Schmidt pointed out. 'Intelligent implants beneath our skins and in our skulls, bio enhancement, brain impulse therapy, and human beings have been using prosthetic limbs to replace those lost due to injury or illness for hundreds of years. That natural progression from enhancements to permanent improvement, projected well into the future, will inevitably create a race of humans more machine than people, and the constant miniaturization of that technology will inevitably make that race ever smaller and more efficient. Look at me, for instance – as a holosap I'm really just an entire dead person inside a quantum chip.'

'Or just dead inside,' Nathan murmured.

Schmidt smiled but did not rise to the bait.

'I suspect that either the controlling species will be more powerful, or this species will be reliant in some way upon its dominant ally. They could possibly be in a sort of symbiotic relationship.'

'That's weird,' Vasquez uttered.

'That's useful,' Foxx countered. 'Divide and conquer.'

'True,' Schmidt said, 'but like any evolutionary species it will have developed defense mechanisms for just such an eventuality. If you recall, when we first encountered this species it was cocooned around an alien vessel and feeding off the metals and power circuits inside. It requires sustenance, energy, which it treats effectively as food. But it cannot travel alone as it has no means of propulsion sufficient to carry it between the stars.'

'Hence the relationship,' Nathan said, 'it's helped by a species that it can treat as a sort of galactic taxi.'

'Precisely,' Schmidt said, and then frowned. 'Which does somewhat beg the question of how they managed to get here.'

Nathan thought for a moment about the shooting stars he'd been seeing.

'You say they're real small. Do you think they'd have the ability to withstand re–entry into the atmosphere of a planet?'

'No,' Schmidt said, 'at least not at the velocities we're used to.' He thought for a moment. 'But if they were extremely small in mass their entry velocity might be low enough that some of them could survive, enough to get onto the surface of a planet and seek out suitable energy sources, from which they could begin to proliferate themselves.'

Schmidt appeared surprised at his own insight and looked again at Chance Macy's silent form inside the cubicle.

'However, if they were protected by a cocoon of some kind, launched with intent…'

'Something that might cause a shooting star in the atmosphere on burn up,' Nathan suggested.

'Why do you keep mentioning shooting stars?' Foxx asked.

'I've seen more shooting stars in the last two days than I've seen in a month beforehand,' Nathan said. 'Is there anyone tracking objects that drop out of orbit?'

'Sure,' Vasquez said, 'CSS tracks everything bigger than a grapefruit that hits the atmosphere, but that's hundreds of objects a day.'

Nathan felt something in his bones, a certainty that he recalled from his days as a detective in Denver all those centuries ago. Sometimes, when a breakthrough in a case was just around the next corner he could *feel it* as though a sixth sense was pulling him toward the perpetrator.

'Humor me,' he said to Vasquez. 'Could you get CSS to check the trajectories of all of these objects that have landed in the past week.'

'You serious?' Allen asked.

'Very,' Nathan replied. 'If we get a connection in locations between these objects arriving in our atmosphere and the murders we've witnessed, we'll know.'

'We'll know what?' Vasquez asked. 'It could be down to nothing more than coincidence. There's hundreds of these objects landing on earth every week, nobody's going to pin this freaking thing down to it.'

'No,' Schmidt said, 'but Detective Ironside has a point. This species appears in many respects to have evolved as a parasite. We can assume that it is many thousands of years more advanced than us and may have developed the means, either independently or in concert with its host species, to travel through space and infect planets. Cocoons of sorts appear favorable to them, either entire vessels or perhaps smaller cocoons that they may well build themselves. If those cocoons are strong enough to allow them to survive re–entry, then we might have been invaded a long time ago.'

'So what's it doing here?' Vasquez asked. 'Why bother with us? Why go to all this trouble of mimicking human forms and killing others off?'

'We are unlikely ever to understand,' Schmidt said simply. 'Who could possibly understand what motivations a species like this might possess? We can't even understand what it's thinking, or whether it actually thinks at all.'

Vasquez looked to one side as a message came through on his ocular implant.

'Okay I got something here,' he said, 'sending it to the display screen over there.'

Nathan hurried over and they all watched as data from CSS spilled onto the screen.

'Four thousand, nine hundred and fourteen objects were tracked as hitting the earth's atmosphere in the last week,' Allen said and whistled softly. 'Wow, that's a lot of suspects to work through Nate.'

Nathan thought fast, driven by the sense that time was somehow running out.

'Okay, wipe off anything that didn't hit the surface.'

The screen changed.

'Okay, you're down to three hundred nineteen objects,' Vasquez said.

Nathan clenched his fists by his side, his brain running overtime as he spoke.

'Right, now access every law enforcement database planet side and call up any homicide victims anywhere that had injuries matching those of the bodies we found in New Washington and San Diego.'

'You think there could be more of them?' Foxx asked.

Nathan said nothing, waiting as the law enforcement databases of every police force on planet earth were scrutinized by banks of super computers. It took a painstakingly long seventeen seconds for the information to appear before them.

'Damn, twenty four cases,' Allen said with a start. 'Desiccated remains, crystal structures in the skin, look at these things, they're everywhere!'

Nathan saw the data before him as clear as daylight.

'India, Australia, Africa, the Americas,' Foxx murmured as she read down the list. 'We've got hits in every continent except Antarctica.'

Nathan stared at the screen for a long moment. 'Now match any of the atmospheric objects remaining to the cities or locations where the bodies were found.'

The data bank altered instantly and everyone saw it at once.

'Twenty four matches,' Vasquez uttered in horror. 'Every city where they hit, they had homicides that match our MO.'

Nathan stood up and ran a hand through his hair.

'It's an advance force,' he said. 'They're infiltrating us from within.'

'But if there's only twenty four of them we don't have much to worry about yet,' Allen said, 'we've got the jump on them, right?'

Nathan could hear the hope in his tones just as he could detect the sense that they all knew he was wrong.

'The twenty four are the killings we know about,' Vasquez

answered. 'Bodies found before they could be disposed of, homicides interrupted or whatever.'

Nathan nodded. 'There could be thousands of others we don't know about yet.'

*

Tamarin Solly stood on the corner of a sidewalk opposite the precinct, a hard light umbrella shielding her from the incessant drizzle on the awful orbiting station. On her ocular implant flashed the occasional message from police communicators, her illegal black market scanner allowing her to listen in on police frequencies.

Crowds hurried by, the throng of conversation competing with the hum of vehicles travelling past overhead. Solly frowned, tucking in closer beneath the umbrella as she tried to ignore the noise. Grounded by birth, she was used to the near silence of Sacramento's suburbs or the quiet hills of Los Angeles, not the rush and chaos of New Washington. But Solly had caught word of what had happened down on North Four, rumors of a police pursuit of something that ran like a bio–enhanced criminal and yet was somehow not. Rumors were sometimes just that, and sometimes they were not.

Finally, she spotted the man she was looking for as he walked out of the precinct building and across the street. Tamarin checked her hair and make up before she struck out and intercepted the young officer.

'Hi!'

She offered the young guy her brightest smile. Although she was nearing her seventies, a healthy dose of cosmetic surgery every once in a while had maintained Tamarin's youthful glow, her hair long and wavy, her eyes clear and bright. She couldn't draw a crowd like she had in her forties, but a young pup like this shouldn't prove too difficult.

'Hi?' the younger man replied with a slightly confused smile.

'I'm Tammy,' she said and extended her hand, 'what's your name?'

'Muammar,' came the reply. 'Is there something that I can do for you?'

The polite reply and cultivated accent suggested money, a rarity on the orbital platforms, and Tamarin quickly changed her tone from cheerful floozie to articulate professional, but she maintained the suggestive pose that she knew all men would respond to.

'I believe that we may have a common interest,' she suggested. 'I was wondering whether you would like to discuss it?' Tamarin allowed a healthy portion of thigh to appear beneath her raincoat, which was open because of the heat emanating up from the deck beneath them, her blouse opened enough to draw the kid's eyes down.

'What interest?' he asked, his voice suddenly slightly dry as he coughed a little.

'Detective Nathan Ironside,' she said. 'I believe that he ordered a signal sweep of some kind a short while ago?'

The kid frowned again, suspicious. Tamarin moved closer to him, one hand on his arm and her breasts brushing close against him.

'I'm sure I can make it worth your while,' she whispered to him, her eyes wide and as honest as she could make them. 'For both of us.'

She ran her free hand lazily across Muammar's crotch and saw his skin flush with color. The kid looked left and right as though he was being watched.

'I can't speak about police matters, I'm only a clerk and...'

'Then we can speak about it privately,' she cut him off. 'I have a hotel room in the black hole, where nobody at the precinct can hear us. I'm sure that I can encourage you to recall the events of the day...'

She offered him a suggestive smile, her body pressed against his as she gently pulled him with her, and to her delight his resistance collapsed and he allowed himself to be led away from the precinct building toward one of several hotels standing near the gigantic North Four arm.

***

XIX

'You're going, all of you.'

Captain Forrester loomed like a gigantic obsidian boulder, supporting his broad shoulders with balled fists as he stood and leaned forward on his desk.

'We need to keep this quiet,' Foxx said as she stood before him in the office. 'Nathan's found a solid match between the projected impact points of these objects and the homicides but we can't be sure of anything yet, and if Global Wire picks this up everything's going to hell. You send us to CSS, they're going to know something's up.'

Captain Forrester shook his head.

'This is too damned important,' he replied. 'Even if nothing came of it it would be foolhardy in the extreme not to have you notify CSS of what you've learned. I'm sending you down to CSS right now, but that thing in there stays here. I don't want to risk moving it until we find out what the big wigs at Polaris Station decide what they want done with it.'

Nathan beamed quietly as Forrester opened up a communications channel with the CSS Headquarters in New York City. Foxx remained cautiously silent as an attache appeared holographically in the room, a smartly dressed young man who worked as a liaison between the Governor's office and CSS HQ.

'I need a direct line to the Director General, CSS,' Forrester announced.

'*I'm afraid that won't be possible, captain,*' the attache replied. '*Director General Coburn is at Polaris Station on essential business and...*'

'You connect me to the director general in the next sixty seconds,' Forrester growled as he pointed one thick finger at the younger man, 'or I'll come down there and plug an aerial into your ass myself. What we have to tell Arianna Coburn could be instrumental in the defense of our planet. But if you have something more important to be getting' on with, do let us know.'

The attache blushed in shock and the connection flickered out.

'A touch less cordial than he was used to,' Foxx suggested.

'Goddamn CSS stooges,' Forrester rumbled. 'I got no time for their airs and graces.'

Nathan smiled. In a world that was in so many ways so different from the one he had left behind, so many things still remained the same: the divide between rich and poor, the war between criminals and the law, the bureaucratic lethargy of politics and governorships and the yawning chasm between the "grounded" and the working man. Even after four hundred years, the working man was still able to get more done in a day than a politician could achieve in a year, with much less fuss and far less ceremony.

The communications channel flickered back into life again, but this time it was not the attache who appeared in the room but a Rear Admiral of the CSS Fleet.

'Captain Forrester, 4th Precinct, New Washington,' Forrester announced himself.

'Rear Admiral Vincent O'Hara, CSS Fleet Command,' came the reply. 'What's this about? We have a major situation up here and I'm getting priority feed through calls from your department.'

Forrester remained as immoveable as ever.

'We have potential evidence of an attempt by extra terrestrial entities to infiltrate the Sol System.'

Nathan noted that Forrester's bold statement got the admiral's attention.

'How so?' O'Hara asked, his tone entirely more agreeable.

'As many as twenty four homicides,' Foxx replied as the captain gestured for her to speak. 'The victim's bodies were consumed from the inside out and only crystals left in their desiccated remains.'

'So?'

'The killer then assumed the identity of the victims,' Foxx went on. 'We captured one this morning here in New Washington. It's capable of shape shifting, of assuming different forms in the same manner as an entity we encountered aboard CSS Titan a few months ago.'

Now, O'Hara was all ears. '*You* were aboard Titan?'

'We get on well with her captain, Admiral Marshall,' Nathan added as helpfully as he could. 'The ship's physician, Doctor Schmidt, is also in the loop and has been helping us identify what's going on.'

O'Hara seemed to dwell on this for a moment.

'I want your detectives up here at Polaris Station as soon as they can get here.'

Nathan raised an eyebrow as Captain Forrester leaned forward again on his desk. 'Why would you want them all the way out there near Saturn, when the murders all occurred down here on..?'

'There is more to this than I can reveal at this time,' O'Hara insisted. 'Your detectives will be required to brief the Joint Chiefs of Staff and the Director General as soon as they arrive. I will send a shuttle to you immediately. O'Hara out.'

The image of the admiral vanished as Forrester looked at them both.

'What the hell is all that about?' Foxx asked.

'I don't know,' Forrester replied thoughtfully, and then stood up straight. 'Why are you both still here? Get going, now!'

Foxx led the way out of the office and hurried to grab her things from her desk as Nathan pulled out his sidearm and slipped it into a shoulder holster beneath his leather jacket.

'Glad I didn't have any vacation booked.'

Vasquez watched Foxx furtively. 'What's up?'

Foxx looked up and saw Allen also watching her expectantly.

'Get packed,' she said. 'We're off to Saturn.'

'Not Tethys Gaol again?' Allen uttered in horror.

'Polaris Station,' Nathan replied. 'We've got a date with some big wigs at CSS.'

Vasquez and Allen exchanged a glance and then scrambled over each other to grab their weapons from their desks as Doctor Schmidt shimmered into existence alongside Foxx.

'Will you be requiring my presence at CSS?' he asked. 'I am due to report back aboard Titan in the morning anyway.'

'Yes,' Foxx said. 'I want us all there. Whatever we're up against here, CSS clearly knows something about it already. We brief them on everything we know, together.'

Nathan was about to lead the way when he suddenly thought of Sula and her mother. He set his bag down and quickly accessed a communications terminal using his ocular implant.

'What are you doin'?' Vasquez asked.

'I can't just walk out of here,' Nathan said. 'I promised I'd call Sula tomorrow so I gotta let her know we're out of town.'

Allen's features softened into a curious smile. 'I love the way he says things like that – *outta town*. Makes it seem like we're all still living in farm houses on the prairie.'

Nathan tossed a screwed–up ball of paper at Allen, who ducked the missile easily as Nathan saw the call request connect and Sula's mother appeared before him in the room.

'Detective Ironside,' Rosaline said formally, placing a thin veil over her surprise and curiosity. 'I wasn't expecting to hear from you today.'

'I know,' Nathan replied. 'I'm afraid something's come up and I'm heading out of tow... off to Polaris Station for a couple of days. I wanted to call and let Sula know before I went.'

Rosaline appeared surprised. 'You're more likely to see her than I am then.'

'What do you mean?'

'Sula didn't call you?' her mother asked. 'She applied for an Ensign's commission in the fleet and was selected for an experience package. She left yesterday.'

Nathan stood in silence for a moment, not sure of what to say.

'Okay, that's great,' he said, overcoming his disappointment that she'd travelled away without telling him. 'Do you know when she'll be back?'

Rosaline shook her head.

'Her posting was for three days on a fleet frigate anchored at Polaris Station but I haven't heard from them yet.'

Nathan lifted his bag onto his shoulder.

'Okay, I'll try to meet up with her out there. Do you know which ship she was sent to?'

'Endeavour.'

***

XX

Ayleea

A loud alarm blared through Tyrone's cockpit as his Phantom fighter plunged into Ayleea's thick atmosphere. A flickering halo of fierce red light burst into life around the fighter's sleek fuselage, forks of flame probing against the canopy as Tyrone fought with the controls to slow the craft's fiery descent.

The distress signal from the ground contact vanished as the Phantom was surrounded by the fearsome heat of re entry. Even the latest communication technology struggled to penetrate such high energy phenomena, and the Phantom did not possess enough signal boost to maintain the link. Tyrone scanned at his instruments, screens that displayed his engine temperatures, shield strength and airspeed as the atmosphere around the fighter became gradually denser.

'C'mon honey, bring me home.'

Tyrone locked the navigation computer onto the communication signal's last known location as the craft plummeted down. He knew that the enemy warship would return eventually. His only hope was to make contact with survivors on the surface, learn everything that he could about the enemy, and hope that the fleet would make it to Ayleea before he was captured or killed. As to the survivors, Tyrone steeled his mind for the worst but maintained a sliver of hope that Fortitude's crew had escaped before their ship had been overrun by the terrifying entity that had consumed it.

The halo of plasma and flame gusted out as the Phantom slowed down to a lower Mach number. Tyrone could see the curve of the planet across the horizon, the sky above already turning a peculiar shade of red as the planet's red dwarf star blazed down upon the jungles far below, the star itself far larger in the sky than the sun Tyrone was used to.

Tyrone had known about the thick forests that carpeted so much of this hot, violent world. A dense atmosphere was protected from radiation by a magnetosphere more powerful than the earth's and the planet's dense iron core was much larger. Born in an ancient nebula along with hundreds of other suns, the powerful little red dwarf star at the center of the Ayleean system possessed only half the Sol System's central star mass, but as a Main Sequence star it often produced bursts of violent solar storms and radiation that bathed Ayleea and would have been close to fatal to most life on earth.

Tyrone saw dense banks of clouds billowing violently upward from the planet's surface, cumulonimbus clouds four times as high and many times more violent than those on earth. They rose up in gigantic, terrifying pillars of pink and orange and red, flickering with lightning bolts ten miles high. Tyrone turned the Phantom away from the largest of them as he sought a passage through them. He reached down and manually reset his altimeter to Ayleea's barometric pressure as he descended, and saw 1412 millibars on the readout as he did so.

The vast thundercloud trains dominated the horizon as the Phantom descended through thirty thousand feet, and Tyrone spotted a narrow patch of clear air buried deep within the violent storms. He knew how dangerous it could be to fly directly through major storm cells on earth, let alone out here on this cruel and dangerous world, but he had no choice as the signal had emanated from somewhere below the buffeting storms.

Tyrone aimed the Phantom for the fragile gap in the weather and saw sprawling tracts of dense jungle beneath it, the leaves of the forests a deep mauve and black. The planet's parent star radiated most strongly at infra red wavelengths, producing little of the blue light common on earth. Here on Ayleea, reds, purple, mauves and blacks dominated the landscape beneath a red sky that gave the impression of a permanent sunset even during the brightest days.

The Phantom rocked violently as it hit turbulence and then suddenly the clouds closed up around Tyrone and his fighter was plunged into darkness. Tyrone switched his gaze to the flight instruments, nothing visible outside the canopy except darkness and the occasional, vivid flare of angry white light as lightning bolts forked through the atmosphere like giant, jagged fingers probing for him. The fighter's wings rocked as though they were being hit by falling rocks and Tyrone gripped the control column tighter and eased back on the throttles as he sought some sight of the ground.

A sudden crescendo of impacts shook him to the core as a cloud of fist sized hailstones pummeled the craft, only her shields preventing the canopy from being smashed in under the blows. Tyrone cried out in surprise and his heart thumped against his chest as the Phantom blasted clear of the hailstones and then sliced downward out of the clouds.

Brutal, rugged jungles of dark foliage loomed before him, steep ravines and hillsides forged by crashing rivers and millennia of storms and savage gales, wrapped in wreaths and ribbons of gloomy cloud. Tyrone's sharp eye scanned instinctively for a landing spot somewhere in the forbidding terrain and he managed to pick out a small canyon wash to his left where a clearing broke from the tree line alongside a turbulent river of dark water.

Tyrone hauled back on the throttles and control column, the Phantom sweeping around in a tight turn as he bled off airspeed and extended the fighter's spoilers and landing struts. The EM Drive spooled up as he came in to land, the wings rocking and the fuselage bucking this way and that on the strong winds as he fought for control.

The Phantom drifted over the eerily black water, like fast flowing oil struck through with rainbow hues, and then it thumped down onto the clearing amid billowing clouds of dislodged dust and sand. Tyrone killed the main engines immediately and then extended the claw grips from beneath the landing struts to keep the fighter anchored to the shore, fearful that the gales would tip the craft over. The sound of the engines and the hum of electronics died down as Tyrone shut off the avionics and batteries to save power, and suddenly he was sitting alone in a silent cockpit staring out at an alien world.

Squalls of rain drummed against the now unshielded canopy,

drenching it in seconds. Tyrone loosened his harnesses and pulled back all four manual canopy restraints before hitting the open switch. The angular canopy opened with a hiss of equalizing pressure and Tyrone felt a hot breath of air waft into the cockpit along with the scent of rotting vegetation and electrically charged air.

The heat hit him hard as he breathed it in, dense and clogging in his lungs as though they were filling with warm water. He sucked in air as he clambered out of the cockpit and jumped down onto the sandy shore, the rain squall passing but leaving millions of impressions in the sand where rain drops had landed with impressive force. He landed surprisingly hard on the beach and his legs almost folded beneath him, Ayleea's mass greater than that of the earth due to its larger iron core. He forced himself to stand upright against the increased gravity and looked for some sign of habitation.

The forest canopy swayed in the hot and buffeting winds like shimmering black towers, the sand of the clearing beneath him coarse and crunching beneath his boots as he walked up the beach. Behind him the water of the river flowed like black treacle, the higher gravity of the world reducing the peaks and troughs in the waves as above the sky flickered with latent energy and the flashes of lightning bolts high in the blood red atmosphere.

Tyrone reached the tree line and crouched down as he pulled out an emergency communicator and activated it. Capable of both broadcasting and receiving on a multitude of frequencies, it represented his only means of detecting the source of the transmission he'd received while in orbit.

Tyrone downloaded the coordinates of the signal and looked at a display screen on the device. He had landed within a couple of miles of the source but he knew instantly that in this terrain the journey there would be extremely tough. Worse, he had heard as a child the stories of the kind of creatures that inhabited this world, stories designed to scare children into being good for their parents or be *sent to Ayleea*. He looked up into the jungles before him, wreaths of vapor swirling around the thick, flat topped trees draped in dense coils of vines and creepers. To his right, in the distance he could see coils of thick smoke boiling up into the atmosphere from fires raging in a nearby city.

'Damn it,' he cursed as he looked back at his fighter.

The Phantom was in good enough shape to fly in this kind of weather but he might not be able to find anywhere to land closer to the source of the signal on this horrendous planet. The origin of the signal was somewhere to the north, or currently east on this world due to its rapidly changing magnetic orientation. Mountain chains dominated the horizon in that direction, weathered into ragged peaks as though he were looking at the upturned blade of a gigantic combat knife, its serrated edges black and...

A noise attracted his attention and he peered into the forest as one hand flashed to the plasma pistol at his side. The darkness of the dense forest was compounded by the pigmentation of the leaves and trees, making the jungle depths seem like midnight even during the day. The glow from the red dwarf star cast an unusual hue across the turbulent clouds above, disorientating Tyrone and making it hard to detect motion, and the rumbling winds disguised any sound.

He knew that he couldn't hope to follow the river to the source of the signal as it headed in the wrong direction, flowing away from the mountains, and its force would be far too great for him to swim against. He turned to his right and saw the flood plain spreading out before him, endless miles of watery swamps stretching toward the oceans.

And then he saw the lights coming toward him.

Four of them, bright white and moving fast, zipping low across the water like insects. Tyrone dashed for the tree line even as he heard a familiar crump of energy and a hail of small plasma shots swept like burning hail across the beach. Tyrone sprinted into the trees as the shots peppered the sand around him, puffs of smoke from the scorched beach leaving pools of glassy black material as the superheated plasma melted the sand.

Tyrone crouched down and aimed his pistol out across the beach as four small, metallic craft raced by. He could hear the whine of their engines as they zipped past and turned as one like a flock of tiny birds. Through beams of weak sunlight slicing through the clouds he saw the mass of objects wheel toward him to the sound of beating wings.

Sentry Drones. The most horrific of battlefield weapons, Tyrone had heard of them being deployed by the enemy during the Ayleean War, and of similar devices being used by the CSS Marines in retaliation. So cruel were the bugs and so horrific the injuries they had caused in combat that in the end an agreement had been signed by both sides in the conflict banning their use.

Tyrone whirled and launched himself into the forest with the speed of the possessed, his legs and arms pumping as he vaulted over a fallen tree. He looked over his shoulder and saw the swarm of ugly metallic creatures accelerate as they plunged into the forest and closed on him rapidly. He knew that they were not biological: the glint of metal on their bodies and wings suggested machines at least the size of his fist and aggressively styled like some kind of demonic hornet.

The humming grew louder and he dared not look over his shoulder to see how close the drones were as he struggled to maintain his pace under the heavy gravity and dense foliage clogging his path. Tyrone tried to keep moving but it was as though his body was shutting down, the extra effort required just to run too much for his muscles. His vision began to blur and he staggered sideways, momentarily off balance as he fought to maintain his pace.

Tyrone struggled along what looked like an animal trail between rows of trees and chanced a look over his shoulder. The swarm of mechanical horrors was closing in fast, and he could see through the feeble shafts of red light beaming down through the trees that they had metallic antennae that probed the air ahead of them, glossy black abdomens and inch long stingers that he knew contained a vile cocktail of poisons designed to paralyze and kill.

He ran harder but his lungs were spent and his legs trembled as he staggered deeper into the forest. The rumble of the winds faded, replaced by the sounds of a jungle that were both familiar and alien:

strange cries, whispering insects, falling branches and the sound of unknown creatures up in the canopy. Sweat drenched his skin and ran in thick rivulets down his face, clogging his vision.

He looked back again and saw one of the bugs within a few meters of him now, big glossy black eyes watching him with a soulless intent, wings beating the air as it weaved between the thick ferns and dropped down under branches before popping back up in single minded pursuit.

Tyrone changed direction again, plunging deeper into the forest in the hopes of avoiding being cut off by the terrible machines. He heard them shift course behind him, dog legging his path as they rushed in with their ugly abdomens and needle sharp stingers rolled up beneath their bodies to point at him. He skittered to a halt, turned, took careful aim and fired his pistol. The shot rocketed out in a bright blaze of plasma and struck the nearest drone square on its ugly face, the metallic creature dissolving in a cloud of incandescent embers as its now headless abdomen plummeted to the forest floor and crashed into thick bushes alongside Tyrone.

The other drones wheeled up sharply and veered away as Tyrone fired randomly at them, scattering them away as he backed up. His back thumped against something solid and he turned to see the great, squat trunk of a tree blocking his path, thick with vines. Suddenly the vines moved and he realized that they were not vines at all. Primeval instinct made him look up and he saw the cruel eyes of some unspeakable creature nestled in its lair amid the branches of the canopy, its thick beak as big as his torso and clicking loudly as its countless arms writhed out and pinned him to the tree before he could escape.

Tyrone screamed as the powerful vines hauled him up toward the clicking beak and he smelled a rancid odor of rotting meat. The tentacles wrapped more tightly around him and he felt his boots lifted from the jungle floor as he was dragged up the rough trunk toward the creature's mouth.

Tyrone writhed as he tried to free his right arm, his pistol pressed against his leg, trapped by one of the thick vines. He looked up and saw the beak clicking, juddering as though in anticipation of a fresh meal as thick drool spilled in copious loops and strings to drench his flight suit.

Tyrone looked down and saw more vines moving to wrap around him and he cried out in horror. He twisted his pistol hand until the barrel of the weapon was pointing as much away from his leg as possible and then he squeezed the trigger.

A plasma bolt roared from the barrel and blasted through the thick vines and he heard the creature emit a deep, guttural roar that reverberated through his chest and the tree itself. The vines flinched and recoiled from the damage and Tyrone felt the pressure released slightly. He hauled his arm up out of the grasp of the tentacles and looked up as the animal's beak brushed against the roof of his skull, a gaping maw of pink tissue and rotting strings of flesh and bone fragments.

Tyrone shoved the pistol inside the creature's mouth and fired straight into it. A piercing scream of pain soared across the forest, loud enough that it rang in Tyrone's ears as he was suddenly released and thumped down onto the forest floor once again. The impact was far harder than he expected, his acceleration in the fall faster than that of earth, and his weakened legs crumpled beneath him as he sank to his knees.

The writhing vines coiled back up into the tree but then the humming noise soared back and he looked up in time to see the drones rushing in again. Wearily he lifted the heavy pistol in his hand and opened fire but the drones zipped left and right, up and down as they rushed in to avoid the clumsy shots.

Tyrone shouted out at them, as though it would do any good, and then one of the drones flipped over in mid air and its fearsome stinger plunged into Tyrone's belly. His cry of desperation mutated grotesquely into one of agony as white pain ripped into his body.

The drone jerked away again and flew off, the rest of the swarm hovering nearby like hyenas circling their wounded, doomed prey. Tyrone folded over the searing agony that ripped across his stomach and travelled up his spine like fire. He knew that he was doomed, Ayleeans likely having sent the drones in to finish him off. Maybe they had survivors too and they'd seen him land. Maybe they would eat him, as apparently they preferred to do with their victims. Maybe they would keep him prisoner for endless years here on this terrible world, or subject him to tortures that he could not begin to imagine.

Tyrone turned the pistol to his own head. The fact that he was contemplating suicide for the second time in one day was not lost on him, but the pain inside his body was already so overwhelming that he could not bear it for a moment longer. At least this way he wouldn't be giving the Ayleeans the satisfaction of gloating over their victim.

Tyrone squeezed the trigger and heard a deafening plasma shot rocket by, but his pain did not subside. The nearby buzzing became panicked as the swarm zoomed up and away from him and several more shots echoed through the forest as the buzzing of synthetic wings mercifully faded away into the distance. Tyrone looked up to see fat, smoldering drips of white hot plasma around the body of a drone just inches from him, embers of molten metal fading slowly to a deep red. An acrid stench of melting circuitry filled his nostrils as he heard the sound of heavy footfalls alongside him.

Tyrone turned his head as a heavy boot thumped down on the pistol in his hand, pinning it to the ground as the barrel of a plasma rifle was pressed hard against his cheek. Beyond it glared the yellow eyes of a towering Ayleean warrior.

The Aleeyan was eight feet tall and bore only a superficial resemblance to a human being. A powerful musculature was visible beneath a hard, leathery skin that was mostly dark brown but flecked with patches of lighter color, almost gold. Dressed in metallic armor that covered approximately half of the Aleeyan's body, the rest was naked but for the thin, skin–like nano shielding that the species traditionally wore. Its head was a tangled mess of thick black hair surrounding a thick, heavy boned jaw, hunched shoulders and a fearsome yellow eye. The other eye was covered by a device that seemed to be some kind of laser sight, a thin red beam flickering as it pierced the drifting mists. The Aleeyan had small, sharp teeth that had been ritualistically filed, its lips thin and regressed as though the creature was showing a permanent snarl, and it wore a large plasma rifle in a long sheath on its back.

Before Tyrone could move or speak, something hard clubbed him on the back of his head and everything went black.

**

XXI

Polaris Station

Nathan walked with Foxx, Vasquez and Allen into a spectacular briefing room that was situated atop the vast station orbiting the planet Saturn. The entire structure was a hard light dome that afforded a tremendous view of the ringed planet, currently awash with sunlight and its baleful eye filling half of the entire view. Nathan saw in the distance a large warship hove to outside the station, its hull a battered mess and being tended to by a swarm of maintenance craft and tugs, and beyond it the entire CSS fleet gathered together, an impressive armada still dwarfed by Saturn's vast sphere and rings.

'Wow, what the hell happened to her?' he asked out loud as he looked at the damaged vessel.

'None of our business right now,' Foxx said as she pulled him toward the center of the room.

A long table was manned by countless military figures, and Nathan instantly recognized Admiral Franklyn Marshall and Rear Admiral O'Hara. Doctor Schmidt was present, as were a couple of Marine guards.

'Detective Foxx,' Marshall greeted Kaylin with a handshake. 'It's been too long.'

'We only ever seem to meet when there's a crisis.'

'I'll hope for a few more then,' Marshall said smoothly, and then turned to Nathan. 'Ironside. How's life in the 25th Century?'

'Great, thanks,' Nathan replied, 'except for the alien invasion. A bit bummed about that.'

'Detectives,' Admiral O'Hara greeted them. 'Franklyn has told me much about your work, for which we're all immensely grateful.'

His skin was dry and rough as sandpaper as he shook Nathan's hand, the grip firm but hot. Nathan waited with Foxx as the high and mighty of the senate and the military sat down, evidently having been waiting for Foxx to arrive.

'Ladies and gentlemen,' O'Hara began, 'as you all by now know we are facing a crisis the likes of which we have no precedent for. Our greatest fear, that the first contact we experienced was a prelude to an invasion attempt, has come to pass. We know that Ayleea has already fallen and that our ships have been viciously attacked by an unknown aggressor. Our only certainty is that this aggressor uses an advance guard of sorts, a sentient species with the ability to transform itself at a near molecular level and assume identities beyond its own.' O'Hara paused as he looked at the men and women arrayed before him. 'We now also know, thanks to the investigative work of these detectives from the New Washington Police Department, that the invasion has already begun.'

A rush of whispers rippled through the crowd as the JCOS and dignitaries digested this new and unexpected information. O'Hara anticipated a flood of questions and so he gestured to Foxx.

'I will leave it to Detective Foxx to explain what's happened.'

Kaylin got to her feet, and Nathan watched as she moved to where she could be seen by all of those watching.

'My team and I recently began investigating a series of murders, both on New Washington and planet side, where the victims appeared to have been desiccated. Their apparently mummified remains had been utterly divested of their internal organs and bodily fluids, leaving only their bones and skin behind. We have since determined that the entities responsible for these killings, of which there have been twenty eight now recorded, is the same extra terrestrial species encountered by Titan and her crew some months ago.' Foxx took a breath. 'They have been here and on the surface of earth for some time and have taken to adopting the form of their victims, ID implants and all. We have no idea how many there are walking among us.'

One of the JCOS spoke up. 'How can this have happened? How could they have slipped through our defenses undetected?'

Marshall spoke, his voice quiet but with sufficient authority and gravitas to be heard throughout the chamber.

'Detective Ironside was able to deduce that the alien beings reached earth through the atmosphere via cocoons of some kind that allowed them to survive re entry. It would appear that they sought out victims at random, presumably to overpower the population while we were sent off to fight other attackers such as the larger alien Marauder ship encountered by CSS Defiance and Endeavour at Ayleea. This tactic should be familiar to you all as we also performed similar…'

Nathan was beaming with pride at being mentioned by Marshall for having solved the riddle of how the alien beings arrived on earth. He almost didn't catch the admiral's last words, but now they echoed through his mind as alarm bells rang inside his head.

'What was that?' he blurted.

The congregation looked at him in surprise as Admiral Marshall ground his teeth in his skull at the interruption.

'What was what?'

'The frigates,' Nathan said. 'You mentioned ships engaged against an alien vessel?'

'Two of our frigates encountered an alien capital ship in orbit around Ayleea, code named Marauder,' Marshall confirmed. 'We believe it to be our true enemy.'

Nathan swallowed. 'CSS Endeavour was there?'

'Yes,' Marshall replied. 'What of it?'

Nathan swallowed and controlled himself. *She's not your daughter.* 'Nothing,' he said finally. 'It doesn't matter.'

Marshall peered at Nathan suspiciously but turned to Doctor Schmidt. 'The doctor here knows more about this enemy than anybody else, and may be the key to figuring out how to prevent them from proliferating.'

Doctor Schmidt stepped forward, his holographic form glowing a soft blue that contrasted starkly with the blackness of space outside.

'We've known for a long time that alien entities can enter our atmosphere at will and have done so for millennia. The British were the first to discover such alien forms way back in 2014, long before routine space travel, ID chips or any of the orbital cities familiar to us all. They sent a balloon twenty miles up and captured microscopic aquatic algae, biological organisms known as extremophiles, living high in earth's atmosphere that could only have come from space. Their findings were published in a paper during the Instruments, Methods, and Missions for Astrobiology conference of that year in San Diego. The entities they described had varied from a colony of ultra small bacteria to two unusual individual organisms part of a diatom frustule and a two hundred micron sized particle mass interlaced with biofilm and biological filaments. The findings of the British team were the first confirmation that life is common in our universe both around and between the stars,' Schmidt went on. 'The seeds of life exist all over the universe and travel through space from one planetary system to another. It was one such seed that caused *The Falling*, the dreadful plague that wiped out six billion humans three hundred years ago and set us on our new path.'

Schmidt gestured to a holographic projection of earth and of various alien bacteria as he spoke. Some of the bacteria had segmented necks connected to teardrop shaped bodies. Others were like small animals, but the majority were spheres that seemed to leak a biological substance that at the time of their discovery had simply been named *"goo"*.

'What frightened the people at the time was that these spheres, each as wide as a human hair, had all been identified via X ray analysis as being made from titanium and traces of vanadium. They had also found that they had a "fungus like knitted mat like covering", a combination known to no species on earth at the time.'

'What does this have to do with the expected invasion?' Admiral O'Hara demanded.

'Nothing,' Schmidt conceded, 'but the use of such a species as a means to degrade a populations' ability to defend itself suggests that our enemy, whomever they may be, are perhaps not much further advanced than ourselves and purposefully use this swarm like entity to soften their targets up, so to speak.'

'Explain,' Hawker said impatiently.

'Our frigates identified a very large, very powerful vessel which attacked them,' Schmidt said, 'and that in itself tells us a lot. The ship was recognizable for what it was; its weapons operated in a similar, albeit more powerful manner as our own, and it was capable of super luminal travel, as are our own. Their technology has a basis in ours, so perhaps might their biology.'

Marshall's eyes narrowed as Commodore Hawker spoke.

'So you're saying they've sent a big swarm of bugs to infiltrate and cause disruption on earth, after which they come in and mop up what remains.'

'Eloquently put,' Schmidt murmured in a dry tone, 'but correct.'

'We were expecting gigantic insects or machines,' Admiral O'Hara muttered, 'not a shape shifting soup.'

'Of course,' Schmidt said. 'Mankind has been raised on a diet of movies featuring insectoid aliens or anthropomorphic beings, but the most likely form of life to spread across the universe in large numbers is cellular bacteria and viruses, perhaps merged with some form of technology. Even on earth, bacteria have always outnumbered larger life forms by billions to one. Your own body contains more bacteria than every human being who has ever lived. Bacteria have been found here on earth, such as *Bacillus permians*, that have been known to survive inside sodium chloride crystals in New Mexico caves for over two hundred fifty million years and been successfully revived, so such entities are more than able to cross the distances between star systems and survive the journey.'

'And now they're here,' O'Hara murmured uncomfortably. 'Last time something like this made it to earth several billion people died, and that was from just what people managed to breathe in. If they're already here and waiting for a thumbs up from their overlords to start massacring the population, our rear guard is already destroyed. It's no wonder the Ayleean defenses collapsed so quickly.'

'The species we've encountered may not have a willfully predatory purpose,' Schmidt replied, 'it may simply be surviving.'

'In what way?' Foxx asked.

'Because if it's a non sentient being then it merely *exists*,' he replied. 'It has no emotion, no cares other than consuming prey and only achieves what we would call consciousness when acting in concert in large numbers. It cannot be reasoned with, or empathized with, it simply *is*. However, its fundamental simplicity means that a coherent defense against it should be well within our capabilities, as we discovered with the superglue fluid I formulated on Titan when we first encountered the species.'

'Easier said than done, I suspect,' Marshall said. 'We barely escaped with our lives from that last encounter.'

Schmidt gestured to a holo display that appeared in the room, showing footage of the entity they had first encountered wrapped around the long dead corpse of an alien vessel.

'The alien entity forms as a fluid devoid of pollutants,' he said. 'Sensors indicated that it is as hard as steel, the near absolute zero temperature of deep space responsible for its rigidity and likely an evolutionary response. If these things first evolved to travel within cometary debris or similar, they could gradually have evolved defense mechanisms against the cold vacuum of space.'

Schmidt gestured to the display as it zoomed in to moving shapes beneath the icy cocoon.

'Channels,' Schmidt replied, 'passages of heat generated by biological processes through which the life forms move and consume the vessel they're aboard. That's their fuel, the metals of the hull, the electrical circuits, the wiring, probably the crew too. They either break the metal down by oxidizing it or by corrosive means, consuming it directly on an atomic scale. The energy gained from this process allows them to power that spacecraft if they feel the need to travel.'

Schmidt slipped his hands into the pockets of pants that didn't really exist, the gesture an endearing sign of his human origins.

'They would not have needed to infiltrate the vessel in great numbers, only sufficiently so that they could replicate, spread and eventually take control. They're a collective intelligence constructed of biological cellular forms and nano scale machinery, able to move freely throughout the vessel without the crew ever having known that they were there until it was too late.'

Nathan stared at the display for a moment.

'And that's what they intend to do on earth,' he said finally, 'undermine us from within, and then the big guns come in and finish us off. That's what must have happened on Ayleea. We need to find these infiltrators, and fast. Maybe we could set up stations using that glue fluid and have people walk through it? The infiltrators would be unable to get through, their locomotion impeded.'

'Hosing down a few billion people might be beyond our capabilities and is certainly not something we'll have the time for,' Admiral Marshall pointed out. 'The enemy know that we're aware of them now, which will accelerate their timescale. We need to do something before we get our backsides taken out from beneath us. What do we know about the individuals who were killed on earth?'

Suddenly all eyes were on Nathan, and he coughed to clear his throat.

'Twenty eight dead and counting, from all continents on the planet,' he replied. 'No known connections between them but we're working on it.'

'Why are they picking these people off one by one?' O'Hara asked. 'And why are they picking them off at random? Are you sure there's no connection between the victims?'

'We can't be *absolutely* sure,' Nathan admitted, 'but right now nothing's jumping out at us. The victims are widely geographically separated and have no connection to each other that we can find. All we can do right now is track down the killers using the ID chips consumed when the victims were killed, which go off–line for a short while before reactivating, and hope to get them all as soon as we can.'

Marshall frowned

'If they're raining down on earth as frequently as you suspect, there could be dozens more arriving on earth every day. You'll never track them all.'

Doctor Schmidt stood forward.

'That's where I come in, Admiral. We know from previous experience that this species can clone cells perfectly, after we witnessed the Ayleean clone that infiltrated Titan. What we also learned at the time was that they clone cells just a little *too* perfectly. Nature does not replicate with absolute precision, and thus slight changes in our DNA and genetic make up is what causes us to look a little like our parents but not *precisely* the same. This genetic drift is what gives us evolution in the hereditary sense. It's possible that I could use CSS protocols for hunting escaped criminals and alter the programming to search for signals evidence from the brains of these clones that exhibit the perfect symmetry this species produces when it clones an entity, and use that as a means to track them down.'

Marshall stared at Doctor Schmidt blankly as he digested what he had said. 'How long will it take?'

Schmidt's eyes flickered as he performed a rapid calculation. 'Two or three hours, perhaps, maybe less if I start the moment we're done here.'

'Do it,' Marshall ordered. 'Right now we need to know everything we can about this species. They could be sufficiently advanced that we're already doomed, but I'm not going down without a fight. We need to find a weak spot in their armor and we need to do it fast.'

Foxx wracked her brain for a rapid solution to the crisis, more aware now than ever of what was at stake as she glanced at the damaged warship outside the station. She knew from school that it had taken intelligent human life around four and a half billion years to appear on earth, and that event had occurred in a relatively stable solar system in a sedate corner of the Milky Way galaxy's Orion Arm. Much of the rest of the galaxy was a turbulent milieu of gravitational waves compressing spiral arms into dense clouds of violent star birth, or superheated to millions of degrees in the galaxy's dark heart, wherein ruled the gargantuan supermassive black hole Sagittarius A.

Life could not realistically be expected to emerge in these dense, hot, radiation bathed furnaces, and so mankind looked to similar areas of the galaxy for signs of life around yellow spectral stars like the sun, or long lived red and brown dwarf star systems, or in globular clusters where millions of suns would fill the sky in a dazzling halo of stars orbited by planetary systems rich in the heavy metals necessary for life.

'They must have been doing this for millennia,' she concluded. 'They're nomads.'

'That is likely true,' Schmidt agreed.

'So you're sayin' that the entity we captured must be old,' Vasquez said, 'really old.'

Schmidt nodded.

'Who knows what this life form may once have looked like, but it has clearly progressed to a state that we no longer recognize immediately as life, not in its current and natural form anyway.'

Rear Admiral O'Hara looked at Nathan and Foxx.

'You must hunt them down, all of them,' she said. 'You must find out how many of these things there are and what they're trying to do before our enemy reveals itself. If you don't, I fear that the fate that befell the Ayleeans will be visited upon us and that there is little time remaining to prevent our extinction. Go, now.'

The men and women at the table stood up and hurried away to perform their duties. Nathan wasted no time in approaching Admiral Marshall.

'Admiral, you said that Endeavour is a ship in CSS and that it encountered the enemy?'

'What of it?' Marshall asked, clearly preoccupied with the task at hand.

Nathan swallowed, suddenly uncertain of how to voice his concerns. 'I have family aboard her.'

Marshall looked at him curiously for a moment. The admiral knew enough about how Nathan had come to be here that the idea of him having any surviving family was remote in the extreme. And yet, here he was. Nathan could see the understanding blossom in the admiral's eyes, but any sense of compassion was devoid from his expression.

'We all have people aboard the fleet,' he replied. 'Endeavour is a military vessel and completed its mission to the best of her crew's ability. You're one of us now, Ironside, and if you have family in the fleet this probably won't be the first time they find themselves in danger. Get used to it.'

Marshall strode off with his lieutenants as Detective Foxx moved to Nathan's side.

'Thanks for the pep talk,' Nathan muttered as the admiral hurried away.

'He's got a lot on his plate,' she said in a meagre attempt to comfort him.

'Sula was on Endeavour,' was all he could say in reply, and then he looked down at Foxx, 'which one is she?'

Foxx's hand closed around his arm in comfort as Allen and Vasquez waited a discreet distance away.

'That one,' Foxx said, and pointed out of the vast viewing ports.

Nathan looked out into the blackness and saw the shattered hulk of the ship he'd noticed when he'd first walked in.

'No,' he gasped and pulled away from her.

'Is there something wrong here?' Rear Admiral O'Hara asked as he strolled over.

Nathan whirled. 'Sula Reyon, eighteen, Ensign aboard Endeavour. Can you tell me where she is?'

Admiral O'Hara raised a questioning eyebrow and turned to his assistant, who quickly accessed a roster and scrutinized it for several long moments.

'Sula Reyon is not on the roster for CSS Endeavour,' the assistant reported.

Nathan's shoulders sank in relief and he sighed as he rubbed his forehead with his hands. Then, he looked up in confusion.

'But she was assigned to the ship before she left earth,' he said. 'Why wasn't she aboard?'

The assistant glanced down at the roster.

'Sula was assigned to Lieutenant Hackett, a pilot aboard Endeavour who had recently been transferred from CSS Victory. Sula was transferred to another frigate for her induction as Hackett was considered an unsuitable mentor for her.'

'Which one?' Nathan asked eagerly.

'CSS Defiance,' the assistant reported cheerfully.

Nathan's train of thought collapsed into disorder and he swayed on the spot as Foxx moved in alongside him.

'Are you sure about that?' she asked.

'Of course,' the assistant said, confused at their concern. 'Sula wasn't aboard Endeavour.'

'No,' O'Hara said, 'unfortunately she must have been transferred just before the two ships were diverted to Ayleea. Defiance is currently missing in action after a combat engagement that Endeavour barely survived.'

'Oh,' the assistant said, and averted her eyes from Nathan's gaze.

'I'm sorry,' Admiral O'Hara said to Nathan. 'As soon as I have any news I will contact you immediately.'

Nathan nodded vacantly but said nothing as Admiral O'Hara turned and walked away from the chamber.

'I only met her a few days ago,' Nathan said softly to Foxx.

'And you'll meet her again,' Foxx encouraged him. 'We don't know what's happened yet, but there's nothing we can do for Sula except our jobs.'

Nathan realized that there was one entity in their possession that might actually know what the enemy wanted from humanity, where the infiltrators might be, and how to destroy them. His fists clenched as he headed for the exit, rage building inside him like an unstoppable wave as he wondered where Sula was and whether she was safe.

'We need to get back to New Washington.'

***

XXII

CSS Defiance

'Approaching destination coordinates.'

The bridge of the frigate was so quiet that Captain Jordyn Lucas could hear the combined breathing of her fellow officers above the faint hum of electronics and computers. The bridge was bathed in red light and the heat was intense, a consequence of Lucas ordering engineering to divert every last watt of power into the engines.

Defiance had leaped out of the Ayleea system on emergency coordinates, a common tactical safety net designed to allow fleet warships to evade dangerous situations at a moment's notice. Both she and Captain Travis Harper of Endeavour had agreed upon a rendezvous point in the event that such a leap was necessary, but when Defiance had arrived there they had found nothing, no sign of Endeavour and no evidence of gravitational waves that might have betrayed her presence.

'How much did you see?'

Captain Lucas looked at Lieutenant Ellen Goldberg, who had recently been released from the sick bay after being checked out and reported to the bridge. The fighter pilot stood with a young, blonde Ensign whom Lucas didn't recognize.

'Not much,' Goldberg said. 'We were close in with Fortitude and she looked intact, but then that stuff just came right at us so we turned tail and ran. We didn't see the capital ship until a moment before she opened fire. That's when Tyrone called a warning to Endeavour but it was too late.'

'Tyrone?' Lucas asked. 'Your wingman?'

'Tyrone *Tornado* Hackett, Flight Leader.' The voice of the Executive Officer, a tall and gaunt man by the name of Walker, was soft but carried with it the weight of his experience.

'A Lieutenant, serving aboard Victory and then Endeavour. It was he whom we left behind at Aylcea.'

Sula saw Captain Lucas briefly close her eyes and nod, apparently consulting her ocular implant before she opened her eyes again. 'Heroic beggar isn't he, for someone who was recently grounded according to his flight report.'

'He's misunderstood,' Ellen said carefully.

'He's repeatedly misunderstood the concept of rank, seniority and duty according to his service records,' Walker snapped back, but even his sharp tones suddenly softened. 'But his flying is of the first order. I've never seen a fleet pilot pull a stunt like that before.'

'Nor had I,' Ellen admitted as she glanced at Sula. 'Tyrone served during the last months of the Ayleean War, and he doesn't trust the Ayleeans. The diversion here only made things worse because he believes that the accord was a mistake.'

'What an officer believes is irrelevant,' Walker snapped. 'Their duty is what matters.'

'So does their courage,' Lucas murmured softly, but was distracted by her thoughts.

Captain Lucas knew that Endeavour's absence meant that she had been so badly mauled by the alien vessel that she had been forced to leap for the nearest colony she could find, her damage preventing her from reaching both the rendezvous point and then onward home to Sol. She also knew from the brief datalink transmissions received before their respective super luminal leaps that Endeavour had been hit just once by the alien vessel, and yet that hit had effectively crippled the frigate and forced her to retreat.

Now Defiance was reaching a second leap point, heading not for Sol but in a wider arc to avoid drawing the enemy closer to home. Lucas could only hope that the enemy vessel would choose to follow her and not Endeavour, that they would be tempted by a fresh target.

'You're playing a dangerous game, captain,' Walker said.

'Service in the fleet is not meant to be a safe game, XO,' she replied, unwilling to show any hint of the crippling doubt she bore on her shoulders. 'Tactical?'

Walker, his hands behind his back, remained otherwise motionless as his eyes swiveled to glance at his display screen.

'We've left a clear trail,' he replied. 'Endeavour successfully veiled her leap signature, which is what we should have done too.'

'Endeavour was crippled,' Lucas replied, keeping her voice down. 'She would have headed for Proxima Centauri or perhaps directly home.'

'Concealed,' Walker reminded her. 'We were already the favorable target once Endeavour had cleared the field.'

'Better safe than sorry.'

'Us, or them?' Walker asked without looking at her.

'Ten seconds,' came the navigation officer's warning.

'Shields up,' Lucas snapped. 'Divert engine power to plasma cannons. I want a salvo ready the moment we drop out of super luminal.'

The officers swiftly complied with the captain's orders and Lucas took a last moment to survey her crew. Their faces in the ugly glow of the emergency lighting looked like shocked angels huddling away from the demonic red glare of some unspeakable creature. All of them had witnessed the destruction of Ayleea and the damage wrought on Endeavour, and now they knew that Defiance was likely only seconds ahead of the huge warship they had encountered barely two hours before.

'Five seconds, four, three, two...'

Lucas grabbed the arm rests of her seat as the red light on the bridge was warped and a bright flare of white light burst from the main display screen. Her guts convulsed as the frigate decelerated from super luminal cruise and rocketed out of its gravity well into deep space.

'All stations, no contacts!' the signals officer called.

'All plasma cannons fully charged, shields up!' came the report from the tactical officer.

'Helm, hard to port!' Lucas snapped. 'Bring us about!'

Defiance heeled over as the frigate turned hard to bring its broadside to bear on any craft following their gravity wake. Lucas watched and waited as the ship turned, circling back to a position directly behind their own gravity well.

'She's not there,' Walker said. 'They didn't take the bait.'

Lucas said nothing, watching both the main display screen and the signals sweep of the local area. She had chosen the spot for a reason, something that her father had once said after a command tour in the Ayleean War: *In space, there's nowhere to hide. It's like fighting in a swimming pool, where everything moves slowly and everyone can see you. You have to make the universe fight for you. You have to find something to help.*

To the right flank, silent and dark, she saw the sensors detect a field of debris that caused distant stars to flicker as unseen objects passed by in the infinite blackness. Virtually invisible to the naked eye, the debris field was the remains of several moons that had once orbited a star that had died long ago, its feeble white dwarf remnant burning several Astronomical Units away and barely brighter than other far more distant stars.

'Open an emergency channel to Polaris Station,' Lucas ordered.

The communications officer obeyed instantly, then Sula saw him frown as he adjusted his controls.

'The channel is open but the interference from a nearby white dwarf star is causing an intermittent connection. We can't signal them in real time, we'll have to keep it open and hope for the best that something makes it through.'

'Time lag?' Captain Lucas asked.

The officer glanced briefly at his instruments. 'An hour, maybe two.'

'It'll have to do,' Lucas replied as she glanced again at the shadowy asteroid belt. The one thing that could save them was now the one thing blocking their line of contact with home. 'Record everything and transmit as of now. We'll send them everything we've learned so far and...'

'Contact, gravity bow shock, zero nine zero, elevation two four!'

'Hard to starboard, port guns to bear, all power to main cannons!' Lucas yelled.

'We can't fight them!' Walker snapped. 'They're too powerful!'

Lucas nodded, almost standing out of her seat as she saw a patch of stars ripple on the main screen as the alien ship's gravity well warped the curvature of space time before them.

'We're not here to fight,' she replied. 'We're here to learn.'

'We're here to do *what?*'

'Contact, vessel, capital class, port bow!'

Lucas squinted as she saw the gravity well flare bright white and the huge alien warship lurched out of super luminal cruise in the same spot that Defiance had, barely five kilometers away.

'Fire all, *now!*'

Defiance shuddered as her port batteries opened up with a salvo of twelve massive plasma charges. Captain Lucas saw the shots rocket away from the frigate, bright blue and white spheres of energy each as large as houses.

The shots crossed the vacuum of space between the two vessels in less than three seconds and slammed into the alien vessel with a ripple of brilliant explosions that tore into her hull. Lucas shot out of her seat and let out a ragged cry that matched those coming from the rest of the crew as they saw the salvo hit home.

'Evasive manoeuvers!'

Defiance lurched and accelerated as it turned, coming around behind the big warship as Lucas peered at the main display screen and saw flickering lines of bright orange flame surrounding the ship's massive hull panels on her port bow.

'I'm detecting damage,' the tactical officer reported. 'She came out of super luminal with her shields down! She's trailing debris and gases!'

'Analyze them!' Lucas snapped. 'And then get us out of here! Helm, take a heading directly toward the stellar remnant!'

Walker stared at Lucas. 'But there's an asteroid field in the way!'

Before she could reply the tactical officer shouted a warning. 'I'm detecting a massive energy surge, she's turning and preparing to fire!'

'All power rear shields!' Lucas yelled as the ship accelerated away from the alien vessel. 'Keep running!'

Walker wrung his hands as he saw on the main display screen the huge ship's plasma cannons glow with vivid yellow light as the huge vessel swung around and then four red plasma charges rocketed from them. The massive shots filled the screen in an instant.

'Brace for impa…'

The shots slammed into Defiance's stern and the entire vessel heaved as her shields took the force of the blows and tried to dissipate the energy across the hull. Lucas threw her hands up to protect her face as wall panels burst outward in showers of sparks and flames licked across the ceiling.

'Direct hits, two impacts astern!' the engineering officer shouted, struggling to stay upright at his post. 'Shields are holding but another hit like that and we're scrap metal!'

Lucas looked at the tactical display on her viewing screen and knew that there was nowhere else to run.

'Head into the asteroid field!' she snapped. 'Right now!'

The helmsman did not hesitate to obey the command, but Walker stormed to her side.

'We can't run in there! Once inside we'll be trapped.'

Lucas strapped herself into her command seat. 'They're on a mission, XO. They won't want to spend hours hunting us in there. It's the only way we can save ourselves.'

'We can jump again!' Walker hissed. 'Get away from them!'

'Where?' Lucas challenged. 'Where the hell would we go? We don't have enough fuel for more than a couple of jumps! If we head further out toward the Rim we'll never make it home and if we approach any of the colonies we're dragging the enemy right to their doorstep. You want that on your conscience Walker, when you see them start bombing our cities from orbit?'

'I want them gone from our damned stern!'

'I want them gone from *existence*,' Lucas growled back at him. 'The only way we can do that is to start figuring out what their weak spot is. Now, get in line or get off my bridge.'

Walker hesitated for a moment, his eyes locked on hers and repressed fury radiating from him like a planetary nebula. Finally, he turned and barked an order across the bridge.

'Maximum pulse power, take us in!'

Defiance surged forward, the helmsman turning sharply to port and then to starboard to spoil their enemy's aim as the frigate accelerated toward the blackened maw of the asteroid field.

'We're leaving them behind,' the tactical officer noted.

Lucas saw it too on the tactical display and nodded. 'We're faster off the mark than they are in sub luminal,' she observed. 'Something to note for future engagements.'

'That's not much use if they can disable us with a single shot once we lose the shields,' Walker pointed out.

'It's handy in avoiding that single shot,' Lucas snapped back. 'Tactical, forward sensors active, all shields to rear.'

'Aye, cap'n,' came the response as the frigate veered toward vast, frigid chunks of rock and ice floating invisibly in the blackened void.

Across the bridge, Sula watched the main viewing screen with Ellen Goldberg as she saw the stars ahead blinking in and out of existence, like crystals sparkling and then vanishing at random in a black sea. She knew what she was looking at but it was hard to picture in her mind, the immense field of debris eclipsing stars in the darkness.

'Helm, three quarter,' Lucas said, her voice calmer now but terse none the less. 'Pick us a route, Weisner.'

'Aye, cap'n,' the helmsman, a young man of perhaps thirty, replied as he gripped the controls more tightly. 'Here goes nothing.'

As Sula watched, the vast chunks of debris sailed past on either side of the frigate, rocks with masses of thousands of tons that were easily capable of tearing off Defiance's hull plating. The ray shielding that protected warships against plasma blasts by absorbing and spreading the power of their impacts and torpedo projectiles by deflecting the missiles was no defense against truly massive, solid objects like asteroids.

The XO stood forward as he watched the immense debris field before them, the distant white dwarf star gleaming beyond it. 'It's an orbital field,' he said.

Sula saw Captain Lucas nod. 'That's why I picked it. It still has the rotational velocity of its parent star, so we can predict the motion of much of the debris.'

The frigate slowed as it eased into the flow of frigid, dark rocks like a vehicle joining a freeway. Sula realized that Captain Lucas was more experienced than she had at first thought, always thinking ahead of their predicament.

And then she realized that their enemy was too.

'Multiple salvos to stern!' the tactical officer yelled. 'They're opening fire!'

The viewing screen of twinkling and vanishing stars suddenly burst into light as plasma blasts smashed into the asteroid field. Huge chunks of debris burst out from impacts amid blossoming fireballs that flickered and died out, and suddenly the orderly rotation of the asteroid field was thrown into chaos as impacted asteroids lurched out of formation into each other in massive collisions.

In the distance, Sula heard the first chunks of debris hammer the frigate's hull with deathly, echoing blows.

***

XXIII

'Hull breaches on decks three, four and six!'

Sula hung on to the command rail as she heard Captain Lucas bellow commands to the bridge crew one after another.

'Close the bulkheads! All power to main shields! Helm, one eighth pulse!'

'Aye cap'n!'

Defiance shuddered as more massive chunks of debris clattered against her hull. Sula could see the concern etched into the expressions of the command crew as they focused on their instruments. The ship was in grave danger and there was nowhere for them to run for help.

'You're digging us deeper into a pit that we cannot escape from, captain,' Walker shouted above the din.

'The enemy is doing that for us,' the captain shot back. 'I won't drag anybody else into this fight just to save our own skins.'

'Two more salvos, astern!'

Captain Lucas barely reacted, her eyes watching the way ahead. 'Maintain course and speed. The deeper we go, the safer we'll be.'

'And the harder it will be to get out again!' Walker yelled.

Sula watched the captain for a reaction but it was as though she were in another world, her eyes fixed to the display screen and her body motionless. *Combat paralysis.* She had heard her late father speak of it on occasion, the moment where there is so much going on and so much stress and danger than the human mind simply shuts down and reboots, unable to cope with the demands of the moment. Her father's fellow pilots had also called it *saturation point.* Sula could see that the XO was standing behind the captain and impatiently awaiting a reply, but none was forthcoming.

'She's lost her stones,' Ellen whispered to Sula, 'can't think straight. If she doesn't make the right call in the next ten seconds, we're done for.'

The frigate shook as the alien ship's plasma shots smashed into asteroids all around them and the debris blasted from the explosions slammed into the frigate's immense hull, but this time there was less violence in the impacts. Captain Lucas gestured to the screen.

'The shots are starting to miss us,' she said, coming awake as though from a dream as she looked at the helmsman. 'Take course starboard four zero – keep that mess they're making between them and us.'

'Aye, cap'n.'

Sula watched as the frigate turned slowly, diving to starboard beneath a truly massive asteroid that could almost have qualified as a small moon itself, smaller rocks tumbling along its flanks as they were dragged in by its gravity.

'That was too close,' Ellen uttered, watching Captain Lucas uncertainly.

The blasts from the alien vessel diminished further as Defiance slowly navigated around to the far side of the large asteroid.

'Damage report,' Lucas asked.

Sula listened with Ellen as the different stations reported in. Defiance had lost thirty per cent of her shield generators and her hull was badly damaged somewhere down on the lower port stern. Her engines had survived the blasts however and were fully functional, although most of the aft plasma cannons were out of action.

Captain Lucas studied the report for a long moment and then looked up to the tactical display. As Defiance's sensors swept the field, so they could see the debris scattered around them and a glowing red icon denoting the alien vessel far behind.

'They're not entering the asteroid field,' Lucas observed.

'That's what people do when they haven't lost their minds,' Walker uttered out of the corner of his mouth.

Lucas did not respond to her XO as she stepped forward, as though moving closer to the screen would somehow reveal something new.

'They're slower in sub luminal cruise and they're not willing to risk their hull integrity by coming in here after us.'

Sula spoke almost without thinking about it from where she crouched with Ellen, her voice louder than she expected. 'They're not leaving, either.'

Captain Lucas turned to look down at her and Sula almost cringed away from the XO's penetrating gaze as he marched toward her.

'Since when are you an expert on military doctrine?' Walker demanded.

Ellen Goldberg stood and blocked the XO's path. 'Since we're fighting an enemy that none of us know anything about.'

Captain Lucas kept her eyes fixed on Sula. 'She's right, there is no doctrine yet. Why do you think they're not following?'

Sula slowly stood up, aware that Walker was still directing an unfavorable gaze her way but willing to take the chance that Captain Lucas was taking her seriously.

'They can't let us escape,' she offered, 'for some reason. We're only one ship and we've already seen what they're capable of doing at Ayleea. Why would they pursue us when Endeavour has already slipped away? If I were in their shoes and planning some kind of invasion of earth, I'd have gone after Endeavour instead and stopped her from sending a warning.'

Lucas said nothing but Walker scowled.

'We split up, standard operating procedure when under attack from a superior force. Divide assets in the hopes that one or the other will be able to get help. Endeavour slipped away and concealed her path, we escaped but did not conceal ours.'

'You're welcome,' Captain Lucas remarked wryly as she glanced at the XO.

Sula kept her nerve.

'That only works if invading earth is the plan,' she replied as she looked at the captain. 'What if they let Endeavour go because they knew she'd run for home? What if they're planning something else?'

Captain Lucas was watching Sula now with an appraising expression but the XO was having none of it.

'That's ridiculous,' he snapped. 'They've utterly destroyed Ayleea and murdered millions of the people there. The Ayleeans are extinct and you're telling us they're sparing us for some other reason that you can't even define?'

The XO's words made Sula shrivel in shame, but then they revealed something to her that nobody else had mentioned. She lifted her chin defiantly.

'You said it yourselves, we don't know what their doctrine is. And since when do we know that they've murdered millions of Ayleeans?'

Lieutenant Goldberg turned and raised an eyebrow at her. 'What more evidence did you want? Their planet is in ruins, their cities aflame and their fleet destroyed.'

Sula nodded in agreement. 'But I saw nothing on the displays to suggest that they'd *murdered* a single person. The cities were empty, so were the jungles. I didn't see any life readings on the displays when you scanned the planet. There was no life because it was *gone*, not because it was dead.'

The frigate's bridge fell into a deep silence as the command crew stared at Sula and she cringed again, fearful that she had been in error. Captain Lucas watched her blankly for a moment and then she whirled.

'Son of a bi... Tactical, replay the original scans of Ayleea again!'

'Aye, cap'n!'

Sula watched as the holo screens displayed a stream of data recording the life patterns on Ayleea as recorded via measurements of gases in the atmosphere, technological indicators and the presence of recognizable ID chips of a similar design to those used in the Sol System.

The tactical officer looked up at the captain.

'There's nothing,' he said in amazement. 'The planet is virtually devoid of biological signatures larger than a cat except in a few isolated areas.'

Captain Lucas frowned. 'You mean there was *nothing* alive down there?'

The tactical officer shook his head.

'The jungles are still there, the forests and everything, but fauna is virtually zero. Historical scans of the planet showed massive life readings at least on a par with earth. If there's anything left now, it wasn't enough to show up on our scopes.'

Captain Lucas turned to look at Sula. 'Why didn't you mention this before?'

Sula blushed as she realized the importance of the things she had noticed.

'You were a bit preoccupied with trying to stop us from being blown up.'

The captain folded her arms and leaned against one of the command consoles. 'Come out here, young lady.'

Sula, somewhat embarrassed, stood up and stepped onto the command platform. Lucas glanced at the XO.

'This is what happens when people use their eyes and ears and minds even when they're in grave danger,' she said.

Sula shrivelled again under the gaze of the command crew. 'I had no duties so I had enough time to look,' she said quickly to the captain. 'Everybody else here was busy trying to stay alive.'

Captain Lucas smiled and rested one hand on her shoulder.

'A born diplomat too. And you're barely out of high school and in a high stress situation. What are you doing here?'

Sula took a moment to recall her life before this moment, her heart thumping in her chest like a war drum.

'Scholarship,' she blurted. 'My father was a fighter pilot.'

Lucas's appraising expression turned cloudy. 'Was?'

Sula's lip trembled and pain pinched at the corners of her eyes but she managed to keep her voice even. 'He died at the Battle of Proxima Centauri.'

If there had been any festering hostility toward her among the command crew it blustered away and died in that moment. She saw the XO close his eyes briefly and step back, all pretense of contempt vanished.

'You didn't tell me that,' Ellen said to her.

'Didn't seem like the time or the place,' Sula replied with a shrug.

'That's why you wanted the Eighty Fourth,' Ellen said. 'Your father flew with them.'

Sula said nothing in reply. Captain Lucas squeezed Sula's shoulder briefly and then let her arm drop away.

'Well, you're in the thick of it now,' she said softly, before looking up at the crew. 'We need a way out of this asteroid field without getting our backsides handed to us by that ship out there.'

Walker stepped forward again.

'It's quite possible that CSS knows what's happening out here. Endeavour must have made it back to the Sol System by now or at least one of the outposts, and Captain Harper would have made it his priority to warn the senate of the situation on Ayleea.'

Captain Lucas nodded, Walker's prior arguments apparently already forgotten.

'We can't be sure that they'll send help,' she replied. 'They'll know that Ayleea is lost but not why, and thanks to Sula here we now know more than they do. We need to know what happened to the fauna on Ayleea and especially the Ayleeans themselves.'

Sula was staring into space as her brain processed a memory and she blurted out a name.

'Tyrone.'

'What about him?' Walker asked her.

'He's still back there.'

Walker sighed.

'It is highly regrettable but Tyrone was likely either captured or killed by the enemy,' he replied. 'There's not much that we can do for him and we don't even know where he might have been taken even if he is alive.'

'The enemy ship followed us,' Sula pointed out. 'It might not have noticed a lone fighter among all that debris around Ayleea.'

'That's unlikely,' Walker replied. 'Their scanners showed tremendous power, easily strong enough to detect a Phantom fighter at those ranges. They would have picked him up in moments, or utterly destroyed him with a single shot. Even if he survived, he'll have suffered the same fate as the Ayleeans and we have no idea what happened to them.'

Sula stepped closer to the captain.

'That's true, but unlike the Ayleeans Tyrone has a CSS ID chip, right? They have a tracker that has a longer range than standard civilian chips. If we could get back into Ayleean orbit we could do a search for his ID implant. If he *has* been captured, and if we can find him...'

'We might find the rest of Ayleea's people,' Captain Lucas finished the sentence for her. 'And that means reinforcements.'

Sula felt a flush of pride at her idea as well as an overwhelming sense of doubt over whether it was the right course of action. The XO was quick to share those concerns in his usual manner.

'Heading back to Ayleea is the worst idea I've ever heard.'

Captain Lucas nodded thoughtfully. 'That's why I like it.'

'Somehow, I knew you were going to say that.'

'We're the only ship to evade the enemy so far,' Lucas said to him, 'and right now they're mysteriously sitting out there waiting for us. Sula's right, there's got to be a reason for that mystery and if there is, the solution to it is probably back at Ayleea. Plus it takes us closer to home and not further away. If we can locate Tyrone, we might figure out what's going on here and it also means we didn't leave a good pilot to whatever horrible fate consumed the Ayleeans without at least trying to bring him home again.'

The XO's shoulders sank.

'You know damned well that I wouldn't oppose a mission to rescue a downed pilot, but right now it's *us* that needs rescuing. How the hell do we get out of here without being blasted into a billion pieces?'

Captain Lucas re took her seat and eyed the viewing panel for a moment.

'We sneak out,' she replied. 'Helm, I want one third pulse power and then I want you to shut the engines down.'

'Seriously?' the helmsman asked in a strangely high pitched voice.

'And I want you to aim directly at the largest asteroid you can see.'

Sula baulked, as did the rest of the crew.

'You're insane,' Walker uttered.

The bridge crew fell deathly silent as they heard the insult, and Captain Lucas slowly turned to look at her XO.

'Probably,' she replied. 'And that's the only thing that's going to save us. Helm, one third impulse and then shut us down! I want every system switched off, cold and dark except for one stern plasma cannon, understood?'

'We'll have no steerage, no shields, no internal support!' Walker wailed. 'We'll be sitting ducks!'

Captain Lucas glared at the officers on the deck around her and they leaped to carry out their orders as Sula stared at the captain, torn between horror and fascination.

'Do you have any idea what you're doing?' Sula asked in a whisper.

'No,' Lucas replied.

Sula stared in horror at the captain, but then Lucas offered her a fleeting smile as Defiance accelerated forward.

'One third impulse,' the helmsman called. 'Shutting down, now.'

The ever present hum of the ship's engines faded away as one by one the command officers called out warnings.

'Shields down, internal systems into standby.'

'Plasma batteries discharged except for one cannon, relay lines down, all defensive systems off line.'

The bridge lights flickered and faded out. Suddenly, the entire ship seemed to fall silent as one by one the various displays and screens switched off. Sula took a hold of the command rail again for balance as utter darkness consumed the bridge, broken only by a handful of blinking stand–by lights winking on and off in various colors.

'Helm is down,' the helmsman replied, 'steerage is almost lost. Are you sure you want to do this, captain?'

Captain Lucas nodded. 'Come to starboard four degrees, then shut down the helm.'

'Four to starboard, aye.'

The XO's voice reached out from the darkness one more time. 'Captain, I must insist one last time that you don't follow this course of action. The enemy will detect and destroy us the moment we leave the debris field, if we don't die beforehand. It's madness.'

'Noted,' Lucas replied, then looked at the engineering officer. 'Open the garbage chutes.'

'You wanna take out the trash *now*?'

'And start dumping fuel,' Lucas added.

'We need that fuel!' Walker wailed in dismay. 'How the hell do you expect to make it home if…'

'It's no good to us if we can't leave,' Lucas murmured, unconcerned.

The engineering officer shook his head in disbelief as he complied with her orders. Sula watched as the frigate moved through the blackness on the main viewing screen, a huge asteroid before them betraying its presence only by the star fields it blocked from view.

'We're accelerating,' Walker noted, 'its gravity is pulling us in.'

'Hold course,' Lucas repeated to the helmsman.

'Steerage lost captain,' the helmsman replied. 'I couldn't change course if you wanted me to.'

Lucas slowly stood up out of her seat as Sula watched the asteroid's immense black bulk block out the view of everything else ahead of them. Another screen showed the view from behind, a stream of fuel trailing behind the frigate and glistening as it froze in the frigid vacuum of space.

'Plasma battery, stand by,' she ordered.

'Standing by, cap'n.'

Sula gripped the rail tightly, watching as Captain Lucas appeared to count down in her mind, her lips moving softly and one hand clenched into a fist by her side as she waited, and waited, and...

'Dump all garbage, port dispenser chutes!'

'Dumping now, port chute!'

A dull, deep boom reverberated through the frigate's hull as the vents opened on the port hull, and moments later Sula heard a dim rushing sound as garbage from Defiance's hull was ejected forcefully into space.

Then, something quite wonderful happened.

Defiance began to turn slowly and drift to starboard. Sula sucked in a breath of wonder as she saw their trajectory changing. 'An equal and opposite reaction,' she whispered in delight. 'The garbage ejection is pushing us clear of the asteroid.'

Captain Lucas snapped an order.

'Fire now! Target the dumped fuel!'

'Firing!' the tactical officer reported.

Sula squinted as she saw three plasma shots rocked out astern and a brilliant explosion lit up the debris field in a brief flash of blue–white light. The trail of ejected fuel lit up in the blast in a brilliant explosion that flared like a newborn star and briefly illuminated the entire asteroid field before dying out to be swallowed once more by the eternal blackness.

'Fuel vents closed,' Captain Lucas ordered.

'Vents closed, aye,' came the response.

In the glare of the fading explosion Sula saw a stream of metallic trash trailing behind Defiance and the ship drifting wide of the asteroid's horizon, yawing slowly to port as she did so.

'The explosion accelerated our drift,' Sula said. 'That's brilliant.'

Captain Lucas kept her eyes on the screen. 'Great minds.'

'We're going to clear the asteroid,' the helmsman said, the joy evident in his voice. 'Shall I re start the engines captain?'

'No,' Lucas said. 'Wait.'

Sula watched as Defiance slowly pirouetted, her bow pointing toward the huge asteroid as she sailed silently past it with only a few hundred meters to spare. The cloud of metallic debris spun through space behind them, expanding rapidly and glinting weakly in the faint starlight as the last clouds of burning fuel flickered out in the bitter vacuum.

'We've accelerated,' the helmsman said. 'The asteroid swung us past in a gravitational slingshot.'

Sula stared at the captain in wonder as the frigate accelerated away from the asteroid, the alien vessel no longer visible behind it.

'You want them to think we've been destroyed inside the debris field,' Sula whispered. 'It's genius.'

'It's bloody risky,' Walker said as he stood nearby in the darkness. 'They might not fall for it.'

'Helm,' Lucas called. 'Rear view screen, visuals only, no sensor scans. Check we're not about to plow into anything hard and dark out there.'

The helmsman replied within two seconds.

'We're good for about two minutes,' he said. 'Then we hit another of the big ones and it's all over.'

As if on cue a clattering sound rippled through the ship as the hull was pelted with a cloud of smaller asteroid fragments.

'Hold course,' Lucas cautioned the crew. 'No shields. I don't want them to detect any emissions from us.'

Walker's voice again pierced the darkness. 'They might *see* us if they wait long enough.'

Lucas nodded, agreeing but not debating the point as she watched the screens and waited. The seconds seem to tick by agonizingly slowly, half lit faces staring into the viewing screens.

'One minute now,' the helmsman said.

The silence deepened on the bridge as they waited. Then the tactical officer spoke softly.

'I'm detecting some kind of sensor sweep on the passive scan,' he reported. 'High energy, but not enough to reach far into the debris field. They're looking for us.'

Lucas smiled.

'Just a little longer,' she promised. 'They're scanning the debris we left.'

'Thirty seconds,' the helmsman whispered, his voice once again a little high pitched.

Sula watched and waited, counting the seconds down in her mind as she saw on the rear view screen another asteroid astern the ship growing rapidly larger.

'Fifteen seconds.'

Sula realized that she was gripping the command rail so tightly that her hands were aching. The asteroid behind them filled the screen as the helmsman grasped the ship's controls and fidgeted in his seat, desperate to act.

'Ten seconds!'

'Hold,' Lucas said firmly.

Sula saw the entire bridge crew reach out to hold onto something, bracing for impact. The asteroid was at least ten times as massive as the frigate and there was no way that...

'Super luminal jump detected!' the tactical officer yelled. 'They're gone!'

'Full power to engines, half impulse!' Lucas snapped. 'Shields up!'

The helmsman re-started the frigate's engines and threw the ship's throttles forward as the entire bridge lit up again and Sula squinted in the sudden bright light. Defiance shuddered as her engines engaged and with a surge the frigate slowed down and arrested her suicidal collision course with the asteroid astern.

'Tactical, scan for contacts!'

There was a moment's pause and then the tactical officer looked up at the captain and grinned.

'Nothing on the scopes, cap'n, our tail is clear.'

Sula felt a wondrous relief that danced across the bridge around her as the command crew relaxed, exchanging glances of admiration for their captain.

'Helm,' Captain Lucas said, ignoring their gazes, 'get us out of this debris field and set a super luminal course for Ayleea.'

'Aye, cap'n.'

Sula watched as Captain Lucas returned to her seat, straightened her uniform and sat down as though nothing had happened. Her voice rang out across the bridge as the command crew hurried to carry out her orders.

'All plasma batteries to full power, all shields charged, all gravitational plating engaged and make sure the engineering team get to the stern and repair the damage we took as best they can. Let's go rescue this lost boy pilot and find out what the hell happened to Ayleea!'

Ellen Goldberg threw one arm around Sula's neck and squeezed.

'Okay, maybe you do have a place here. Let's hope that miserable son of a gun Tyrone appreciates our efforts on his behalf.'

***

XXIV

Ayleea

The thick foliage surrounding Tyrone was laden with a dense odor of decay. He could hear the sound of movement in the jungles and heard the sound of footfalls around him but he could see nothing for his eyes were blindfolded. Normally, he would have accessed a sensory display in his ocular implant to give him an impression of where they were going, but the Ayleeans had attached a device to his neck that scrambled the implant. Tyrone was effectively blind, and with his hands bound behind his back he stumbled and staggered through the forest.

His captors numbered four, and they had wasted no time in silencing Tyrone with a brutal blow to the side of his head. Bound and blindfolded within sixty seconds, they were now moving at a rapid rate through the forests, the grunts and snarls of his captors driving him on. The only thing that had confused Tyrone was the fact that they had applied a salve to the drone wound in his belly that had miraculously quelled the pain and reduced the swelling within minutes, allowing him to walk again. At least they didn't want him dead, yet.

About all that he could tell was that they were descending deep into a valley system, heading ever downhill. The heat was stifling, Tyrone's flight suit drenching him in sweat as he staggered along. The Ayleeans stopped periodically to drink, allowing Tyrone the chance to quench his thirst before they set off again. His head pounded from dehydration and his sense of balance was weak and untrustworthy, but eventually he felt the ground beneath their feet level out and the sound of rushing water once more.

Something sharp prodded him in the chest and brought him to a stop. Moments later, the blindfold was torn from his eyes. To his surprise he barely squinted as the light hit him, so pale and weak down here that he found he could see perfectly normally in the half darkness.

They were standing in the depths of a ravine, soaring mountains reaching up into dense clouds tumbling end over end thousands of feet above them that glowed with red light from the sky above. Moist, warm air was rising up to hit cooler flows near the peaks, condensing out as rain that never reached the surface and merely coiled in endless vortexes like angel's wings. The forest was thick on either side of them, a black mass of squat, tightly packed trees and vines, while before Tyrone was a plunging waterfall. The deluge crashed down at what looked like a ridiculous speed, the water tumbling far faster than that on earth and thundering down into a wide lake upon the shore of which they stood.

'Do we kill him?'

The four Ayleeans stood back and watched Tyrone for a moment in silence. Their leader had spoken, easily identified by the yellow chevrons on his body armor.

'The elders want him alive,' another growled.

'I'm in favour of that,' Tyrone offered.

'You were not told to speak!' the Ayleean leader snapped and stepped forward as he slammed one bunched fist into Tyrone's belly.

Tyrone gasped as he dropped to his knees, coughing in the hot air.

'We must not harm him,' said another as Tyrone struggled to recover his breath. 'They were here, the humans, but then they left us again.'

'I'd have expected nothing less,' snarled another. 'Their peace charter was never more than a prelude to war. I say they brought this upon us deliberately. We should kill him now Shylo, before it is too late.'

Tyrone sucked in a lung full of hot air.

'We got hit too,' he rasped, his head pounding. 'Our frigates barely made it out.'

The leader of the Ayleean gang, Shylo, grabbed Tyrone's collar and with one massive arm hauled him to his feet.

'Where did they go?' he growled at Tyrone, his huge disfigured face inches away so that Tyrone could smell his rank breath and see festering wounds on his leathery skin.

'Tactical egress leaps into super luminal,' Tyrone replied breathlessly. 'They'll probably try to make it back to Sol without being followed.'

The Ayleean released Tyrone, who swayed unsteadily on his feet.

'Where they will close ranks and leave us to die,' he growled.

The more aggressive Ayleean in the group pulled a broad, ornate knife from a sheath on his back that was as long as Tyrone's arm, the blade dulled with dried blood.

'Let me open him up, one limb at a time.'

Tyrone sensed the indecision in the group and knew that he had to speak. 'I answered your distress call.'

Shylo peered at him. 'What distress call?'

'The one sent from this location,' Tyrone replied. 'I landed because I couldn't get aboard my frigate in time for it to jump. I figured I'd stand more of a chance down here.'

'You stand more chance of being sliced into tiny pieces,' the aggressive Ayleean sneered at him.

'You think I want to be here?' Tyrone snapped. 'If I'd known you were an Ayleean force I'd have landed somewhere else!'

The Ayleean lunged forward with his blade raised but Shylo blocked his companion forcefully, stayed the blade with one thick hand. Shylo reached up to his chin with his other hand and stroked it, long nails rasping against tough skin.

'Where did the capital ship go?' he asked.

'Jumped out of the system after our frigates.'

One of the other Ayleeans pointed at Tyrone. 'He could be one of *them.*'

'One of what?' Tyrone asked.

Shylo pointed up to the sky with one long finger. 'The ones who came from above, who infiltrated our people. They took our forms, and when they attacked we were broken from within.'

Tyrone winced. 'Shape shifters? Like an icy gray material, right?'

Shylo nodded and Tyrone saw the other Ayleeans taking notice of what he was saying.

'We heard rumors,' Tyrone said, 'about some highly classified briefing, that an unknown substance that possessed a fluid form had infiltrated one of our capital ships. They called it "goo" and although it was destroyed, the CSS leadership feared that it would return. They said that an Ayleean ship had also been infected.'

Shylo nodded. 'That is true.'

Tyrone jerked his head up to the skies above them. 'Whatever the hell is going on here, it's not CSS behind it. We sent a senate vessel, Fortitude, here to sign the final peace charter with Ayleea. We lost contact with her two days ago and so two frigates were dispatched to check things out. We thought that elements within the Ayleean leadership might have reneged on the deal and taken the ship.'

A low series of discontented growls rippled through the Ayleeans but Shylo silenced his companions with a wave of his hand.

'Enough,' he muttered. 'There was no back tracking on the deal, even though some of the Ayleean Council opposed the charter. When Fortitude arrived our fleet had already been destroyed from within.'

Tryone suddenly felt cold despite the cloying heat of the jungle. 'They infiltrated your fleet?'

Shylo nodded. 'Everything, thousands of them.'

Tyrone felt the first surge of panic bolt through him. 'We have to warn them! You've got to get a message to Sol!'

'Our signals are blocked,' Shylo replied. 'Their armada prevents our escape.'

'Armada?' Tyrone echoed. 'We only encountered one vessel, a big one.'

Shylo watched him for a moment longer, and then he gently

pushed his companion's blade away from where it hovered beside Tyrone's head.

'Come,' he said, 'you must tell the elders what you know.'

Tyrone was pushed in the direction of the waterfall as Shylo led the way, and Tyrone knew instantly that he would have to negotiate the dense, dark waters despite the incredible force with which they were falling.

'I'll never survive moving through that,' he said as they neared the falls, the air thick with swirling mists that coiled and tumbled on the hot air.

'We're not going through,' Shylo growled as they moved across the slippery rocks, the water flowing and churning lethargically beside them like black oil.

'That's a relief.'

'We're going under.'

Before Tyrone could answer two of the towering Ayleean warriors took an arm each and Tyrone let out a howl of despair as they suddenly leaped off the rocks toward the thick, churning water. Tyrone took a deep breath and then they plunged into the fluid and vanished beneath the surface.

It was all that he could do to keep the air in his lungs as he hit the water. It felt like treacle and his legs folded up beneath him as they plunged feet first beneath the waves. The Ayleeans dove down with powerful strokes, Tyrone dragged with them like a dead weight through the thick water. He tried to open his eyes but it was as though they were glued half shut and he could barely see anything but the churning surface above them. He felt the blows of the waterfall drive them down deeper and his lungs felt as though they were about to burst, only the chill of the water a relief from the incessant heat of the jungle.

Tyrone dribbled a few bubbles out from his lips, hoping that he would be able to keep the water out, and then he saw lights appearing in the water above them. The Ayleeans twisted upward and kicked with powerful strokes and suddenly the three of them burst from the surface of a wide, limpid pool into an underground cavern.

Tyrone gasped for air, felt it hit his lungs cool and clean as the water plummeted off his face in thick, fast falling drops. The two Ayleeans dragged him from the water and hauled him onto the rocky shore as he got his first good look at the hidden cavern.

Candles and torches glowed in their thousands, lodged into crevices in the rocks, and their flickering lights revealed the vast walls of the cavity. Tyrone blinked in amazement as he realized that the walls of the cavern were covered in artwork, paintings of some kind that depicted hunting scenes and dancing figures, as though they were the relics of some prehistoric past that he knew had not existed for the Ayleeans on this world. Their species, as divergent as it seemed, had arrived here just two hundred years previously.

Shylo strode from the lake, water streaming down his body like rivulets of flaming embers as they reflected the lights. From the depths of the cave system Tyrone saw countless eyes watching them, reflecting the candles and torches in their shining cornea. Many were short, perhaps four feet tall, furtive creatures hiding behind rocks and whispering to each other. Children, Tyrone recognized, hundreds of them.

'This way,' Shylo ordered.

Tyrone was marched up the rocky shore and onto a path that had not been hewn through the rocks by tools but worn down by the passing of countless feet over centuries. Tyrone watched as adult Ayleean warriors stepped forth from the darkness, heavy spears and swords in their hands and anger in their gruesome faces. The dim, flickering lights and the angry, half shadowed faces gave Tyrone the impression he was being marched through Hades. The Ayleean children leaped with primate–like agility from one rock to another, keeping their distance but with growing curiosity as Tyrone was led toward the back of the cavern, where resided a knot of elderly looking Ayleeans, their graying locks the only betrayal of their advanced years.

Shylo slowed as he reached them, and then he got down onto one knee before the group and bowed his head. The eldest of the senior Ayleeans stepped forward.

'Again, you have come through for us, Shylo. Stand, old friend.'

Shylo got to his feet and the elder rested one gnarled, leathery hand on the warrior's shoulder.

'Were you tracked?'

'No,' Shylo assured him, 'but we encountered a flock of drones we had to destroy, so it can't be long before they find us.' Shylo looked over his shoulder. 'The human is called Tyrone, and he answered a distress call.'

The elder nodded and then Shylo stepped aside as the old Ayleean moved to confront Tyrone. Tyrone was shoved down onto his knees by his companions before they too bowed down. Tyrone winced as his knees hit the rocks, the elder moving to tower over him, yellowing eyes glowing like discs of fire in the candlelight.

'My people go hungry,' he growled down at Tyrone. 'Our cities burn, our farms gone, our people missing. Give me a reason not to let the children gorge themselves on your remains.'

Tyrone looked up into the old Ayleean's eyes.

'We're all dead anyway, from what I hear. One more meal won't make a difference.'

The Ayleean leaned forward, peering down at him. 'Tell that to starving children.'

Tyrone looked left and right and realized that even the youngest of the group wore blades in their armor, some of them now stroking the tips of the weapons in anticipation.

'The jungles out there,' Tyrone said, 'there was food, I saw it. Lots of it.'

The elder stood up and gestured to the walls of the caverns around them.

'Our people lived like this when we first came here,' he announced grandly, 'after we had been forcibly ejected from earth and Ayleea became our home.'

'Nobody was forced out,' Tyrone corrected him. 'Werner Ayleea led the colonies of the damned here by choice.'

The elder tilted his head in acquiescence despite the growls of anger echoing around the cave. The Colonies of the Damned, as they had been known, were the derogatory names given to those who carried still the hideous deformities that scarred humanity in the wake of The Falling.

'After we had lived like rats in the wastelands of earth for a century after *The Falling* had been cured, our disfigured forefathers felt very much as though they were being forced out,' he replied. 'Here on Ayleea we had our own world, a home of our own, but it is a dangerous world and we were forced to survive as primitive hunter gatherers as we learned to adapt to Ayleea's jungles. Now, we cannot use our plasma rifles for the enemy can detect the energy they produce when fired. Yes there was life and food here, but in two days it has almost all gone.'

Now, Tyrone's voice was no longer defiant.

'What happened here? What did they do?'

The elder looked back down at Tyrone and his voice filled the cavern.

'We are cattle,' he replied simply. 'All life on this world, all life on earth, everything is seen by them as a source of food, and their time for harvest has come.'

***

XXV

New Washington

Nathan hurried off the shuttle from Polaris Station onto the busy spaceport deck with Kaylin Foxx, Allen and Vasquez and was immediately confronted by a pair of squad vehicles manned by two anxious looking officers.

'What gives?' Foxx asked as they approached.

'You need to come with us,' one of the officers, a sergeant, told her in a hushed whisper. 'It's talking.'

The voice that answered was not Foxx's.

'*What's* talking?'

Nathan turned and saw news anchor Tamarin Solly hurrying toward them, her team following and with one of them carrying a sonic amplifier.

'A suspect in a murder case,' Vasquez replied, 'and we don't have anything to say yet so if you'll be on your way we can…'

'What of the reports that the police are hunting not one but several serial killers both here on New Washington and across the planet?'

Nathan managed to keep a straight face and not reveal anything but Lieutenant Allen stared at Solly in amazement. 'How the hell did you know about other victims in..?'

'It's my job to know,' Solly glowed with delight as she realized she'd hit the jackpot with the cameras running. 'How many victims are there? Should people be double locking their doors at night? How can the two killers be working together both up here and down there, and how are the victims being found?'

'Captain Forrester will make a statement as soon as we have sufficient information,' Foxx replied coolly as she climbed into the squad vehicle.

'Captain Forrester is refusing to talk to us.'

'Wonder why,' Nathan murmured as he climbed into the vehicle alongside Foxx.

'And you four have just flown in from Polaris Station. Why does the CSS have an interest in this, and is it connected to the fleet's amassing in orbit around Saturn? And what's talking at your precinct station? The public has a right to know if…'

The door hissed closed and the squad vehicle hummed into life and lifted off the platform, forcing Solly to back up.

'Damn it, this is getting out of hand,' Foxx said as the vehicle turned and soared through the port toward one of the station's arms, wherein a brightly illuminated tunnel allowed shuttles and Mag Rail services into and out of the spaceport. 'They're following everything we do and it's only a matter of time before they figure this out.'

Nathan watched as the squad car pulled up and climbed vertically up and away from the spaceport, although Nathan began to feel the effect of the station's centrifugal gravity pull him toward their destination as though they were diving rather than climbing.

'I've seen people like Solly before and they're like a dog with a bone,' he said. 'They won't let go until they've got everything they can out of it. Only way we can shut her down is to either tell her the truth in return for the first scoop on the story when the time comes, or we deliver false information to her to send her off the trail.'

Foxx shook her head.

'I just want her off our case.'

'You could arrest her.'

'Are you kidding?' Foxx uttered. 'On what charge?'

'For being an amazing pain in the a…'

'Are we suggesting that we silence a free press?' Foxx cut him off.

'No,' Nathan replied in measured tones. 'Just curbing their excesses, for the benefit of one and all.'

Foxx ruminated on the idea as the squad car slowed and pulled out of what was now a vertical dive down the tunnel toward North Four. It moved smoothly into the flow of traffic above the city streets, descending in a gentle turn for the roof of their precinct building.

As soon as they had landed Foxx and Nathan hurried to the interrogation room to find Schmidt already in place, one hand supporting the elbow of his other arm, the hand of which was thoughtfully stroking his chin.

'Give us the lowdown doc',' Foxx said as they walked in.

Schmidt looked at them sideways and raised an eyebrow. 'Behold, it speaks.'

Nathan looked at the figure in the hard light cubicle, still imitating Chance Macy, watching them and precisely mirroring Schmidt's thoughtful pose.

'What's it said?' he asked Schmidt.

'Does it matter?' Macy asked.

Nathan noted that the entity's voice was not that of Macy, but of somebody else.

'It doesn't have enough information on Macy to replicate him entirely,' Schmidt said by way of an explanation. 'So it relies on what it does have. The voice you're hearing is probably that of Samuel Freck, its last victim.'

'Freck,' the figure echoed.

Instantly, the form's color vanished like a rainbow fading away and for a moment it was partially opaque. Nathan watched in fascination as the shape changed, became slimmer as it adopted a slightly awkward stance and then the color reappeared once more and he was looking at a perfect replication of Samuel Freck.

Foxx walked closer to the cubicle. 'It's learning,' she said.

'Doesn't everyone?' Freck replied directly to her.

Nathan saw Foxx recoil from the cubicle as Schmidt spoke.

'The entity as you all know is built from intelligent smaller components, like cells. It's overall intelligence however is a sum of its parts. Alone, the cells are nothing, rather in the same way that a lone termite is nothing. Bring sufficient numbers of them together, however, and they can coordinate their actions and achieve remarkable things.'

'Like homicide,' Foxx murmured cynically.

'That thing's a freak,' Vasquez uttered as he walked in with Allen, regarding the being with disgust.

Freck's face dissolved into rage. 'I ain't no freak man!'

The expression, the movement, the fist slamming against the wall of the cubicle was so perfectly performed that had Freck's friends not known he was already dead, Nathan reckoned that they would have been completely fooled.

'How the hell are we ever going to detect these things?' Foxx uttered. 'There's no way to tell them apart, it's perfect.'

Nathan thought for a moment as he looked at Freck and then a sudden realization hit him, hard. He turned to Foxx.

'Can you shut off the sound to that thing so it can't hear us?'

Foxx nodded, but it was Schmidt who answered. 'Yes, we can eliminate all electromagnetic interference from all points outside of the cubicle by creating a sonic wave interference patter…'

'Just do it, Einstein.'

Schmidt inclined his head. 'It is done.'

Nathan pointed at the being inside the cubicle.

'This doesn't make sense,' he said. 'Freck died on the surface but Erin Sanders died here on New Washington.'

'Yeah?' Vasquez said, 'So what?'

'So how the hell does Erin's killer know what Samuel Freck looks like?'

Doctor Schmidt looked at the captured being in surprise and then back at Nathan.

'A most astute observation, Detective Ironside. Are you feeling all right? Dizzy spells, fever, headaches?'

'He's right,' Allen said as he consulted his ocular implant's data stream. 'Erin Sander's ID implant never left New Washington and Samuel Freck hasn't been in orbit for months. Neither show any sign of being within a thousand miles of each other in their lives.'

'I'll be damned,' Foxx uttered, 'they must be communicating.'

Doctor Schmidt nodded and appeared to access his internal files before he spoke.

'When we captured one of these entities on Titan, they were taken sufficiently far away from their own kind that they were unable to communicate effectively. They ended up using internal heat fluctuations to send a warning sign.'

'Like a sort of Morse Code,' Nathan said.

'A what code?' Allen asked.

'Never mind,' Schmidt cut in as he studied Freck Seavers' mimic in the cubicle. 'All that matters is that these entities communicate, and if they communicate…'

'They can be tracked,' Nathan finished the sentence for him, 'and they can be found.'

'Trouble is,' Vasquez pointed out, 'we don't have any idea of how they do it so we don't know what we're looking for. And if they're communicating then how come this thing didn't know Chance Macy's voice?'

'Because Chance Macy is still alive,' Doctor Schmidt replied, 'so we must assume that the entity that killed Freck only *saw* Chance but did not have the opportunity to hear his voice and thus replicate it.'

'Then how did it know where to find him?' Nathan wondered out loud. 'Did it target Freck specifically, or did it simply pick up the first person it could find as a vehicle to get into the city for some other purpose?'

Schmidt pondered that for a moment. 'Logic suggests the second assumption,' he said finally. 'Freck was a random target and the entity was in fact driven by a different, ulterior motive.'

Nathan looked at Samuel Freck's mimic inside the cubicle and had a thought.

'Schmidt, can you get Captain Forrester to use the police signals corps to scan for a wide spectrum of signals emitting from this building, maybe even track any responses that come in?'

'Yes,' Schmidt replied. 'But why would you want to do that now? This entity is not going to just signal its companions and do the job for us.'

'Says who?' Nathan replied as an idea formed in his mind. 'Let's not go hunting for these signals, let's get Freck's killer here to do it for us.'

'How the hell you gonna get it to tell us that?' Vasquez asked. 'It can't even talk much, plus we're in North Four and the black holes in communication around here won't let them broadcast anything so easily.'

Nathan froze as he considered that for a moment.

'The black holes,' he echoed thoughtfully. 'I bet we don't have any evidence of these things operating in areas of limited communication either.'

Doctor Schmidt scanned the data banks of the currently known victim locations and smiled ruefully.

'You must visit the sickbay soon, detective. You're in danger of becoming intelligent.'

'They stay in contact because, like you said doc', they're limited in intelligence as individual operatives,' Nathan went on. 'They can't operate efficiently without each other's knowledge, without sharing information and data, and that might even mean they have a central controller, someone in overall charge of them.'

'If we can identify such a controller,' Foxx said, 'we could hijack the signal and prevent the invasion attempt, or at least give CSS a fighting chance.'

'Reinstate the sound to the cubicle,' Nathan said.

Schmidt activated the sound once more and Nathan spoke clearly.

'Okay, if this thing can't tell us what we need to know then the solution is simple. We just use the victim's ID chips to locate them and we shoot them on sight, and we can detect those not yet reported missing using your new scanner, Doctor Schmidt.' Schmidt appeared mystified but said nothing as Nathan went on. 'We have enough police and military here and on the surface to kill them all. Sure we may catch some collateral along the way but, y'know, the needs of the many outweigh the needs of the few and all that. When the invasion begins we'll have the advantage of surprise over whoever is controlling these things because they'll be out of action but their overlords won't know it. As soon as the enemy fleet arrives we hit them hard with all four of our concealed *ultra quantum interstellar plasma hadron overdrive* cannons and wham!!' Nathan punched his right fist into his cupped left hand. 'One enemy fleet totally annihilated.'

To Nathan's amazement Freck's eyes widened in what appeared to be embarrassment and suddenly his figure returned to the shape and form of Erin Sanders. Sanders' mimic stood rigidly upright and its eyes closed. In an instant, Nathan saw that it began pulsing with a strange light.

'That's it!' he snapped. 'Get everything we have tracking for a response signal!'

Foxx, Allen and Vasquez stared in mystified wonder as Schmidt opened up the scanners and began collating the data.

'What *ultra quantum interstellar plasma hadron overdrive* cannons?' Foxx asked in a whisper.

Nathan shrugged but said nothing as the being before them pulsed with energy. Nathan noted the temperature inside the cubicle rising as Erin's form turned a dull red.

'High frequency sub space modulating signal detected,' Schmidt said suddenly, 'emitting on all available...' Schmidt stopped talking suddenly as his eyes opened and he looked at Foxx. 'On all available military channels.'

Foxx and Nathan exchanged a glance and before they could speak Allen cut across them.

'Maybe the victims planet side all have close relatives or friends inside the CSS and military networks?'

Nathan felt his blood run cold.

'That's how they did it,' he said out loud. 'The Ayleean fleet didn't get destroyed in battle and Ayleea didn't burn under an enemy attack. The infiltrators provoked the Ayleeans to kill their own and they destroyed themselves.'

Schmidt's voice cut across them all.

'Divide and conquer,' he said. 'The signal the entity just sent may be that which starts the invasion process.'

***

XXVI

Nathan barely had time to think about the consequences of what he had done when a priority signal appeared inside the room with them, bearing the emblem of the CSS.

'It's a military signal,' Schmidt warned. 'We cannot reveal anything that we've learned, or it may alert the enemy to what we know about them. We can't trust anybody.'

Nathan nodded, and a moment later Schmidt allowed the signal to open and a holographic Rear Admiral O'Hara flickered into existence in the room alongside them.

'Detectives,' he said with a somber voice that immediately put Nathan on edge.

'What is it?' Foxx asked, sensing the same air of regret as Nathan.

The admiral was standing with his hands behind his back, his jowls resting on his chest as he looked directly at Nathan.

'We have had word from Defiance,' he said simply. 'A brief contact that would have been sent about an hour and a half ago, from a neighboring system to Ayleea.'

Nathan's heart sank as he stared at the admiral, knowing somehow that whatever he was about to hear, it was not good.

'Tell me,' he insisted.

'I can show you,' O'Hara said. 'I'm truly sorry, Detective Ironside.'

The admiral's image was joined by a vivid scene of the bridge of a fleet frigate that Nathan assumed was Defiance, her captain a stern looking woman who was shouting commands to her crew. The connection was weak, the image trembling and distorted, but it was clear that they were under attack.

Nathan could not hear any sound, only the moving images as the ship was repeatedly hit by plasma blows from an unknown source. He stepped toward the holographic display, peering into it as he saw glimpses of the bridge, of the lights flashing in and out, of explosive discharges from panels being blasted from the walls. And then he saw her, crouching by the command rail, her long blonde hair vivid against her CSS uniform.

'Sula,' Nathan gasped, reaching out for her by instinct.

The frigate's deck shook and trembled beneath the attack and then the ship's transmission was cut brutally short and the image vanished. Nathan stared into the empty space where Sula had been moments before, and then he looked at the admiral.

'The frigate entered an asteroid belt,' O'Hara explained. 'Although we have no visual data, we do have digital information that made it out. The frigate was pursued further, and approximately five minutes after it entered the asteroid field there is a sharp spike in electromagnetic interference followed by a complete cessation of all transmissions.'

Nathan swallowed.

'Just spit it out,' he said, his throat dry.

'The spike was a major detonation from within the field, equivalent in signature to the ignition of plasma fuel on a massive scale. Analysis of that signature and also of considerable metallic debris detected in the field before the data transmission broke off confirms the destruction of CSS Defiance with the loss of her crew.' O'Hara sighed. 'The enemy warship pursuing her left the area shortly after the event.'

Nathan closed his eyes. In the silence that followed he realized that everybody was watching him, could feel their gazes burning into him. He heard his own mantra revolving around in his head. *She's not your daughter.*

'Again, I'm truly sorry for your loss, detective,' O'Hara went on. 'You'll be required to help prepare for the defense of our planet and also to continue to try to root out the enemy within. We will arrange contact with Sula's mother to...'

'I'll do it,' Nathan replied, opening his eyes. 'I'll tell her.'

He felt Foxx move closer to him as the admiral nodded in agreement, and without another word the transmission shut off. The silence weighed heavily on him for a brief moment, and then he whirled to Schmidt.

'Can you get the uniforms to transport Erin's mimic to the airlocks at the spaceport?' he asked as he pointed to the trapped infiltrator. 'Quickly?'

'Yes of course,' Schmidt said, 'but why would you want to…?'

'Just do it, and bring that fluid you hosed it down with!' Nathan snapped and then hurried out of the interrogation room.

Foxx followed him with Vasquez and Allen as he marched toward the main office.

'This isn't the way, Nathan,' Foxx said urgently as she jogged to keep up with him. 'We need that thing alive and you know that killing it won't bring Sula back to…'

'I know that!' Nathan insisted. 'Just trust me! We can't finish this if we can't talk to anybody at CSS! We have to find a way to identify who has been replicated!'

Foxx didn't reply as they got into the squad vehicle. Nathan remained silent as she took off and lit up the lights and sirens, the squad cruiser accelerating up and away through the streams of traffic cruising above North Four and climbing vertically into the North Arm.

Nathan did not look at the spectacular scenery this time, his mind utterly empty but for an image of Sula and the cheeky, mischievous grin that had reminded him so much of his daughter. He barely noticed Foxx landing at the spaceport and activating the gravity cells on her boots before she climbed out of the vehicle.

'I need to know what you're going to do,' she said as he climbed out and started walking.

Nathan did not reply, climbing out and striding with absolute conviction toward the airlocks that lined one side of the spaceport's landing bays. Protected by hard light barriers and solid steel doors, access could be granted only by a security officer manning a guard post outside the airlock.

Nathan flashed his detective's shield at the officer and was met with a gesture to stop him as the guard stepped out.

'Can't let you through I'm afraid guys, I haven't had clearance from...'

Nathan acted without conscious thought. He stepped into the guard's left and wrapped one arm around his throat as he twisted him around and closed the other arm over the first and then squeezed hard.

'Nathan!'

The guard struggled in his grip but Nathan lifted him almost bodily off the deck and the pressure around the guard's throat partially closed the arteries in his neck. After a few seconds the guard's struggling body fell limp and Nathan lowered him gently to the deck and then dragged him back into his guard house.

'What the hell are you doing?' Foxx demanded, one hand moving instinctively to her sidearm.

Nathan grabbed the guard's pass and turned, accessing the hard light barriers and door controls on a panel nearby. The barrier vanished and the solid doors hissed as they opened.

Nathan turned and saw Doctor Schmidt crossing the spaceport behind them, with the hard light cubicle and the trapped entity within now being pushed along on a gravity pad by two uniformed officers. The officers pushed the cubicle into the airlock as instructed by Doctor Schmidt, and set a canister of hemostatic agent down alongside it.

'Detective Ironside,' Schmidt said as he joined them and blocked the entrance to the airlock, 'this time I really think that you're in danger of going too far and I...'

Nathan walked straight through the doctor and into the airlock, Schmidt flinching and then brushing himself down in disgust.

'Do you have *any* manners?'

Nathan saw the infiltrator standing before him inside its hard light cubicle, once again having taken the form of Erin Sanders. Beside the cubicle was the cylinder of compressed hemostatic agent which Nathan picked up in one hand and activated with a flip of a switch.

'Guess what?' Nathan said to the infiltrator, 'I'm gonna let you go.'

Even as he said the words he noted the expression of concern on the face of the infiltrator. Its eyes moved to the cylinder in Nathan's hand and then back to his, and whatever it saw in his eyes he could tell it didn't like.

'You wouldn't let me go,' it said simply in the female voice that was like Erin's but didn't sound quite right.

'You sure about that?' Nathan asked, and then with one hand he reached out to a control panel and shut off the hard light cubicle.

'Nathan, what the hell are you doing?!' Foxx screamed as she drew her pistol and aimed into the airlock.

The infiltrator looked at Nathan and frowned, not moving despite there being nothing now to contain it.

'You're not gonna run away?' Nathan asked, one hand on the trigger of the dispenser in his hand, the cylinder heavy and humming with energy as he held it pointing at her.

He saw the infiltrator swallow, an endearing sign of the human traits it was picking up. Nathan, a seasoned interrogator of suspects, knew fear when he saw it.

'You intend me harm,' the infiltrator said.

'No,' Nathan frowned, shaking his head as though offended. 'No harm, only an endless nothingness.'

The infiltrator smiled now. 'I cannot die, for I am not one.'

'I know,' Nathan said, 'let me help you with that.'

Nathan lifted the cylinder and fired, a stream of amber colored fluid hosing out and splashing across the infiltrator. The figure did not move as it was drenched in the thick fluid, Nathan knowing that it would not be able to escape or change shape as it was smothered. The fluid hardened almost immediately, not solid yet but thick and dense, sufficiently so that the entity could move only slowly.

Nathan shut off the dispenser and set it down on the ground beside him. Then he stepped back out of the airlock and slammed the steel door shut. He turned the locks and secured them, then opened a communications channel with the infiltrator trapped inside.

'You're alive,' Nathan said. 'I know that you live and that you wish to continue to live, that you fear dying because I can see it in you. You say you can't die, not really, but then nothing ever does, does it? It just breaks down and becomes something else. So, what I'm gonna do is deny you that right.'

The infiltrator frowned, confused.

'Consciousness,' Nathan whispered to it, malice surging like poison through his veins. 'Scientists and psychologists argue about what it is but I reckon it's all about having enough neurons in place to know who and what you are. People don't remember life as a baby, or in the womb, because our brains haven't developed enough to be truly conscious. But when the two halves of a human brain join up by the time we're two years' old, memories start to form. We're no longer blindly responsive to stimuli, we can *think*. We're *conscious*. That's what you are, right now. But when we die that consciousness is lost and we cease to exist. It doesn't bother us any more than the fourteen billion years we didn't exist in this universe before we were born. But, imagine, if we were to die but be aware of it and yet powerless to change it, an endless prison that will last for the life of the universe, countless trillions of years, dead and yet alive at the same time.'

The infiltrator's face collapsed as it realized what he was about to do.

'Don't do it,' it said, once again using Erin's voice.

Suddenly, Nathan realized what was wrong with the infiltrator's rendition of Erin's voice, the depth of it, the strange twist to its chords. It had only heard Erin speaking once and she had been in terrible pain, her voice twisted with agony just before it killed her.

'Nathan, you can't do this,' Foxx said.

'I can do whatever the hell I want,' Nathan snapped without looking at her. 'To hell with this thing. Once that airlock's open the hemostatic fluid will freeze as hard as rock. I'll fire that thing out there into the cosmos and it'll move in a straight line for the next billion years with nothing to come near it.' Nathan smiled at the infiltrator. 'How long do you think it will take for your consciousness to break down into utter insanity?'

The infiltrator's features collapsed into true panic. 'You won't do this, it's not in your nature!'

Nathan grabbed the emergency evacuation lever, a thick steel handle painted in bright yellow and black chevrons.

'Try me,' he snarled and hauled on the lever.

'Okay I'll talk!'

'Then talk, *now*!' Nathan yelled. 'Everything! How do we locate all of you?!'

The infiltrator's expression warred between rage and desperation, and then it blurted its response in a flourish of self loathing.

'Water, that's what sets us apart. We are as much machine as we are living beings, and our cells can no longer hold sufficient water.'

Nathan frowned. 'That's it?'

'That is why we draw the fluids from our victims,' came the response. 'We use it both to conceal our true identity and to retain life. Without hosts, we will perish.'

'Who leads you? Who is in command?' Nathan yelled as he leaned his weight against the evacuation lever.

'I don't know!' the infiltrator shouted. 'We have Sentinels, leaders in high places but the identity of their hosts is never revealed. We all operate alone!'

Nathan turned to look over his shoulder at Foxx.

'Erin Sanders, the reports said she treated drug addicts on North Four.'

'Yeah, but there was no connection to Freck Seavers or any military networks.'

'But what if there didn't need to be?' Nathan said as he used his ocular implant to access the reports on Erin Sanders. 'You recognize any of the names on the list of patients Erin worked with?'

Foxx's gaze drifted slightly as she scrutinized the same display and then her eyes widened.

'Paul Montgomery.'

'Who's he?'

'He's the son of the Governor of New Los Angeles,' Foxx explained. 'He got addicted to Shiver and was admitted to a North Four clinic by his father, who had revoked his son's wealth and ordered him to be treated like any other orbital citizen on threat of losing his inheritance. It was all over the news a few months back.'

'Okay,' Nathan said, 'and Freck went to a prestigious college, right? Wouldn't there be sons and daughters of governors and politicians and even military figures in the same colleges too?'

'Lots of them,' Foxx responded without hesitation. 'San Diego's climate draws them in from across the world. It's one of the top colleges globally.'

'That's how they got in,' Nathan said. 'They weren't looking to get to kids like Erin and Freck. They were targeting the people those kids came into contact with, their co–workers, their bosses and parents.'

The infiltrator glared at them both from within the airlock.

'If you pull that lever, I will still be able to let every single infiltrator on the planet know about what you've done before I am frozen. They will know you're onto them, detective.'

Nathan looked the infiltrator in the eye.

'That's the idea.'

Nathan hauled down on the emergency evacuation handle and he heard the infiltrator's scream as the airlock opened and the atmosphere within was vacuumed out in an instant in a whorl of vapor and ice crystals. He saw Erin Sander's form turn pure white as it froze along with the hemostatic agent enveloping it, an icy coffin from which the infiltrator's tortured expression stared wide eyed at Nathan as it tumbled out of the airlock and into the chill embrace of deep space.

Nathan pushed up and closed the airlock once again. He turned and looked at Doctor Schmidt.

'That enough for you to locate them all?' he asked.

'I'm on it,' Schmidt replied. 'I can use body temperature data to start isolating the infiltrators and broadcast the result to every human being alive.'

'If we have any time left!' Foxx snapped as she turned and dashed for the squad cruiser. 'Damn it Nathan, you know you just started the invasion, right?'

***

XXVII

Allen and Vasquez arrived near the airlocks to see Foxx running with Nathan toward them.

'What gives?' Vasquez asked, looking at the airlock as two uniformed officers helped an unsteady looking guard to his feet.

'Get your guns and get ready,' Foxx ordered them as she jumped into the squad car.

Nathan knew that he had provoked whatever pre–invasion mission the beings had and he could tell that the team would be more than annoyed about it, but now they had a lead, something tangible they could follow.

'You *provoked* it into activating the invasion?!' Detective Allen said in horror as Foxx explained what Nathan had done.

'It wouldn't have made any difference,' he said as they walked swiftly through the spaceport. 'It'll be much harder for them to hide now. If we didn't get them out into the open they'd have taken us down from within.'

'They might do that already, Nathan,' Foxx pointed out as the squad vehicle took off and Foxx guided it toward the North Arm.

'Where are we going?'

'Back to the precinct,' Foxx snapped. 'The only way we're going to prevent these things from committing mass murder is to obtain their precise locations and that's not going to happen off the signals you provoked it to send because you can bet your arm they'll seek to find new hosts as fast as they can.'

The central panel between Foxx and Nathan shimmered into life and Schmidt appeared as a small hologram between them.

'I have initiated a scan for all individuals who exhibited a response of any kind to the signals the infiltrator attempted to send from the precinct building. It's only a short range protocol but it might pick up a few of them.'

Nathan accessed his ocular implant as they flew down the North Arm and saw locations pinging up all over the orbital stations.

'Damn it they're everywhere!' Allen said over the radio. *'We've got sixteen signals here in New Washington alone, twenty three in New Chicago, more in New London.'*

'I've got eighteen in New Moscow,' Vasquez added.

The two squad cars reached the precinct building within minutes, both landing rapidly. Nathan burst into Captain Forrester's office alongside Foxx and spoke before she did.

'Signals corps! Have them tie the signals emissions from interrogation room four to the ID chip of any recipient planet side!'

Forrester blinked in surprise but he saw the urgency on their faces and he relayed the command instantly.

'What the hell's going on?' he uttered as soon as he was done.

'Genius here just started Armageddon,' Vasquez said as he jabbed a thumb at Nathan.

'I got our captive to signal all other entities that have infiltrated our society,' Nathan snapped in his own defense. 'The signals corps can track them now, once they've matched the signal to the receiving ID chip.'

'And if those entities then go and murder somebody else and switch identities?' Allen challenged as he hurried into the office behind Vasquez.

'It's possible,' Nathan agreed, 'but it'll take time to do that and if we can grab them before they make the switch, we're golden.'

'That's a hell of a risk,' Forrester pointed out.

'So is waiting for the invasion to begin! We also know that the infiltrators have a bit of trouble holding their water.'

'They do *what* now?'

'Trust us on this,' Foxx insisted. 'Send a signal to all CSS stations that the entities appear to be attempting to infiltrate government, law enforcement and military positions. That's how they're going to overpower us. It's what happened on Ayleea! If we can't get the upper hand here on earth we're going down and it'll happen real fast. We need to deploy everyone and everything as fast as we can and wipe these things out before they try to take hold.'

Forrester nodded, apparently stuck for words, but then Vasquez spoke for him.

'Oh man,' he said softly, 'I think we're too late even for that.'

Nathan turned as Vasquez hit a switch and a holo screen shimmered into view. Upon it, Tamarin Solly spoke to them as though she were in the room alongside them.

'It has become clear that police forces across the orbital stations, the globe and the CSS fleet at Polaris Station are mobilizing against a threat that appears to be facing mankind. I have heard from a reliable source at CSS New York City that there are beings among us who are not of this earth, who intend to infiltrate our society and attack us from within. In a shocking development, we understand that the police were involved in a pursuit and capture of just such an entity and even now have it in captivity but have chosen not to inform, or warn, the public!'

Foxx stared in horror at the transmission.

'How the hell did she figure this out so damned quickly?!'

Nathan thought back to the crime scenes and he realized quickly what was happening.

'The entities have infiltrated our media and government organizations,' he said. 'If one of them is placed highly in CSS they could have informed Solly of what's happening to create panic.'

'Or Solly could be one of them herself,' Vasquez suggested.

'No, she'd have been identified by now on the signals sweep,' Allen replied. 'She's got inside information somehow.'

'It is believed that there may be over four thousand alien entities living among us and that they may have been here for some time. According to one source, they may have even been here for centuries.'

'Damn her!' Foxx snapped, one hand moving instinctively for her plasma pistol. 'She's fomenting just the kind of panic the enemy will want. This is how it begins.'

'Chaos behind enemy lines,' Vasquez agreed with her, the quote sounding to Nathan like something from the detective's Marine days. 'Disrupt and destabilize,' Vasquez went on. 'We've go to shut them down, right now, be *seen* to be doing something or the people will start to take matters into their own hands and before you know it everybody will think everyone else is some kind of alien.'

Nathan hurried across to the office windows and looked out onto the sparkling, rain soaked streets. Shafts of sunlight were sweeping across the cityscape as the station revolved, earth's vast and baleful blue–white eye glowing brightly as veils of rain drifted across the packed streets and sidewalks. From his elevated vantage point, Nathan could see some people standing and listening to Solly's broadcast beaming live into their ocular implants. Others, he noted, were already running while others still changed direction sharply, diverted by the rapidly spreading news.

'Damn it. Schmidt, do you have anything yet?'

Doctor Schmidt spoke clearly, analyzing events as he always did with a sort of detached and clinical appraisal, as though he were watching a drama show and not real life.

'Solly's broadcast appears to be designed to create panic and confusion and mistrust, with the signal being received by some four thousand or so individuals on New Washington alone.'

'The same must be happening across the orbital stations and planet side,' Foxx said as she looked out onto the streets with Nathan. 'We can't help them now.'

'Yes we can,' Nathan said as he turned to Schmidt. 'There must have been a single part of that infiltrator's signal that was the same for all recipients and transmitters, that went to the one it called a Sentinel?'

Schmidt assessed the data and nodded.

'Yes. A very low frequency signal propagating from a planet side source.'

'Do you have a location?' Nathan asked.

'I'm trying to lock it down now,' Schmidt said as he focused.

'You think that's where the main player in all of this is?' Foxx asked Nathan.

'Gotta be,' Nathan replied.

Schmidt turned to them.

'You had best hurry,' he said. 'The replying signal was emitted from CSS Headquarters, New York City.'

Nathan and Foxx exchanged a glance.

'Coburn,' Foxx said. 'It must be somebody close to her.'

'Do we have an ID?' Nathan asked.

'No,' Schmidt said, 'Of all signals identified, a quarter belong to military personnel and cannot be accessed.'

Nathan was about to turn and run with Foxx from the office when an emergency announcement was broadcast across all of New Washington's districts and into the ocular implant of every single citizen. He turned and stared into the face of Commodore Adam Hawker, the British commander's stoic expression and cold blue eyes strangely emotionless as he spoke.

'*Lock down protocol has been initiated,*' Hawker droned. '*All citizens are advised to remain in their homes and offices. Repeat, lock down protocol has been initiated. All flights into and out of the station are cancelled and all control of the response has been handed to military command. For communications safety, all holosaps will be shut down until further notice.*'

'What?!' Nathan shouted, and whirled to the doctor. 'Can you get that infiltrator data out to the surface before you're shut off?'

Doctor Schmidt's shoulders sagged.

'All communications with the surface have been cut off and there is no time for me to complete my work,' he said.

Before Nathan could reply he saw Doctor Schmidt smile a strange, sad smile and then his projection flickered out and in the blink of an eye he was gone.

Nathan took one look at Foxx and he knew what she was thinking.

'Hawker,' he said. 'He's one of them. He's shutting down all lines of communication.'

'And he's with Arianna Coburn right now,' Foxx said. 'If they infiltrate the CSS at that level the people will be putty in their hands! We need to get down there!'

Nathan knew that the station's lockdown protocol would prevent any craft from legally leaving or entering either the station or earth's atmosphere. That meant they would have to figure out another way down to the surface.

'Where's Betty?'

Betty *Buzz* Luther was a patrol officer with a formidable reputation for what was euphemistically termed "tactical flying". A sergeant and significantly older than most other officers still on the force, she also had a reputation for being willing to break the rules.

'Let's go,' Foxx said as she checked her sidearm.

Nathan followed Foxx out of the office and up a stairwell toward the roof.

'What are we going to do when we get down there? It could be anybody, any one of her staff, even Coburn herself?'

Foxx shoved her way through the door onto the roof and Nathan heard the panic from the streets below as people ran this way and that, already consumed by terror that they or their loved ones were being consumed and infiltrated by hellish beings from another world.

'I don't know,' Foxx admitted as she reached for her personal communicator and cursed as she saw that it was receiving no signal. 'Do you know where Betty lives?'

'East Three,' Nathan replied as Foxx changed direction toward their squad cruiser. 'You think she'll be able to commandeer a shuttle?'

'Only one way to find out.'

***

XXVIII

Ayleea

'We're cattle?' Tyrone uttered.

The cavern was filled with nothing but the sound of crackling flames from torches burning in endless ranks like ragged stars in the night. Despite the heat of the jungles outside Tyrone felt cold now as he listened to the elder's reply.

'The worlds that we know as homes are to them, farms,' he said. 'We didn't know it but they have been watching us for centuries and mankind for much longer. It is written in your history books, the stories about flying discs in the skies that nobody could identify.'

'UFOs,' Tyrone nodded.

'We had them here too, from time to time,' the elder said as he pointed with one crooked finger up to the sky somewhere outside. 'Until our vessels became more powerful, more numerous, and then suddenly they appeared no more in our skies. We thought that was a good thing, because we didn't understand what they were. Now, we know that when they disappeared it was the beginning of the end for our people.'

Tyrone realized that he had never heard an Ayleean speak in such tones of defeat and resignation. A proud warrior race who thrived on the belief that they had prevailed against all odds and human brutality, they had never been defeated in battle for a want of courage. Only mankind's superior technology and cunning had quashed the Ayleean's savage spirit.

'What were they, these UFO's?' he asked.

It was Shylo who answered.

'Shepherds, effectively. They monitored us just like they monitored humanity for millennia. Our ancestors all thought that they were watching us with some noble aim of contacting us when we were suitably advanced to warrant their intervention. The truth is that they were waiting for life to become abundant enough and our technology to be advanced enough that they could harvest everything for themselves.'

Tyrone frowned.

'There has been life on our worlds for millions of years,' he said. 'How come they didn't do this a long time ago?'

The elder rested his hands on a thick cane, the length of which was studded with what looked like hundreds of razor blades.

'Efficiency,' came the reply. 'Why not wait for a species to advance technologically before plundering a planet? We think that the species behind this is not all that far advanced compared to us, but had just enough of an advantage to overpower us in battle and conquer us by subterfuge. We were infiltrated long before this happened.'

'Shape shifters,' Shylo spat. 'Cowards who hide rather than fight. When they revealed themselves among us they slaughtered thousands of our most experienced soldiers, commanders and High Councilors. They switched off our defensive shields, our weapons guidance systems, our communications, everything. Then they turned many of our own weapons against us. There were so many, and by the time we realized what had happened and attempted to mount a defense, the big warships arrived and finished the work that their shape shifting accomplices had begun.' Shylo averted his eyes from Tyrone's, shamed at their defeat. 'It was over within twenty four hours.'

Tyrone looked at the few hundred Ayleeans gathered inside the cavern, and then he looked at the elder.

'They killed them all?'

'No,' the old Ayleean responded. 'They were taken away in massive transport ships, perhaps to be enslaved, perhaps to be consumed. We don't know which. All that we do know is that we and perhaps a few small pockets of survivors around the planet remain. The infiltrators were only the first wave. After them came the octopeds.'

'The what's?'

'The infantry,' Shylo explained, one fist clenching and un-clenching in slow rhythm, 'the real enemy, the species that inhabits those capital ships. They are crustaceans of some kind, multi legged with exoskeletons, predators. They overwhelmed us in numbers and forced us back into the jungles, taking our families away from us.'

Tyrone heaved his legs up beneath him and stood, his hands still manacled behind his back.

'The human survivors, where are they?'

The elder frowned. 'There are no humans on Ayleea.'

'I picked up their distress call,' Tyrone insisted. 'They were definitely human.'

Shylo looked at the elders. 'The drones that attacked him, how could they have known where he would be?'

'They could have tracked his fighter when it landed,' the elder offered.

'But the drones have only a short range,' Shylo argued, 'and we did not detect any distress signals.'

Tyrone began to feel a cold pit forming deep in his belly. 'If the infiltrators sent a fake signal to draw me in, they might have done so to draw you out.'

Shylo nodded. 'They must know roughly where we're hiding out, and so would have drones dispatched from the nearest city.'

The elder sighed, his massive chest sinking as he spoke. 'They have again used deception to outwit us. The drones you destroyed will have led them out here, and they will search for us.'

Tyrone nodded.

'You sure can't stay here forever,' he said. 'They'll find us eventually.'

'And we will stand and fight to the death!' Shylo snarled.

A rumble of low growls of approval echoed like warring demons through the darkness of the cavern, but Tyrone shook his head.

'That's what you did the first time. How's that worked out for you?'

'You insult our courage?!' Shylo roared, his voice booming across the cavern.

'It's no insult to speak the truth. This isn't the time to fight,' Tyrone said. 'This is the time to think.'

'Thinking has got us nowhere!' Shylo snapped.

'Fighting didn't exactly save the day either,' Tyrone pointed out as he gestured with a tilt of his head to the cavern around them.

'We cannot defeat this enemy,' the elder said. 'They are too powerful.'

'And yet here you are,' Tyrone said, 'not dead yet, right?'

The elder watched him but said nothing.

'There has to be a way out of this,' Tyrone said. 'I saw the remains of the fleet and I saw Fortitude. She looked undamaged.'

Shylo's carved fangs bared in disgust. 'That is their prize.'

'Who's prize?'

'The shape shifters,' the elder replied. 'From what we understand they have no means to transport themselves across space quickly, and so they occupy vessels as a cocoon and travel aboard them. Presumably in return for assisting our attackers by infiltrating and weakening our defenses prior to the attack they get a new home, your ship Fortitude and what's left of our fleet.'

Tyrone lifted his chin, determined to get the hell out of Ayleea.

'We have a way of defeating the shape shifters,' he said.

'Impossible,' Shylo spat. 'They cannot be detected, we never know who they are!'

'You don't need to,' Tyrone insisted. 'All we need is a clotting agent, like a glue. The shape shifters tried to board one of the CSS flagships months ago and were repelled because the fluid devised by our scientists prevented them from moving or changing shape.'

The elders looked up sharply at Tyrone, eyes widened.

'The goab trees,' one of them whispered.

'What?'

'The trees,' Shylo said, his anger suddenly replaced by curiosity, 'the infiltrators would not follow us into the trees sometimes during the invasion. We did not understand why, but if the goab trees were the reason…'

'The sap,' the elder said, and then turned to Tyrone. 'The goab tree is coated with sap that runs in thick rivers down its trunk twice a day to protect it from the sun's radiation. Our ancestors used it as a fuel in times of emergency and it burns in our torches now.'

Tyrone looked at the torches and felt the first glimmer of hope flicker into life within him.

'This sap,' he said, 'it's readily available?'

'The goab trees grow in thick forests everywhere,' Shylo confirmed, 'but they are also home to predators that use the jungle canopy as a home and defend the trees in return.'

'Yeah,' Tyrone said, 'I've met one, and it didn't take kindly to being hit with a plasma bolt.'

Tyrone made his decision. Although he hated it, a glance at the Ayleean children still watching him from the shadows convinced him that one way or the other, these people were every bit as desperate as he was. There was no longer a choice. He would ally himself to them until he got a chance to get away. You couldn't be too choosy about your allies in time of war, he reminded himself.

'They destroyed your cities, but I take it there may still be transports available?'

The elders nodded. 'The planet is large and so are the cities. They rounded up most of our people but many areas remain untouched.'

'Then this is how we do it,' Tyrone said, raising his voice loudly enough to be heard across the cavern. 'You can decide to sit here cowering in the dark, but that's not who I understand the Ayleean people to be. The enemy will find us here, sooner or later and by your own admission you'll fight until your deaths, so why not fight for your lives instead? If we can make it to a transport then we can make it to Fortitude and fight our way out of here.'

'The drones will see us,' Shylo replied. 'They're everywhere.'

'But the enemy is not,' Tyrone said. 'There was only one capital ship up there in orbit, and one thing I did notice about them is that they're powerful but slow, cumbersome. We don't number enough people to fill a large vessel. A smaller, fast transport like Fortitude will easily out manoeuver that capital ship. The only danger will be getting control of Fortitude before the capital ship returns and blasts it to hell.'

The elder leaned down to challenge him.

'And the small matter of that ship being entirely consumed by shape shifting entities?'

'We blast our way in,' Tyrone said, 'and we use the sap as a weapon to force the infiltrators back. If there's enough of it out here in these forests, we should be able to overpower them and run for Sol.'

'And do what?' Shylo asked. '*Beg* for help?'

Tyrone raised an eyebrow at him. 'Your fleet just got wiped out in a single day. The CSS fleet is bigger and more powerful but I don't think you'll need to beg for anything. The more ships we can bring to the table, the better.'

'Your senate vessels have no armor or weapons,' the elder pointed out.

'No,' Tyrone conceded, 'but it's much faster than that capital ship up there. If we can take control of her, we'll be out of here in no time.'

The Ayleeans looked at each other for a moment as though weighing up the consequences of taking action or not taking action.

'Our people,' the elder said. 'If we leave Ayleea, we leave other survivors to their fate.'

'If you don't leave you'll be joining them sooner than you think,' Tyrone replied. 'You want to meet them having been shepherded there by infiltrators without a fight, or do you want to take a shot at coming back here with the CSS fleet behind you and the chance not just to join your people but to liberate them too?'

Shylo looked at the elders for their guidance and slowly they nodded to him. He lifted his huge curved blade and turned to his people.

'Prepare the weapons. We leave, in one hour!'

Tyrone cringed in surprise as a hellish roar went up from the Ayleeans, their horrendous shrieks of bloodlust amplified by the confines of the cavern and their wild eyes gleaming like cruel stars in the darkness.

***

XXIX

The city crouched in the darkness, dwarfed by the immense mountain ranges soaring into the turbulent clouds tumbling by far above. The glow of the sunset was a vivid orange that silhouetted the mountains and their saw tooth peaks.

Tyrone could see that the city itself was aflame. Thick columns of smoke spiraled up into the sky from fires that outlined the shape of tower blocks and the landing pads of a spaceport, some of which had collapsed. A tremendous fusion of modern technology and native resources, the city looked as though it had merged with the jungles over decades. Colossal steel and concrete pillars were entwined with dense foliage and vines, not the result of abandonment but a deliberate attempt to entwine nature with civilization.

'The foliage is what's burning,' Shylo said as he crouched alongside Tyrone. 'The city is still strong.'

'But empty,' Tyrone said as he observed their destination through a high powered lens built into his ocular implant.

'They took everybody and everything,' one of the elders said from behind them. 'Took them up in their capital ships.'

Shylo had explained on the journey that the alien capital ships had arrived outside of their fleet's location in orbit. After the last defeat in battle against the CSS, the fleet had remained inside Ayleean space to effect repairs. They were still there when the attack came.

Tyrone had listened as the Ayleeans told him how their own people turned against them in their thousands, shutting down power supplies, shield generators and weapons systems aboard all Ayleean vessels and even on the surface. Rendered defenseless in a matter of minutes, the Ayleean fleet was subjected to a merciless barrage that shattered what was left of their warships within minutes.

'They destroyed everything before the fleet could fire a single shot in reply,' Shylo had said as they had climbed a narrow ledge on a mountain side, a thousand foot drop just inches from them and Tyrone clinging to the rocky walls as he listened. 'There was no defense against the orbital bombardment that followed, and only those of us who were not in the cities at the time of the attack survived the first onslaught.'

As the capital ships had descended so they had targeted all of the defensive structures with pin point accuracy, apparently using their own infiltrators as guidance for their weapons. In the first few minutes the entire strategic and tactical network of defense installations the Ayleeans had constructed were neutralized.

Then came the capital ships. Descending from orbit in the pre'dawn they targeted the cities and began collecting the Ayleean people in massive vessels that the Ayleeans had named *harvesters*.

'Did you see them?' Tyrone asked.

'Yes,' Shylo nodded, 'we saw them. Every warrior in every city took to the streets armed with whatever weapons they could find and engaged the enemy directly, but it was no use.'

Tyrone listened intently, trying to gather and memorize as much information about the attack as he could. He knew for sure that what had happened on Ayleea would happen again on earth, soon, and he had little time to figure out a suitable defense and get word to CSS.

'What about the aliens themselves?' Tyrone asked. 'Were they armed?'

Shylo gripped his plasma rifle tighter as he replied.

'They move fast, too fast to easily shoot at, and they have twin whiplash spines on their shoulders that they use to poison victims. They moved in groups, too many for us to counter but they carried no actual weapons like plasma rifles.'

Tyrone rolled his shoulders as he digested the information. 'Sounds great.'

Shylo looked at him curiously.

'Sarcasm,' Tyrone replied without looking at the warrior. 'Right now, all we've got to worry about is the drones. You picking anything up yet?'

The elders behind him were each holding passive scanners used to detect the presence of the cruel automated drones that had been turned against their creators.

'Nothing yet, but they're in there somewhere.'

Tyrone waited for a moment as he took one last sweeping look at the city, and then he saw what he was looking for.

'There, the western platform.'

Shylo and the others looked through the smoke, and there upon the landing platform was a large shuttle. Tyrone could see that it was more than large enough for the two hundred or so Ayleeans in the group behind him, each of them laboring beneath the burden of a container filled with the thick sap of the goab trees.

'We could make it directly there,' Shylo observed. 'The route is clear.'

Tyrone looked at the city between them and the landing platform. There were no streets in the conventional sense. Instead, the city was arranged in irregular blocks that conformed to the terrain beneath them and passage through the city was via aerial walkways or by swinging using thick vines. Although the process seemed archaic it was possible for a citizen to cross from one side of the city to the other in less than fifteen minutes, so used to a life among the trees were the Ayleeans.

'Can we all make it there within thirty minutes?' Tyrone asked.

Shylo nodded. 'Yes, provided we are not blocked in our path by the drones. Why thirty minutes?'

Tyrone checked the sky above them. He knew that Ayleea orbited much closer in to its parent star than earth, but that its rate of rotation was also somewhat slower. The daylight would last perhaps another hour.

'You said that the enemy attacked in the pre dawn,' he said.

'That's a common time to attack any enemy,' Shylo pointed out, 'when they're asleep and their body clock at its lowest ebb.'

'Yeah, for humans that works, but maybe these creatures prefer hunting at night. If you're right and they're aquatic, they probably evolved in low light conditions beneath the waves. In about twenty minutes that sun is going to breach the trough between those two peaks and shine straight down on the city. The smoke and the glare of the sunlight might help confuse the aim of your enemy if you come out with the sunlight behind you.'

Shylo looked at Tyrone and raised an eyebrow in surprise.

'It might also affect the drones' ability to see us coming.'

'Two birds, one stone,' Tyrone replied. 'Let's move.'

Shylo waved the Ayleeans on and they descended down the hillside, staying below and behind a ridgeline that led down toward the blackened surface of a boulder strewn river winding its way past the city. Tyrone could see numerous bridges crossing the water along the way, some of them burning but others intact and giving access to the city.

'That way,' Shylo whispered as he pointed to one of the larger bridges. 'We will cross more quickly on that one.'

Tyrone was about to agree when he thought again.

'No,' he replied, 'we use them all. I don't want the whole group in one place or it'll make us an easier target to hit. Use the bridges further down, then we can cut back up toward the landing platform with the sun behind us. Don't charge your weapons unless the enemy show themselves.'

Tyrone crept down toward the water as Shylo used hand signals to break up the following group into smaller units, each heading for a different bridge as Tyrone crouched down behind a large, damp boulder and surveyed the city. He could see now the burning vines and trees, a thick smog of smoke drifting across the buildings on the hot wind. Each of the landing platforms on the far side of the city were on elevated towers perhaps a hundred feet high, draped with vines as well as metal ladders. In the interior of the pillars he could see elevator shafts but it was unlikely that they were functional given the devastation he could see everywhere else. Buildings were pockmarked with the scars of plasma fire, craters smoldering where the capital ships had blasted defensive structures into oblivion.

Shylo crouched down alongside him.

'We are ready.'

Tyrone checked his plasma pistol's magazine one last time. 'Okay, once we move we're committed so as fast as you can. I'll cover the bridge below us from here, and have your sharp shooters do the same.'

Shylo nodded, and then with a broad gesture with one thickly muscled arm he waved his fellow survivors forward. Instantly, the Ayleean flooded silently out from their hiding places and rushed onto the bridges.

Shylo leaped up and sprinted away, surprisingly agile for such a big warrior as he leaped across rocks and landed on the nearest bridge at a run. Tyrone heard the rumbling of hundreds of footfalls on the bridge, the black water beneath them rippling as the water trembled in concert with the vibrations.

Tyrone's gaze switched to a movement in the water as one of the boulders beneath the surface was dislodged by the vibrations and began moving with the flow of the water. Even as he saw it he spotted another moving, and then another, and with growing horror he realized that Shylo had been right about the alien invaders: they were aquatic in nature.

'Enemy, below!'

Tyrone shouted the warning as loudly as he could even as the surface of the water burst as dozens of grotesque creatures crashed out of the waves to shrieks of war lust, their gray backs looking just like the boulders around them. Tyrone saw them emerge from the water, eight legged monstrosities something between a giant crab and a rhinoceros. Their bodies were scaled with thick, gray plates laden with lumps and bumps like the thick hide of a whale, their legs segmented like those of an insect but also covered in the strange armor. He could see the coiling, writhing whiplash spines that Shylo had mentioned, black eyes between them searching with a soul less gaze for their next victim.

'Covering fire!' Shylo bellowed as he sprinted across the bridge.

Tyrone activated his pistol and fired at the enemy nearest Shylo, saw the blast hit its back and burrow deeply through its armor to burn into its flesh in a puff of gray smoke. The creature shrieked in agony and turned to look Tyrone in the eye as he fired again and again.

The Ayleeans flocked across the bridges, bright flares of plasma fire zipping this way and that as they opened fire on the animals now swarming up onto the bridges, their long legs twisting around support pillars and hauling them out of the water.

Tryone checked his left and saw several Ayleean sharpshooters picking off the enemy one by one as they emerged from the water, a hail of plasma fire hissing as it rained down on the grotesque creatures swarming out of the river.

'Move, now!' Tyrone shouted. 'Change positions!'

The Ayleeans did not respond, firing endlessly at their enemy.

'Change positions, covering fire!' Tyrone yelled above the crescendo of gunfire.

The creatures swarmed up the hillside, clambering up the rocks below the shooters and then rushing their positions. Tyrone felt his heart plunge as he saw one of them rush into the hiding place of an Ayleean rifleman, moving far too quickly for the warrior to turn and shoot it at close range.

The warrior's rifle was smashed aside by one of the creature's legs as another pinned him down. Tyrone flinched as he saw both of the poisonous spines plunge into the Ayleean's chest. The warrior screamed in agony and then he was silenced as rows of razor sharp teeth crunched through his face and skull and it burst like a ripe watermelon.

Tyrone leaped out of his position and backed up the hillside by ten paces before he jumped back down into cover and began firing again. He could see the survivors streaming into the city and flocking toward the landing pads, and he fired in support of Shylo and his comrades as they protected their people against the sudden onslaught.

Tyrone aimed carefully at one charging creature and fired, the shot smashing into the back of its body and striking one of its hind legs. The creature faltered as it screamed in pain, its leg dragging behind it.

'Go for the legs!' Tyrone yelled above the din of battle at Shylo. 'Take their legs ou…!'

Tyrone jerked backward as something flashed before him and screamed as a huge creature scrambled up the rock face and blocked his aim. A vast gray bulk of hardened keratin armor topped by vicious serrated teeth and beady black eyes glared down at him, thick legs straddling the rocks either side of his hiding place as two writhing spines reared back and then rushed toward him.

***

XXX

Tyrone hurled himself forward as the spines plunged down and he heard them smash into the rocks behind him as he crouched beneath the creature's belly and pushed his pistol up underneath its jaw and fired twice.

The plasma shots blasted into its squat neck and Tyrone yelled out in pain as searing plasma splashed across his hands. He jerked back from the scorching plasma spray as the creature writhed in agony and then sprawled over his hiding place, squashing him beneath its bulk. Tyrone saw its head slumped against the rocks before him, black eyes staring back at him but now lifeless as the lethal spines drooped uselessly against the rocks.

Tyrone crouched in horror as he saw more of the creatures rush past as they stormed up the hillside, heard tortured screams of pain as the Ayleean shooters were taken down by the advancing horde. Quickly he shut his plasma pistol off as he realized that the dead body of the creature above him was effectively shielding him from view of the rest of their attackers. Tyrone crouched down and turned, watched as Shylo and the other Ayleeans advanced into the city, the sunlight streaming down through the clouds behind them and making them harder to see for the pursuing creatures advancing toward them.

The Ayleeans took to the vines and the trees, soaring through their city above and beyond the octopeds' reach with a grace and skill that Tyrone realized that he admired. He cussed under his breath, reminding himself of what they had been capable of during their wars with humanity, but he couldn't help himself silently willing them on.

Tyrone watched, and then his heart sank as he heard a vibrant humming noise. He turned and saw clouds of drones plunging down the mountain side toward the city, their ugly black abdomens gleaming in the sunlight. They raced past nearby as Tyrone watched helplessly, and then they were gone across the river and the noise subsided. He could still hear the crump and whistle of plasma energy and the cries of battle but he could see nobody now, the battle moving toward the landing pads. Carefully, Tyrone checked around him and then he clambered from beneath the dead octoped and turned to look over the river behind him.

The rocks were littered with dead octopeds and also the remains of Ayleeans, their bodies torn apart in a bloody frenzy during the attack. Rocks were stained red with the blood of the fallen, and bizarre splashes of deep purple blood leaking from the veins of their attackers.

Tyrone knew that he could neither save nor reach Shylo and his people. If he was lucky and they reached the shuttle, perhaps they might have turned around and picked him up but he doubted it, the Ayleeans as treacherous as they were ugly. No, now his only chance was to reach his Phantom fighter, its plasma cannons his ticket out of here aboard the shuttle: *comply or die*, as he used to like to say. Tyrone turned to run up the hillside and head for the shore where he'd left the fighter, and then he heard a distant cry

He looked over his shoulder and saw on the far side of one of the bridges an Ayleean infant, perhaps a few years old. Within inches of the child was the octoped he'd injured with his earliest shots, its scorched and twisted legs dragging behind it as it crawled toward the stricken Ayleean child.

Tyrone hesitated. He could make it out of here unseen if he kept running.

The Ayleean child crawled backward and away from the creature, too young to fight.

Tyrone stared in horror, unable to tear himself in either direction. The Ayleean infant would one day grow into a warrior who might kill countless humans. It might grow to hate us. There was nothing that he could do right now. The needs of the many…

The child cried out, its wailing tinged with fear.

'Damn it.'

Tyrone made to switch on his plasma pistol, but then he saw the clouds of drones diving in and out of the smoke and he knew that he could not betray his presence. Tyrone shoved the weapon into its holster and leaped from his hiding place. He ran down the hillside and onto the bridge, sprinting for the child as the octoped dragged itself ever closer. Tyrone pumped his arms and ran as hard as his legs would allow him, but the gravity on Ayleea was too much and he knew that he could not get there in time.

The octoped saw him coming, and in a moment of horror Tyrone saw it judge the distance and make a strange cackling sound that seemed almost like laughter. The octoped's spines reared up over the infant Ayleean but its eyes were locked onto Tyrone's and shining with the mindless satisfaction of pure hatred.

The spines rushed down and Tyrone hauled his pistol from its holster as he crouched down and fired twice. Two plasma bolts ripped into the creature's face and neck in a cloud of hissing flesh and it recoiled backward, screeching loudly as Tyrone dashed in and lifted the Ayleean child bodily from the ground.

He turned to run, and as he did so he saw a dozen sentry drones zip upwards out of the smoke, hovering briefly as though sniffing the air before they turned and accelerated toward him.

'Oh no, not again.'

Tyrone started running, but his legs were already weakened and he knew that he would not get far before the fast moving drones would overhaul him and cut him off before moving in for the kill. He reached the end of the bridge and set the child down before pointing up the hillside.

'Get out of here,' he ordered the child. 'I'll hold 'em off as long as I can.'

The child stared up at him in confusion, it's yellow eyes bleary with tears.

'Go!' Tyrone yelled as he heard the drones rushing in. 'Now!'

He pushed the child away and whirled, aimed and fired at the nearest of the drones. The shot hit it square in the face and it spiraled down to clatter onto the rocks nearby as three more dove in toward him. He fired twice but he knew that he could not hope to hit them all.

From beside him something flashed past through the air and to his amazement a tightly weaved net opened up across the sky, weights spinning at its corners as it expanded. The three drones slammed into the net and it closed around them, trapping their winds as it plunged down into the river. Tyrone looked to one side and saw the Ayleean child snarling, one fist clenched in joy as it watched the drones hit the water and sink in a tangled mess beneath the waves.

The child looked up at him, smiling broadly, and then it reached up and took hold of his hand before waiting expectantly. Tyrone sighed and pulled the Ayleean child with him. Maybe he could use the kid as a bargaining chip when the Ayleeans fled the system.

'C'mon,' he said to the child. 'I've got an idea.'

He hurried back the way they had come, climbing over the ridgeline and down the far side, jogging along as beside him the lithe Ayleean child leaped from rock to rock. Bounding ahead, he could finally understand the Ayleean's physical prowess in battle. They were so used to dealing with Ayleea's gravity that when boarding CSS warships in battle it must have seemed as easy as walking on air.

Tyrone followed the child along the pathway, but when the child began to head for the caverns Tyrone called to him and pointed to another way. They followed the river around the base of the mountain as fast as Tyrone could manage, every step seeming twice as difficult until after twenty minutes of frantic trekking Tyrone finally saw the spit of land he had been looking for, jutting out from the jungles toward the churning surface of the black river. His heart leaped in his throat and he was about to sprint for the Phantom still parked on the shore when he saw the four drones hovering around the fighter.

'Wait, bugs!'

The Ayleean child grabbed his hand and prevented him from rushing in as he too spotted the enemy drones circling the fighter.

'We've got to get in there,' Tyrone said.

'The bugs,' the child insisted, 'they get you first, then you're no good to me.'

Tyrone almost laughed. 'I like the way you're thinking kid, but if we don't get aboard that fighter, we're never gonna get off this rock.'

Tyrone shook the child free and pulled out his pistol. 'Stay right here.'

Tyrone ran down onto the beach, stumbling as his weakened legs struggled with his increasing momentum. He hit the beach hard as the drones detected his approach and changed direction. Tyrone looked behind him at the sun setting behind the mountains and he staggered to his left, putting the brilliant orb of the star directly behind him and illuminating the drones while blinding them.

Tyrone saw them zip left and right, hoping to flank him and get the sun out of their sensors. He crouched down and opened fire on two of them to his right, catching one lucky hit but missing the other as on his left the other two drones circled around. Tyrone saw his chance and dashed for his fighter as the drones closed in from either side.

He was half way there when the drones changed direction away from him. Tyrone turned, and then he saw the Ayleean child on the beach far behind him.

'No!'

The child shouted to him, waving its arms to attract the drones. 'Hurry!'

The drones lunged in as the child suddenly crashed into the black water and with great swings of his arms sent water spraying in bright sunlit plumes up into the air, drenching the first drone as it flashed past and climbed away again to avoid the water.

Tyrone fired at the drones and drew one of them toward him as he ran for his cockpit. The Phantom detected his approach and he saw the canopy opening as he ran the last few yards across the beach. He heard the hum of the drone behind him as he scrambled to the fighter and hurled himself up, one boot landing on a footrest as he powered himself up and vaulted into the cockpit. Tyrone slammed down into the seat as the drone rushed up to him and he aimed and fired once.

The shot slammed into the drone and smashed it aside in a mass of melting metal and smoke. Tyrone lowered his pistol and then he heard the scream. He looked past the smoldering remains and saw the Ayleean child stagger out of the water with one of the cruel drones attached to his chest.

'No!'

Tyrone hit the Phantom's emergency scramble power switches, heard the powerful ion engines begin to whine into life as he shouted at them to work faster. The avionics came on line before him and the weapons began charging. As soon as he dared he engaged the anti gravity plating and the Phantom lifted off the sandy beach and he turned the fighter around as the drones rushed toward him.

Tyrone flipped the safety cover on the cannon switch and fired once, and four bolts of plasma rocketed away from him and blasted two of the drones into embers as the last zipped to one side and rushed in. Tyrone hit the canopy switch and the drone slammed into the canopy frame with a clatter of metal on metal, clutching on and watching him with a cruel, black eye. Tyrone ignored it as he hovered across to the child's body on the beach and settled the fighter down again. He activated the fighter's shields and the drone was suddenly hurled away by the charge and crashed against the nearby rocks.

Tyrone opened the canopy again and leaped from the cockpit to the child's side. The kid was laying on his back, its chest plate pushed aside by the drone attack, and with a start Tyrone suddenly realized that the child was a girl. Her eyes stared up at the darkening sky as her chest heaved rapidly.

'C'mon,' he gasped as he lifted her up, straining against her weight as he made his way back to the cockpit.

Gently he lifted her into the fighter's seat and then climbed up behind her.

He barely heard the drone above the noise of the Phantom's idling engines as it rushed in behind him, and he realized that it had not been destroyed by the shields. Before he could turn to face it the drone's fearsome stinger plunged between his shoulder blades and Tyrone gagged as pain ripped through his body. On instinct he turned and jumped down, letting his back slide against the edge of the Phantom's footrest to rip the drone from his back.

The metallic hornet buzzed and lifted off, ready to strike again. Tyrone grabbed a rock in his fist and whirled as the drone rushed in. He reached out and grabbed the machine by its face, slammed it against the Phantom's fuselage and smashed the rock down on it with the fury of the insane.

The drone's stinger missed his arm by a whisker as Tyrone slammed the rock against its body again and again, shattering its circuitry and bending the stinger into a useless chunk of twisted metal. The drone's wings stopped beating as its body was crushed and dented by the blows and it dropped onto the beach at his feet. Tyrone lifted one boot and stomped on the machine twice again for good measure before he dropped the rock and clambered wearily into the Phantom's cockpit once more.

Tyrone slid in beneath the Ayleean child's limp body as the canopy closed and managed to lever himself into position as he pulled the seat harnesses over himself and the girl. He reached around her waist and grabbed the control column as he lifted off, pain pulsing through his body like lances of fire as he struggled to maintain focus.

The Phantom lifted off and he guided the fighter across the ridgeline to where the city sprawled in the river valley the other side. The shadows were falling fast now and he could see endless ranks of octoped creatures swarming through the city in pursuit of the fleeing Ayleeans.

Flashes of plasma fire flickered through the streets near the landing pads and he could see the shuttle still there, Ayleeans clambering up the vines and hurrying to board her, others still fighting on the ground beneath the pad's pillar in an attempt to cover the escape of the women and children.

Tyrone took careful aim and with a grim delight he opened up on the octoped hordes with the Phantom's powerful cannons. Streams of high energy plasma bolts ripped into their ranks and he saw the city light up as the shots decimated them in billowing clouds of flame, smoke and severed body parts. He saw the Ayleeans far below him punching the air and firing at the octoped masses as they began pulling back, leaving their dead behind as they climbed with gusto up the vines toward their shuttle.

Tyrone circled around, lined up again and this time he hosed the octoped hordes down from the front, his plasma rounds smashing through them in bright explosions, killing dozens with every shot. The octoped ranks scattered off the platform and away from the onslaught, the scorched bodies that remained billowing flames and smoke as Tyrone pulled up and strained to look over his shoulder.

In his helmet he heard a crackle and a sudden, clear Ayleean voice ragged with joy and despair at the same time.

'Phantom this is shuttle one one four clear of the pad.'

'Copy one one four,' he replied. 'Let's get out of here. I have one injured, correction, two injured.'

'We've got two dozen,' came the reply, *'but there will be medical equipment aboard Fortitude.'*

Tyrone nodded and looked down at the child slumped against him. Her chest was fluttering weakly and his own pain was increasing with every passing moment.

'Roger that,' he replied, his voice raspy. 'I have the lead, stay close.'

With grim relief Tyrone opened the throttles and the Phantom accelerated away from the smoking remains of the city as she pointed her nose upward and began to climb into the blood red sky toward the stars flickering faintly beyond the turbulent clouds.

***

XXXI

Tyrone blinked as his vision blurred, the stars shimmering and smearing across his field of vision as the Phantom fighter soared clear of Ayleea's atmosphere. The Ayleean child in his arms was hot to the touch, her breathing coming in ragged, rattling gasps that were becoming weaker with every passing moment.

'I've got Fortitude on my passive sensors,' he gasped as the last of the sunlight vanished over the planet's limb, Ayleea in darkness far below him.

'We're right behind you.'

Tyrone guided the Phantom in toward the faint signal from the Senate cruiser, the same IFF beacon that Endeavour had pinged that he could now detect without having to betray his position using active radar. They would have precious little time to get aboard the cruiser before she was overwhelmed by the strange shape shifting substance used by the invaders to quell resistance.

'Thirty seconds,' Tyrone said.

The Phantom rocketed through the deep blackness, and ahead he saw the stars being eclipsed by a long field of debris orbiting the planet. The occasional shooting star of burning wreckage flickered by below as Ayleea's gravity began drawing the shattered hulks of warships down to their doom.

Fortitude's beacon was transmitting from the far side of the debris field, the Phantom's computers triangulating her position and displaying it to Tyrone on a small display mounted before him. He kept most of his systems switched off, hoping that he could sneak in as close as possible.

'Switching to stand by now,' he ordered. 'Engines off.'

Tyrone cut the power to the Phantom's engines and shut down all unnecessary systems as soon as he was lined up directly with Fortitude. In the vacuum of space the fighter required no constant source of thrust to travel, allowing Tyrone to sneak up behind the cruiser without being detected until the very last instant.

Tyrone, his own breathing becoming hoarse in his throat and incessant pain throbbing through every fiber of his body, flipped the safety cover off the trigger on his control column and prepared for battle. The Phantom fighter was able to transmit override frequencies to the senate cruiser as they were both CSS vessels that recognized each other's identity. That would allow both the fighter and the shuttle behind to land aboard her. However, what happened when he opened that landing bay was anybody's guess as the enemy would know he was there the moment he sent the signal.

Fortitude appeared before him, her sleek and silvery hull glinting in the faint starlight and distinct from the dark, foreboding hulls of the Ayleean warships around her. Despite the chaotic nature of the debris field the cruiser looked undamaged but for minor dents in her hull caused by low velocity collisions with other wreckage in the debris field.

'Just a little further,' Tyrone whispered to himself.

He saw the cruiser's stern before him, her shape enhanced by the displays in the cockpit to help him pick her out in the deep blackness of the planet's shadow. The Phantom was drifting at high speed toward the stern landing bay, barely seconds away now. Tyrone took a deep breath to clear his senses and then he hit a switch in his cockpit and suddenly the fighter went "fangs out", her fire control radar activating as the engines spooled up, her shields switched to active and her plasma cannons charged up.

Tyrone emitted the emergency landing signal and instantly the cruiser's stern bay doors began to open. He saw her interior lights beam out into the darkness, power still available to the ship, and he knew that if they could fight their way in they had a chance.

'Doors open, landing protocol now!'

Tyrone switched the Phantom over to its autopilot to land the fighter as he gripped his plasma pistol tightly and watched as the fighter sailed through the hard light atmospheric shielding into the empty bay and touched down on one of the smaller landing pads. He craned his neck over his shoulder and saw the Ayleean shuttle touch down nearby.

Tyrone opened the canopy on his fighter as the engines shut down and he punched the harnesses clear as he clambered out of the cockpit on unsteady legs, ready for a fight. He saw the shuttle's main ramp open and Ayleeans pour out into the bay, plasma rifles at the ready as they fanned out.

'I need a medic!' Tyrone snapped as he dropped to one knee, exhausted.

Shylo burst from the shuttle and hurried across.

'You are hit?'

'Stung,' Tyrone gasped, 'but I have a passenger who needs a medic, now!'

Tyrone stood up and climbed onto his fighter as the Ayleeans flocked out of the shuttle, and he hauled the child's body out. Almost immediately he heard a shriek of anguish as one of the Ayleeans rushed forward and dropped his rifle as he tore the child from Tyrone.

'I got cut off in the attack on the bridges,' Tyrone said to Shylo. 'The kid was there too. She helped me take off, but she took several stings.'

Tyrone watched as the Ayleean rushed away toward the elders, who were already grabbing ingredients of some kind from a satchel and were busily grinding away some mysterious potion that Tyrone took to be an antidote of some kind. The focus was on the child, but it was Shylo who looked away to one of the landing bay entrances and spoke, his voice carrying above the commotion.

'They are coming.'

Tyrone turned to face the entrance as the Ayleeans lined up either side of him. His breath was coming in short, sharp gasps and he could feel sweat dripping from his face despite the cruiser's cool atmosphere and normal gravity.

All of a sudden one of his legs gave way beneath him and he stumbled.

Strong hands caught his fall, and he looked up to see Shylo and another warrior holding him. They lifted him upright again but said nothing, maintaining their grip on him to prevent him from collapsing.

Tyrone turned to the sound of footsteps emerging from the entrance to the landing bay, and before him strode Senator Isabel Gray, her son Samuel and a phalanx of armed CSS guards. Tyrone's eyes widened as he stared at them.

'Senator?'

Senator Gray motioned for them to lower their weapons. 'Stand down,' she said, 'there is nothing to fear here.'

The Ayleeans didn't move as Tyrone staggered forward. 'Why are you here?'

'We did not leave Fortitude,' Senator Gray said. 'We were waiting for rescue.'

'Why didn't you signal me when I flew past you before?'

'You were but one ship,' Gray replied with a gentle smile. 'We could not betray our presence here aboard Fortitude.'

'You could have run.'

'The capital ship was here and it would have caught us easily.'

'It's not here now.'

'And we wish to leave, urgently. Come, the ship is ready and we have avoided any permanent damage. But we must escape before the capital ship returns.'

Tyrone hesitated.

'The capital ship has been gone for several hours,' he said, and on an impulse: 'CSS Titan and Pegasus were both badly damaged and had to leave. They won't be coming back.'

Gray smiled.

'Titan was only partially hit,' she insisted. 'She will return with more ships and we can meet them.'

Tyrone shook his head. 'Titan was never here and nor was Pegasus. Senator Gray would have known the difference between Ships of the Line and frigates. It was you who sent the distress signal, wasn't it, to send me down there and locate the hiding Ayleeans?'

Senator Gray's face folded into fury and she pointed at the Ayleeans as she screeched at the top of her voice.

'Seize them and kill all those who resist!'

From out of sight behind her surged a wave of silvery, pulsing material that rushed like a fluid into the landing bay and washed past Senator Gray and her soldiers, absorbing them as it moved and splitting into two forms that began flanking the Ayleean force.

'Fire!' Tyrone shouted.

The Ayleeans opened up with their plasma rifles on the advancing wave as Tyrone saw Senator Gray's form dissolve into the crystalline soup that surged toward them. Almost immediately the front of the wave churned up into the form of multiple octopeds that leaped out at them, oblivious to the wave of plasma fire rocketing toward them.

'Fall back!'

Shylo waved his men back and they began retreating by sections, each covering another with rapid plasma fire that smashed into the advancing octoped creatures in showers of burning embers as their shape shifting cellular forms were melted by the blasts.

Tyrone fired twice at the nearest form and saw his plasma bolts sear a hole straight through it, only for that hole to be instantly filled in as the wave of material advanced toward them. Tyrone looked over his shoulder and saw the Ayleeans rushing forward with what looked like slingshots that they swung over their heads.

'Get down!'

Tyrone ducked at Shylo's command and the slingshots let go, each one as large as a man's head and filled with a syrupy concoction of goab tree sap. The missiles arced over Tyrone's head and slammed into the advancing octoped ranks. Tyrone saw the thick fluid instantly stiffen the shape shifting bodies as they tried to move forward, binding the cellular material together into glutinous lumps that sagged and drooped under their own weight.

'Fire!'

The Ayleeans opened up once more with a barrage of plasma fire, carefully avoiding the areas where the wave had been hit with the sap. Now, their plasma shots seared through the octoped ranks and drove them back toward the landing bay walls either side of the Ayleeans.

Tyrone saw an opportunity and yelled a command.

'Forward!'

Tyrone dashed for the landing bay entrance as the Ayleean force rushed away from the shuttle behind them and followed him into the wide corridor. Tyrone turned and began firing in support of the Ayleeans as they evacuated the landing bay.

'Get everyone out of the bay!' Tyrone yelled.

The Ayleeans tumbled out of the landing bay and ran down the corridor as the warriors behind them fired in retreat at the roiling masses of alien fluid now turning to pursue them once more, laboring under the burden of the goab sap. The slingshots fired once again, splattering the mass with more glutinous sap and further hindering its progress.

Tyrone saw the shape shifting forms looking at themselves and the thick sap restraining them, saw one of the octoped aliens transform again into Senator Gray and scream in fury as she pointed at him.

Shylo fired at her and the plasma blast smashed through her face in a cloud of burning embers as he retreated through the corridor entrance with the last of the Ayleeans. Tyrone, his heart racing and his skin drenched with sweat, hit the emergency close switch and the entrance slammed shut.

The corridor was filled with the sound of heavily breathing Ayleeans as Tyrone opened a panel on the wall beside the now closed doors and accessed a terminal. He input his ID code and security pass, and moments later another smaller hatch turned green. He pulled it open and grabbed a handle inside that was emblazoned with black and yellow chevrons.

Tyrone turned to see the form of Senator Gray once again, this time with her face pressed up against the door windows and rage etched into her semi opaque features. Tyrone looked at her and smiled through his pain.

'Have a nice day.'

Tyrone hauled down on the handle and instantly the landing bay doors opened as the hard light shielding was shut down. An emergency protocol in the event of on board fire in the bay, the opening doors and disabled hard light shielding evacuated the landing bay instantly.

Senator Gray's rage turned for a brief instant to horror and Tyrone saw her scream as she and the entire mass of shape shifting goo was sucked out of the landing bay in a rush of vapor and ice crystals as the air was frozen solid in an instant.

Senator Gray's scream was frozen in place as she vanished and tumbled out into deep space amid a sparkling cloud of frozen shape shifting octopeds and shapeless masses.

Tyrone slumped against the wall, holding himself up by the hand still gripping the emergency handle. He turned as he saw the Ayleean elders move alongside him, and one of them held a pouch made from the black leaf of a tree from Ayleea. Something foul smelling inside the pouch made him recoil, but the elder pushed his head down toward it.

'Breathe it,' he insisted.

Tyrone sucked in a deep lungful of the putrid smelling juice sloshing about inside the pouch and he almost vomited. But almost instantly the stench dissolved into something entirely different, a blissful sense of peace. Tyrone felt the pain in his body subside and he smiled dreamily as he let go of the handle. Strong hands caught him once again as the elder yanked his flight suit aside and slapped more of the strange concoction over the wound in his back, further easing the pain. Tyrone looked up blearily at Shylo.

'Man, you can gimme some more o' that sugar,' he mumbled.

Shylo gripped Tyrone's collar.

'We need you to fly us out of here,' he snapped. 'A CSS ship will not respond to Aylccan commands, remember? Our ID chips will not allow it.'

'Shhuuurrre,' Tyrone whispered, 'it's a ciece of pake. Man, I've got this.'

Shylo rolled his eyes and glanced at the elder. 'I told you, humans can't cope with the seed of a Clysco Bat.'

The elder shrugged, and as Tyrone looked down he saw the Ayleean child standing on her own two feet and smiling up at him. Feeling immensely pleased with himself, Tyrone clicked the fingers of one hand.

'Take me to your leader! I mean, to the bridge!'

Even before they could move, an Ayleean shouted a warning down the corridor.

'The capital ship! It's back!'

***

XXXII

Tyrone staggered onto the bridge, his boots barely touching the deck as he was carried between the muscular arms of two Ayleean warriors. Fortitude's bridge was almost completely dark, only emergency lighting available as Tyrone was dragged unceremoniously to the captain's seat and dumped into it.

Shylo leaned close to him.

'Tyrone, focus. We need you to access the main computer and give us manual control of the ship before we're overrun by that material or the capital ship.'

Tyrone struggled to think straight, his head swimming and his body numb from the strange concoction of chemicals now warring with the venom coursing through his veins. Sweltering hot one moment, frigid with cold the next, his heart fluttered in his chest as he stared blankly at the controls before him.

'We need access, now!' Shylo snapped, and pointed ahead.

Tyrone looked up to where the main display was showing the view ahead of the ship. Unlike most warships, the view ahead aboard Fortitude was through an actual window rather than blast shielded display panels. There, out in the bitter vacuum, Tyrone saw a shadowy warship looming toward them, its shape identifiable only by the stars that it eclipsed as it moved.

'Hurry!'

Tyrone sucked in a lungful of air and felt his head clear just a little as he pulled himself upright in his seat and looked around him. His training kicked in and he spoke almost without thinking.

'Protocol eight one three alpha niner, initiate!'

The ship's computer scanned Tyrone's ID chip and immediately the ship's bridge hummed into life as computers reengaged and the lights flickered on.

'Lieutenant Hackett, Tyrone, oh four seven delta three three one, computer override on DNA and chip analysis.'

The ship's computer calculated in an instant its response, the soothing female voice filling the bridge.

'*Access denied, alien presence detected aboard the ship, recommend lockdown protocol effective immediately.*'

'Damn it, those things must still be aboard the ship!' Shylo snapped.

'Belay that order,' Tyrone replied to the computer. 'Identify alien presence and location.'

'*Multiple Ayleeans detected on bridge, deck level three, four and...*'

'Disregard Ayleeans!' Tyrone cut the machine off.

'*No other unidentified persons aboard the vessel.*'

'All Ayleeans are fugitives from a global attack,' Tyrone insisted as he looked at Shylo, 'and are now allies of CSS. Scan Ayleea if you don't believe me. The enemy is directly ahead of us, off the port bow and we're about to be attacked!'

A deafening silence filled the bridge as Shylo hissed.

'They're going to fire!'

Even as he said it the alien capital ship loomed into clearer view and her vast bulk suddenly was illuminated by internal lighting as it charged its main cannons. Scanner alerts swept the senate cruiser as she was scanned prior to attack.

'Damn it!' Tyrone yelled. 'We need control now!'

The ship's computer replied, its tone as genial as ever.

'*Ayleea scan complete, all life forms assessed, destruction evaluated. Assessment concurs with Lieutenant Hackett's report.*'

'Give the Ayleeans the bridge!' Tyrone yelled, almost laughing in exasperation and disbelief as the enemy vessel's plasma cannons glowed deep red.

'*Negative, Lieutenant, control may only pass to a certified CSS officer of sufficient rank to...*'

'Give me control, now!' Tyrone yelled.

'You have control, lieutenant.'

Tyrone leaped out of the captain's seat and virtually hurled himself onto the main throttles at the helmsman's station. Fortitude surged forward as her engines engaged and the cruiser accelerated out of the debris field as four massive plasma blasts rocketed away from the enemy ship and zipped past behind the cruiser to slam into the debris field in a frenzy of explosions.

'Hard to port!' Shylo yelled.

Tyrone pushed the helm over as the massive stern of a wrecked Ayleean warship loomed out of the darkness to be illuminated by Fortitude's running lights. The cruiser heeled over and the distant sound of metal scraping along metal shuddered down the hull as the cruiser slipped free and turned toward deep space.

'We've got to get out of here,' Tyrone gasped as he slumped off the controls. 'Somebody get the shields up?'

Shylo's Ayleean warriors quickly dispersed to the various stations across the bridge even as the cruiser shook violently as a plasma blast slammed into the debris field somewhere behind it. Tyrone saw them scan the various stations and quickly familiarize themselves with the controls, their language not so far removed from that of CSS that they couldn't read.

'We have no weapons, only shields,' one of the warriors pointed out.

'You have ships without weapons?' Shylo asked in horror.

'This was a diplomatic mission,' Tyrone said defensively. 'Would you have rather we showed up aboard Titan?'

'The enemy vessel is turning to pursue us!' one of the warriors yelled.

Tyrone gripped the controls of the helmsman's station as he gritted his teeth to focus more clearly. 'They won't keep up with this bird. Open a channel to Polaris Station, emergency frequency at full power.'

The Ayleean behind the communications panel began scrutinizing the display before him as Tyrone pushed the throttles wide open and the cruiser accelerated away from the debris field. Despite the gravitational plating Tyrone could feel the ship's acceleration and he heard Shylo gasp as he reached out for the command rail to steady himself.

'Navigation,' Tyrone called, 'plug us in a super luminal route home, direct to the Sol System. We need to warn them of what's happening as fast as we can.'

The warrior nodded as he began sweeping his big hands over the controls as two of the elders approached Tyrone.

'Are you sure you can get us there without us being intercepted?'

Tyrone grinned as he glanced at the tactical display and saw the big capital ship being left behind.

'This is a senate cruiser,' he said. 'They're not armed, but they're built for high speed diplomacy and VIP transport. There's nothing in our fleet that can keep up with them, even in super luminal. Once we jump, we'll be long gone. Trust me, there's nothing that can go wrong now.'

A voice called out across the bridge.

'New contacts, dead ahead, enemy capital ships!'

Tyrone's confidence wilted as he saw two massive capital ships rush out of super luminal cruise right ahead of them in bright flashes of light.

'You were saying?' Shylo uttered as he peered down at Tyrone.

'Turn us around,' the elder insisted.

'We can't turn around, the other one's behind us,' Tyrone snapped. 'We're gonna have to make the best of it.'

'You can make the best out of a situation like *this*?'

Tyrone didn't reply as he twisted the controls and the senate cruiser rolled along its trajectory in a graceful manoeuver known as a barrel roll as a salvo of plasma blasts rocketed toward it from the enemy capital ships. The shots zipped past the cruiser on all sides, detonating nearby as they went and shaking the ship from bow to stern as she raced past, the rolling flight path spoiling the enemy's aim.

Tyrone gave a whoop of delight as the ship levelled out and raced past between the two capital ships, which were now line abreast and could not fire at Fortitude without risking hitting each other. The senate cruiser accelerated through the gap and soared free as the two lumbering capital ships began to turn.

'We're out of here! Navigation, you got my destination coordinates plugged in yet?'

'The coordinates are set but we have no super luminal power,' came the reply. 'The engines must have been damaged during our escape from the debris field.'

'The hull,' Shylo growled. 'It was hit by debris when we departed the field.'

Tyrone cursed as he glanced at the cruiser's engine displays. Without the Higgs Drive they wouldn't be able to leave the Ayleean system at all. Even at maximum sub luminal velocity it would take the cruiser decades to reach Sol.

'Two more contacts, dead ahead!'

An alarm blared as Tyrone saw two huge white flashes burst into life before him and two more massive capital ships lunged out of super luminal cruise and opened fire almost immediately.

'Brace for impact!'

Tyrone yelled the warning as he hauled the controls to one side and the cruiser soared to starboard as plasma bolts rocketed toward it in flaming red flares.

The cruiser pulled up and right but the shots were launched far too close to avoid entirely and the cruiser shuddered as it took a direct hit to the stern. Tyrone heard the blast and felt the ship rock from one side to the other as her hull was shattered by the immense impact.

The ship echoed with alarms as Tyrone tried to maintain control, the lights flickering and work stations blasting out sparks from electrical overloads as circuits were melted and control linkages severed.

'We're hit, badly, all stern sections ablaze!'

'Shields are out!' called another Ayleean. 'The enemy are turning to engage us again!'

Tyrone looked at the engine displays and saw that two of the upper engines were entirely destroyed, only the lower pair remaining.

'Divert all power to the remaining engines!' he yelled. 'Get us out of here!'

'The enemy are preparing to fire!' the Ayleean warned. 'They're almost within range!'

Tyrone desperately sought a way out of their predicament, but he knew with a sudden overwhelming sense of defeat that there was no escape now. They could still outrun the capital ships, but there was nowhere to run to but the cold embrace of deep space and a legacy of sailing through the silent void for millennia. They would all die of old age, starvation or hypothermia long before they even left the system.

'Communications channel established with Sol!' another Ayleean shouted above the blaring alarms.

Tyrone knew what he had to do.

'Open the frequency!'

A moment later and Tyrone was on his feet as he saw an image of Rear Admiral Vincent O'Hara before him, the perfectly formed holographic image seeming to be standing on the damaged bridge with him.

'Admiral!' Tyrone said, without any preamble. 'We are under attack! Ayleea is gone. The enemy harvests the life on planets for unknown reasons. They are octopedal, amphibious and predatory, but their ships appear to have been taken from other species. They use a shape shifting species as an advance guard to infiltrate their enemies – you cannot trust anybody!'

O'Hara replied, his transmission flickering with distance and interference from the pursuing capital ships.

'Can you reach home?' he asked. 'Can you make it back to Sol?'

'We have no super luminal engines!' Tyrone replied. 'And we're being pursued by five, repeat, *five* capital ships! We need assistance, immediately!'

Admiral O'Hara watched Tyrone for a long moment and he spoke, but Tyrone could not hear the admiral's words. The signal began to flicker and before he could say anything more it broke up completely.

'The capital ships are opening fire!' an Ayleean warned him. 'Brace for impact!'

Tyrone barely heard the warning, staring out of the main viewing panel as he realized that they had won a battle only to lose the war. In a flash of vivid light he saw the universe outside the viewing panel flare brilliant white and he knew that his time was over.

***

XXXIII

CSS Defiance

'Destination in thirty seconds, captain.'

Sula watched as Captain Jordyn Lucas sat down in her seat in the center of the bridge and surveyed the command stations. She could see from the expressions on the faces of the crew that they were as ready as they could be for whatever awaited them on Ayleea. Sula felt something of a burden of responsibility for having brought them back here, especially after it had almost cost them their lives, but the chance to bring Tyrone home and learn something more about their unknown enemy had been enough to sway the crew behind her.

'Twenty seconds.'

'All power to shields and weapons,' Captain Lucas ordered. 'Open a communications channel with Polaris Station ready for when we go sub luminal. Whatever happens out there I want somebody to see it and learn from it.'

Sula took hold of the command rail, ready for the deceleration from super luminal into normal cruise and knowing now that Defiance would initiate evasive manoeuvers as a matter of course the moment she dropped out of super luminal cruise.

'Ten seconds.'

Strangely Sula found herself wondering what Nathan Ironside would be doing at that moment. She recalled his interest in her, in her family, in what she was doing. His concern for her welfare had been comforting, a meagre flame of warmth to fill the frigid void left after the death of her father. Only now, as the ship was heading back into danger once again as her father had done so many times, could she appreciate what it meant to have somebody to care for her and her mother, somebody who did so for no other reason than kindness.

'Five seconds.'

Captain Lucas gripped the rests of her seat more tightly.

'Here we go, stay sharp.'

Sula watched the main display screen as the engineer counted down the time.

'…three, two, one, *now!*'

Defiance surged as she dropped out of super luminal cruise, the display screen flaring bright white and then settling down to reveal a blanket of stars twinkling in the darkness of space and the planet Ayleea, entirely in shadow and only the faint blue ring of her atmosphere illuminated by the sun on her far side. Sula squinted and could make out the fiery scars of burning cities glowing in the darkness.

'Hard to port, full pulse power!' the helmsman called as he turned.

'All plasma batteries charged, shields at maximum!'

And then the tactical officer cried out.

'Multiple contacts three thousand meters, elevation three fiver niner!'

The helmsman responded instantly, turning Defiance to bring her main guns to bear on whatever was out there. Sula saw the display screen switch instantly to latch onto the detected targets and heard a gasp as they were identified as five enemy capital ships coming straight at Defiance.

'There are five of them?!' Walker stammered.

'And they're–engaged,' Lucas confirmed as she saw flickering exchanges of plasma fire. 'Helm, take us in at maximum impulse and fire off a salvo as we pass. Don't give them time to shoot back!'

'Aye, cap'n!'

Walker gasped in horror. 'You're engaging them?'

'I'm coming to the aid of whomever they're attacking.'

'Captain, priority IFF distress code, it's Fortitude!'

Lucas shot up out of her seat as the main display screen zoomed in on Fortitude, the sleek cruiser trailing debris and escaping gases as she fled directly toward them just ahead of the lumbering capital ships, only two of her engines functioning.

'Damn it she's crippled,' Lucas snapped. 'Covering fire, immediately!'

The tactical officer complied immediately and Defiance's starboard batteries opened up as the frigate heeled over hard to port. The plasma shots rocketed toward Fortitude and flashed over her bridge before zipping into the distance and smashing into the bridge of the nearest attacking capital ship.

*

Tyrone Hackett saw the bright flare of light and closed his eyes, waiting for the unimaginable pain of plasma fire obliterating his body and that of every Ayleean on the bridge around him.

The cruiser shook but he felt nothing, and he opened one eye.

'CSS frigate, dead ahead!' Shylo yelled. 'They're opening fire!'

Tyrone saw flashes of plasma fire rocket toward them as Defiance surged from the brilliant flare of her rapidly fading gravity well and fired. The shots rocketed over the cruiser and smashed into the pursuing capital ships and Tyrone let out a whoop of delight and stood up out of his seat.

His legs promptly gave way beneath him again and he slumped back into the chair as Defiance turned away before them.

'Open a channel,' Tyrone gasped. 'That's our ticket out of here.'

*

Sula watched as the main display screen in Defiance's bridge flickered and an image of Lieutenant Tyrone Hackett appeared on the screen. He looked ill, sheened with sweat and his eyes drooped with what looked like exhaustion.

What took you so long folks?'

'Identify yourself!' Captain Lucas snapped.

'Lieutenant Tyrone Hackett, CSS Endeavour, now aboard the senate cruiser Fortitude. We are unable to jump to super luminal, have civilian casualties and require immediate extraction.'

Sula leaped to her feet as she saw the lieutenant's ragged face on the screen. A quick glance at the tactical display revealed that Fortitude was mortally damaged and would not stay ahead of the capital ships chasing her for much longer. Defiance had slid into a formation position alongside the smaller cruiser but she too would become a target before long.

Walker spoke openly on the bridge. 'Captain, we're no match for a single one of those capital ships, let alone five. If we remain here to assist Fortitude, we put ourselves in range of their guns.'

'Would you have me leave them there?' Lucas challenged.

Walker lifted his chin slightly. 'Better to lose one ship than two.'

Beside Hackett's face on the screen, the angry, leathery face of an Ayleean warrior appeared and sneered out at Walker.

'I wouldn't have expected anything else from a human,' he snarled.

Walker recoiled. 'There are Ayleeans aboard the cruiser!'

'They're with me,' Tyrone snapped. 'They're the only survivors. Fortitude's crew is gone.'

Captain Lucas looked at Walker. 'They could be shape shifters too.'

Sula felt the first hint of panic hit her as she realized what Lucas was suggesting.

'They could be infected,' Walker agreed. 'There could be more of them aboard, even if Hackett is genuinely there. If we let them all aboard us…'

Captain Lucas glanced at the screen and Hackett's sickly features. The lieutenant gave her a withering glance as he pointed at his own face.

'You ever see one of the shape shifters look as bad as this? I took a direct hit from a sentry drone, twice, to get this far. You wanna quarantine us when we get aboard then go ahead, but if we don't leave in the next five minutes you're gonna be sweeping up the few atoms of us that'll be left so how about you make up your damned minds?'

Captain Lucas wrestled with indecision as Sula watched her, and on an impulse Sula turned to Tyrone on the screen.

'What did you say to me me the last time you saw me, when you insulted me?'

Tyrone looked at her and she saw the uncertainty on his face. The bridge crew on Defiance looked accusingly at Tyrone as he stumbled on his response.

'Well, I, er, y'know, I....'

'A clone wouldn't know what happened because you hadn't met one yet,' Sula snapped impatiently. 'I figure they can only replicate objects and forms, they can't replicate memories. What did you tell me to do?!'

Tyrone sighed.

'I told you to take a hike Ensign, because only big boys get to play with big toys.'

Sula couldn't prevent the smirk that twisted her face into a smile as she glanced at Captain Lucas.

'Is that so, lieutenant?' Lucas asked in a stern voice. 'We will have to discuss that when you and your team get aboard.'

'Yeah, about that, now's a *really* good time!'

'The capital ships are almost within range of Fortitude,' the tactical officer informed Lucas. 'One shot and her hull will be compromised. She'll be blown apart.'

Sula looked at the captain and she sensed the thoughts flashing through her mind one after the other as she sought a way to achieve the impossible, realized the incredible stress the command of a frigate in battle placed upon its captain.

'If we stop to board her we're all dead,' Walker reminded his captain.

'If we do nothing *they'll* all be dead,' Lucas replied without looking at him.

Sula began hopping up and down as she sensed the answer staring them in the face.

'How many are there aboard Fortitude?' she asked Tyrone.

'Couple hundred,' Tyrone replied, 'all Ayleeans plus me.'

Sula nodded. 'Fortitude was in orbit, so you must have got aboard her somehow.'

'Shuttle,' Tyrone replied, 'but that's not nearly fast enough to get us the hell out of here and…'

Sula turned to Captain Lucas. 'I have an idea.'

'Let's hear it,' Lucas replied.

*

'This is insane!' Shylo snapped.

Tyrone didn't argue as they hurried to the landing bay and opened the hatches once more, the atmosphere inside the bay re stabilized. The two hundred or so Ayleeans flocked to the shuttle as Tyrone headed for his Phantom.

'I don't like it either but it's the only chance we have. Get aboard and head straight for Defiance as soon as those doors open, understood?'

Shylo grunted an unintelligible response as he hurried away toward the shuttle and stormed up the boarding ramp. Tyrone leaped into his cockpit and started the engines as the canopy closed, firing up the plasma cannons for good measure as he checked the systems and hoped against hope that Sula's idea would work. Fortitude had shut down her engines and turned about, and was now effectively flying backward, her bow pointing at the pursuing capital ships.

The shuttle's boarding ramp closed and Tyrone watched and waited as the automated computer evacuated the air once more from the landing bay and disabled the hard light shielding before opening the main doors.

A rush of vaporized, frozen air was drawn out of the bay in writhing whorls of misty ice crystals and suddenly Tyrone could see deep space beyond and the stern of Defiance directly ahead.

'Go, now!' he snapped across the communications channel.

The shuttle blasted out of the landing bay at full power, rocketing past the Phantom as it launched itself toward Defiance. Tyrone saw the frigate's stern landing bay open as he rocked the fighter's throttles forward and accelerated out of the landing bay even as he saw Fortitude's remaining engines re engaging their power as they had been programmed to do the moment the launch bay doors opened.

The cruiser slowed dramatically in its backward flight as the Phantom soared from the landing bay toward Defiance. Tyrone craned his neck around his head rest and saw the cruiser suddenly accelerating away directly toward the pursuing capital ships.

'Go Fortitude,' he whispered in delight.

The unarmed cruiser rocketed away and began turning directly toward the nearest of the pursuing capital ships, following a pre-programmed course. The lumbering vessel began to turn to try to avoid the missile now plowing toward it at maximum pulse power, but the high velocity and immense mass of the warship was no match for the agility of the smaller cruiser and the attack so unexpected that it was unable to bring its massive guns to bear on the smaller vessel.

'It's working!' Tyrone yelled.

He turned the Phantom slightly for a better view, and moments later he saw the five capital ships break away from each other as Fortitude rushed in to the leading ship and smashed into her with all of her twelve thousand tons of hull.

*

The deck of Defiance was filled with a chorus of cheers as Fortitude vanished amid a blossoming fireball of brilliant white light and flame. The bridge of the capital ship dissolved into a flaming mess as the collision shattered the huge vessel and broke her hull just aft of the bridge.

Sula felt the tension go out of her chest and shoulders as the crippled warship slowed, explosions ripping through her hull as she came apart at the seams. Alongside her the other warships were turning back onto course to pursue Defiance, but Sula could see that there was no way they would catch up with the frigate as the shuttle and the Phantom fighter landed in her stern bays.

Sula had told Fortitude to use her bow thrusters to turn about, and then to launch the shuttle and Phantom fighter out of her rear bay before sending Fortitude flying into the enemy via remote guidance from Defiance in an attempt to force a collision. The cruiser's momentum gave the slower shuttle an edge over the pursuing warships when she launched, and the collision attempt would scatter the five ships giving the shuttle and fighter time to land and escape.

'Both craft are aboard, landing bays closed!' the tactical officer said.

'Jump to super luminal, effective immediately!'

Defiance surged as a rainbow spectrum of light filled the bridge and the display screen flared bright white, and then the frigate blasted its way into super luminal cruise and the display screen went pure black. A few more cheers rippled across the bridge as Sula ran a hand through her hair in relief.

Captain Lucas leaned back in her seat and glanced at Walker.

'A fire ship, huh?' she said.

The XO peered at Sula with interest. 'You're quite inventive for a youngster.'

'And quite destructive too,' Lucas observed with an appraising smile. 'I like it.'

Sula managed a faint smile. 'Now what do we do?'

Captain Lucas straightened her uniform and turned to the

helmsman.

'No sense in hiding now,' she said. 'Plot a course for Polaris Station, maximum velocity. We need to tell them everything we can about the enemy, and hope to hell we're not too late.'

***

XXXIV

New Washington

The panic in the air was tangible, as though alive and shrieking like banshees through the streets as the city went into lockdown for the second time in a year. Nathan could hear distant sirens echoing mournfully across the city as he dashed for a squad vehicle on the roof.

Lieutenant Foxx jumped into the cockpit with Nathan just behind as Allen and Vasquez took the rear seats. Within moments the craft took off, the doors closing even as the EM Drive kicked in and blasted whorls of rainwater away from beneath the vehicle.

Foxx flew the craft up into the flow of traffic rushing through the sky lanes and then flew directly up North Four's arm toward the spaceport at the station's heart. Nathan felt the station's gravity fade rapidly away as they flew into the port and saw the shield doors firmly closed, all traffic blocked from getting in and out.

'How the hell are we going to get past that?' Allen asked.

'I don't want to know,' Foxx replied as she aimed for a landing spot alongside a City Defense Force patrol shuttle parked nearby. 'Because that'll be down to Betty.'

The City Defense Force was a small unit attached to the police and CSS. Equipped with militarized spacecraft, they were mostly charged with anti smuggling duties, tracking down traffickers in body parts, illegal biomechanical enhancement packages and of course the drug of choice, Shiver, still widely available on North Four's tougher streets.

'Detective Ironside,' Betty greeted them as they climbed out of their squad vehicle. 'The city's on lockdown and there's chaos everywhere, so I guessed you were on duty.'

'Not me this time,' Nathan assured her, raising his hands in innocence.

'We need a ride to the surface,' Foxx said. 'It's urgent.'

'Is it ever anything else with you two?' Betty asked. 'You've noticed that the shield doors are down, right?'

There was no suggestion in her tone that she couldn't help them, only a statement of fact. Betty *Buzz* Luther was one of the most experienced precinct pilots in the force, with over fifty years' service behind her and a reputation for reckless flying that had traumatized more than one officer over the years.

'We need a way through,' Vasquez said, slightly nervously. 'You got any ideas?'

Betty offered him a withering look. 'You're asking *me* that?'

'We're kinda worried about it,' Allen offered.

Betty produced a pair of flying gloves from her pocket and pulled them onto her hands as she smiled sweetly at him.

'Don't you worry yourself,' she offered. 'I've got this.'

'You *can* get us out?' Nathan asked in surprise.

'How do you think drugs sometimes get smuggled in?' Betty asked as she climbed aboard the CDF shuttle. 'There's always a way.'

Nathan climbed aboard the shuttle and within moments they lifted off and turned, Betty aiming not for the main landing bay doors but for gigantic vents mounted in the walls of the landing bay.

'The heat exchange system?' Foxx uttered.

'It's really *big* inside there,' Betty enthused as she flew the shuttle toward the nearest of the vents. 'Took us a while to figure out how the smugglers were getting packages inside the station.'

'People have flown through here before?' Vasquez asked as the shuttle slipped through the hard light shielding on the vents and the walls closed in around them.

'Of course not,' Betty admitted airily without even the mildest sense of irony. 'They send automated drones through. Nobody would be crazy enough to actually *fly* through one of these.'

Nathan saw the confines of the venting system close around them and he looked at Foxx with a concerned expression on his face, but she shook her head to silence him.

'How long?' she asked Betty.

'Oh, not long,' Betty replied cheerfully. 'We just need to blast our way out one of the emergency ducts before we get crushed inside the vents.'

'Whoa wait a minute there,' Vasquez said, 'crushed in the what now?'

Before Betty could reply they saw a huge set of blades before them spinning in the darkness. Nathan grabbed the edges of his seat as Betty chortled.

'Hold on now, this bit's gonna be a little tricky to get right!'

The shuttle rushed toward the huge fan that filled Nathan's vision and he let out a howl of terror that mingled with more from the rear seats as Betty suddenly pushed forward on the control column and then rolled the shuttle hard over to starboard.

The shuttle dived and rolled, matching the rotation of the enormous fan and then it slipped through between the blades and was suddenly hauled to the right by some unseen force. Betty stamped down on the rudder pedals and the shuttle slewed around into a tight tunnel illuminated by white running lights above their heads.

Nathan flinched as the shuttle slammed against the metallic side of the tunnel with a clanging of metal on metal and then was carried along on some kind of turbulent airflow.

'Whoopsie!' Betty chortled as the shuttle shook and vibrated as it travelled along the tunnel.

'Where the hell are we?' Allen asked.

'This is the ventilation system that acts as a coolant for the city outside the North Four arm,' Betty explained. 'It works because one side of the station is always heated by the sun, while the other is cooled by the shadow of deep space. That creates convection, which creates a flow of air that smooths out the temperature variations inside the city and also circulates some of the build up of water vapor in the atmosphere. The turbulence inside the tunnels is what's shaking us about a bit.'

The shuttle rushed along the tunnel and then turned sharply at the end. Nathan looked at the endless curved surface of the tunnel passing them by and realized they were now following the outside rim of the orbital station.

'How can you shoot us out of here? Won't it breach the station's atmosphere?'

'Nah,' Betty scorned with a wave of her hand. 'Bulkheads separate the sections of the tunnel and will seal off any breach. Secondary, smaller tunnels keep the air moving around the breach until it can be fixed.'

Foxx frowned but said nothing as Betty wrestled with the controls.

'Shuttle zero delta five report your position.'

Nathan looked at the communications suite as Betty replied politely.

'Zero delta five is outside the southern quadrant, checking the exterior panelling.'

'Zero delta five, we have you located inside the station.'

Betty smiled.

'Young man, will you next be telling me my bra size and what I had for breakfast this morning?'

Nathan listened to a long, silent pause before the controller replied. *'Ah, no sir, I was merely...'*

'Your scopes appear to be malfunctioning,' Betty cut across him. 'There may be some interference out here, stand by while I check it out.'

Betty turned the shuttle as it was dragged along by the turbulence and Nathan saw what looked like a square panel in the surface of the tunnel up ahead. She glanced over her shoulder at Lieutenant Foxx.

'You sure you wanna do this?'

'We have to,' Foxx replied. 'CSS Headquarters could be in danger.'

Betty nodded, turned, and without further hesitation pulled a trigger on her control column.

Nathan saw two bright plasma bolts blast out and impact the panel as they flew past. The panel was smashed from its mounts in a cloud of burning embers and almost immediately a vortex of frozen air rushed out of the cavity in writhing coils of icy mist. The shuttle slowed as the direction of the airflow in the tunnel altered drastically and Betty hurled the throttles open. The shuttle accelerated into the new flow of air and rushed out of the station and into the vacuum of space as Betty keyed her microphone.

'Control this is zero delta five, we have a plating breach in sector three. I can see it from out here. It must have been causing the sensor confusion you had a moment ago.'

The reply came back after a moment's pause.

'Roger, zero delta five, breach identified. We're shutting the section down.'

'Copy that, control. Zero delta five is returning planet side.'

Nathan looked at Betty and smiled. 'You've got a real sly side to you, you know that?'

'I do.'

Foxx leaned forward in her seat. 'Something's not right.'

Nathan frowned as he looked at her, but he knew that her instincts were rarely wrong and almost immediately he realized why.

'Zero delta five, what is your operating identity and patrol tasking?'

Betty smiled tightly. 'Oops.'

'Where are you supposed to be, Betty?' Foxx asked her.

Betty looked over her shoulder apologetically. 'Traffic patrol on South One.'

'How did you get this shuttle?' Vasquez asked.

'It's complicated,' Betty replied, and then became defensive as Foxx's features paled. 'You said it was urgent!'

'I didn't tell you to steal police property!'

'We're not stealing, just borrowing.'

'Zero delta five, dock immediately or we will be forced to open fire on your

position.'

Vasquez slapped his head in disbelief. 'Oh, you're kidding me.'

Nathan looked at Foxx. 'They think we could be shape shifters.'

'They'll shoot us down if we don't comply, but if we don't get down there to CSS then this whole invasion will get going.'

Betty took the matter into her own hands and opened the throttles. The shuttle surged away from New Washington toward the vast blue–green sphere of the earth even as they saw a pair of bright stars rocketing toward them.

'I think we're being intercepted,' Nathan said as he saw the two points of light resolve themselves into CDF armed patrol vehicles. 'We need to get out of here.'

Betty pushed the control column forward and the shuttle dove away from the orbital city, accelerating rapidly both under its own engine thrust and the gravity of the planet drawing it down. Nathan saw the vast surface of the earth spread below them, the shuttle diving directly downward and the armed patrol vehicles swiftly gaining on it.

'Shuttle zero delta five this is ARU Flight, reduce speed and turn port immediately or we will be forced to shoot.'

Foxx didn't wait for Betty to reply, instead punching a transmit button on the center console herself.

'This is Lieutenant Kaylin Foxx, New Washington PD. We have information that the Director General of the CSS may be in danger and we need to get units to the surface immediately.'

There was a pause that seemed to last an age, and then a reply crackled over the channel.

'This is ARU Flight, heave to immediately or we will be forced to…'

Betty shut the channel off and looked at Nathan. 'Any chance they could be shape shifters?'

Nathan knew that it didn't matter now either way.

'Head for the surface,' he said. 'Can you outrun them?'

'No,' Betty admitted as she leaned around in front of Nathan and checked the position of the incoming Armed Response Unit craft. 'But I can outsmart them.'

The pair of patrol vehicles soared in toward her and Betty hit a switch on the console before her as she turned away from their pursuers. Almost immediately Nathan saw a cloud of sparkling material trail behind the shuttle and the two patrol vehicles veered away sharply and overshot their target.

'What was that?' Nathan asked.

'Dust particles,' Foxx replied, 'designed to clog up the instruments and engine intakes of drug dealing vehicles. The particles are magnetically charged and attracted to the hulls of spacecraft.'

Nathan peered out of the windows and saw both patrol vehicles swinging around in broad turns to resume the pursuit.

'They're not quitting.'

Betty kept her eyes on the instruments before her as she accelerated at full throttle toward the atmosphere.

'Hold on to your hats,' she uttered as the patrol vehicles closed in.

Nathan flinched as a stream of plasma bolts rocketed past his window with bright flashes. Betty jerked the controls and the shuttle veered right and away from the attack, and then moments later she hauled back on the control column and the shuttle reared up. Nathan felt a mild sense of G force pushing down on him under the aggressive manoeuver and then suddenly the shuttle shook violently as the patrol vehicles pulled up and away.

The shuttle shuddered again and Nathan saw the fearsome glow of red and orange flames flickering from beneath the shuttle as it slammed against earth's upper atmosphere.

'They won't pursue us through the atmosphere,' Betty said as the shuttle shook violently in the ferocious turbulence of re entry, 'but they'll launch interceptors to meet us from the surface.'

Foxx leaned forward and rested one hand on Betty's shoulder.

'Whatever it takes. We have to get down there.'

Betty nodded and gripped the controls tighter.

'You asked for it.'

***

XXXV

CSS Headquarters

New York City

Arianna Coburn paced up and down in the senate conference chamber, in front of broad windows that looked out over the East River, rivulets of rain spilling down from the dark gray clouds tumbling past overhead, the city a metallic blur in the mist. For a moment, it seemed to her as though the sky itself were crying, reflecting her own anxiety as she awaited news from the fleet.

The nearby spaceport was devoid of life and she could see from her vantage point high above the city that the streets and parks were empty. The citizens were already hunkering down, the reports on Global Wire of what was happening on the orbital stations and here on the planet sending them into a frenzy of paranoia where anybody, even their own friends and family, could be the enemy.

Nobody could have predicted this, she told herself. Nobody could have known that the enemy would have been among mankind for so long, perhaps even for centuries, watching, waiting. She turned to a series of holograms levitating before one wall of the chamber, each showing images from mankind's distant past that she had requested be displayed so that she could study them.

Arianna stared at an image of an oil painting from the year 1710, by Flemish artist Aert De Gelder. The graceful picture depicted *John the Baptist and Jesus*, and shining down on them a silvery disc emitting rays of light. Another image nearby portrayed the *"Glorification of the Eucharist"* painted by Bonaventura Salimbeni in 1600. In the center, two men sat either side of a metallic sphere with two probes that looked uncannily like mankind's earliest satellites. More images abounded, artwork, archaic photographs taken by witnesses to strange phenomena in the skies hundreds of years before the CSS had even existed, and records as far back as ancient Egypt describing fleets of unknown craft traversing the skies long before humanity had built its first aeroplanes. The words of countless conspiracy theorists echoed through her mind: *They have been here for a very long time, watching and waiting. Everybody knew it, but nobody thought to do a thing about it.*

The entrance to the chamber shimmered and vanished as a man walked through, and Coburn turned to see Commodore Hawker striding toward her. He turned as the doorway rematerialized behind him and sealed it shut.

'What is it?' Coburn asked.

Hawker walked toward her as he gestured to the city outside. 'They could be anywhere, or any one of us. We need to be cautious.'

Arianna nodded but then a thought crossed her mind. 'They could be you or I.'

Hawker smiled faintly in agreement. 'I think that if that were the case, one or the other of us would not be standing in this room. Their invasion, or whatever it is they're planning to do, has already begun and we have precious little means to stop them.'

Coburn turned and looked out across the city and then up toward the angry skies roiling overhead. A lone gull had braved the storms and was wheeling near the building, searching for morsels of food or perhaps somewhere to shelter from the coming storm. It was oblivious to the greater storm gathering on the horizon, one that all life on earth faced.

'There's nothing that we can do,' she whispered.

Hawker frowned. 'There is always something that we can do, even if it means leaving the system and returning later.'

Arianna turned to him. 'We cannot evacuate three billion people from the planet in a matter of hours, and what of the colonies?'

'I wasn't talking about the entire population, Arianna.'

Arianna stared at Hawker for a long moment. Despite her fear for the future she had not yet considered implementing the Savior

Protocol.

'We can't,' she said. 'We just can't do that.'

'There may be no other option,' Hawker pointed out. 'Nobody wants to talk about it but we've seen what happened on Ayeela and if we don't do something to mitigate this crisis before it overwhelms us then we will go the same way that they did. We will become extinct, Arianna.'

Arianna turned away from him and closed her eyes, unable to bear the thought of what the commodore was suggesting.

The Savior Protocol had been created a century before, when the newly formed CSS had decided that humanity could not risk facing extinction again as it had once had with *The Falling* centuries before. To aid in this, a system had been devised where the majority of the senate and congress, along with their families and selected military personnel, would evacuate the planet should a Global Extinction Event occur again.

Ever since then a small flotilla of twenty spacecraft, all equipped with super luminal drives and all capable of carrying at least two hundred passengers, had been kept on stand by in orbit around Mercury Station, a solar observatory post on the planet closest to the sun where few civilians ever travelled. The presence of the flotilla was a closely guarded secret, as nobody was under any illusion about how the public would react if they knew that there was a private fleet of ships ready to whisk their leaders away at the first hint of trouble.

'The Savior Protocol is there to protect the future of the human race,' Hawker said, apparently sensing her discomfort. 'Not to provide the lucky elite of the grounded with an escape plan while leaving the masses behind. Unless every human being alive today possessed a super luminal transport we could never hope to save everybody anyway.'

Arianna lifted her head as she thought of Admiral Marshall.

'Unless we stayed, and we fought.'

'That, my dear, is what the Ayleeans did,' Hawker pointed out.

'That didn't turn out so well for them. Look, believe me when I say that I find the protocol as unpalatable as you do, but staying and fighting isn't what a government does best. Surviving is what they do best, and survive we must, even if we are down to our last few hundred survivors. We've been there before and prevailed.'

Arianna shook her head.

'We would be viewed as cowards,' she said. 'We do not yet know if this invasion force will even reach earth. The public are in panic over the possibility that there could be an advance force among us, but Global Wire have grossly exaggerated the threat to the point of invoking civil war on the streets and…'

Arianna stopped in mid sentence and stared into the middle distance as a sudden and troubling thought occurred to her.

'What is it?' Hawker asked.

'Global Wire,' Arianna whispered, 'they've been fomenting propaganda, false news, inflating minor stories into major issues for the people for months now.'

Hawker frowned. 'That's the media, Arianna, it's what they do and…'

'No,' she insisted, 'this is different. You know as well as I do that one of the first tasks in an invasion is to insert specialist troops behind enemy lines to observe the enemy, find weakness, spread disinformation and create chaos before the main invasion force arrives.'

Hawker nodded. 'Yes, of course.'

'What better way to do that than to plant the seeds of defeat long before the people even realize that they're in danger? The media have been responsible for eroding public trust in government for months now. Look at the people, hiding in their homes, distrusting everybody, fearing everyone and everything. They couldn't fight now if they wanted to, and if an invasion force landed outside the city there would be nobody to oppose it.'

'We can't place responsibility for the crisis in the hands of the media alone, Arianna.'

She barely heard Hawker as she realized what had happened.

'The people are immobilized,' she said, 'only the shape shifters can move freely because they would presumably take forms of various types and not just humans, things that we wouldn't recognize as a threat or even a...'

Arianna's blood suddenly ran cold in her veins and she turned to the broad windows. Outside, wheeling on the buffeting winds, the lone gull drifted back and forth. Its beady black eyes watched her and suddenly she knew without a doubt that the enemy was relying on humanity's reaction to the crisis to complete its objective. *Divide and conquer.*

'We need to make a news statement immediately,' Arianna said as she turned back to Hawker. 'Having us hiding out in our buildings and fearing each other is precisely what the enemy wants us to do!'

Hawker struggled to keep up with her pace of thought.

'But you said it yourself, the enemy could be anybody. It could be me.'

'Then stay here and lock the door!' Arianna snapped as she marched for the exit. 'I'm going to tell the people what's really happening.'

Arianna reached the chamber door but came up short as it failed to open for her. She frowned in confusion and Hawker's voice reached out to her.

'You handed all control to the military, remember Arianna?'

Slowly, she turned and looked at Hawker, who stood calmly with his hands behind his back.

'Open it, commodore,' she ordered him. 'Millions of lives may depend on what you do now.'

'Yes,' Hawker said as he lifted his chin and steeled himself, 'and to let you out of this building and perhaps see you occupied by one of those creatures out there would further their aims immensely. In fact, letting you out there to spread a message that might cause even greater chaos could also play into the hands of our enemy, and as I said, I can't quite be sure of who you really are.'

Arianna struggled to understand why the commodore would suddenly turn against her.

'You think that I'm an imposter? I haven't left your sight or anybody else's since this whole thing began!'

'But you did before it began,' Hawker pointed out, 'as did we all. They have been here for a very long time, Arianna, and anybody could now be on the verge of causing the fall of mankind. I cannot, *will not*, let you leave this room.'

Arianna nodded and sighed.

'I understand, Commodore,' she said.

Hawker relaxed visibly. 'Good, let's sit down and discuss…'

Arianna pulled a plasma pistol from beneath her robes and took aim at Hawker. The commodore's eyes flew wide and he hurled himself behind the large table as a plasma bolt blasted from the weapon.

***

XXXVI

'Interceptors, ten o'clock low!'

Foxx pointed at the display screen in the center of the shuttle's console as two angry red blips appeared on it, rocketing up on an intercept course from the surface below them.

'They look like Corsair fighters,' Vasquez said from the rear seat. 'They'll take us down in no time if we don't reach NYC first.'

Betty glanced at the radar scope and then ahead of them to where the last of the heat glow from re entry was dissipating.

'They'll get there first but they don't know that we're headed for CSS HQ,' she pointed out. 'Maybe I can tease them out of there.'

'How you gonna do that?' Nathan asked, almost not wanting to know.

Betty grinned as she pushed the shuttle into a steep dive. 'We're gonna do some flyin'!'

Nathan felt his guts rise up into his throat as the shuttle plummeted out of the high atmosphere toward a vast weather system spinning off the North American coast. Nathan saw towering cumulonimbus clouds circling a central eye, and he knew instantly what he was looking at.

'That's a hurricane,' he said.

'It's a major depression,' Betty corrected him, 'probably the remains of a hurricane cell that's spun up here from Florida. Best thing we can do is get down in there and hope the interceptors don't try to follow us.'

'Are you kidding?' Detective Allen said from the back seat. 'Even you're not crazy enough to try to pull a stunt like that!'

'You sure about that?' Betty asked as the shuttle plunged toward the turbulent clouds below. 'Hold on!'

The shuttle soared downward and the blanket of thick clouds rose up before Nathan through the windshield until they plunged into their embrace and the horizon vanished. The shuttle's wings rocked violently as turbulence slammed into the fuselage and Betty fought for control as they plunged down.

Nathan caught glimpses of towering white pillars of cloud against the blue above them and then there was nothing but the pure white and gray cloud surrounding them in a featureless haze. He looked out to his right and saw the shuttle's wings rippling and flexing on the wind currents, then looked left into the cockpit and saw Betty focusing intently on her instruments as she flew the shuttle manually through the storm.

'You're not going to use the autopilot?' Vasquez asked, his voice higher in pitch than usual and his knuckles white on the rests of his seat.

'Autopilot is for wimps,' Betty replied without looking back at him, 'and the avionics can be used to lock the fighters onto our position. We need to get right into the storm so that the electrical interference hides our location.'

The clouds outside grew darker suddenly and without warning.

'Man, it just got real dark out there,' Nathan gasped.

'We're in the shadow of a cumulonimbus cloud,' Betty replied. 'That's where the real action is and they form chains in systems like this, so there should be some more up ahead somewhere.'

The darkness deepened and the shuttle rocked more violently but Betty did not alter her course. Nathan saw the altimeter wind down through ten thousand feet and almost before he realized it the shuttle plunged headlong into an intense thunderstorm.

The darkness outside the windshield was split by a thunderous barrage of hailstones that pelted the screen with ice and scared Nathan half out of his wits. He reared up in his seat, one hand grasping his harness and the other pressed against the console before him as the hailstones hammered the fuselage around them like thousands of boots sprinting across a tin roof. The shuttle veered this way and that, tugged by powerful updrafts as it plowed through the center of the violent storm.

'You see!' Betty shouted jubilantly above the thunderous hail. 'We're losin' 'em!'

'We're gonna lose our lives too if we stay in here much longer!' Vasquez called back.

Betty didn't reply, cackling in delight as a flash of lightning illuminated her face like a grotesque demon. Nathan flinched as lightning bolts flashed all around them, reaching out for the shuttle as it plunged through the hailstorm and then the hammering of the ice changed to the hiss of rain as the shuttle descended further.

'Okay, here we go,' Betty chortled and banked over, relying entirely on her instruments for navigation in the thick cloud.

The shuttle began to turn, but with the turbulence and the darkness Nathan couldn't tell if he was right side up or upside down. The craft was jostled and rocked as it plunged through the thick cloud banks surrounding them.

'Once we punch out of the cloud to land those fighters will be back on us in no time!' Betty said to Foxx above the noise of the rain hammering the fuselage. 'They share a datalink with the more powerful radars at CSS and they'll pick us up real quick, so you'll all have to get off and run when I touch down.'

Foxx nodded.

'You too Betty,' she replied, 'there's nothing up there for you now anyway. This is the end of the line, and for all of us if we're too late.'

Nathan reached down and with one hand checked his plasma pistol, tucked as ever into its holster under his left arm. He had no idea what was awaiting them but if Hawker was an alien imposter then the entire defensive network of the planet could be under threat and the invasion might begin at any moment.

'Sixty seconds,' Betty said as she watched the instrument console before her, the glow from the countless dials and screens a soft green in the otherwise dark cockpit.

Nathan saw veils of rain pelting the shuttle's windscreen as it descended, but some of the darkness began to subside and he looked down to his left to see slate gray ocean waves churning with white crests through veils of cloud racing past beneath them.

The shuttle descended down below the cloud base and Nathan saw New York City crouched on the horizon, its soaring towers lost in the low cloud and misty rain, its parks rain sodden and dark. Street lights glowed and he could see the immense domed superstructure of the CSS Headquarters looming before them.

'Thirty seconds,' Betty said. 'The defenses could open up at any moment so brace yourselves!'

The shuttle bucked and rolled in the heavy turbulence and Nathan heard the engines whining in protest as Betty rocked the throttles back and forth to keep the craft airborne as it closed in on the CSS landing pads. Even from this distance he could see the gun emplacements that were discreetly positioned beneath the landing pads, able to shoot at approaching enemy craft while using the pads as natural shielding against attack.

They waited, but suddenly he realized that there was no plasma fire coming forth from the platforms.

'They're not shooting,' Vasquez said in confusion. 'We're within range.'

'Maybe they believed what we told them?' Allen suggested.

Lieutenant Foxx shook her head as she looked at the shuttle's sensors.

'They're not doing anything,' she said. 'Betty, switch the communications back on.'

Betty obeyed as they closed in on the CSS building and instantly the cockpit was filled with the bland static of an empty broadcast. Nathan looked around at Foxx.

'Why wouldn't they be broadcasting?'

Foxx drew her pistol and made ready to disembark. 'Because the safety systems have been shut down,' she replied. 'Everything's been shut down. It's started. The enemy are opening us up for the invasion.'

Betty swung the shuttle up into a climb that brought it level with the nearest platform as she extended the shuttle's landing gear.

'We'll touch down here and then…'

Her voice was cut off by a blast of plasma fire and the shuttle rocked as plasma bolts smashed into it and crashed into the landing platform before them. Nathan saw explosions billow against the building and wash across the shuttle in waves of flame as Betty hurled the throttles open and veered hard to starboard away from the attack.

Alarms blared in the cockpit and pierced Nathan's ears as two CDF fighters rocketed past overhead their position. He looked across at Betty and saw her face creased with the effort of controlling the shuttle.

'We're hit!' she shouted as the shuttle lurched awkwardly to one side. 'I'm going for a lower platform, be ready to get out before those fighters come back!'

The shuttle's engines clattered and smoked as the shuttle careered around in a wide circle, leaving a trail of smoke that swept past the windscreen as Betty kicked in a boot full of left rudder and aimed for a landing pad right in front of them. The shuttle strained and the remaining engine screeched as it tore itself apart and the shuttle crashed down heavily onto its landing gear which promptly collapsed beneath it.

The shuttle ground to a halt on the landing pad to the sound of screeching metal as Betty hit the emergency exit switches and the side panels opened automatically.

'Thank you for flying Air Luther, have a nice day,' she groaned as she nursed where the side of her head had hit the console in front of her.

Foxx, Vasquez and Allen vaulted from the shuttle as Nathan unbuckled from his seat and jumped out after them, his pistol in one hand as he turned and reached out for Betty.

'Come on!'

Nathan grabbed Betty's hand and hauled her out of the cockpit and out into the rain as he heard the fighters swooping in from the clouds above them. He ran hard, forcing Betty to keep up as he heard a crackling sound and saw two plasma bolts rocket down from the fighters and hit the shuttle square on.

Nathan threw himself down onto the wet landing pad and Betty thumped down alongside him as the shuttle exploded. A wave of heat washed over Nathan and a cloud of scorched metal fragments pelted the walls nearby as the shuttle was blasted to pieces and a hail of debris clattered down around them.

Nathan looked over his shoulder and saw the shuttle's ruined fuselage engulfed in flames as he staggered to his feet and helped Betty up. Together, they hurried across to the exit where Foxx and Vasquez were struggling to open the door with Allen.

'Everything's shut down,' Allen explained as they joined him in the shelter of the doorway. 'Nobody's come out to meet us and we can't call in as there's no communications working.'

Nathan knew that something major had happened already.

'They could have sent armed troops to arrest us,' he said, 'but they didn't, which means Hawker doesn't have total control over everybody inside.'

'There can't be many of them,' Vasquez agreed, 'just enough to shut the building down. Only Hawker could do that, and maybe Arianna Coburn herself.'

'Let's focus on what we *can* do,' Nathan said. 'How long until you can get through that door?'

'It's gonna take a few minutes,' Vasquez replied. 'I haven't had to hot wire a modern door for a long time and CSS sure build 'em tough.'

Nathan frowned. 'Have you thought of knocking?'

'Say what now?'

Nathan stepped past him and reached up, and with one hand he knocked loudly on the heavy metal door. The sound was loud enough to hear above the rain clattering down on the landing pad behind them, and for a few moments there was nothing but that to hear.

'There's nobody in there.'

Nathan smiled. 'A shuttle just blew up on this landing pad,' he replied. 'Somebody's gonna be watching.'

A few more moments passed and Nathan knocked again, more loudly this time. Almost immediately a voice replied from a speaker above the door.

'What do you want?'

'To come in,' Nathan replied. 'We're under attack out here.'

'The building's on lockdown, nobody is allowed in or out.'

'Case you hadn't noticed there's an invasion going on,' Foxx called out. 'We know that there are infiltrators inside the building and we know how to identify them!'

'Sure you do, and if we just let you in you'll start sucking our insides out! Get lost or we'll blow the landing pad!'

Nathan stepped closer to the speaker.

'This is precisely what they want,' he insisted. 'They want to divide and conquer, to keep us from trusting each other. Right now every defensive system on earth is being shut down and it's being done from inside the building! If we don't get inside there and put a stop to it there's going to be nothing to save us from the invasion!'

There was a momentary pause.

'How do we know you're telling the truth?!'

'It's water,' Nathan called back. 'The shape shifters don't hold much water because they're more machine than biological, they don't have much fluid inside their bodies. It's the only way we have to tell them apart!'

There was another long pause.

'Who do you think the infiltrators are?'

'Commodore Hawker may be one of them,' Foxx replied. 'Where is he right now?'

'He's in lock down with the senate chamber.'

'Damn it,' Nathan said, 'we need to get in there right now. You can escort us under armed guard if you want but at least let us check that Director General Coburn is not under any threat!'

There was another pause that felt as though it lasted for ages, and then suddenly the hard light door shimmered out of existence and Nathan found himself staring down the barrels of six plasma rifles.

***

XXXVII

Nathan threw his hands in the air as six heavily armed CSS guards confronted him, their heads ducked down behind rifle shields and the weapons humming with restrained energy.

The guards silently waved them inside the building as one of them spoke in a gruff voice.

'Turn around, hands on your head and walk backward into the building. Any of you make a move for a weapon, we'll fry you all right here and now!'

Nathan obeyed, but he saw something flitting through the clouds outside and he knew they were out of time.

'Those fighters are manned by infiltrators,' he said, 'they just blew up our shuttle and now they're coming back.'

Nathan walked quickly backward inside the building, Foxx and Betty hurrying with Allen and Vasquez until they were all inside. One of the CSS guards jogged forward and peered outside to see a pair of Corsair fighters rocketing in toward the platform. The fighter's plasma cannons lit up and instantly the soldier sealed the door shut and backed away.

Nathan flinched as he heard the plasma rounds smash into the exterior of the building, dull booms echoing down the corridor in which they stood, but the hardened shell of the building was more than a match for a fighter's weapons.

'They intercepted us when we left New Washington,' Foxx said by way of an explanation. 'We barely got down here with our lives.'

The rifles didn't waver from pointing at them as the squad leader replied.

'Doesn't mean they're the infiltrators.'

'We need to reinstate the holosaps,' Vasquez said. 'They're the key to identifying all of the infiltrators.'

'The holosaps were shut down by Commodore Hawker to secure

our communications channels.'

'That's the point,' Foxx said. 'They're the only sentient beings immune to the invasion. The infiltrators couldn't allow them to be active because they would be able to continue work on identifying who was who. One of them was on the verge of cracking the case when they were shut down.'

The soldiers looked at each other uncertainly.

'Guys,' Nathan said, 'if we were the infiltrators, do you think we'd be advocating using the help of the one species that could undermine us?'

The soldiers exchanged one more glance, and then the squad leader lowered his plasma rifle and gestured with a nod of his head down the corridor.

'Director General Coburn could take control of the holosap lockdown from the military if there was sufficient evidence for concern,' he said. 'She's in the senate chamber.'

Nathan didn't hesitate, taking the lead and hoping fervently that the guards themselves were not infiltrators playing a careful game. He knew that they could gun the entire team down in a flash as they followed, their weapons humming with energy just waiting to be unleashed.

'How long has the senate been on lockdown?' Foxx asked the squad behind them as they hurried down the corridor.

'About an hour,' came the reply. 'Commodore Hawker gave the order.'

'Hawker,' Vasquez spat. 'He's gotta be behind all of this. If he's with Coburn he'll probably try to turn her too, and with her gone anything could happen. If she gave the order to throw open the doors to the invaders people would do it, they trust her so much.'

Nathan was about to reply when one of the soldier's radio speakers crackled.

'Shots fired!'

'Where?' the squad leader demanded.

'The senate chamber!'

'Damn it,' Foxx uttered as she broke into a sprint. 'We're too late!'

*

Arianna Coburn saw her double shot hit the conference table and splatter white hot plasma across the surface as Commodore Hawker ducked and rolled out of sight behind it. The plasma hissed and bubbled as it dripped off the hard light table in glowing globules to fall onto the floor.

'Open the door, Hawker,' Coburn snapped.

The commodore remained low, crouching under cover of the table.

'I cannot do that,' he replied, his voice oddly calm considering that she had just attempted to kill him. 'You'll kill them all.'

'*I'll* kill them all?' Coburn stammered. 'You're one of them, aren't you? You're an infiltrator.'

'Don't be bloody ridiculous, Arianna!'

Coburn tried to spot Hawker but he was using the long table as cover and moving quickly to avoid exposing himself to her aim. Coburn saw him move right toward the exit and she fired twice again, the weapon spitting fearsome crackling balls of energy that smashed into the table once more and forced Hawker back into hiding. She changed direction, blocking his path toward the exit.

'You're an infiltrator,' she repeated. 'There's no reason why you would want to flee now other than to ensure that the leadership of earth are removed from the equation!'

'That's not what this is about,' Hawker pressed from his hiding place.

'The Commodore Hawker that I knew would never have run from a fight.'

She heard a gasp of resignation coming from the old British warrior.

'Commodore Hawker won't be running from the damned fight, Arianna. He'll be staying right here. It's you, and the senate leaders, who need to be removed from the equation in order to ensure that *somebody* survives!'

Arianna shook her head ruefully, surprised at just how cunning this creature was, how well thought out its arguments were. She wondered briefly why something capable of being so convincing would ever need to kill in the first place.

'You don't seriously think that I believe that, do you?' she asked. 'You could have made the same suggestion without coming here and trying to lock me inside this building while my planet is invaded by whatever horrific beings are behind it all.'

'Arianna,' came the pleading response, 'if anything it is more likely you who is the infiltrator. You're the one who's been suffering under the stress of the whole situation and now you're the one trying to kill me!'

'You're the one trying to invade my world!' Arianna shouted. 'What the hell did you expect, a red carpet?! You're murdering our citizens just to take their form and…'

Arianna's train of thought ground to a halt as a new awareness hit her like a freight train. She stared into the middle distance as she realized what she had deduced. *Murdering, for no reason other than to take the form of others. Cunning enough, that they would never need to kill in the first place.*

'Why would they kill, when they could just replicate a person's ID chip on the black market?'

Her voice was a whisper, soft in the otherwise silent chamber. Sure, the infiltrators might not have any empathy for human life but she and the JCOS had received reports from witnesses that the strange shape shifting entities showed a genuine fear of dying when confronted with their own mortality. Killing to take an identity was one thing, but hadn't Detective Foxx said in report that one of the beings had taken the form of a person that they had not murdered? If they could do such a thing, then surely they could have taken human forms and obtained illegal ID chips among the outer colonies *before* coming to earth? The colonies were less well policed, a haven for drugs and crime. She looked across to where Hawker was hiding.

'Why would you kill and expose yourselves to the chance of identification when you could have just...?'

Hawker wasn't there.

Arianna whirled and her pistol arm hit something solid as Hawker loomed before her and smashed her arm aside. Strong, wiry hands twisted the pistol from her grasp and she cried out as pain bolted through her wrist and shoulder.

Hawker held her in place, her arm twisted back on itself as she was bowed over at the waist in sympathy to the pain. The commodore turned the pistol over in one hand and pressed it against her temple.

'My apologies, Arianna,' Hawker said, 'but I will not let you leave this room.'

'Then you've done your work well,' she spat at him. 'Divide and conquer, commodore?'

'I am not doing any such thing, I'm trying to...'

Hawker's response was drowned out as the solid door to the senate chamber suddenly exploded inward in a shower of sparks and the hard light door behind it fizzled out. Hawker yanked Arianna in front of him and kept the pistol pressed to her head as he saw six CSS troops storm into the chamber, followed by four detectives and what looked like an elderly patrol officer.

'Put the weapon down, hands on your head!' the squad leader yelled.

'On your knees!' bellowed another.

Hawker remained standing, switching his gaze swiftly from one person to the next as he tried to figure out what the hell was going on.

'Stay back!' he warned, and pressed the pistol more closely to the director general's temple.

Detective Ironside raised his hands palm up to Hawker and shook his head.

'Take it easy,' he said quickly. 'Nobody wants to get shot here. It's over, Hawker, we know you're behind all of this. Put the weapon down, okay?'

Hawker narrowed his eyes as he tried to keep his eyes on all of the intruders.

'You won't get away with this,' he hissed. 'I know what you all are. You were all at the JCOS briefing at Polaris Station, you knew everything.'

Detective Vasquez raised an eyebrow. 'Are you kidding me?'

Hawker saw the six CSS soldiers glance in surprise at the police detectives.

'You had inside knowledge,' Hawker went on. 'You came back here and you started the invasion early because you knew we were onto you.'

Detective Ironsides almost laughed. 'We were the ones doing the investigating! If it wasn't for us, nobody would have known that the infiltrators were here at all!'

'Indeed,' Hawker agreed, 'it's tough to arrest a killer if you're wandering around looking for yourself.'

'We captured one of them,' Foxx added.

'A clever ploy to lead us off the trail,' Hawker retaliated. 'And that meant the infiltrator had access to you, all of you. It could have obtained your identities at any time!'

'I fired it out of an airlock,' Nathan said.

'So you might say, but none of the rest of us saw it! It could be anywhere!'

Foxx threw her hands to her head.

'Damn it, this is getting us nowhere! The whole purpose of the infiltrators is to set us against ourselves and it's working! Commodore Hawker, we have evidence that you're a Sentinel, a leader of the infiltrators.'

Hawker stared at Foxx for a long moment, genuine surprise and fear wracking his body.

'But I haven't done anything!'

'You're holding a gun to the director general's head, sir,' Detective Allen pointed out.

'But she's one of *them*!'

'And we think *you're* one of them!' Foxx insisted.

Hawker pulled Arianna closer to him, the gun still firmly against her temple.

'If you kill me I'll take her with me,' he insisted.

'If we were the enemy, that would play right into our hands,' Vasquez pointed out. 'Removing government from play weakens the structure of our society. You're not winning any fans here, Hawker.'

From beneath Hawker's grip Arianna spoke, her voice trembling.

'They kill us for our identities but they don't need to,' she gasped. 'Something's missing. Why would they kill to do that, when they could more easily adopt identities using black market ID chips?'

'Because then there would be two of each person wandering around,' Foxx replied. 'Sensors would detect that too easily.'

'But not if they were separated by light years, as per the colonies,' Arianna said. 'It might take weeks or even months for the data to filter through. They could have travelled here and settled in among us without the risk of being exposed due to their murders being interrupted and the police turning up.'

Commodore Hawker's grip eased without conscious thought. 'They must *need* something,' he said. 'Something from us, from our bodies, to be able to function.'

Arianna Coburn turned her head to him as far as she could.

'They,' she said. 'You said *they*.'

Hawker stared down at the director general, and at the pistol he was pressing against her skull, and he realized suddenly what had happened.

'Oh hell,' he whispered, and then looked up at the armed guards watching him. 'But any one of you could be...'

Nathan Ironside stepped forward, blocking the aim of the CSS guards.

'The thing that the infiltrators need is body tissue as a disguise and water, that's why they kill and assume human identities. The only way to solve this is to reactivate the holosaps. They can figure out who's who without fear of being replicated. You're the one who shut them down, Commodore, so we figure it must be you who's behind all of this because you're the one calling the shots.'

Now, Hawker stared at Ironside for a long moment. 'I did not make that order.'

Detective Allen frowned.

'We know that you did, we all saw the broadcast.'

'Yes,' Hawker agreed, 'I broadcast the order, but it did not come from me.'

Hawker looked down at Arianna and he suddenly released her as he stared at Nathan. Nathan thought back to their meeting with the JCOS at Polaris Station and then he realized. *The handshake, dry and rough, as though the skin were parched. The infiltrators cannot hold water for long.*

'Admiral O'Hara,' Hawker whispered. 'O'Hara gave me the orders to be broadcast in his absence. He also ordered the *holosaps* to be shut down.'

Nathan stepped forward and took the gun from Hawker.

'Where is O'Hara now?'

Hawker directed a fearful gaze at Nathan.

'He's at Polaris Station in command of the fleet,' he replied, 'and he shut down all communications to avoid betraying their position to the enemy.'

'I don't think that's what he had in mind,' Nathan said. 'He did it so that he could take control of the fleet.'

***

XXXVIII

CSS Titan

Admiral Jefferson Marshall strode onto the bridge of the fleet's flagship and surveyed the crew as they worked at their stations. Over thirty men and women served aboard the flagship's bridge and another three thousand in the armory, flight deck, galleys, war room, engineering and maintenance sections. A floating city in the depths of space, Titan had been at the forefront of the last few battles of the Ayleean War, one of three Ships of the Line newly constructed to strike fear into the hearts of the Ayleeans.

Now, the Ayleeans were no more.

'Tactical?'

Titan's Executive Officer, Olsen, a fleet commander with thirty years' experience replied with the efficiency of the born and bred military officer.

'Battle ready on all fronts, admiral.'

'CAG?'

The Commander of the Air Group replied with brisk, clipped tones.

'All flights ready, all launch catapults prepared with pilots awaiting orders.'

Marshall nodded as he stepped up onto the command platform and settled into his seat. Before him was the usual broad display screen, now showing vast tracts of deep space where the fleet had gathered outside of the Sol System as per tactical protocol. Although the natural temptation was to position close to earth to protect it directly, Marshall and every other commander knew that it would be like standing in front of a gun and hoping one could duck the plasma round when it came out of the barrel. The Ayleeans had been completely overwhelmed, their fleet shattered. CSS would not allow the same calamity to overtake its warships, which would monitor relay stations just outside Sol's heliosphere and wait for their enemy to arrive.

'On our turf, but on our terms,' Marshall whispered to himself.

On the main tactical display beside the viewing screen he could see Titan's location at the head of more than thirty warships, all cruising under the colors of many flags. Although CSS was an organization that embraced all nations and all creeds, thousands of years of territorial patriotism was a hard thing to breed out of people. Much of planet earth was now given over to nature, with cities perched on the largest rivers but most small towns and urban areas long gone along with the borders that defined them. However, that did not stop the people from considering themselves as Russian, British, American or whatever other flag they may perceive themselves to have been born under. Even those born in the orbital cities who had never once visited the earth defined themselves by which country their station orbited above, and their cultural dialects and accents remained recognizable and were even deliberately maintained by people for whom an identity distinct from others was considered a birth right. Ironically it was only here in deep space, far from any sense of home, that all men and women became what they had always been and served only one flag: that of humanity.

'Priority fleet wide signal, incoming!'

Marshall's reverie was broken by the communications officer's call, and almost immediately a perfectly formed hologram of Rear Admiral Vincent O'Hara shimmered into life on the command platform before Marshall. He waited as the admiral stood with his hands behind his back and his chin held high to address every ship in the fleet.

'We have been here before,' he began solemnly. 'Our ancestors fought to survive conflicts, disease, social strife and inequality countless times in history, and always we have fought each other. Even in the wake of *The Falling* we fought each other, struggled to build new futures in isolation, segregated those who suffered more than we did. Now, for the first time in our history, we stand together side by side to defend our homes against an enemy for whom we have given no slight, against whom we have mounted no attack. An enemy who does not know us, does not understand us and shows no indication of doing anything but destroying us.' O'Hara paused thoughtfully. 'Ayleea has fallen, their species extinct. They were unable to defend themselves against the onslaught that overtook them. We must not fall prey to the same fate that they did: they let their enemy in without knowing it.'

Admiral Marshall listened, aware that the bridge of the warship was utterly silent, the crew hanging on the admiral's every word.

'We here are united and we must remain so. The enemy will seek to divide us, and we must resist. No ship that comes out of the Ayleean system can be trusted, for all there have been infiltrated by our enemy and represent the greatest danger to any military force: an enemy within. They must be treated just like any other enemy ship and destroyed if they make it back to Sol, for the security of the fleet and of our defense of earth.'

Marshall frowned as he thought of Captain Travis Harper and of Endeavour's narrow escape from the clutches of the enemy.

'It is almost certain that our enemy will arrive soon and that their attack on earth will begin in earnest. I trust that every man and woman in the fleet will do their duty, that you understand that the safety and security of every human being alive in this universe of ours rests in your hands.' O'Hara placed one hand over his left chest. '*Defensionem ut impetum.*'

In response, the crew automatically mirrored his actions in chorus. 'Defense as attack.'

Admiral O'Hara's transmission cut out and Marshall leaned back in his seat.

'A touch one sided,' Olsen murmured alongside him, quietly enough that the rest of the crew wouldn't hear. 'Endeavour got away okay.'

'That's what I was thinking,' Marshall said. 'What happened to Harper anyway?'

'He was taken away for debriefing at Polaris Station,' Olsen replied.

'I think that Admiral O'Hara did it personally.'

'I promised him a command on his release,' Marshall said, 'and gave him Victory with O'Donnell as his XO.'

Marshall glanced at the tactical display and saw the frigate CSS Victory nearby. Most of Endeavour's crew had been transferred to Victory to bolster her ready for the battle, while others had been posted to a cruiser named CSS Valiant. Marshall found himself watching the vessels with an intense gaze but he couldn't figure out why the ship suddenly seemed so important to him.

'Enemy.'

The word was whispered by the tactical officer as a simple warning. There needed to be nothing more said, the single word enough to inform Marshall that an enemy signature had been detected by Sol's most outlying relay stations.

'Battle status, now.'

Marshall snapped the order and instantly Titan's bridge lighting became subdued to a dull red that alerted the crew that battle was likely imminent.

'This is it,' Olsen said. 'How do you want to play the game?'

'To win,' Marshall replied, an old habit of theirs before committing to battle. 'Tactical?'

'Multiple signatures,' came the terse reply. 'At least twelve of them. They're too distant to calculate mass, all moving super luminal toward Sol.'

Could be warships, could be scouts, Marshall reflected. Either way, it didn't matter. They weren't CSS or private vessels otherwise the call of "enemy" wouldn't have been used. These were vessels entering Sol space that were not recognized as human, and that meant they had to be destroyed.

'Can you calculate their destination?' he asked.

The tactical officer nodded as he scrutinized the data on his screens.

'Looks like they're heading for Polaris Station, admiral.'

That made sense, Marshall reflected. Their plan was probably to overwhelm the military response before advancing upon an undefended earth.

'Prepare for super luminal leap,' Marshall ordered. 'Ambush trajectory, Alpha Group and Delta Group. Beta and Charlie to act as a rear guard and reinforcements.'

'Aye, cap'n.'

Alpha and Delta group each had a single capital ship, in this case Titan and Pegasus respectively, along with two frigates each and a small armada of cruisers and destroyers. A third ship of the line, Poseidon, led Beta and Charlie Group. Marshall's plan of attack was simple, and he spoke it out loud.

'We don't know our enemy's strengths or tactics or their weaponry for that matter,' he said to Olsen. 'We'll ambush them, hit them hard, and then escape if necessary.'

'Guerrilla warfare,' Olsen nodded in appreciation. 'Works for me. Fighters?'

'We hold them in stand by,' Marshall replied. 'I don't want to commit to a long slog against the enemy until we know what they're capable of. One capital ship almost took out two frigates with two shots. Let's not give them the chance to hit back too soon, eh?'

'Aye captain,' Olsen nodded.

Titan's mass drive hummed into life as the helmsman responded automatically. Wired directly into the ship's controls and data linked to Marshall's ID chip, the helmsman reacted quite literally with the speed of Marshall's thoughts. Although the Admiral frequently called orders to the helm by force of habit, the helmsman was already executing a manoeuver by the time Marshall opened his mouth, saving precious fractions of a second in battle.

'Super luminal in three, two, one..., now!'

Titan's bridge surged with a light spectrum and the huge warship blasted into super luminal cruise along with the fleet close behind.

*

CSS Defiance

'Five minutes to Sol.'

The tension on the bridge was palpable as Captain Lucas rapped her fingers on the armrest of her chair and watched the tactical display. Although it was entirely blank she knew in her heart of hearts that the enemy was right behind them.

'There was nothing else that we could do,' the XO, Walker, said to her. 'We had to run and we had to come home.'

Lucas nodded in agreement but said nothing. Sula watched the captain but held her tongue. She felt an overwhelming need to comfort Lucas despite now knowing that the captain was more than capable of shouldering the burden of command. None the less, Sula knew now what CSS crews faced in battle, what her father had faced time and time again in the massive dogfights against Ayleean warriors like the ones who now were aboard their ship.

The bridge entrance opened and Sula turned to see Lieutenant Tyrone Hackett walk in with a customary loose limbed stride, flanked by two Marines who kept their eyes on him and their rifles at port arms. Captain Lucas shot out of her seat.

'Lieutenant,' she said as he approached. 'Tell me something that doesn't involve us losing battles.'

Tyrone's gaze met Sula's and lingered there for a moment before he walked by. Ellen held out a clenched fist and Tyrone bumped it with his own and a brilliant smile.

'Where would you like me to start?' he asked the captain.

'Anywhere damn it, just get talkin' and don't stop until you're done.'

Tyrone took a brief moment to order his thoughts.

'The enemy are octopedal in biology and appear to have an aquatic or amphibious nature and origin,' he said. 'That much was clear when we encountered them. They're fast, aggressive and it seemed to me they take pleasure in attacking other species. You could sort of see it in their black eyes, the beady little bast…'

'Arduous as your battles may have been we need information,' Lucas cut him off. 'Are they attacking us for a reason?'

Tyrone nodded.

'Yeah,' he replied, 'Shylo and the elders said that the invaders treated them something like cattle. It was like a harvest or something, and that the Ayleeans were mostly loaded onto ships along with other lifeforms on the planet and shipped off somewhere.'

'Cattle?' Sula uttered.

'Yeah,' Tyrone said. 'Looks like we're on the menu for something. Either they use other species as slaves or they have them for dinner. Either way, it's a fair bet that whatever's waiting for us on the other side of harvest day isn't hugs and kisses.'

Captain Lucas nodded. 'What of their ships?'

'I don't know much,' Tyrone said, 'but the Ayleeans reckoned that the octopeds didn't build the ships they're travelling in. Their biology doesn't match up with the ships they're using too well, suggesting they were taken from other species during similar invasions.'

Captain Lucas punched a clenched fist into the palm of her hand as she looked at Walker.

'That means they'll have weaknesses,' she said. 'They won't be able to operate their ships as well as the original builders, and that might be why they need to weaken their victims from the inside *before* they can invade.'

Sula saw the XO nodding in agreement, perhaps the first time that he had done so since they'd embarked on their mission.

'Stands to reason,' he said. 'Those capital ships are very powerful and should be more than a match for our fleet if they had more than, say, half a dozen of them. But if they're merely hitching a lift on somebody else's ride…'

Captain Lucas turned away from them and looked up at the display screen, even though it showed nothing but an absolute blackness as deep as oblivion.

'Where is Shylo?' Tyrone asked. 'And the elders?'

'They're being held in the landing bay under armed guard,' the XO replied.

'Captain, the Ayleeans got me out of there,' Tyrone said. 'They're on our side, so there's no need to keep them locked up.'

Walker shook his head.

'We can't take the risk that they'll attack us themselves. They just lost their planet and their people and they're not the most trusting of species at the best of times. Letting a couple hundred of them just wander around a CSS frigate during time of war would be tantamount to suicide.'

'They have children, lives,' Tyrone snapped. 'They're as much people as we are.'

Sula stared at Tyrone and couldn't help the smile that spread on her features.

'Wow,' she said, 'what did they feed you down there, hot shot? You sound like you actually *like* some of them.'

Tyrone cast a withering glance in her direction.

'Like is too strong a word,' he replied. 'But tolerate, yeah, definitely. I wouldn't be here if they hadn't got me out and besides, you could use their help.'

'How so?' Captain Lucas demanded.

Tyrone turned to her. 'How many Marines you got aboard Defiance?'

'Two hundred,' Lucas replied, 'plus fourteen Special Forces.'

'Any one of those octopeds is worth four men in a fight,' Tyrone replied. 'And the Ayleeans below decks are the only ones who have engaged them in open battle, hand to hand. How much do you think they're gonna be worth if this comes down to a boarding fight?'

Captain Lucas bit her lip uncertainly and Sula instinctively came to Tyrone's aid.

'Captain, if Lieutenant Hackett can so completely change his tune regarding how he feels about the Ayleeans, then either he's learned something new about them or he's under the influence of the kind of drugs I think we all could use right now.'

A ripple of bitter laughter rattled around the bridge. Captain Lucas eyed Tyrone for a moment and then she nodded, to the XO's dismay.

'Release them from custody,' she said. 'Bring their leader to me.'

Tyrone whirled to carry out the order, but not before he flashed Sula a smile that caused her skin to flush a deep shade of crimson.

'Ensign?' the captain snapped.

Sula almost jumped out of her skin and turned to Lucas. 'Yes ma'am?'

'We may be about to go into battle and you're not signed up for this,' she said. 'I want you on a shuttle off the ship as soon as we get a picture of the battlefield, understood?'

'But I can help,' Sula said. 'I already did!'

'And I appreciate it,' Lucas replied, 'but I won't fight this ship with one hand behind my back. Your time will come but it's not now, okay?'

Sula's shoulders sank but Lieutenant Goldberg stepped up alongside her. 'That would be a tactically unsound decision, ma'am, based on Ensign Reyon's performance so far.'

'I concur,' said a voice behind her, and she turned to see Tyrone move alongside his wingman. 'We're stronger together, right?'

Captain Lucas shook her head.

'Don't say I didn't warn you,' she said as she turned to the bridge crew. 'Bring the ship to battle status!"

***

XXXIX

CSS Titan

'Sub luminal in twenty seconds, captain.'

Admiral Marshall stood on the command platform, as was his habit, his chair ignored behind him as he prepared himself for battle. With no information available when in super luminal cruise, he was reliant on the picture of the developing battlefield that he had just before they'd engaged the mass drives. Multiple targets, all heading directly toward Saturn on a trajectory that suggested they would attempt an ambush at close range.

'Prepare all stations for a frontal assault,' he ordered. 'We can't let them slip through too close to earth or any of the orbital stations.'

'Aye, captain,' Olsen acknowledged, the bridge crew carrying out their tasks with a quiet discipline and lack of ostentation that masked their anxiety.

Marshall had been in this position a couple dozen times in his career. Although the bridge seemed quiet he could detect the tension, a live current in the air seething unseen between them all. They were on the verge of open battle and virtually every officer aboard the ship had seen recordings and read books about the last, great battle fought by a CSS fleet action at Proxima Centauri, against the Ayleeans. Some seventy vessels were engaged in that final, titanic engagement that cost the lives of thousands of CSS personnel and many more Ayleeans. Marshall could recall vividly the tremendous exchanges of plasma fire, the vast cloud of ionized debris and gas like a planetary nebula flickering with diabolical lightning as the warships engaged each other at close range. Like all battles, tactics and strategy only took you so far. Eventually, inevitably, it came down to a slugging match at close range as the opposing sides tore chunks out of each other until a final, deciding blow was delivered.

That blow, fortunately for the CSS fleet, had been the destruction of the Aylcean flagship *Riizoor* when a series of well placed and timed bombardments ignited the plasma store deep inside her hull. The entire armory and most of her engine bays had been obliterated in a blast so powerful that for several minutes the battle itself subsided, the tremendous and instantaneous loss of life subduing even the most brazen of warriors.

The Ayleean cause had been doomed from that moment onward.

Marshall knew that his enemy possessed warships of greater power than his own and that his only chance of defeating them in battle was to create a similar, devastating attack. Not for him would there be a traditional engagement. This time it was hit hard and run fast, and then come back again to keep their enemy on their toes, keep them confused and unable to use their superior firepower to dominate the battlefield.

'Ten seconds, captain.'

Marshall cracked his knuckles and straightened his uniform.

'It's time, ladies and gentlemen,' he said simply, avoiding the convention of sharing elaborate words of inspiration at a time when he knew many may lose their lives. 'May providence favour us, the enemy fear us and the battle go our way, because this is *our* home. *Defensionem ut impetum.*'

'Defense as attack!' snapped the bridge crew, and on cue the navigation officer called out the countdown.

'Four, three, two, one, *now!*'

The bridge blurred in a spectrum of light as the massive capital ship decelerated out of super luminal. The main viewing screen flared brilliant white and then showed a vast field of stars and the distant disc of Saturn looming nearby. In an instant, at a glance, Marshall was able to orientate himself to their location and picked out earth as a speck of light no brighter than a distant star in the blackness.

Marshall's eyes flicked to the tactical display and even before he could give any orders he saw the rest of the fleet flash out of super luminal behind Titan and then the tactical officer shouted a warning.

'Multiple gravity wells, all cardinal points! They're coming!'

Marshall glanced at the tactical display and saw the fleet moving into ambush positions, forming the "horns of the bull" to envelop the enemy within a barrage of plasma fire. He looked at Olsen, the XO.

'All weapons on full charge, we hit them as soon as they arrive.'

'Aye, cap'n!'

The star fields before the fleet suddenly rippled as several gravity wells shimmered into existence, the space time "bow shock" of the incoming enemy vessels telegraphed a few seconds before they emerged from super luminal cruise. Marshall felt the old tension rise to a new peak, the agonizing waiting finally over and the chance to act upon him.

'For what we are about to receive, may providence make us truly thankful,' he murmured.

A moment later and the rippling star fields burst with brilliant flares of white light and Marshall saw not one, or two or even three but a dozen massive Marauders surge out of super luminal and rush into position before the CSS fleet.

'All vessels, fire now!'

Marshall shouted the command as he clenched one fist before him, determined to get the first strike in. From Titan and all of the fleet's ships a seething barrage of blue–white plasma rained inward toward the newly arrived Marauders and he saw the salvos begin to impact in brilliant explosions that rippled like lighting across the vast ships.

'Direct hits, all quarters on all vessels!' the tactical officer yelled jubilantly. 'We're detecting shield deficiencies and power surges across the enemy's fleet!'

'Good!' Marshall yelled. 'Reposition and hit them again, keep moving and...'

'Incoming fire, brace for impact!'

Marshall heard the command but he could not quite believe it as he could see the enemy fleet and they had not yet fired a single shot.

'Where away?!'

The reply came just before the impact.

'Port bow captain, it's one of ours, it's Victory!'

Before Marshall could reply the CSS frigate's lethal barrage plowed into Titan with the strength of fallen angels. Marshall saw on the main display screen the massive broadside fired from barely a hull length away.

The bridge shuddered as Titan reeled under the blows and the ship's electrical systems burst outward in showers of sparks and flame as she was overwhelmed by the sheer level of energy washing across her shields.

'All ships, break off the attack!' Marshall yelled. 'Get clear of each other! The fleet has been infiltrated!'

'All lines of communication are down!' the communications officer yelled as another savage barrage slammed into Titan. 'The fleet's channel codes have been flushed and we're being jammed! We can't talk to each other!'

Marshall stared in horror at the tactical display as he saw the fleet begin to break formation, ships veering away from one another as they began firing in desperation at the attacking vessels, both those of the enemy and those of the CSS fleet now firing upon their comrades in arms. Marshall heard in his mind the words of Doctor Schmidt taunt him from afar: *divide and conquer, captain.*

Polaris Station. Suddenly Marshall knew without a doubt what had happened, that his entire fleet had been deliberately manoeuvred into this precise position. Olsen had said that O'Hara had debriefed Captain Travis Harper himself, and now Harper, a long time friend of Marshall's was firing on Titan with frenzied salvos that were battering the warship's port flank. The command codes were in the hands of Admiral Vincent O'Hara and he had shut them down, replacing them with new codes and thus opening every ship in the fleet up to the infiltrators or to be controlled by O'Hara directly from Polaris Station.

Arianna Coburn had been right, the enemy had been among mankind for a very long time, at least long enough to infiltrate the highest positions in the military.

'We're getting a distress call planet side!' shouted the tactical officer as Titan's hull groaned under another salvo and the lights flickered weakly. 'Their shields and plasma guns around CSS HQ are all down. Everything's being shut down!'

Marshall saw in his mind's eye Ayleea, so totally overwhelmed that it had lost its entire fleet and then its entire population, and now he knew how. Utter, complete and total destruction of the defense and command infrastructure from within. He looked at the display screen and saw the enemy capital ships cruising at a leisurely pace past the battle toward earth as the CSS vessels broke up in disarray around them.

'Pegasus is firing on us!'

'Return fire!' Olsen yelled. 'All batteries open up on...'

'Belay that order!' Marshall snapped, knowing that Pegasus had been on Rim patrol until recently and could not have fallen prey to the same infiltration as Travis Harper. 'That ship's been taken over but the crew are still with us!'

Olsen stared at Marshall in horror as what had transpired overcame him too. Not only were their ships firing on each other, they could not fire back without killing their own people.

Titan rocked as Victory's barrage smashed into her hull and the shields went down as the bridge was plunged into a blackness broken only by the showers of flaming wreckage crashing down around Marshall. The main display screen flickered out as the links were severed and he turned to the tactical display nearby to see the enemy Marauders slowly turning to engage them.

The final blow.

They would hit the CSS vessels hard now, starting with those not under their control like Titan. Marshall gripped his seat for support as the massive ship shuddered and trembled beneath the plasma blows raining down upon her from Pegasus.

'Tactical?!'

'We've got nothing, captain! Shields are at seventeen percent, hull integrity is collapsing, hull breaches on four decks and we've lost contact with the engine room!'

Marshall glanced at the displays still working nearby and saw the Phantom fighters waiting on the catapults.

'Launch the fighters, all of them!' Marshall called. 'Maybe they can take out the Marauders' gun emplacements!'

'Aye, cap'n!'

Marshall saw wave after wave of Phantom fighters rocket out of the launch bays as the main display screen flickered back into life. His heart sank as he saw the star fields now strewn with debris from a battle where the enemy had yet to fire a single shot. Allied frigates, corvettes and capital ships fired upon their own in a raging storm of plasma that zipped and rocketed back and forth between them as a vast cloud of ionized gas and debris grew in the light of the distant sun's glow.

'Fog of war!' Olsen called out. 'Captain, we have to retreat!'

'We stay and we fight!'

'We're only fighting our own people! We'll lose the battle no matter what we do now! We have to fall back and try to protect earth!'

Marshall agonized as he saw several Marauders turning toward them, their huge plasma cannons lining up to deliver the fatal blasts that would annihilate the CSS fleet in a single action, one ship after another.

***

XL

Polaris Station

Nathan felt a surge and his vision blurred as the shuttle decelerated out of super luminal cruise and the vast baleful eye of Saturn loomed out of the darkness before them. Her rings filled his field of vision as he sat in the rear of the cockpit, Betty at the controls and Foxx seated next to her.

'They're not going to want us here,' Betty said. 'Arianna Coburn handed control of the military to O'Hara and he's closed down any means of warning the fleet. All communications channels are shut off.'

'We have to get aboard,' Nathan said. 'There must be somebody out here who will listen to us.'

Betty shrugged, her head wound hastily bandaged. 'It's out of my hands, I've never served in CSS and neither have any of my family.'

'What about Admiral Marshall?' Nathan asked Foxx.

'He'll be aboard Titan,' Foxx replied. 'Our only hope now is Doctor Schmidt.'

Nathan turned to see the holographic form of Schmidt sitting alongside Allen and Vasquez in the shuttle's main cabin, although whether a holosap actually needed to "sit" was debatable. Commodore Hawker had succeeded in "reviving" the good doctor before they had left CSS Headquarters using source codes stored in the building.

'Can you get us in there?' Nathan asked.

Schmidt nodded, his entire existence currently reliant upon the power from the shuttle's engines.

'I can get you aboard, but as soon as I access the appropriate communications channels I will no longer be isolated aboard this shuttle and Admiral O'Hara will be alerted to my presence.'

Foxx turned to Admiral Hawker, who was sitting alongside Schmidt in the rear of the shuttle.

'You can get us close,' she said. 'O'Hara doesn't know you're wise to what he's been doing. They'll let you aboard if they think you're still on side.'

'The fleet is in terrible danger,' Hawker protested. 'I should be at my command and he'll know that.'

'So tell as much of the truth as possible,' Nathan replied. 'Tell him that the fleet is in danger and you wish to serve there, even if it means accepting defeat. You think that Polaris Station should be evacuated and as many human lives saved from the invasion as possible.'

'He'll see through it,' Hawker baulked. 'If O'Hara's been an infiltrator for so long, he'll not take any chances.'

'It's common sense and it's believable,' Vasquez pressed, 'given the circumstances. Once we're inside Polaris, we cut Schmidt loose and hopefully he can override O'Hara's shut down protocols and get the fleet back on line.'

'How long will you need?' Nathan asked Schmidt.

'Moments,' he replied, 'but Admiral O'Hara's infiltrator will likely have converted the codes he's used into physical form, something that cannot be traced using computers in order to prevent him from being remotely bypassed as we are trying to do. The only way we can pin him down will be to literally take them from him, and in that I cannot help you.'

Foxx watched as Betty guided the shuttle toward Polaris Station.

'We need to land close to O'Hara.'

'The station shields are down,' she said in surprise. 'O'Hara must have shut everything down to hasten the invasion and the fleet's defeat.'

'Including the fleet's defenses and probably earth's too,' Hawker spat in fury.

Vasquez pointed to the uppermost tip of the vast station.

'That's the control and conference rooms,' he said. 'The highest point of any military structure is where you'll likely find the top dogs.'

'If we try and land there O'Hara will likely see us coming and have us blasted into shrapnel,' Allen pointed out.

'Then we're gonna have to be quick about it,' Foxx said and glanced at the pilot. 'Betty?'

'I'm on it,' she replied as she guided the shuttle in. 'We're cleared to land in Delta Bay Fourteen, but I'll pull up at the last moment and put us in Alpha Three. That's as close as I can get you to the conference rooms.'

Foxx nodded and checked her pistol.

'We don't know how many of these infiltrators there are aboard the station, and those that are not infiltrators will likely think that we are once the shots start flying. This needs to be fast, understood?'

'I get it,' Allen said, 'but we can't just start shooting. We don't know who we need to hit.'

'That's where I come in,' Schmidt said. 'I cannot alter O'Hara's physical codes, but I can broadcast the ocular implant update I coded as soon as we get aboard, based on body temperature. From Polaris Station the update will reach all implants almost instantaneously across the system and within an hour or so on the colonies. Everybody will know the difference between friend and foe because they'll light up like Christmas trees.'

Nathan pulled his pistol out as Betty slowed for a landing, the vast mushroom shaped form of Polaris Station filling the screen before them.

'I want O'Hara,' he said to Foxx in a low voice.

'Don't make this personal,' she replied. 'O'Hara is dead. The thing in his place probably wouldn't understand revenge even if you do manage to kill it.'

'I saw the look on that thing's face when I sent it out of that airlock on New Washington,' Nathan insisted. 'They fear death, just like we do.'

Foxx closed her eyes before she replied.

'I've been here before, Nathan, when I lost my parents,' she said softly, 'and trust me, no matter what you do or what you achieve, that hole inside you will never, ever be filled. Sula's gone, Nathan. All we can do is try to prevent others from suffering the same fate.'

Nathan gripped his pistol tighter but said nothing as Betty lined up for landing.

'Here we go,' she warned them.

At the last moment she opened the throttles and pitched the shuttle steeply up, climbing clear of the delta deck bay and up to the alpha decks. Almost immediately an alarm blared as officers inside the control towers bellowed at her.

'Be prepared for a frosty reception!' she chortled.

The shuttle landed inside the alpha bay just before the blast doors crashed down to seal it and Foxx hit the emergency open button on the main exit. The doors hissed open and she jumped out with Nathan, Allen and Vasquez right behind them.

'You there!'

Nathan saw four armed CSS guards dash into the landing bay.

'Gentlemen!' Commodore Hawker called to them. 'The station has been compromised and we're here to...'

The guards opened fire as Foxx yanked the commodore into cover behind the shuttle's fuselage as a stream of plasma shots rocketed past and burst against the shuttle's hull.

'Damnably rude of them!' Hawker blustered.

'Damnably,' Foxx agreed as she fired a couple of shots over the shuttle's nose to keep the guards occupied. 'We can't kill these guys. Where's Schmidt?'

Nathan looked up and saw the doctor's glowing blue form materialize in an office alongside the landing bay.

'He's live and in the system,' he replied.

Schmidt's ephemeral form began accessing the station's data streams as Nathan ducked down, a salvo of plasma fire spraying searing hot globules across the landing bay deck nearby.

Vasquez and Allen fired back, their shots going high as Commodore Hawker yelled out again.

'Stand down! We're here to identify the infiltrators!'

'You're the infiltrators!' came the reply. 'Admiral O'Hara has already identified you and you landed illegally!'

'Admiral O'Hara is the enemy!' Hawker yelled back above the gunfire.

'This is getting old real fast!' Foxx snapped as she fired again. 'Schmidt, you done yet?!'

Nathan glanced across at the office and saw that the holographic form had vanished already.

'He's not there!'

'Damn it!' Vasquez snapped. 'They must have shut him down already!'

Nathan was about to ask what the hell they were going to do next when a ferocious barrage of plasma fire showered down around them. Nathan ducked down and away from the lethal blasts and heard the drumming of countless boots on the deck. Before he or Foxx could respond, an entire platoon of Marines rushed around the sides of the shuttle, weapons aimed at them.

'Put your weapons down!'

Nathan knew that they couldn't hope to shoot faster than the troops now surrounding them and he immediately set his pistol down.

'We're here from New Washington,' he said quickly. 'We have a way of identifying the infiltrators.'

'Sure you do,' the Marine lieutenant snapped. 'Face down on the deck, all of you!'

'He's telling the damned truth!' Hawker snapped. 'Don't you know who I am?'

The Marine sneered at Hawker.

'Right now I don't know who anybody is, so get on your face or

I'll blow it off right here and now!'

Hawker blanched and lay flat on his chest as the Marines scowled down at them.

'What do we do with them?'

The lieutenant appeared to weigh up whether to imprison them when a hologram shimmered into life and Rear Admiral Vincent O'Hara stood before them, his hands behind his back.

'Good work,' he said as he saw the Marines standing over Hawker and his companions. 'Have them detained immediately before they can do any more damage. Ensure that they are kept inside a hard light quarantine unit so that they cannot infect anybody else.'

'You're the infection!' Hawker snapped. 'Why have you shut off the defensive shields to our entire fleet and this station?'

'I have done no such thing,' O'Hara replied. 'I am trying to reinstate the power as we speak, and no doubt you were hoping to stop me.'

Nathan looked up at O'Hara from where he lay on the deck with a Marine's boot between his shoulder blades.

'We know what you've done, but we're one step ahead of you!'

'It doesn't look that way to me, detective.'

'Then reinstate the holosaps,' Nathan snapped. 'They're our only defense against the infiltrators because they cannot be mimicked.'

Admiral O'Hara shook his head

'Until the communications channels are secure we cannot afford the risk.'

'They were never breached,' Foxx replied. 'You shut them down to prevent us from broadcasting a fix to ocular implants that would identify infiltrators to everybody!'

O'Hara frowned. 'I would have done no such thing.'

'Then reinstate the holosaps,' Nathan repeated. 'If you are who you say you are, we can identify infiltrators immediately before the fleet is destroyed.'

The Marines glanced at O'Hara, who shook his head in pity.

'Nice try, but I won't compromise the security of our military channels until I'm sure every last infiltrator is safely under lock and key. You'll just use the channels to further doom our fleet. Take them away!'

O'Hara's hologram vanished and Nathan looked at the Marine lieutenant.

'Reinstate the holosaps,' he said. 'They're our only hope. Don't take my word for it or O'Hara's. Just do it and you'll see!'

The Marine's eyes narrowed as he considered the request. He glanced at his corporal, who shrugged uncertainly. 'The admiral will string you up by the balls if you disobey a direct order.'

'So will I if you don't,' Commodore Hawker growled. 'Do it, you have nothing to lose. If we're infiltrators, why would we ask you to do the one thing that will expose us? Use your damned head, man!'

The Marine watched them for a moment longer and then turned to his corporal.

'Do it,' he said, 'quietly.'

The corporal hurried away to the nearby office and descended the steps. Nathan watched him walk inside and move across to a control panel. Moments later, Doctor Schmidt's hologram flickered back into life.

'I'd better not regret this,' the Marine growled at Foxx as he watched her down the barrel of his rifle.

'You won't,' she replied. 'Just watch.'

Nathan saw Doctor Schmidt gesture to the Marine corporal and then suddenly Nathan's ocular implant flashed and he saw an update bar rapidly flicker before him. Moments later, he looked up at the Marines and saw one of them with an angry bright red border flashing around his body.

'Enemy!'

Nathan saw the Marines recoil from the soldier in their midst, who whirled and aimed at the lieutenant. The soldier was cut down in a hail of plasma fire before he could pull the trigger and Nathan saw his body collapsing amid a cloud of swirling embers and hissing material that was clearly anything but flesh and bone.

'Holy mother of...' The Marine lieutenant stared at the smoldering pile of molten slag now starting to crawl across the landing bay deck away from them. 'Fry that thing, right now!'

The Marines encircled the remains and opened fire, plasma rounds decimating the remaining material into a lifeless stream of molten cells. Nathan got to his feet as the Marine lieutenant saw Commodore Hawker stand up.

'Commodore!' he snapped to attention. 'You have to realize that we had no idea that...'

'Silence!' Hawker snapped. 'I am more than aware of the dilemma you faced. Right now the important thing is to locate Admiral O'Hara. He is one of them, an infiltrator, and he must be stopped!'

Doctor Schmidt materialized before them, his features creased with anxiety.

'The fleet is in danger of being defeated and O'Hara has disappeared. As expected, I cannot find the codes.'

***

XLI

Nathan set off at a run with Foxx and the Marines alongside him. Already he could hear across the station the sound of plasma fire as infiltrators were identified among the staff and gunned down with extreme prejudice.

Nathan reached an elevator shaft and leaped inside, the doors closing as two Marines joined him with Foxx. The elevator climbed away as Vasquez, Allen and Commodore Hawker waited for another elevator to become available.

Nathan flinched in surprise as Doctor Schmidt shimmered into existence alongside them.

'The fleet's ships are being controlled from here, Polaris Station,' he informed Nathan. 'Roughly one third of our vessels are engaging their own allies and the enemy is moving into position to finish the job. CSS Victory appears to be entirely controlled by infiltrators.'

Nathan gripped his plasma pistol more tightly as he willed the elevator to travel faster.

'Can we get word to the rest of the station that Admiral O'Hara is the source?'

'I fear that it would do little good,' Schmidt replied. 'The admiral is dead and I don't think that our intruder will maintain his likeness for long now that the secret is out.'

The elevator's hard light doors opened and Nathan rushed out onto a long corridor that led to the main conference room where O'Hara had been holding court. Already he could see that the doors had been sealed shut from the inside, red beacons signalling that they were locked.

'Can you open those doors?' Nathan asked as he ran with the Marines.

'I can do one better than that,' Schmidt replied as he vanished from view.

Foxx ran up alongside Nathan, her pistol held double handed before her and always looking far too big for her small hands.

'What's he doing?' one of the Marines asked.

'Having a look,' Nathan guessed in reply, and was rewarded as Schmidt appeared before them once more.

'O'Hara is not inside and nor is the intruder. O'Hara's ID chip is located inside the room but has been abandoned.'

'Damn it,' Nathan cursed, fury boiling through his veins. 'He must be somewhere. Can we track his form?'

'He could have broken up into several different pieces and without proper scanning equipment it could take hours to find him,' Schmidt said. 'Right now we have no way of knowing how to reverse whatever he has done with the override codes.'

Foxx looked at her data display and cursed.

'The communications links are back up, but the fleet's taking a pounding and they're not going to last much longer. If we don't get Admiral Marshall his full fleet back it'll all be over no matter what happens here.'

Nathan struggled to conceive a way out of their predicament but no matter what he considered nothing seemed capable of averting the tragedy that was unfolding outside.

'There's *nothing* we can do?' he asked Schmidt again.

'The codes were comprehensively altered,' Schmidt reminded him. 'O'Hara can do what he likes with the fleet's vessels and we cannot stop him until we can access the codes.'

'Then how is he doing it?' Nathan asked. 'Where is he able to place these commands? The ships can't fly themselves, right?'

'No, but they can be commanded to attack other vessels on autopilot and the crews locked out of the command interface,' Schmidt replied. 'It was an emergency measure designed to prevent a boarding force from taking permanent control of an allied ship by turning her against an attacking force if control was lost. Of course, nobody could have foreseen the codes being used against us by what we thought were our own people. Only the highest ranking and most loyal members of military rank were entrusted with them. If I hadn't been shut down I might have got new codes to them by now.'

Nathan stared at Schmidt and a new thought blossomed into life.

'If the ships were entirely shut down, would they reboot under new command codes?'

'No, the codes are hard wired in and the ship's computers will remember them.'

'Damn it, there has to be a way!'

Schmidt shrugged apologetically.

'I'm afraid that the whole system was designed to prevent an enemy from successfully boarding our ships and using them against us,' he said. 'The whole point of the safety system is that there *isn't* a way out of it.'

'Maybe if we find out where O'Hara is emitting the signals from we could shut them down?' Foxx suggested.

'It wouldn't make a difference to the ships themselves,' Schmidt countered. 'They will continue on in the absence of any further commands from Polaris Station.'

Commodore Hawker looked at the entrance to the conference chamber and turned to the Marines.

'Blast those doors. I want in there.'

The Marines did not hesitate to obey, rushing toward the doors and setting up a series of explosive charges around the control mechanism in the wall alongside them.

'O'Hara's infiltrator is not in there,' Schmidt said, 'I already looked.'

Nathan tucked himself against the wall as the Marines retreated from their charges.

'I don't care, maybe we missed something. He couldn't have gone far.'

Moments later the charges detonated, blasting a small hole in the wall and frying the circuitry inside. The hard light doors' opaque surface vanished and one of the Marines jogged forward and checked the power cables.

'It's down,' he reported.

Nathan hurried through the open doorway and into the chamber and saw before him the large room. The long table was still there and surrounded by chairs hastily vacated by the JCOS team as they left to join their ships.

Nathan surveyed the room for a long moment but he could see nothing out of place.

'It must be here, somewhere,' he said. 'It must be something physical, something that O'Hara could have held in his hand or worn somehow.'

Foxx frowned as she looked around. 'O'Hara took off, he might have taken it with him.'

Nathan turned to Schmidt. 'You said communications were back on line. Can you check to see if any of the station's sensors are detecting anomalous intruders present?'

Schmidt paused a moment, his eyes almost glazing over as he accessed the station's data banks and sensor arrays.

'Negative,' he replied finally. 'Every member of staff has been accounted for, and seventeen infiltrators destroyed. The station is clean.'

'Except for O'Hara,' Nathan said as he looked about them. 'He must be in the room.'

'But there's nobody here,' Foxx said, 'and his ID chip is here on the table.'

'They're shape shifters, remember,' Nathan said as he looked about.

His eyes fell on the chairs around the table and the moment they did, he knew what had happened. There had been twelve chairs around the table when he had last been here, but now he counted fifteen scattered before him. Worse, the table was sheened with an oddly glossy surface as though it had been recently wiped down.

'The furniture,' he said.

Before anybody could respond one of the chairs changed shape and a wickedly sharp blade whipped out and pressed into Commodore Hawker's ribcage as the chair began wrapping around him like a snake entwining itself around a tree. Hawker gasped in horror and Nathan took aim but already he could see that Hawker could be killed in an instant as Admiral O'Hara's form mutated from inanimate materials into something recognizably human. As he watched he saw the material move like a fluid from the surface of the table, slithering and rippling as it joined up once again with the other two chairs and transformed until O'Hara stood before them, his right hand a blade pressed against Hawker's ribs and the other arm about the commodore's neck.

'Don't shoot,' Nathan said as the Marines' rifles pointed at O'Hara.

The infiltrator smiled. 'It is too late.'

'It's never too late,' Foxx replied.

'The invasion is already over,' came the reply, recognizably O'Hara's voice but the tone and delivery sneering and cruel. 'Your fleet is doomed and the rest of you will not survive the day.'

'What the hell do you *want* with us?' Nathan asked in exasperation.

Again, the cold smile.

'You are *corvu,*' it said as though Nathan should understand what that meant. When it saw the confusion on their faces, it used another word. 'You are fuel.'

'Fuel for what?' Vasquez asked.

'For everything,' came the reply.

Nathan frowned as he saw the blade pressed against Hawker's body. The entity could have killed him in an instant but it had not done so.

'It's a distraction,' Nathan realized spontaneously. He stepped back and holstered his pistol. 'It's playing for time for some reason and won't kill the commodore yet because it *can't*.'

Foxx glanced curiously at Nathan but she followed his lead and stepped back, lowering her pistol. The malicious glimmer on O'Hara's face fell slightly.

'You are doomed,' he insisted.

Nathan ignored him and turned away to look at the table alongside them. Upon it were scattered data pads, probably left there when the JCOS had left for their posts. Vasquez, Allen and Foxx all saw the direction of his glance at the same time and they pounced on the data pads and began trying to open them.

'They're all password protected,' Foxx snapped.

Doctor Schmidt stepped forward.

'Put them all in a pile on the table,' he ordered.

'You're doomed!' O'Hara snapped again. 'I will kill him.'

Nathan deliberately ignored the entity but he glanced instead at the Marines.

'Keep your weapons trained on it. If it moves, kill it.'

The Marines obeyed instantly, much to the commodore's distress. Nathan watched as Doctor Schmidt bowed over at the waist and his head vanished into the pile of data pads Vasquez and Allen had piled up on the table. He remained there for several seconds and then he emerged.

'Pad four, password echo echo one nine three.'

Foxx grabbed the pad and entered the password and immediately the screen lit up as Admiral O'Hara let out a shriek as he released Hawker and leaped toward Foxx. The Marines fired instantly and the blasts hit the entity directly in the chest and hurled it backward in a cloud of smoldering embers and incandescent cells. The creature wailed as it struggled to recombine itself as Nathan whirled to the soldiers.

'Containment unit, now!'

The Marines rushed forward and tossed a high energy projection unit that unfolded as it flew through the air. It landed over the entity as it writhed on the deck, and in an instant a hard light cubicle formed around it and sealed it inside as Nathan hurried to Hawker's side.

'Are you okay?'

The commodore nodded as he got to his feet, relief in his eyes. His relief turned to confusion as he saw the look on Nathan's face.

'You could at least look a little more cheerful that I'm okay?'

Nathan wasn't looking at the commodore. As he had helped the old man to his feet so he had looked out of the broad windows before them that displayed Saturn's immense panorama, and there he had seen something truly terrifying.

'We're out of time,' he said.

They all turned, and there against the flare of the sun loomed an immense, wedge shaped craft at least twice the size of Polaris Station. Nathan stared in horror at the vast spaceship, its hull flickering with tiny pin prick lights. Flanked by four Marauder capital ships, the immense vessel was moving directly toward them and gradually blocking out the light from the sun as it did so.

'A harvester of some kind,' Commodore Hawker said. 'That's what O'Hara must have been talking about. Look at the size of it.'

Nathan turned to Schmidt, who was already accessing the data pad's internal codes.

'Do you have them?' Nathan asked.

Schmidt's head finally popped up and he nodded.

'I'm rewriting the codes as we speak.'

'Then stop speaking and send them, now!'

***

XLII

CSS Titan

'Brace for impact!'

Admiral Marshall reached across for the command rail, his vision blurred as blood trickled down his forehead from a cut. The great ship's deck heaved as another devastating broadside slammed into it from a nearby Marauder and the lights on the bridge flickered out once more.

'Hull integrity critical!' shouted the tactical officer. 'Engines almost out!'

Marshall could see the main display panel showing the fleet in total disarray, the Marauders cruising through the cloud of debris and firing on any vessel within range.

'Plasma cannons are depleted and we don't have enough energy to recharge them!' Olsen called, his own features wracked with desperation. 'We're out of options!'

Marshall saw the Marauders turning slowly before them, huge plasma cannons coming to bear on the frigate Valiant. Even before he could cry out a useless warning he saw the massive cannons loose off a series of shots. The huge rounds plowed through the debris field and smashed into the badly damaged frigate and suddenly the entire ship vanished amid a brilliant supernova of searing white light. Marshall threw his hands up to shield his eyes as the frigate was consumed by the blast and exploded in a fearsome fireball that expanded rapidly out into the frigid cosmos.

'We lost Valiant!' called the tactical officer. 'Pegasus is still out of control, Illustrious and the Russians are pulling out!'

Marshall could see the smaller ships turning away from the fight and fleeing, firing back at the huge Marauders as they went. The big vessels turned slowly to pursue the frigates, and Marshall felt the old rage of his youth fire up once more inside his belly.

'Helm, full power, take us closer to that Marauder!'

The helmsman was already responding to Marshall's thoughts, Titan turning onto an intercept course with the lead Marauder.

'What the hell are you doing?' Olsen stammered. 'You're following a pursuit course?!'

Marshall didn't reply as he used his communicator to contact the ship's compliment of Marines.

'Sergeant Agry, prepare your Marines for a boarding assault!'

Olsen stared in disbelief at the admiral. 'A *what*?!'

'We're out classed and out gunned!' Marshall snapped. 'The only chance we have is to take one of those capital ships for ourselves!'

'Are you out of your mind?!' Olsen raged. 'We can't take them on! We're losing the battle and we're on the verge of losing the war!'

Marshall said nothing as he turned to the helm, watching as Titan accelerated in pursuit of the Marauder. The ship shook as another of CSS Victory's broadsides caught it a glancing blow astern.

'This is insane!' Olsen shouted, but suddenly a realization dawned in his eyes as he stared at Marshall with a strange expression.

'What?' the admiral asked, off guard.

'You don't want to board them,' Olsen gasped. 'You want *us* to be boarded!'

'What?'

'You're one of them,' Olsen said as he pointed at Marshall. 'Why else would you order the fleet's flagship on a suicide mission?!'

'Because I wouldn't order another to do something that I'm not prepared to do myself,' Marshall shot back. 'You're either with me or you're guilty of treason and dereliction of duty, Olsen. Get in line or get off the bridge!'

'The hell I will!' Olsen shouted as one hand moved for the service pistol at his belt.

'Don't do it,' Marshall warned.

Four Marine guards around the bridge tensed up, their rifles held at port arms but all of them teetering on the verge of intervention as the ship's internal lighting flickered as the power surged in and out.

'I'm relieving you of command,' Olsen said as he drew his pistol.

'It doesn't matter,' Marshall said. 'Our fleet has been sabotaged, Olsen. The only way out of this is to take away their advantage, to neutralize the capital ships. We can't win the battle any other way.'

'We're not attacking that capital ship and boarding her!'

'Defense as attack,' Marshall said as the bridge rocked again, Titan shouldering another massive salvo of plasma shots. 'That's our motto.'

Olsen wavered as he looked at the tactical displays and saw the Marauder beginning to turn away from them. Marshall saw it too and he screwed his brow up as he watched the capital ship veering away from them.

'They're turning,' the tactical officer called. 'They're pulling back.'

Marshall turned to the main display and saw the big Marauder actively trying to get away from Titan, and suddenly Marshall was hit by a revelation as he looked at the big ship's hull.

'I'll be damned,' he uttered. 'Helm, get us as close as you can to her!'

The ship was already turning and accelerating as Olsen pointed the pistol at Marshall.

'I said I'm relieving you of...'

'They've got a weak spot!' Marshall cut him off and pointed at the screen. 'Look at them, damn it! Those huge cannons and the smaller plasma batteries! It doesn't make tactical sense because if we get close in with them, they can't shoot us with their main guns and our own sabotaged ships can't hit us without risking damaging the Marauders!'

Olsen looked from the tactical display and back to the main viewing panel.

'And if they board us we'll lose Titan to them! The battle will be lost and earth exposed!'

'The battle is already lost!' Marshall bellowed, finally losing patience and storming across the bridge to confront Olsen. 'We've fared no better than the Ayleeans because we're fighting on their terms! It's time to change the battlefield before we all die! For the last time, are you with me or not?!'

Olsen struggled, the pistol pressed against the admiral's chest as he wrestled with the dilemma. A wrong move now would cost them the battle, the war and most likely every living being on the earth.

'Damn it,' he uttered as he lowered the pistol. 'You better be right about this.'

'It's my job to be right,' Marshall snapped back.

He turned as Titan moved inside the arc of the Marauder's guns, the enemy capital ship fully twice as big as Titan. Instantly, the intense barrage of plasma fire ceased as both the Marauder and CSS Victory were denied the ability to maintain their attacks.

Marshall clenched the command rail with both hands, both elated that his gamble had paid off and anxious of what the Marines would find when they entered the enemy ship.

'The Marauder's hull integrity?' he demanded.

'Seventy eight per cent,' came the tactical officer's reply, 'and it's sectioned and double plated, probably ten to fifteen feet thick.'

Marshall nodded. The main screen now showed the Marauder's underbelly, a vast maze of interconnecting panels built not of identical forms but connected in a seemingly random pattern. Marshal squinted, peering at the unusual shapes.

'Keep scanning,' he ordered. 'Look for any kind of weak spot like exhaust vents, poorly fitting panels, anything.'

Moments later, the tactical officer responded.

'I've got something,' he said. 'A vent of some kind, it travels directly from the hull exterior into the belly of the ship, probably an exhaust. It's closed but we can get through it.'

Marshall nodded.

'Do it,' he ordered. 'Send the Marines in, full attack!'

*

Gunnery Sergeant Jenson Agry stood near a massive sealed hatch on Titan's upper decks and surveyed the one hundred strong Marine platoon before him. Titan's interior shuddered from small plasma blasts and internal fires, the lighting flickering weakly in and out as he spoke, his voice distorted by the atmospheric mask he wore.

'We have no idea what we're going to find in there,' he said, 'but we do know it's likely we will encounter the shape shifting material that invaded Titan some months ago. We're equipped to deal with that, so I want the glue tanks in first under heavy weapons escort, then the rest of us right behind. We secure the entry spot, hold position and ensure Titan can't be infiltrated before we allow more troops in and advance, understood?'

'*Hoo rar!*'

'If we can't secure the position we will be forced to order Titan to break off and leave us behind,' Agry added. 'We won't be able to risk letting the enemy aboard her.'

Corporal Ben Hodgson stood at the front of the Marine platoon along with twenty or so of the men who had survived the last encounter with the "goo", as they had taken to calling it. Agry nodded at them and stood aside, and immediately they went to work.

The Marines accessed the huge doors behind the sergeant and exposed a circular room with a top hatch, ten feet across and specifically designed to be used to board enemy vessels. The entire deck of the room was an elevator, while outside a hatch on Titan's massive hull were grappling hooks and plasma cutters designed to sheer through even the toughest hull plating.

The Marines boarded the elevator, half of them equipped with the anti goo tanks and the rest with heavy plasma guns. Moments later, Sergeant Agry activated the boarding protocol and the hatch closed as above them he heard the plasma cutters grind into the hull of the Marauder.

Immediately, the elevator platform began ascending. Agry checked his heavy plasma cannon one last time and then activated it. The plasma battery hummed into life, heat haze rippling up from the magazine as he looked up and saw through an observation panel clouds of sparks and whirling embers as the Marauder's hull was sheered through.

Moments later the cutters burst into the ship's interior and folded away like the petals of some grotesque metal flower blossoming inside the Marauder and the elevator rose up the final few feet and hatches opened on either side.

A rush of gas flooded across them as Sergeant Agry jogged out into the Marauder's interior with his Marines either side of him and promptly felt his boots leave the deck as zero gravity kicked in.

'Zero zero!' he ordered.

The troops activated small thrusters on their combat suits designed for *zero zero* combat: zero gravity, zero breathable atmosphere.

They were in a corridor of sorts but it wasn't like anything he'd seen before. The walls were forged from some kind of moss like material and the corridor itself was not straight but winding, while other corridors extended vertically up from their position and were illuminated only by a bizarre bioluminescent glow from something alive in the walls.

The air was moist, vapor spiraling in myriad clouds of droplets as Agry looked about him and tried to figure out what to do next. They were at a natural disadvantage in these poorly lit conditions, forced to fight on their enemy's terms and turf and…

'Enemy!'

Agry looked ahead and saw something moving in the misty confines of the tunnel before them. Moments later the dim illumination within the tunnel blinked out into utter, complete blackness and Agry's heart thumped against the wall of his chest like an incarcerated prisoner begging to be freed as he heard a hellish screeching sound rush upon them.

'Infra red!'

Agry's ocular implant flickered into IR vision and he almost panicked as he brought up the heavy gun at the roiling wall of creatures racing toward him in a gruesome flood. His brain had the chance to notice multiple legs, clicking beaks of some kind and bulky, horned bodies before his IR vision exploded with bright pulses of white plasma as the Marines opened up on their foes.

The screeching reached a new crescendo and Agry lost all sense of what he was looking at as the heat flares from the plasma shots blended into a fierce white light that blinded him to where the enemy was.

'Glow sticks now! IR off!'

Agry fired into the white mass of noise as with one hand he tossed a glow stick ahead of him. His ocular implant switched off at his mental command and he saw the blackness of the tunnel return to be illuminated by the glow from numerous luminescent tubes spinning through the tunnel away from him to collide with more creatures rushing upon their position from in front, behind and above.

In an instant he knew that they simply did not have enough firepower to hold their position, and he knew they could not let the creatures into the breaching pod behind him for fear that they might get aboard Titan.

Sergeant Agry knew the fight was already over and that he would never be able to secure their position against so many enemy, but he kept firing anyway.

***

XLIII

CSS Titan

'They're pinned down!'

The XO's voice rang out across the bridge as Marshall saw the communications feed from Sergeant Agry's Marines inside the enemy ship. He could hear the desperate gunfire and could see the gruesome creatures screeching and charging this way and that in the dim light as the soldiers tried to hold them at bay.

A scream of agony pierced his ears and he saw a Marine yanked from his position by one of the creatures, its thick beak shearing off the soldier's leg as though it were made of butter as two cruel stingers plunged into his chest and pierced his body armor. The Marine screamed in pain and then quivered in the grip of the creature as some vile cocktail of venom surged through his body and poisoned him, white foam spilling from his mouth. A hail of plasma fire rained down on the animal and drove it back but the shots also peppered the injured soldier and killed him.

Sergeant Agry's voice rang out above the din of battle.

There's too many of them!

Marshall stared in dismay as he realized that the Marines were about to be overpowered and that there was nothing he could do about it. Olsen's hand rested on his shoulder.

'Admiral,' the XO said softly, his voice strangely audible despite the noise of battle filling the bridge. 'We're done here.'

Marshall turned to Olsen. He knew that there was nothing else that they could do, no other plays left in the game other than to pull away and physically use Titan and the other fleet vessels as battering rams to try to smash the enemy ships to pieces.

'We're done,' he agreed, unable to look his XO in the eye.

There was nothing more he could do for any of them, either the

Marines aboard the Marauder or the people on earth. With a heavy heart, Marshall turned to the tactical officer and gave what he felt sure would be his last command.

'Withdraw,' he said, 'before our hull is breached.'

The tactical officer nodded solemnly, the voices of the fighting Marines echoing back and forth across the bridge as he reached out to disengage the boarding pod mechanism and fall back from the Marauder.

'New contact, bearing oh seven elevation five, CSS identification!'

Marshall looked up at the communications officer, the final vestiges of hope drained from his mind and body.

'Who is it?'

The officer looked up at him in surprise. 'It's Defiance, sir!'

Marshall raised an eyebrow. 'Defiance was destroyed in the…'

'They're requesting a channel, captain!'

'Open it!' Marshall snapped.

On the deck before him Marshall saw the holographic form of Captain Lucas standing before him.

'Admiral, Captain Jordyn Lucas, CSS Defiance!'

Marshall hesitated, uncertain of who he was looking at. 'Captain, right now I cannot rely on anything that you say due to our predicament regarding infiltrators that have been exposed here on earth. They replicate human appearance perfectly and we have evidence that your ship was destroyed in an explosion and…'

'Admiral, with all due respect shut the hell up and listen!' Lucas snapped, shocking Marshall into silence. 'The enemy ships were built by a different species to the ones that are inside them now! We've analyzed them and we believe that they were designed as mining vessels, not warships!'

Marshall stood up straighter.

'Mining vessels? We call them Marauders.'

'That's what their plasma cannons are designed for.

They're *not* warships! The plasma cannons are designed to blast asteroids and rock, to extract minerals from within them. The creatures aboard them now are scavengers and they're hiding behind the power of the capital ships. We're on our way to you now and we've brought some help.'

As Marshall watched, he saw a young man appear in a CSS flight suit flanked by two towering Ayeelan warriors.

'You want us to help even the odds there, admiral?' the pilot asked.

Before Marshall could reply, CSS Pegasus pulled up and away from them and the communications channels filled with the voices of the captains of other ships.

'This is CSS Pegasus, we have regained control. Repeat, we have regained control! Launching all fighters and redirecting attacks onto Marauders!'

'This is CSS Vanquish, we have regained control, vectoring for flank attack!'

'This is CSS Delphi, we have regained control, request orders!'

Admiral Marshall pushed himself off the command rail.

'Titan, belay my last and hold firm!' he snapped. 'Delphi, Pegasus and Vanquish, attack all targets and get in close! Get inside their guns and rip them apart! Defiance, your assistance would be most welcome. Board her with us and send your reinforcements immediately, we have Marines under fire in her lower decks!'

'Bright lights!' the CSS pilot with the Ayleeans said.

'Say what now?' Olsen asked.

'Bright lights!' the pilot repeated. 'The enemy are of aquatic origin and avoid bright light! It's their weakness!'

A ripple of excited anticipation surged through the ship as the bridge crew leaped into action and Marshall watched as Defiance rushed in alongside Titan and climbed into position to board the huge Marauder. Marshall turned to the viewing screen where Sergeant Agry's Marines were under fire.

'Get some damned spot lights to those Marines, now! And start jamming all of the enemy's communications, order Polaris Station to do the same! I want that enemy blind in more ways than just one!'

*

CSS Defiance

Tyrone Hackett jogged along at the head of the Ayleean warriors, leading them through the frigate as crew members staggered back and out of their way, shocked at the sight of the heavily armed Ayleean troops moving through the ship.

Tyrone reached the boarding hatch even as it was opening, and he ducked inside as Shylo and another twenty Ayleeans crammed inside, each dragging canisters of hemostatic agent and heavy, powerful flashlights alongside their plasma rifles.

'Twenty this time, no more!' Tyrone called out as more of the warriors tried to force their way in, eager to join the battle. 'We'll leave the hatch open topside and you can all climb up once we've secured the position!'

Although Tyrone had not given the command a second thought, he was somewhat surprised to see the warriors back off from the hatch entrance without argument, gripping their weapons tightly as the hatch doors closed.

'You're a natural leader,' Shylo growled down at him. 'But my men should be ashamed to obey commands from a mere human.'

'Yesterday you would have said they should kill me for giving them orders,' Tyrone replied, and smiled up at the warrior. 'You've gone soft, Shylo.'

Shylo glowered down at Tyrone as the boarding hatch rose up and the cutters did their work in a frenzied shower of embers, and then Tyrone activated his plasma rifle and looked up.

'Here we go! One for all and…'

The boarding hatches burst open and Tyrone saw a frenetic tumble of octopedal predators scrambling over the roof and plunging down into a misty corridor before them, beyond which he could see the flashes of plasma weapons and the screams of both human and alien combatants.

'…one for all!'

Tyrone rushed out with nineteen Ayleean warriors behind him all screaming with bloodlust as they opened fire into the enemy hordes. The octopeds screeched in agony and alarm cries went up among them as they turned to face the attack from behind and were met with a hail of plasma fire and brilliant, blinding white lights.

The octopeds' black eyes squinted and shied away from the brilliant illumination as the Ayleeans pored out into the corridor.

Tyrone went down onto one knee, propping his elbow on the extended knee and firing on automatic into the frenzy of entangled gray limbs and cruel black eyes. The stench of burning flesh and skin filled the corridor, a cloud of acrid blue smoke searing his eyes as plasma rounds blasted into the bodies of their attackers.

Tyrone checked behind him and saw more of the octopeds crawling over the top of the boarding hatch, but even as he shouted a warning so he saw dozens of Ayleeans flooding up and out of the breach, firing as they went and cutting the fresh intruders down.

Tyrone kept up his firing as Shylo and several other Ayleeans charged forward with long, polished blades in their hands that flashed in the white light beams. The towering warriors plunged into the fray with screeches of fury, their weapons crunching deep into the enemy's bodies or slicing clean through limbs and necks.

Tyrone backed up as thick, oozing purple blood snaked in pools like oil across the ship's decks, more Ayleeans rushing past him and plowing into the octopeds in a wave of fury that pushed them back. Tyrone ceased fire and grabbed a communicator as he yelled a warning. 'All CSS boarding forces, Ayleens in the vicinity are allied, repeat: they're allied, do not shoot!'

The flashes of plasma fire up ahead blazed through the thick smoke and mist like thunderstorms flashing in distant clouds as Tyrone edged forward. Before him in the corridor was a mass of twitching limbs, of gray bodies heaped upon one another and laced with streams of blood that spilled from deep wounds. The last of the Ayleeans thundered past him as they boarded the vessel and sprinted up and over the grim mound of corpses, rushing into battle as Tyrone's communicator crackled.

'Marine Force One, we're pinned down!'

Tyrone saw the Ayleeans rushing into the octoped creatures in a frenzy of clashing limbs, weapons and teeth, and beyond through in the fog of battle he saw what looked like CSS troops fighting toward them from the other direction, the bright lights blinding them just as effectively as it was blinding the octopeds.

'Oh no.'

Tyrone vaulted up onto the heaving mound of bodies and grabbed his communicator.

'Marine Force One, allied dead ahead! Repeat, allied ahead!'

Tyrone heard nothing but static on his communicator and he shoved it into his belt and clambered up over the amassed bodies as he fought to catch up with the agile Ayleeans as plasma shots flashed over his head and screams echoed all around him.

A thick segmented leg swept across his vision and slammed into his chest and he was hurled against the wall of the corridor as his pistol clattered onto the back of a fallen octoped. Tyrone's head smacked against the solid wall and his vision blurred as a wounded octoped crawled from the grisly mass of corpses, three of its limbs missing and one side of its head a bloodied tangle of purple blood and shattered gray exoskeleton.

The creature's bony limb pinned him in place by his chest as a second slammed into his throat. Tyrone's eyes bulged and his senses swam as the injured creature pushed against the bodies of its fallen comrades in an attempt to squeeze the life out of Tyrone.

Tyrone's right hand fumbled for a combat knife in his ankle sheath but he couldn't reach it and his vision was swimming with light and color. The octoped's shattered face sneered in agonized fury, blood pulsing ever faster from the hideous wounds to its skull as it leaned in and tried to break Tyrone's neck, unable to use its stingers which had been shrivelled and burned by plasma fire.

Tyrone's vision began to dim and he flailed for his knife, lifted his leg upwards toward his hand and suddenly he felt the handle of the blade brush his fingertips. He yanked the thick bladed weapon out and slammed it deep into the limb pinning his neck against the wall of the corridor.

The octoped squealed in pain but it did not release him, growling and pushing even harder. Tyrone twisted the blade with the last of his strength, seeking the nerves and blood vessels in the limb, and a fresh gush of purple blood spilled like glutinous ink across his hands as he ruptured an artery deep within the creature's body.

The octoped snarled in anger, pushed harder against the wall, but Tyrone felt the strength go out of the limb and suddenly it fell away from his neck as the other limb against his chest weakened. The octoped sagged, the rage still visible in its eyes but it's grim features collapsing as it slumped before him.

Tyrone dropped onto his knees, his voice ragged through his damaged throat and his breathing tight and whistling as he reached for his communicator. He tried to speak but no sounds came forth, his vision starring as he tried to reach the Marines he knew were just meters from where he crouched.

*

'Keep firing!'

Sergeant Agry's voice was barely audible above the din of battle as he fired two plasma rounds into the face of a charging octoped and watched the creature's bones and flesh melt away in a sizzling cloud of burning flesh as the animal slumped onto the deck before him.

'There's too damned many!'

Corporal Ben Hodgkins was pinned with four of his men across the far side of the corridor, the Marines firing in controlled and coordinated bursts to maintain a constant stream of withering plasma fire on the charging hordes before them.

'Keep firing by sections!' Agry yelled. 'Don't let your weapons overheat!'

The octopedal animals poured like a tangled gray flood over the fallen bodies of their brethren, a wave of wild black eyes and gnarled fangs and scuttling legs. Agry fired again, counting in his head both the number of rounds he had remaining and the pauses between each section firing.

The Marines were split into four sections of five men each, rotating their firing duties to prevent their plasma rifles from overheating and allowing their positions to be overrun by the enemy, but even such professional tactics were no use against so many.

'Fall back by sections!'

Agry fired two more rounds that seared through the belly of an octoped and sent it reeling in agony, trailing a cloud of blue smoke and savage black plasma wounds tearing its flank open. He glanced over his shoulder and saw the rear–most section of the platoon fall back ten paces down the corridor and then open fire once more.

Agry ducked low and dashed back toward them under their covering fire before taking up position again and firing on the first enemy he saw.

Through the thick smoke and vivid, flashing light of plasma blasts he saw an octoped rear up to leap toward them, its thick limbs clawing the air and its even thicker hind legs coiling to pounce. The creature shook under the tension in its muscles as Agry aimed to shoot it square in its chest.

In the light he saw something moving behind the octoped, and then the creature squealed and arched its back as blood sprayed in black arcs from its hind legs and it toppled over sideways. Agry saw a towering figure slashing left and right, a heavy blade severing the octoped's tendons and rendering it disabled as blinding beams of white light broke through the clouds of smoke clogging the air.

The figure raised the blade again and brought it crashing down into the octoped's skull, the creature slumping dead.

Agry's breath caught in his throat as he saw the figure rise up, humanoid but taller, a shaggy mane of hair and bright yellow eyes hungry with blood lust as it pounced on the next octoped before it and slashed down with savage blows, severing entire limbs with each devastating attack.

Ayleean.

Even as Sergeant Agry thought it so he saw dozens more Ayleean warriors pouring over the mound of dead octopeds, their blades flashing in the brilliant white light as they screamed and charged and crashed into the octopeds from behind. The charging creatures suddenly found themselves cornered between two forces and Agry saw the sudden surprise and anguish in their expressions.

'Hold your fire!'

Agry's command rang out in the corridor but it was several seconds before the Marines responded and their streams of plasma fire ceased. Agry crouched with his plasma rifle aimed into the hordes as they were decimated by the charging Ayleeans, the warriors coated with glistening sheens of purple blood as they hacked and slashed their way through the enemy, one of them doing so despite his other arm hanging by tenuous threads from his shoulder, his eyes wild with unstoppable bloodlust.

Three of the remaining octopeds reared up to charge at the Ayleeans and Agry switched his aim and fired upon them. The Marines behind him followed suit without orders, the hail of searing plasma fire cutting the octopeds down into smoldering shreds of burning tissue amid roiling clouds of blue smoke.

The plasma fire ceased, the corridor thick with smoke and the smell of blood and burning flesh. Agry kept his weapon in place, aimed down the corridor as through the smoke strode the Ayleean warriors. They walked side by side, blocking the corridor, advancing with chests heaving from the exertion of battle, eyes wild.

'Er, sergeant?'

Hodgkins glanced across at Agry uncertainly, his own rifle trained on the Ayleeans.

Agry glanced behind him at the boarding chute, a clear way back into Titan for an invading force.

'They could be shape shifters,' said another Marine.

Agry gripped his rifle tighter and called out.

'Stay where you are! Don't come any closer!'

The Ayleeans kept moving, driven by rage and the need for combat, their huge weapons smeared with blood that drooled from the tips of the blades.

'Don't make me shoot!' Agry yelled.

The Ayleeans paused, standing no more than five meters from the Marines, a wall of muscle and rage and hate glaring at them, their eyes flickering in the dim light and reflecting the flames licking around plasma scars in the walls. Slowly, the Ayeelans' blades lifted up, pointing at the Marines, a known sign of a challenge in Ayleean culture.

Agry wasn't about to waste any time second guessing their intentions, and he took aim at the lead warrior.

'Platoon, fir…!'

'Wait!'

The cry sounded like a cat that had just noticed its own tail was on fire, a bizarre and high–pitched squeal that was loud enough to cause everybody to look at it. Agry peered past the Ayleeans and saw a CSS pilot stumbling toward them, covered in blood and with a small white kerchief waving frantically above his head. To Agry's amazement, the pilot shoved his way past the towering, bloodied Ayleean warriors and waved the flag at him as he spoke.

'Th…. wth…mee.'

Agry squinted at the pilot. 'Say what?'

The pilot pointed at the Ayleeans and then pointed at himself. 'Wth... me.'

Sergeant Agry glanced at the Ayleeans, still poised to attack. The pilot turned and grabbed the leading warrior's blade and pushed it down as though he were a naughty child, pointing at him as though to warn him to behave.

'What the hell?' Hodgkins uttered.

Sergeant Agry stepped out of cover and stood up as the pilot staggered toward him, one hand moving to massage his throat. His voice was thin and wheezy, but now Agry could hear him more clearly.

'They're with me,' he said, 'they're with Defiance. We survived, and so did they.'

Agry looked over the pilot's shoulder suspiciously, but then his communicator crackled.

'Marine One, we have regained control of the fleet, be advised, allied aboard with you, allied and Ayleean!'

Agry heard the relief and surprise from his men, and he looked at the pilot and the Ayleeans with renewed hope.

'I have no damned idea what's happened here and I don't want to know,' he growled, and then louder so that the Ayleeans behind them could hear. 'Let's go take this ship for ourselves!'

A thunderous crescendo of screams seared the air as the Ayleeans waved their blades in the air and rushed past the Marines toward the ship's bridge.

***

XLIV

CSS Titan

Admiral Marshall watched as the CSS fleet began to turn in unison once more, and he heard the captains of the various ships reporting with joy as they recovered control of their vessels. Somewhere, somehow, Detectives Foxx and Ironside had come through once more.

'This is it!' Olsen said as he clenched a fist. 'This is where we turn it!'

Marshall watched as the massive harvester spacecraft hove slowly closer, its four flanking Marauder guards easing out from their formations to engage the CSS fleet. With so many of the capital class enemy ships facing them, even a fully united CSS fleet was already heavily out gunned and he knew that in a straight out fight with the gargantuan Marauders they would be utterly destroyed.

Titan, this is Marine One, we have the Marauder's bridge! Repeat, we have the bridge!

A cheer went up from the crew around Marshall and he looked about him with immense pride rising up like a swollen river inside him as he realized that Sergeant Agry's Marines had also prevailed. Titan's bridge was bathed in blood red light, half of her decking and wall panels blown out and with a faint haze of smoke in the air from fried electrical panels, but she was holding together and so were her people.

He looked at the Marauders closing in on them, and he knew what he had to do.

'Admiral Marshall to all vessels, heave to and cease fire.'

Olsen's joy collapsed into confusion and he stared at Marshall in horror.

'Admiral?'

Marshall stepped off the command platform and strode to the

center of the bridge deck.

'All vessels, heave to and cease fire immediately,' he repeated.

Marshall could sense the dismay on the bridge as his crew stared at him, wondering why on earth that he would choose to capitulate, to surrender at the moment that victory became possible.

Olsen hurried to Marshall's side. 'Admiral, we can win this!'

Marshall shook his head. 'No, we can't.'

'Damn it man, we have the fleet back! We can take them on!'

Marshall stood for a moment amid the silently tumbling waterfalls of sparks and the dull red glow of battle. He could hear the sound of other ships still engaged by the enemy, the commands of fighter pilots and bridge crews echoing around the bridge, but right now all he could think about were words that Arianna Coburn had said Doctor Schmidt had emphasised to her and others. *Divide and conquer.*

He turned to Olsen. 'Disengage from the Marauder and order Defiance to do the same. Drop our shields and shut down our plasma batteries.'

A rush of gasps filled the bridge and Olsen stared at Marshall in horror.

'But we've taken control of the Marauder and…'

Olsen's eyes widened as Marshall watched him, and understanding suddenly blossomed like a newborn star in his eyes.

'How about we give them some of their own medicine, XO?' Marshall suggested with a grin.

Olsen almost stumbled over his own words as he whirled to the crew. 'You heard the man! Disengage from the Marauder, send word to Defiance to follow our lead!'

Marshall turned to the communications officer.

'Send word to Agry's Marines,' he ordered. 'Find out if they think they can control that ship.'

The officer nodded in reply as Olsen hurried to Marshall's side.

'How close do you reckon we can get?'

Marshall judged the position of the harvester space station. 'Probably not close enough before they realize what's happening. Even a sustained barrage probably won't be enough to break her hull, she's just too damned big.'

Marshall kept one eye on the tactical display and watched as Titan slowly disengaged from the Marauder, Defiance likewise descending away from the capital ship with her shields down and her plasma batteries draining of their charge.

'*Admiral Marshall?*' Captain Lucas's voice echoed across the deck from Defiance. '*I take it there is a method to this madness?*'

'I want them to think we're beaten,' he replied. 'Let them drop their guard and let them think our Marines failed to take the Marauder.'

There was a long pause and then Captain Lucas's holographic form appeared before the admiral on Titan's deck.

'Get this wrong and we'll be right before their guns.'

Marshall nodded. 'Right where we want to be.'

Lucas peered at the admiral curiously. 'I'm all for out of the box, admiral, but I'm not sure what you've got in mind here and our Marines are now trapped aboard that Marauder.'

Marshall gestured to the tactical display before him.

'You got under their guns and so did we,' he replied. 'They didn't fire on us while there was a danger of them hitting their own. Same tactic, but this time we hit that harvester with everything we have from close range.'

Captain Lucas bit her lip as she thought about the idea. 'It's too big.'

Before Marshall could reply, he heard Sergeant Agry's voice cut in.

'*We have control of the Marauder. It's not going to be pretty, but we can do some good here.*'

'Good,' Marshall said. 'Charge her cannons, and open fire on Titan.'

'*What?!*' Olsen yelped.

'Break away from us and hit us with one shot on the port stern,' Marshall continued and then turned to the XO. 'Direct all shields to that quarter to protect us from the blow. I want the enemy to think the Marauder is still theirs. Make it happen!'

Captain Lucas pressed on.

'Insanely clever, or just insane,' she said, 'but even with that ship on our side, we can't guarantee we'll take out something as large as that harvester!'

Marshall knew that she was right, but then another voice piped up from somewhere on Defiance's deck.

'Use her like we used Fortitude.'

Lucas turned and Marshall saw a young blonde Ensign standing close behind the captain.

'Say what now?' Olsen asked, looking wearier by the moment.

Captain Lucas replied. 'We used Fortitude as a missile to take out one of the capital ships pursuing us out of the Ayleean system. It bought us enough time to leap out and get away. That Marauder is a quarter the size of the harvester but if it was on target at full pulse power...'

Titan rocked violently as a plasma salvo slammed into it from close range, and Marshall crashed sideways against his seat as he looked at the display screen and saw the nearby Marauder's plasma cannons glowing from where they'd opened fire.

'Some warning would have been helpful!' Marshall roared.

'*Oops,*' Lieutenant Hackett's voice crackled over the Marine's communications frequency.

Marshall turned to his crew.

'Do it,' he said to Olsen. 'Tell the Marines to program that Marauder onto a collision course, full power, and then get the hell off that ship!'

Marshall turned back to Captain Lucas as Titan's crew swung into action.

'Don't fire until they're almost on top of us,' he said. 'Lead us in, captain.'

'Aye, admiral.'

Marshall watched as the CSS fleet slowly began to break up under the barrage of plasma fire coming from the Marauders, scattering as though defeated and in disarray. He saw Pegasus turning away from the fight, her vast hull trailing a sparkling stream of metallic debris and gases, Defiance descending away from them as though disabled but turning slowly toward the incoming Marauders.

'Captain, we have a signal coming from CSS Victory!'

Marshall raised his chin.

'Open the channel.'

For a moment nothing happened, and then on a screen on the bridge appeared a face that they all recognized. Captain Travis Harper's features looked identical to the man they had all once known, but instantly Marshall knew that he was looking at something else.

'Your fleet is lost,' the entity said, it's eyes devoid of humanity, utterly without remorse. 'The battle is over. Surrender your forces and stand by to be boarded.'

Marshall kept his tone defiant as he replied.

'We demand the safe passage of all human beings and civilian vessels and the...'

'You are in no position to make demands,' Harper cut him off. 'Any delay in your surrender will result in your fleet's destruction, as occurred on Ayleea.'

Marshall ground his teeth in his jaw.

'Very well,' Marshall snapped and turned his head toward Olsen. 'Order the fleet to stand down and wait to be boarded.'

Olsen turned slowly and relayed the command. Marshall turned back to the entity.

'What the hell is it that you want with us?'

Travis Harper's features took on the appearance of contentment, as though victory was guaranteed, but it was an expression that looked oddly out of place. Harper's mannerisms and nature had never been that way, the captain a humble man who had risen through the ranks to his first command.

'You will be cared for,' came the reply, and then the entity leaned closer to the screen. 'Give us the new codes for your fleet's vessels.'

Marshall looked at the position of the huge harvester spacecraft now dominating the viewing screen before them. The escorting Marauders were moving to surround the fleet with the Marauders already present, the CSS fleet stationary amid a glowing cloud of heated gas and vast, sparkling veils of spinning debris. The Marauder under CSS control was facing directly toward the huge harvester, barely two hull lengths away, and the CSS ships were arrayed around it.

Marshall suppressed the urge to smile as he again looked at Olsen and directed a barely perceptible nod in Travis Harper's direction.

'Let 'em have it.'

Olsen spoke to the Marines aboard the Marauder. 'Give them all what they deserve.'

*

Tyrone Hackett heard Olsen's command as he stood on the bridge of the Marauder, the deck littered with the remains of octopedal crew.

Before them were a series of hexagonal screens, as though the bridge were the gigantic eye of some kind of insect, and beyond were multiple images of the same scene of the huge harvester craft. Whatever species had built these spacecraft saw the universe in a very different way to human beings and the species that had taken the vessel.

'Roger that,' he replied.

Tyrone looked down to where holes in the mossy control panels had been filled with metallic instruments to allow the octopedal species to control the ship. Before them, it appeared that some kind of biological appendages would have been inserted into the cavities to control the ship more directly. Now, with the octopedal species somewhat similar to humans in having limbs and digits, it had taken Tyrone and the Marines only a few minutes to figure out the basic controls.

'Hit it!' he ordered the Marines.

Without hesitation the soldiers opened up the throttles and aimed directly for the massive harvester vessel. The Marauder surged forward as it accelerated directly toward the bridge of the spacecraft facing them.

'Lock the harvester as a destination and then blast the communications console so they can't take back control!' Tyrone yelled. 'Then let's get the hell out of here!'

The Marines set the controls and then leaped up, the Ayleeans firing plasma rifles at the communications panels.

Tyrone checked one last time that they were locked into the enemy spacecraft, and then he turned and ran with the Marines and Ayleeans as they fled for the boarding hatches.

***

XLV

CSS Defiance

Captain Lucas watched as the frigate cruised beneath the huge Marauder and straight into the frenzy of plasma fire streaming from the enemy Marauders as they realized what was happening and tried to prevent the collision of the two enormous spacecraft.

'Keep us steady, full power to all shields!'

The frigate shuddered as a salvo of plasma shots pounded the shields, the Marauder above them taking several direct hits on its starboard plasma rail. Defiance shook and gyrated as its shields struggled to cope with the blows and a couple of panels sprayed sparks in fiery rain to scatter across the decks.

'They're almost here!' the tactical officer called. 'I've got multiple ID chips heading for the boarding tubes!'

Captain Lucas stood up out of her command chair, unable to continue while seated.

'Take us in close, get the hatches ready to open as soon as we dock!'

Before the reply could come a sudden terrific blast hit Defiance square on her starboard flank and the frigate's lights flickered out as explosive showers of sparks and electrical energy burst from her panelling. Captain Lucas shielded her eyes as she was hurled to one side by the impact and smashed into a control panel.

The frigate heeled over beneath the blows, and Sula knew in an instant that they were being directly targeted. She grabbed hold of the command rail and staggered across to Captain Lucas, and as she did so she saw CSS Victory charging toward them.

'They're trying to hit us to take the Marauder out!' she yelled above the din of explosions bursting all around them. 'We can't stay here!'

Captain Lucas struggled to her feet, blood oozing from a cut on her temple as she tried to assess the information flooding in to her on the remaining tactical displays.

'Shields are almost out!' Walker yelled. 'Hull breaches on two decks and we've lost atmosphere in one of the engine bays! Another direct hit and we're history!'

Lucas clenched her fist and slammed it down onto the control panel.

'Damn it! Pull us out, maximum pulse power and evasive manoeuvers! Target Victory!'

Lieutenant Goldberg stormed up to Lucas.

'We can't leave Tyrone and the others behind!'

'We can't reach them either!' Lucas yelled as she hauled herself to her feet. 'What good are we to them if we get them out but are then blown to hell before we can escape? We need to hit Victory first, hard!'

Ellen Goldberg looked at the captain for a brief moment and Sula saw the anguish on her face. There was no way the frigate could remain in place, her hull too easy a target for the nimble frigate Victory and…

Sula grabbed Ellen by her arm. 'Can you fly a shuttle?'

Ellen seemed momentarily hurt. 'Of course I can fly a damned shuttle but why would I want to get into one of those damned things and…'

Ellen's eyes lit up as she realized what Sula was getting at. Captain Lucas pushed the pilot away from her.

'What are you waiting for, get out there!'

Ellen turned and dashed for the bridge exit, and on impulse Sula dashed after her and they ran together down a corridor bound for the launch bays.

'What the hell are you doing coming with me?' Ellen yelled as she ran.

'My job! I'm here as your assistant, right?'

'This is a combat mission and you're not qualified to be…'

'You gonna fly out there, dock, open the hatches, get everyone inside and then get out of there all on your own?'

Ellen cussed under her breath but didn't reply as they dashed onto the flight deck and Ellen headed toward the nearest flight–ready shuttle. Sula leaped into the craft behind Ellen and hit the hatch closing mechanism as Ellen jumped into the captain's seat and flipped a series of emergency start switches.

Sula strapped into the co–pilot's seat as she saw an array of instruments glow in multi color confusion before her and heard the shuttle's engines whine into life. Ellen applied power and the shuttle lifted off the deck, turning toward a set of bay doors that were already opening.

Ellen opened the main throttles and the shuttle surged out of the bay and into the blackness of space just in time for Sula to see immense plasma charges rocketing toward them from the huge harvester craft, and more coming in from either side from the surrounding Marauders and CSS Victory.

'Hang on!'

The shuttle rocked and bucked as plasma blasts rushed by, Defiance diving downward steeply to avoid the salvo that smashed into the Marauder's plasma strakes amid vivid explosions that illuminated the shuttle's cockpit as Ellen pulled up again and aimed for the Marauder's steel belly.

Ahead, the harvester was looming large enough to fill the entire screen and would have been a tremendous sight were it not so utterly terrifying. The Marauder above them was accelerating every second, and already Sula could see that the harvester was turning away in an attempt to avoid the collision.

'Hurry!'

Sula leaned forward and looked up out of the shuttle's screen to see two ragged metallic protrusions poking out from beneath the huge capital ship.

'They're right above us!' she said.

'I've got them,' Ellen replied. 'Get in back and stand by the main hatches. This needs to be real quick!'

Sula unstrapped herself from her seat and dashed out of the cockpit and into the rear of the shuttle, which was large enough to hold fifty fully armed Marines. She moved to the center of the craft and looked at the side hatch, which was a universal fit for all CSS docking hatches and boarding tubes.

Sula moved to stand by the emergency release claws and hoped that Ellen Goldberg was half the pilot everybody said she was as a shower of plasma blasts hammered the ship above them.

*

Tyrone dashed down to the lower decks, Ayleeans running all around him in the same direction with the Marines struggling to keep up.

The huge Marauder was accelerating constantly and he knew that they could have only a minute or so before the ship slammed into the harvester capital ship and was torn apart by titanic forces. He staggered over the first of the inert corpses of the octopeds blocking the corridor, the Ayleeans vaulting lithely over the top and crashing down on the deck the other side like a stampede of antelope across the African veld.

Tyrone hauled his fatigued body over the gruesome mound and saw the Ayleeans all waiting on the other side around the boarding hatches.

'What are you waiting for?!' he demanded as he slid to the deck.

Then he saw Shylo pointing at the closed hatches.

'They have gone!'

Tyrone saw the bitter chill of the vacuum of space on the other side of the now sealed hatch windows, saw below him nothing but the hatch interior and then stars and occasional flashes of light as plasma blasts hammered the hull outside.

'Damn it, what the hell happened?!'

Sergeant Agry moved alongside them and shrugged.

'Welcome to the world of the soldier, fly boy. We're expendable, and Defiance probably couldn't take much more of that attack.'

'I knew it!' Tyrone cursed and threw his plasma pistol at the wall. 'I knew they couldn't be trusted. Damn it, they could've hung on for just a couple more minutes but *oh no*! They had to leave us stuck here in this floating coffin!'

'Somebody might make it back for us,' Corporal Hodgkins pointed out.

The ship shook as another massive salvo plowed into it and Tyrone struggled to stay on his feet.

'Nobody's coming for us! What kind of suicidal, half witted lunatic would show up here now?

Shylo pointed out of the window. 'Somebody's here.'

Tyrone peered out of the windows and saw a CSS shuttle appear and turn sideways before moving in close to the docking hatch. He grinned as he looked at Sergeant Agry.

'I *knew* they wouldn't let us down.'

The corridor shook again and this time large metal panels burst from the walls and Tyrone heard the hiss of escaping vapor and atmosphere as the hull began to fail all around them. He hugged the wall of the boarding hatch and hoped to hell that they would all make it out in time and…

Tyrone looked at the hundred fifty or so remaining Ayleean warriors and the twenty Marines around him, and he realized that even now they could not all make it out.

'A shuttle that size only holds fifty,' Corporal Hodgkins said above the din around them.

Tyrone looked at the docking shuttle and then at Shylo. The towering Ayleeans all exchanged glances, and then without a word they all stepped back from the hatch. Tyrone pushed off and shook his head.

'No, no way! We go together, all of us!'

Shylo said nothing but he raised one hand and placed it over his chest, wherein beat his massive heart.

'You have done enough,' he said, his customary low growl somewhat tempered by something that sounded dangerously close to emotion. 'You must go.'

Something clanged against the Marauder's hull below them with a dull boom and he saw the boarding hatch windows mist briefly as atmosphere returned to the interior from the docking shuttle. The boarding hatch hissed open once more as Tyrone saw the Ayleeans all take a further pace back from their only means of escape.

'We'll fit!' Tyrone shouted above the noise of battle. 'We'll fit somehow!'

Shylo didn't bother responding to Tyrone, knowing full well that they could never fit a hundred seventy into one shuttle. As one, all of the Ayleeans raised their hands and placed them over their chests, watching silently as the hatches opened and a young girl with blonde hair burst out.

'We've got thirty seconds!' she yelled.

Tyrone turned and stared at her in amazement. 'Sula?'

'All of you, get your asses in here now!' Sula yelled, and then she saw the ranks of Ayleeans. 'Oh.'

Sergeant Agry wasted no time and grabbed two of his men and shoved them by their collars into the hatch.

'Go, now, *move!*'

Sula saw the Marines tumble into the hatch until they were all gone, and then she whirled to the Ayleeans.

'Thirty in, now! That's our limit!'

None of the warriors moved, and Tyrone looked at them for one more moment and then placed his hand over his chest. Shylo nodded, and then Tyrone turned for the hatch with Sula.

'Anybody want a lift?!'

The voice came from behind Sula on the far side of the hatch, and they whirled to see a rangy man with shaggy hair and a detective's shield staggering toward them through the smoke and debris.

'Nathan?!'

Sula's eyes flew wide and she dashed toward the man and threw herself into his arms as Tyrone stared in bewilderment.

'Who the hell is this?!'

Nathan Ironside pointed at the Ayleeans and then jabbed a thumb over his shoulder. 'Second shuttle, room for all, move *now*!'

In an instant the Ayleeans blasted past Tyrone and Shylo knocked him physically into the boarding hatch with one shoulder as he passed by, twenty more warriors piling in behind him and hauling the hatch shut behind them as they plunged down into the shuttle waiting for them.

*

'What the hell are you doing here?!' Sula yelled as she ran and jumped into the second boarding hatch.

Nathan plunged in after her as ranks of Ayleeans poured in behind him.

'We saw Defiance return so we came looking for you!'

They landed hard inside the shuttle and then scrambled out of the way as Ayleeans thumped down all around them. Nathan staggered into the cockpit alongside Betty and strapped in as he yelled into the back.

'Grab a seat and hang on!'

The Ayleeans crammed into the shuttle as Sula crawled into the cockpit and sat on a seat behind Nathan. A rough, deep Ayleean growl from the shuttle's interior reached his ears.

'The hatch is closed, go, now!'

Betty *Buzz* Luther punched the release mechanism switches and the shuttle disengaged once more as the Marauder's bow smashed into the huge harvester with a brilliant flare of light that burst like a new born star before them and illuminated the cockpit. A rippling series of explosions tore down the length of the Marauder's hull as Betty hauled the shuttle around and slammed the throttles wide open.

The little spacecraft shook as it flew away from the impact, explosions rippling across the vast hull above them and hurling flaming debris across their flight path as Betty fought for control and turned away from the onslaught.

'Incoming, starboard!'

The warning from an Ayleean in the rear of the shuttle alerted Betty to the plasma bolts rushing toward them from starboard. She pushed forward on the control column and the shuttle plunged into a steep dive. The huge plasma bolts thundered past behind and above them and smashed into the Marauder as tremendous blasts tore her hull open.

The shuttle whirled away from the blasts and turned for open space as Nathan craned his neck around and looked behind them to see the Marauder's million ton hull tearing down through the harvester's immense bulk amid countless explosions and clouds of twisted metal plates spinning and spiraling into space. All around them the ships of the CSS fleet and the other Marauders banked hard and turned away away from the carnage.

And then Nathan threw his hands up before his face as the entire scene vanished into a brilliant halo of light so bright that his eyes streamed as he turned away.

***

XLVI

CSS Titan

'Direct hit!'

A ragged cheer went up across Titan's bridge as Admiral Marshall lowered his hands from his eyes as the tremendous blast faded enough for him to see the Marauder plunge deep into the harvester's hull. The entire vessel had smashed down at a forty five degree angle as the larger harvester had attempted to avoid the collision, and the increased velocity in the last few seconds before impact had driven the Marauder straight through the harvester's hull like a knife through the heart.

Marshall stood up and saw the Marauder's massive plasma strakes plowing through the harvester's bridge deck and a spreading network of brightly burning ruptures expand out from all impact points like a glowing spider's web. The Marauder's own engine bay had erupted during the collision as shockwaves reverberated through her hull and shook her cores loose, the cause of the blinding blast that had seared the vision of everyone watching.

Marshall shook himself from his torpor and yelled an order.

'All vessels, engage the nearest Marauder to Titan! Join forces, get under their guns and drive them back one at a time!'

Titan began to heel over as the helmsman changed course to charge at the nearest Marauder to their position. As the warship swung around so Marshall saw Pegasus turning toward the same ship, and almost at the same time their respective hulls lit up with devastating barrages of plasma fire. The salvos tore in toward the Marauder between the two CSS capital ships and slammed into her from both sides at once.

The huge Marauder briefly disappeared amid the blasts that rippled down her flanks, and even from five thousand meters Marshall could see on the display screen clouds of debris and flaming explosions flickering in the darkness as she was hit.

'Hull breaches and escaping gases detected!' the tactical officer yelled. 'She's hit!'

'Keep at her!' Marshall ordered as he clenched his fists beside his body. 'Give her everything!'

As Titan and Pegasus opened up again on the Marauder so Marshall saw Defiance and a stream of other frigates, corvettes and the British carrier Illustrious sweeping in from all directions around the battlefield. Streams of plasma fire ripped across the glowing cauldron of ionized gases and tumbling debris of the battlefield to smash into the Marauder. Marshall saw the big vessel fire back twice, her massive guns simply not equipped to engage so many targets at once, and the huge blasts sailed between Illustrious and Pegasus to pass harmlessly into deep space.

'Again!' Olsen yelled, forgetting himself in the heat of the battle. 'Hit her again!'

To Marshall's amazement the crew joined in, chanting again, *again, again!* Titan shuddered as her starboard batteries opened up in unison with those of Pegasus, the smaller ships circling the Marauder and firing continuously, looking like cruel gray sharks in a black sea circling some gigantic, wounded prey.

The plasma salvos consumed the Marauder and then suddenly her stern erupted in a savage double blast that caused an expanding shockwave to ripple visibly through the gas cloud. It hit Titan but was barely noticeable as Marshall saw the huge ship's engines explode with a violent expansion of pressurized gas and burning fuel.

Another cheer went up from the crew and Marshall slammed his fist jubilantly down on the command rail.

'All ships target the next nearest Marauder! Keep it together and stay close enough that they can't hit us without fear of hitting their own!'

Olsen glanced at the captain.

'They might try the same tactic, admiral,' he warned.

Marshall shook his head.

'No, Defiance was right, they're not warships. They don't have enough weapons for close engagement compared to us, they *have* to fight from a distance to win.'

As Marshall watched he could see the fleet turning and accelerating toward a second Marauder but to the starboard flank he could see CSS Victory, plasma salvos streaming from her port guns toward Pegasus.

'Tactical,' he ordered, 'turn all guns on CSS Victory.'

A somber mood enveloped the bridge at the order.

'Aye, captain.'

Moments later, Marshall watched as Titan unleashed a savage barrage of fire that streamed in toward Victory and slammed into her. The frigate, already damaged and trailing glittering debris in her wake, burst like an eggshell under the blasts and suddenly vanished amid an immense explosion that split her hull in two.

'Victory is down,' the tactical officer said, the regret clear in his tones. 'Enemy, dead ahead.'

Marshall turned his attention to the Marauder closing in on them at the bow. The enemy ship's immense plasma cannons glowing with restrained energy as she lined up her first shots while shouldering immense plasma salvos from Pegasus, which was passing her port flank.

'Stare her down and keep moving!' Marshall ordered the fleet. 'Hit her as soon as we're within range. All power to bow shields and prepare to get in close!'

'Aye, admiral!'

The Marauder closed in, her hull glowing both in the light from the nebula of battle and from fires across her flanks. Marshall braced himself for the attack, and then he saw the Marauder suddenly heel over and begin turning away. Even as he realized that she was turning so the tactical officer cried out.

'They're disengaging!'

Marshall turned to the tactical display and saw the Marauders splitting out of the battle in multiple directions, scattering to prevent any one of their remaining vessels becoming a target for the CSS fleet. The bridge crew burst into cheers once more, this time echoed across the communications channels as the crews of other ships in the fleet joined in with a gross but most welcome misuse of CSS fleet resources.

Marshall finally felt the tension drain from his shoulders and chest, the stress of battle beginning to subside as he watched the Marauders turn tail on the immense glowing clouds of ionized gas and burning debris. A few moments later, their hulls were surrounded by rippling gravity wells and then with flashes of bright white light they vanished into super luminal cruise.

'Victory,' Olsen yelled and clapped the admiral on the back.

Marshall nodded, his mind echoing with a single quote that he could not for the life of him recall who originally spoke it, but that had endured for centuries.

United we stand, divided we fall.

*

Polaris Station

Nathan stepped off the shuttle with Sula, Foxx, Vasquez and Allen onto a crowded landing bay filled with crews all disembarking from warships now moving in to dock for repairs. A flotilla of smaller fast corvettes from the British fleet had been dispatched to discreetly follow the enemy Marauders, to ensure that their flight from the battlefield was not a ruse to tempt the CSS fleet to drop their guard. As far as Nathan could gather, the Marauders had not yet dropped out of super luminal and were a long, long way from the Sol System.

'Detective Ironhead!'

Nathan saw Doctor Schmidt awaiting them on the deck, and

beside him a woman with bobbed dark hair and a smoldering gaze that could have melted metal from a distance.

'Ah,' Nathan said as he looked down at Sula.

'Ah,' she echoed.

Rosaline stepped away from the doctor and hurried to Sula before throwing her arms around her daughter. Nathan changed direction, deciding that he would be better off avoiding Rosaline for the time being until Sula explained exactly what had happened out there in the Ayleean system.

All around Nathan could see family members of serving CSS crew who had been flown out to the station to meet their loved ones. Detective Jay Allen held his wife, their infant child between them, Sula was with her mother, and even Vasquez was in a passionate clinch with an exotic looking woman who was evidently his current squeeze, the dark skin of her arms laced with chrome tattoos.

'Your time will come,' Foxx said as she noticed the direction of his gaze.

'That an offer?'

'Don't get cute with me.'

'I don't see anybody rushing to your side either,' Nathan said, and then noticed the little shadow that passed behind her eyes. 'You know I didn't mean that in a…'

'I know,' Foxx said.

Among the crews disembarking from shuttles and fighters were a tight knot of a hundred fifty blood–soaked Ayleen warriors who looked as though they were on the verge of panic, surrounded by humans who were all giving them a wide berth but for one. A single CSS pilot stood with them.

Nathan walked over to the pilot, who peered up at him.

'Nice timing on the rescue there,' he said. 'Are you Sula's father?'

'No,' Nathan replied. 'Her father was a pilot, like you. He died at Proxima Centauri.'

Tyrone Hackett's features shadowed with something that looked like a volatile fusion of realization and regret as the pilot's gaze flicked to Sula, who was standing nearby and arguing with an older woman.

'Damn,' was all he could say.

'I'm a family friend,' Nathan said. 'Just wanted to thank you for looking out for her.'

Tyrone blinked. 'I'm afraid she saved my ass…'

'As far as I understand it,' Admiral Marshall said as he strode to join them on the flight deck, 'you both saved a lot of people over the last two days. You should be proud of yourselves.'

Nathan managed a smile as the admiral shook his hand vigorously, the old man clearly beginning to suffer the after effects of battle, which for him meant showing emotions other than grumpiness. Then, the admiral turned to look at the towering Ayleean warriors huddled together and watching the events surrounding them with suspicious gazes.

Tyrone Hackett gestured to their leader.

'This is Shylo,' he said. 'He led the Ayleeans against our enemies. We wouldn't have got this far without them.'

The flight deck fell a little quieter as word spread and hundreds of CSS officers and enlisted personnel saw the admiral standing before the Ayleeans, their leathery skin smeared with purple blood from the enemy and red blood of their own.

Shylo's yellow eyes peered down at the admiral, a man who had led Titan into many battles in the Ayleean War and was responsible for taking the lives of countless Ayleeans. Marshall stared back at the huge warrior, and then he stepped forward a single pace and extended his hand.

'United we stand,' he said simply. 'Divided, we fall.'

Shylo stared down at the admiral for a long moment, and then one bloodied hand reached out and took the admiral's.

'Holy crap,' Vasquez uttered.

Slowly, one by one, the CSS officers and enlisted moved forward and began mingling more closely with the Ayleeans as Marshall kept his grip on Shylo.

'I understand that this is all that's left of your people on Ayleea,' he said.

Shylo nodded, saying nothing. The admiral took a breath.

'Once we get you settled in here, how about we figure out a way to find the rest of them and take back Ayleea, together?'

∗∗∗

XLVII

New Washington

Nathan sat in silence on his couch and stared at the lights of the city surrounding him, the walls of the apartment set to panoramic and thus transparent, giving Nathan the impression that he was sitting on a rooftop in the open air. To his left and right, the station's giant city-filled rim rose up like a metallic wave to soar overhead, the giddying backdrop of earth's vast blue, green and white surface turning slowly as the station rotated, brilliant sunlight casting moving shadows over the endlessly changing city scape. He could see showers falling to drench North Four's shadowy streets far above and to the right, shafts of sunlight casting rainbow hues through the downpours, while closer by beams of slow moving sunlight bathed the streets of Constitution Avenue and the Capitol Building.

Nathan could see all of that, but his focus instead remained on the *Lucidity Lens* before him. He knew that he could don the slim silver device, which attached to the forehead and stimulated lucid dreams as it placed the user in a mild state of sleep, enabling the user to control their own dreams and thus creating the ultimate virtual reality – one where there was no actual difference between the lucid state and reality itself. Nathan had heard the early adopters of the technology had died while using the lens, so enthralled by their virtual world and convinced of their own health and vitality within it that their real bodies had succumbed to dehydration, starvation and sickness. Laws enacted as a result allowed only two hour stretches inside the lens before it automatically cut off, although it was believed that "hacks" for the device allowed longer sessions. Many missing persons reports back at the precinct suggested heavy use of the lenses before the users vanished, some believed to carry out lengthy sessions that had ultimately resulted in their demise in some squalid den somewhere beyond the reach of law enforcement, like digital drug addicts.

Nathan had been just such an addict, unable to relinquish his memories of his true home and the family who had been dead for so many centuries, but now he had found a new focus, people who were alive now, who had become as important to him as his wife and daughter from so long ago.

A soft beeping intruded into his thoughts and he looked at the door to see Rosaline Reyon standing the other side. From her perspective, the door would appear opaque just like the apartment's walls. Nathan stood up and straightened his shirt.

'Enter.'

The hard light door shimmered out and Rosaline walked in, the door reappearing behind her.

'Detective.'

'It's Nathan. Please, take a seat.'

Rosaline sat down on one of the couches, a respectable distance from Nathan. He sat down and tried to relax.

'Sula okay?' he asked.

'She's planet side,' Rosaline said with a soft smile that was somehow filled with regret. 'Her little adventure cemented in her mind the idea that she wants to serve in the fleet. She's about to start her training at CSS HQ.'

'You must be very proud,' Nathan said. 'She already received a commendation for her service as an honorary Ensign aboard Defiance.'

Rosaline looked at her hands, folded in her lap. 'I am,' she said unconvincingly.

'We can't control what our children do,' Nathan said, 'even if we fear for them. They have to choose their own path.'

'That's what her father would have said,' Rosaline replied with an uneasy smile.

'It's what any decent father would say,' Nathan added. 'Sula has a strong sense of duty and great determination. A service in the fleet is just the kind of thing that suits her personality.'

'That's what scares me,' Rosaline said. 'I almost lost her, and she isn't even yet a commissioned officer. They say on the news that we're at war again, that there is something out there that wants to take our planet away from us.'

Nathan knew that there was little point in denying it.

'Ayleea fell, but we rallied here and now the Ayleeans are on our side. The enemy didn't destroy the peace accord, they only strengthened it. They strengthened all of us.'

'Doesn't feel that way to me.'

Nathan found himself wishing that Foxx were here, riding shotgun for him again.

'What do you want me to say, Rosaline?'

Sula's mother squirmed slightly on her seat, as though she were even more uncomfortable than Nathan.

'I want you to promise that you'll look out for her. You work closely with the fleet, you will see her more than I will.'

Nathan raised an eyebrow in surprise. He had expected Rosaline to order him to stay away from Sula, not get more involved.

'I can do that.'

Rosaline nodded, and apparently satisfied she stood up and headed for the apartment door, eager to escape. Nathan hesitated, and then spoke on impulse.

'I won't let her down,' he said. Rosaline turned at the door to look at him. 'I can't be her father but I can be her friend. People are happier when they don't feel alone, right?'

Rosaline appeared surprised as she opened the door.

'That would be more than enough for her, and for me, Nathan.'

The apartment door shimmered out and Rosaline walked through and down the corridor outside. Nathan watched as the door rematerialized, and hoped that he could live up to his own promise.

*

CSS Headquarters

New York City

Director General Arianna Coburn stood before the senate, hundreds of senators gathered before her in their seats around the amphitheater. Beside her, sitting on chairs nearby, the commanders of the fleet had taken new places that had not been filled since the height of the Ayleean War. Behind her, likewise seated, were over a hundred Ayleean warriors, their metallic armor and leathery skin contrasting with the white robes of the senators' ranks.

'Senators,' she began, 'just two days ago, we found ourselves of the brink of annihilation for the third time in our history. Although we repelled an attack that cost the Ayleean people their world and perhaps their lives, we now know that we face an uncertain future. There are species out there who would wish us harm for their own gain, and they will stop at nothing to achieve their objectives. We now know that they view other species as something they call "corvu" – food.'

Ripples of disgust and fear fluttered across the senate, and Coburn waited for them to calm before she continued.

'We will stand against them, as we have always stood against a threat against our survival, but we no longer stand alone. Despite their heavy losses the remainder of the Ayleean people have willingly joined us to oppose and to fight against the invasion of our worlds. The peace accord with Ayleea was not ended with the invasion, but strengthened by it. We shall not again be divided. We shall not be conquered. I have it on the authority of the Joint Chiefs of Staff that the enemy has not fled forever, that they will return with more ships and that they will endeavour to defeat us once more.'

Arianna turned to the Ayleean warriors behind her, their leader Shylo now standing at their front as she spoke.

'To this end, I am officially allowing the entry of Ayleeans into the fleet, to serve us all and to spearhead our newest mission: to retake Ayleea and the colonies from our enemy, and to bring an end to this invasion for once and for all.'

The entire senate stood, and as Shylo and the Ayleeans placed their hands over their chests so the senate mirrored the action. Arianna Coburn turned to the senate and spoke once more.

'We are once again at war,' she said, her voice tinged with regret but growing in intensity, 'at a time when we thought that we were on the verge of peace. Rally your people, speak to them at every opportunity. I want every single person on earth, on every orbital station, in every colony on every moon, planet, prison and mining vessel we possess to know that from this day on we will fight for every last inch of our territory and that nothing and nobody will ever stand in our way. *Defensionem ut impetum!'*

The senate amphitheater trembled as hundreds of men, women and Ayleeans stood and applauded as one, a hymn of war rising up toward the wintery skies over the city.

***

ABOUT THE AUTHOR

Dean Crawford is the author of nineteen novels, including the internationally published series of thrillers featuring *Ethan Warner*, a former United States Marine now employed by a government agency tasked with investigating unusual scientific phenomena. The novels have been *Sunday Times* paperback best-sellers and have gained the interest of major Hollywood production studios. He is also the enthusiastic author of many independently published Science Fiction novels.

To get a free copy of Dean Crawford's novel *The Nemesis Origin* and notification of his publication dates and special offers, just sign up to his mailing list at:

www.deancrawfordbooks.com

Printed in Great Britain
by Amazon